THE DAY OF THE BUTTERFLY

THE DAY OF THE BUTTERFLY

Norah Lofts

ISIS
LARGE PRINT
Oxford

First published in Great Britain 1979
by
The Bodley Head Ltd.

Published in Large Print 2013 by ISIS Publishing Ltd.,
7 Centremead, Osney Mead, Oxford OX2 0ES
by arrangement with
The Author's Estate

CIP data is available for this title from the British Library

ISBN 978–0–7531–9174–3 (hb)
ISBN 978–0–7531–9175–0 (pb)

Printed and bound in Great Britain by
T. J. International Ltd., Padstow, Cornwall

PART ONE

CHAPTER
ONE

When Mrs Westcott first heard the singing in the street she frowned slightly. A notice at the end of the cul-de-sac plainly announced that beggars and hawkers were forbidden. Park Drive clung hard — almost desperately — to its reputation as a desirable, genteel place. Admittedly Mr Mayhew, who lived at Number 10, had once challenged a man who was singing, asking had he not seen the notice.

The man, made bold by drink, said, "Placards don't mean nothing to me, guvnor. Bain't a scholar. Another thing, I ain't begging. I'm giving 'em a bit of a song. If they like to chuck out a copper or two thass their affair."

Mr Mayhew, who was a lawyer, was bound to allow that the man had a point there. None the less he threatened to fetch the constable if the man didn't stop singing. He shambled away and at the street opening, within arm's reach of the notice, burst into song again; still to the same tune but with words of unimaginable obscenity.

The singing this morning was different, very sweet and clear. More than one voice and all young. It was an old country song about May Day and it took Mrs

Westcott back some years, to her childhood in Talbot St Agnes, where May Day was still properly celebrated. Of course she and Felicity and Gerald — children of the Rectory — had not been allowed to join in the singing or the dancing round the maypole on the green; their father objected to May Day; heathen, he called it, pagan, but even he could not prevent his family from listening and now, eighteen years later, in the breast of an intensely conventional, completely unsentimental woman a faint, a wistful echo was struck. Enough to take her to the bow window and look out, curious to see who else in London remembered *If in the Merry Month of May* . . .

Once at the window she went rigid with horror. There in the street, coming from the little private-public garden which closed the cul-de-sac at its upper end, was her own nursemaid with James and Dorothy and the baby in the perambulator. They were not only singing at the top of their voices, but capering; the two children going around the perambulator as though it were a maypole, and Daisy Holt, the nursemaid, was literally prancing, turning round and round, changing hands on the perambulator's handle at each turn. And to make matters worse — if worse they could be — they had all changed hats. James was wearing Daisy's sedate streamered cap, Dorothy was wearing James's sailor hat, and perched on the over-abundant, too-nearly-red, hair of the nursemaid was Dorothy's small leghorn with its demure wreath of forget-me-nots.

The most disgraceful, a really shocking, exhibition.

4

Mrs Westcott's first impulse was to throw up the window, lean out and shout, "Stop it!" But that would not do. Up and down Park Drive that evening — and for long after — people would be saying: "And then Mrs Westcott leaned out of the window and yelled, as well she might!" Controlling herself with difficulty, Mrs Westcott left the window, crossed to the fireplace and jerked the white china handle which activated the bell at the foot of the basement stairs. Emily came, running and breathless.

"Go and tell Daisy to come in at once. Go out by the front; that will be quicker."

She moved to the window in order to see that her order was briskly executed. Further mortification met her. Emily plainly conveyed the message and Daisy laughed, reached out a hand and grasped Emily's, pulled her into the dance. Emily, clumsy and graceless, circled the perambulator once and then came to her senses, looked up at the drawing-room window and said something which put a stop to the unseemly behaviour. The singing stopped and hats were changed. Then the perambulator and its satellites crossed the road, making for the area steps of Number 6, and passed out of view. Mrs Westcott returned to the dusting of the drawing-room which the noise had interrupted. She must, she admonished herself, be very careful, for the scene had upset her so that her hands quivered. She was, naturally, much annoyed with Daisy but her real rage centred about her sister who had so warmly recommended the girl . . .

There were, of course, nursemaids to be obtained in London; but good ones were rare and tended to be handed about as though they were jewels, kept within the family, so to speak. Without such contacts and, let facts be faced, without much money, one was forced back upon inferior people and Mrs Westcott had had a long, sorry experience with such. Her eldest son, Julian, now fifteen and at Harrow — terribly expensive — had been attended in rapid succession by a nurse who drank, a girl who was flighty and became pregnant and then by another who stole. Mrs Westcott, younger then and not yet fully imbued with the Park Drive ethic, had taken charge of him herself, defiantly pushing her own perambulator, later holding a toddler's hand until she was so far advanced in her second pregnancy that it was positively indecent for her to be seen out of doors by daylight. Then, through an agency, she had obtained a nurse named Mary: a sound woman who had stayed with her through three pregnancies. Those children had died. All from typhoid, though there was no epidemic.

By the time James and then, hard on his heels, Dorothy, needed a nursemaid, Mary was herself dead and Mrs Westcott had struggled on, hopeful, despairing, until the thought occurred to her that her sister, Felicity, could help.

Everybody, on the subject of nursemaids, agreed that a country girl was the ideal; better health, better manners, better morals.

Between Mrs Westcott and her sister was the gulf of six years in age and the wider one of social difference. Felicity had made a splendid marriage and was now

Lady Langton, rich, comfortable and secure in the Hall, Talbot St Agnes. Mrs Westcott, less pretty, less vivacious, had been obliged to settle for less; had faced the hopeless choice of being an old maid, her father's unpaid curate for ever and ever, or marrying beneath her. A man in trade. Not even, alas as it proved, successful trade. He imported and sold China tea, and more and more people were going over to the greatly inferior Indian kind. Their income was now rather less than it had been when they were married, and all prices had risen steeply; so Mrs Westcott, asking Felicity's aid, had been forced to the humiliating statement that she could not afford more than ten pounds a year. Felicity had sent — straight out of her own kitchen — Daisy Holt, a good, clean, modest, healthy fifteen-year-old, daughter of the estate carpenter.

The girl had come to London in March; was obviously healthy, seemed willing enough, seemed at first rather homesick and shy, but she had settled nicely. The children liked her. Even more important, really, she got along well with Mrs Bell, the cook, and with Emily. They'd been, until this morning, as happy a household as possible in the circumstances, penny-pinching in a house that was inconvenient and awkward.

Now this disgraceful behaviour. Daisy must be reprimanded.

CHAPTER
TWO

Daisy took the reprimand badly.

"I don't see what I did so wrong."

"That is what I am trying to explain. I heard this hullabaloo in the street — doubtless everybody else did. Imagine how I felt to find you and Master James and Miss Dorothy, shouting and cavorting."

"Keeping May Day. I'd been telling them how we used to. Then I showed them and I can't see what harm."

"Then I must put it more plainly. Well brought up children do not make public exhibitions of themselves . . ."

"Poor little sods!"

"*What* did you say?"

"Poor little sods. So they are. Mustn't make a noise in the garden because of that old bitch next door complaining. Mustn't even play ball up there," Daisy jerked her head towards the bigger garden at the end of the street, "because of the flowerbeds and that old . . ."

"Be careful of your language!"

". . . gardener," Daisy said. And something flashed, mocking and derisive in her eyes. Mrs Westcott noticed for the first time that in the girl's left eye was a greenish-brown fleck; almost a defect. In a less pretty face it would have been slightly sinister, akin to a squint.

"The gardener is responsible for the upkeep of the pleasure-ground shared by a number of people," she said stiffly. "He can no more allow unruly behaviour there than I can approve of it in the street."

"But we wasn't unruly."

"Are you arguing with me?"

"I ain't agreeing."

"To make matters worse, you persuaded Emily to join in this unseemly display."

"Once round the pram!"

Only twice in her years as mistress of the house — once from the nurse who drank, and once from a cook more hot-tempered than most — had Mrs Westcott encountered such an attitude from an employee. A wave of outrage swept over her, but she controlled it.

"I am waiting for you to apologise."

"I don't see what for."

Insolent and stubborn! But even then Mrs Westcott might not have taken a decision so self-damaging, had not Daisy's hair, loosened by the change of headgear and by the dancing, not broken away from its pins and come down. It was wonderful hair. Out there in the sunny street it had seemed too red; here in the curtain-shrouded drawing-room it was bright chestnut, gleaming and shimmering in waves past the girl's waist.

Jealousy, one of the crueller emotions, pierced the woman who had had her forty-first birthday and whose once plentiful hair was growing dull and thin. Mrs Westcott was not sexually jealous; her husband, not the best provider in the world, was at least faithful, even uxorious, and in two months had hardly glanced at Daisy; but the sight of that waterfall of hair inflicted a hurt to feminine vanity and made it essential to retaliate.

"Unless you apologise, *at once*, I shall have no choice but to give you notice."

"But I still can't see," the stubborn girl said.

"That will *do*! You will leave at the end of the week." No, the penalty could be increased. "Better still, at once." It was acceptable behaviour to deal thus summarily with offenders, and provided one paid a week's wages one's conscience could lie easy. It was being done every day, in shops, in factories as well as homes. Mrs Westcott did not pause to wonder how a girl, seventy miles from home, with three shillings and eightpence in her pocket, could possibly manage. She had other things to think of; by yielding to a fit of temper — in retrospect quite irrational — she had condemned herself to looking after her own children until Daisy could be replaced. James and Dorothy were past the real baby stage but Sophie was less than a year old.

It would mean the Agency again, or an advertisement, or the hitherto-fruitless business of asking round among friends. One thing was certain, she would not seek help from Felicity. Felicity obviously thought that anything would do for poor Sybil — that had always been the theory. One day, when she had time, she would write to Felicity and tell her what had happened, how grossly unsuitable. Cursing and swearing,

10

answering back, insolence, vulgar behaviour in the public highway.

Daisy went lightly down the stairs into the basement.

"I got the sack."

Mrs Bell stopped the mincing which made scrag end mildly edible and said, "Never!" Emily dropped a potato and said, "What for?"

"Dancing in the street."

Emily put her scarlet wet hand to her mouth and said, "Law! So did I! She gonna sack me too?" There was genuine apprehension in her voice.

"Of course not. You was led astray!" The green fleck danced. "And I did worse. I let slip a bad word. I called the children poor little sods. And so they are. Never no fun."

"Maybe," the cook said, "but bad language ain't gonna alter *that*." She minced the remainder of the meat, put it into a saucepan, added water, and set it on the stove.

"Now look here, my girl. You make yourself tidy and go straight upstairs and apologise. Wring out a tear or two if you can. Go down on your marrow-bones. Ask Madam to forgive you."

"What for?"

"Swearing. And all the rest."

Mrs Bell was a sensible woman, toughened by fifty years in a hostile world, and if Emily or anybody else had stood there in Daisy's shoes she would have said, "Well, you got what you asked for." But for Daisy she had had from the start a weak spot. She was pretty, but that didn't count. On the whole Mrs Bell distrusted the pretty; it was the liveliness, the something different. A breath of fresh air blowing through the stuffy basement. Mrs Bell was unfamiliar with the word *charm*, all she knew was that when Daisy came into a room it seemed to light up — and she could mimic anybody so that you simply had to laugh. The place wouldn't seem the same without her.

"And where d'you think you're gonna lay your head this night?"

"I'll find somewhere. Wouldn't hurt me to sleep in a park this weather."

"Don't talk like a bloody fool! This ain't the country, bear in mind. You'd be set on, raped, robbed, maybe killed even."

The cook wondered why she should bother. The girl surely must know. Granted she'd only been in London a couple of months, but she could read; and almost every day the papers reported assaults on women, mainly but by no means all of what was known as the unfortunate class.

"Don't you fret your dear old head about me," Daisy said, with such warmth of voice and with such a sweet smile that Mrs Bell could not resent the word *old*. "I'll be all right."

"Thass where you make your mistake, girl. You walk outa here, no job, no home, no money and before you can blink you'll be on the streets." Did the young silly understand what that meant? Really, she looked so blamed innocent, and ignorant. It was like talking to a kitten. Still, she must try.

For a decent, respectable woman, a good cook when there was anything worth cooking, Mrs Bell knew a great deal about the seamier side of life. She ended her lecture, ". . . then you get a dose of the clap and finish up with no nose."

Emily, who had taken no part in the argument, ventured to intervene.

"Excuse me, Cook, but they don't end like that always. My cousin Lou didn't. There was a gentleman, real toff, too, took such a fancy to her, he married her."

Lou had blazed such a trail that Emily would very willingly have followed it, had she not been handicapped from the start. Born with one shoulder higher than the other and no chin; known as Hunchy, or Rabbitface; doomed even in domestic service to inferior places like this where they were glad of what they could get. She looked at Daisy with no twinge of envy. She liked Daisy for no particular reason except that she was gay and high-spirited, and kind with it. This place wouldn't seem the same without her.

"I've heard about your cousin. She was one in a thousand. You now, Daisy, be ruled by me for once. Bundle up that hair and go and say you're sorry."

"Be damned if I will!"

Despite the vigour and the expletive, there was no malice in her refusal to apologise. She bore Mrs Westcott no grudge. Indeed she had almost forgotten how the row had started, and she was equally unconcerned about the future. Except that ending with no nose was funny. She touched her own and laughed.

Her good advice ignored, Mrs Bell washed her hands of the matter. "Very well, go your own way. And may you never regret it."

CHAPTER
THREE

Daisy had almost nothing to pack: Mrs Westcott had provided her uniform and her own wardrobe was scanty, consisting mainly of handed-down clothes from the Langton family, all, with one exception, the sensible, dull things judged suitable for a servant to wear. The exception was a muslin dress, white with a lavender pattern and a lavender satin sash. This she had not yet worn in London because until today the weather had been cool. She would wear it on this glorious day of freedom.

Emily came in, panting a little from the climb.

"Daisy, don't go sleeping out. That'd be dangerous, even for *me*."

"I'll find somewhere, don't you worry."

"I been thinking. Lou was at a place called Kitty's. Mrs Hammond. It's in Sparhawk Lane, off Leicester Square." Daisy, so pretty and now in a pretty dress, might be as lucky as Lou had been. "And look, you take this." It was a shilling, hot and damp.

"Bless you, my dear. I couldn't. I'm all right. She paid me. But thanks just the same." The coin fell on to the worn linoleum as Daisy put her arm round the little hunchback and gave her a warm, hearty kiss. A moment to remember. Very few people kissed girls whose teeth stuck out so far.

Stepping out into delicious, if dangerous, freedom, Daisy carried her few clothes, her brush and comb, tied into the head shawl in which she had arrived in London. She had not owned a hat since she was five and had gone to church with her mother. Her mother had been an excellent manager, and an estate carpenter earned more than an ordinary labourer, so Daisy had had a good, almost a privileged start in life. But her mother had died and her father had quickly remarried, choosing a woman who was not only a bad manager but a regular producer of children — five in five years.

Until she was ten and old enough to go into regular service, Daisy had done the various jobs of which children were deemed capable and which brought in a few pence. She'd picked stones, acted, with a set of clappers, as a bird scarer; anything which came to hand; transient work inculcating a day-to-day state of mind. And although she had stayed at the Hall and made some small progress — from kitchenmaid to housemaid — it had been an existence without aim. She was fond of food and quite interested in the preparation of it, but even if she had entertained ambition in that direction it would be years and years before she was middle-aged enough to be a cook. Long before that something marvellous would have happened. Even her ideas of what the marvellous thing would be were curiously imprecise and not directly linked with prettiness. Being, as everybody said, so pretty was actually rather a burden; a pretty girl, to keep out of trouble, not to get taken advantage of, had to be extremely careful.

She had thought it was marvellous to be chosen by Lady Langton to be sent to London, suddenly promoted to the status of nursemaid. It had been a disappointment to find life in London deadly dull and to be not only homesick for the country and for the lively company of the servants' hall, but more or less hungry all the time. Mrs Westcott, in order to keep up appearances, was obliged to practise many small economies.

Well, that was all over now. She was free and it was May Day and although London was virtually unknown territory she set out gaily, the wonderful thing just around the corner beckoning and whispering.

Emerging from the cul-de-sac she did not turn left, to an area of streets, closes, cul-de-sacs, all much like Park Drive, but also containing a little cookshop in which, on her free evenings, she had fed well if extravagantly for eightpence. She turned in the other direction and was presently in a street of shops. Wonderful shops, full of wonderful things at which she could look with admiration but no envy. She was hungry. Maybe with so little in her purse she shouldn't spend much on food. But she would get something, because something would turn up.

What turned up almost immediately was a coffee stall on a corner. Sausages! They were cooking in an iron pan over a brazier and they smelt delicious. So did the coffee, bubbling away in a copper urn. She was the only female patron, but that did not disturb her, she was too much engrossed with the food. Between the brazier and the urn there were rolls, already half split, and a pyramid of pies.

The stall was a favourite resort of cabmen, for the side street offered standing room for horses and vehicles. Daisy had already learned not to look at cab-horses, they were almost invariably too thin and dejected. Poor things, did they ever see a green meadow?

The man who ran the stall fished out the sizzling sausages with a long-handled fork, slipped them into the rolls and handed them over, very quick and dexterous. Before it was Daisy's turn to be served her presence had been noticed, inspiring in all but the most jaded a little curiosity and more admiration. Curiosity because she was difficult to place; it was rare to see a woman bareheaded; rare to see a decent woman at a coffee stall. The admiration was a natural tribute to her shining beauty, enhanced now by the excitement of being alive and out of doors on such a beautiful day.

At the very front of the stall there was a chipped basin containing mustard and another of rough sugar. One of the men, chancing his arm, said, "Mustard, miss?"

Even in the country, pure as Mrs Bell seemed to think it, one did not grow to be fifteen and pretty without mastering the art of discouragement.

"No, thank you," she said, very cool and distant. To the men — all Cockneys — her voice was puzzling too. Not Cockney; not upper-class either. But definitely

18

deterrent. In fact Daisy was thinking, Why the Hell shouldn't I? I like mustard with sausages! She reached out and helped herself. Then stood, apparently but not really oblivious of them all, and ate two of the rolls and a pork pie. After that she drank a cup of coffee, not nearly as nice as it smelt.

By that time there was a little lull, custom came in fits and starts at this corner. The stall-owner, as curious as his customers, thought he had the answer. Pulling the sausage pan a little aside, he said, "You up from the country?"

"Yes." Too much trouble to explain that she had come up two months ago.

"Got a job?" At such a moment she was capable of very quick thinking; if she said *No*, would he offer to employ her, or know of somebody who would? If she said *Yes* would she be missing a chance?

"I'm not quite certain, yet. I'm having a look round."

He was anything but a fatherly man yet he felt the same uprush of protectiveness as Mrs Bell had experienced.

"You want to be careful," he said. "Pretty girl like you. No hat. And eating alongside cabbies at a place like this."

"There is nothing wrong with this place — except the coffee." To soften that remark, she smiled and added, "The food is very good."

"Whatever you do," he said earnestly, "don't take a sewing job." He had noticed her hands, which were what he called dainty. Other people in the past had noticed her hands, slim and shapely and apparently impervious to rough usage. "Sewing is slow starvation. And if anything millinery is worse."

"I'm not much good with a needle," she said, giving him another smile. New customers arrived, all in a bunch, all in a hurry, as usual, and when he next looked up she had gone. Later he discovered that she had left her pitiable bundle.

Now and again, over the years he remembered her. Pretty as a flower, a bit simple-minded, bound, he felt, for trouble.

Daisy remembered him for exactly as long as it took her to find a hat. No hat, he had said in a way which meant that to be without a hat was wrong, somehow. And now that her attention had been called to the matter, she could see that everybody else wore something over their heads. Even a beggar woman, gaunt and pallid, with a stick-thin child in her arms, had a sort of rag over her head, tied under her chin. Daisy gave her a penny before setting out on the search for a hat which must not cost more than a shilling. She gave another penny to a blind man and another to a sweep whose blackened shoulder she touched for luck.

That she should be a bit vague about money was understandable. Until two months ago she had never had any. Or needed any. She'd started work for her keep, her clothing and two pounds cash a year. Then three, four and five. Her father and the new young family had needed it all and she had handed over, unthinking, ungrudging. Sent to London — no choice in the matter — she had promised to send money home, but, shameful to say, she had not yet done so.

20

The failure had made her feel careless, selfish; but she'd had to have one good meal now and then; and she'd had to buy shoes because those that went with the uniform simply did not fit, too short and too wide, and the pair she had brought with her couldn't stand up to the wear of pavements and gravel paths.

It was the prices, not the grandeur of the shops that intimidated her. Imagine fifteen shillings or a guinea for a hat! The idea that she would like to be a shop assistant came and went; to be with, to handle beautiful things would be pleasant. Then she heard a stout overdressed woman speaking haughtily to a meek girl who seemed to be doing her best, and she thought, No, that wouldn't suit me; I should answer back! When it came to her turn to be served she took pains to speak in the friendliest possible way; and although the girl thought her insane, asking was there a plain hat for about a shilling, she responded. "Why'n't you try a market? They're very cheap."

"Where is one?"

"Cross the road, second street on your left — that way."

"Thank you. Isn't it a beautiful day?"

"For them that can get out and enjoy it," the girl said, but she spoke wistfully, not resentfully.

She had no difficulty in placing Daisy; her feminine eye took in the quality and cut of the muslin dress which had been made for Miss Langton of the Hall. Superior dress, countrified voice, friendly manner, and wanting a cheap hat; obviously a dress-lodger, a kind of prostitute, sent out in clothes provided by the madam of the house. Somehow she'd lost her hat and daren't go back until she'd found a replacement. Well, good luck to her; she'd need it!

The market could be heard, and smelt, before it came into view. Then the narrow alley took a turn and debouched into a much wider street lined on both sides with stalls, and swarming with people, all of the poorer kind who shopped late in the afternoon because there were bargains to be had then. Earlier in the day respectable housewives who liked value for money, but also liked the pick of the produce, did their shopping there, moving purposefully. It was not worth the while of the entertainers to be active then; now they were opening up, shouting, banging drums, clashing cymbals to draw attention from the crowd. Daisy watched her first Punch-and-Judy show, and saw her first monkey with its tragic eyes, doing little antics on top of a barrel organ. It had been taught to beg and she gave it a penny.

Except for the entertainers, who wisely avoided too much proximity, stalls seemed to cluster together according to what they had to offer. Wearing apparel was not immediately visible, but she would find it. She picked her way through filth, glad that her dress was a trifle short. She found a stall which specialised in female stuff, bonnets, hats, gloves, stockings, shawls, even handkerchieves.

That something in her which was later to be recognised as natural good taste had made her visualise, when she thought of a hat, as one trimmed, if trimmed at all, with a ribbon or a flower of the same lavender colour as her sash and the patterns on the dress. But that was a subtle, upperclass colour; here there was crudity; in dyed cotton; red, harsh blue, grass green and something between yellow and orange. So it must be white.

Ordinarily the fat woman who owned this stall would have been impatient with somebody so hard to please and positively angry when the difficult customer made a snatch at the hat practically at the bottom of the pile and said, "This will have to do. I'm sorry, I have disturbed them all. I'll put them back." Oddly she was not; she was glad that the girl had found what she wanted. From somewhere about her bulging person, her voluminous clothing, her disrupted stall, she produced a square of looking-glass not much bigger than a playing card and offered it, saying, "Would you like to see yourself?"

To her reflection Daisy could not give much attention for stockings, handkerchieves and a few toilet articles at the other end of the booth had made her think, jerk to attention and realise that somewhere along the way she had lost — or been robbed of — her bundle. God almighty! Now here she was, as the saying went, with just the clothes she stood up in. What a plight! Exuberance soon overcame dismay, however, and she thought, They weren't worth much, anyway; I'll have prettier things one day.

When she had paid for the hat — cheap coarse straw with a cotton ribbon — she had fifteen pence left in her homemade, cloth reticule. She reckoned that a bed would cost about a shilling, so she could afford just a bite of food, for despite what she had eaten at the coffee stall, she was hungry again. In this place the variety and the quantity of food available was confusing; there were familiar things, sausages, pies and sandwiches, others unknown; jellied eels, smoked eels, and eels in pies, shrimps, winkles and whelks. Talbot St Agnes was too far inland for such things, and at Park Drive they were regarded as strictly working-class fare. Daisy walked along, feasting her eyes, and growing more hungry. She decided to try whelks.

Absolutely delicious, but not, alas, very filling; she could have eaten a hundred, but the one saucerful had cost twopence and she was left with a penny and the choice between spending it on a slice of bread and butter, substantial, or a mug of tea to quench the thirst the whelks had induced.

No harm in just asking! No harm in smiling coaxingly at a man on the far side of a packed counter.

"I have one penny left. Would it be possible for me to have *half* a mug of tea and *half* a slice of bread and butter?"

The age-old Cockney taste for a quip was irresistible.

"You tell me 'ow to 'alf a mug, miss, and I'll 'and it over."

Some people within hearing laughed and Daisy flushed, not as the man thought, with embarrassment, but with temper. One thing she hated was to be laughed *at*. She liked to make people laugh by little jokes, mimicries, even clowning, but being laughed at she simply could not abide. There was nothing she could do about it here, though, and she was prepared to turn away and act dignified, when the man relented.

"'Ere you are," he said, and filled a mug to the brim and handed over a whole slice of bread and butter, bread very thick, butter very thin. Just what she wanted.

Now for Leicester Square and Kitty Hammond's. The end of a wonderful day.

CHAPTER
FOUR

In the open square itself the sunlight still lay as though reluctant to bring the sunlit day to an end, but Sparhawk Lane, too narrow to accommodate more than foot passengers, and lined with old crumbling houses whose upper floors jutted out until they almost met overhead was already cloaked in dusk, a dark tunnel. It reminded Daisy of Waywood, back home where in search of flowers, nuts or blackberries, you could step from a clearing where the sun shone, into the dense shade of the old forest.

There had been times in her brief childhood when she had been a bit scared of Waywood, especially after dusk. Some very strange, uncanny tales were told about it and of course she had been too young, and too ignorant to distinguish between folklore, superstition, and reality. Some people believed that wolves still prowled about the densest thickets; the ghost of a girl who had drowned herself in one of the pools had been seen floating on the surface, and another ghost, that of a little boy who had been lost or deliberately abandoned there, had been heard wailing. Daisy had believed everything until, aged about eight, out with other children, blackberrying in the clearings, she had wandered in the wrong direction and been lost herself. There had been a time of panic; alone in Waywood with night coming on! The worst thing was to run about aimlessly, she knew. So she sat down with her back against a tree, ate all her blackberries and fell asleep. After that the wood held no terror for her though she added to its sinister reputation by claiming to have seen and heard all the dreadful things — and more.

She stepped into Sparhawk Lane without trepidation, her only concern to find Mrs Hammond's house or somebody who could direct her to it. There seemed to be nobody about, and the houses on both sides of the street were deserted; windows and actual doors boarded over. A very curious street indeed. And here, in the very heart of London, as silent as any path in Waywood.

The man seemed to come from nowhere; huge, menacing in the gloom.

"Where're you going?"

"To Mrs Hammond's."

He had been standing in a doorway, very similar to the boarded-over ones she had passed, but he reached out and opened the door so that light from within streamed over him, and over her. He was quite the ugliest man — the ugliest human being — she had ever seen. His face looked as though it had been put through a mangle, everything too flat and too wide. Yet, when the first jolt had passed, she did not feel that he was hostile.

"What's your business?"

Her natural impulse was say, "*My* business". But it behoved her to be civil, since he was the only person in this deserted street of whom she could ask guidance.

"I was told that at Mrs Hammond's — Kitty Hammond's — I could get a bed for the night."

To her astonishment, he laughed, his wide flat face becoming uglier as it creased.

"You'll get that all right."

"Where is it, then?"

"Here," he said. "Come in." Thus invited she stepped into what seemed to her to be a palace; a just-literate girl's muddled concoction of the Cinderella story, fortified by a lively imagination and glimpses of the Hall at Talbot St Agnes lit up for a party. The hall had three archways, those to the right and straight ahead opening upon spacious apartments, not at the moment too brightly lit, but enough to show up the sheen of silk and satin; to the left a staircase rose, carpeted in dark crimson. The hall itself was floored with marble and brilliantly lit by a chandelier whose dangling prisms shone with rainbow colours. The staircase took light partly from this source, and partly from another chandelier on the landing.

"Go up there," the man said, "and you'll find Mrs Hammond somewhere about, prob'ly in the gallery. You meet anybody, say you've passed Sam."

She had the country person's sense of direction and it seemed to her that in mounting the stairs she was in effect going back up the lane and was now on the inner side of those boarded-up doors and windows. In this supposition, she was correct. Kitty Hammond's night house, said by travelled men to be the most luxurious and best in the world, operated behind a blank face.

Treading the moss-spongy, velvet-smooth carpet, Daisy thought that this was not what she had expected a lodging-house to be — but then she had never seen a lodging-house and Emily had said Kitty Hammond's and this was it, so it must be all right. The door guard, looking up, thought, Beautiful mover, too. Beauty of face and grace did not always go together. And he should know; he'd been Kitty's chief door guard for eighteen years and since Kitty's trade, when you really boiled it down, was *women*, Sam was as expert in his field as a horse-trader.

The only gallery of which Daisy had any knowledge was the Long Gallery at the Hall, and she had seen it seldom, since she was a kitchen maid and little concerned with what was known as the front of the house. That gallery was a long place, like three rooms placed on end, the walls were hung with pictures. The gallery here was utterly different; a kind of shelf running round a huge room and bulging out in one place into a kind of sitting room, several small chairs, some tables, flowers, green things in pots, and one huge chair in which sat the most enormously fat woman Daisy had ever seen. The gallery and the bulge were twelve stairs lower than the landing on which Daisy stood, and from it some more steps led down to — Daisy thought — one of the rooms she had just seen through one of the archways.

Without turning her head — and it was indeed difficult to imagine her making any kind of movement

29

— the woman called, "Who's there?" Her voice was low, deep, gruff.

"Daisy Holt."

"And who the hell may she be?"

"Sam passed me." It was the only thing Daisy could think of to say. It was the right thing.

"Come and let me have a look at you." Daisy descended the stairs, rounded the massive chair and submitted herself to inspection.

Literally hundreds of girls had passed through Kitty's hands, and many acknowledged Society beauties were known to her by sight, for hers was also a house of assignation. However, in all her experience Kitty had not seen a girl of low birth, or high, quite like this one who now stood before her, utterly unselfconscious. Like a flower.

In fact Daisy was completely puzzled, for Kitty Hammond nowadays went through the tiresome process of getting properly dressed only once a day and when she dressed it was for the evening, her vast bulk wrapped in satin or velvet according to the season, jewels everywhere, around her neck, on her huge, sagging bosom, on her fingers, in her ears, even in her hair. And apart from this dazzling glitter, Kitty's appearance was extraordinary. She'd once been a prettyish girl and her face was still there, quite small and ordinary above the jowls and the three chins, like a . . . like a mask, or, more like, a face painted on to a turnip for All Hallows.

"So you're Daisy Holt. What's your real name?"

"That is my real name."

Kitty asked because she saw all the hallmarks of an abscondee from a decent home. Perhaps even from school. (Kitty had two daughters who had gone to schools for young ladies and she thought she recognised the white muslin.) Such girls were more nuisance than they were worth; first there was the possibility of inquiries; secondly the certainty of choosiness.

"How did you hear of my place?"

"From Emily."

"I've known a dozen. Emily *who*?"

"I don't know." Emily was just Emily and, being completely illiterate, never received a letter. "The truth is, I got the sack this morning, and Emily — she worked with me — said if I come here I'd get a bed. I thought you let lodgings. Now I think you might need a maid . . . I know I was sacked, but it wasn't for thieving or anything like that."

"What was it for?"

"Dancing in the street."

An oddity, if ever there was one.

"So you can dance?"

"Not like people in ball-rooms. Just like at Harvest Homes and May Day."

"Show me. Down there," Kitty said, indicating the room just below, an expanse of dark shining floor.

"D'you mind if I sing? It goes better." Daisy was practically certain now that Mrs Hammond was eccentric — a word used for rich people with funny ideas. Old Lady Langton had been very eccentric indeed and such people must be humoured; nasty with

31

it, too, so much so that Sir Alfred and his wife were said to be thinking about putting her in an asylum.

Humouring eccentricity, Daisy walked down the few stairs and in the core of this centre of depravity danced and sang in a way which would have surprised Mrs Bell who thought the country innocent and pure. Even, *If in the Merry Month of May*, which Daisy had sung that morning in Park Drive was not without its sly innuendo and there were coarser ones; "*Clap the horns on Billy's head*", for example, might sound like a song about a goat, but in fact concerned itself with cuckoldry as frankly as any Restoration comedy.

The old fat woman in the gallery could entertain such a thought while giving her close attention to the girl. Something quite extraordinary, she saw at once. Country dancing was country dancing, the recreation of clodhoppers, but here all was grace, movement melting into movement with such ease, such seductiveness that even to her mercenary, jaded mind, something of enchantment came and she thought, Too good for the ordinary run of trade. She knew that most men came to her house for a body, as attractive as possible and available at a price. A high price. A touch of the exotic lent spice and Kitty could supply that, too; she aimed to have a mulatto or two, a full-blooded negress, a Chinese girl with feet no more than three inches long, always on call. The trouble with most of them was they didn't winter well.

For real perversions Kitty did not cater. She had her own standards and never employed a girl under the age of twelve; for homosexuals of both sexes she had not

32

only scorn but an unacknowledged fear because such people needed no middle agent and if the world were full of them, where would she be?

She had not only her own standards, but ambitions. Most madams were content to run a whorehouse with as little expense and as much profit as possible; she had never been satisfied with that; she liked to think of herself as an entrepreneur; she had helped six likely girls onto the stage, and three with good voices into the Opera. She liked to arrange marriages, foster liaisons, but perhaps most of all she liked to entertain, priding herself upon providing not only the best food and wine in London but the latest novelties. She had spies everywhere, she read the papers, she heard gossip and she had not only made a fortune for herself, but started several other people on their way, faith-healers, conjurers, purveyors of quack medicines, and of beauty preparations. Men said, rightly, that at Kitty's you never knew quite what you would find — apart from the girls, and even they were exceptional, hand-picked.

Even as she watched Daisy performing, she was planning something new in the way of entertainment; something at once pleasing to the eye, provocative of lust and a bit of a gamble.

"Stay like that!" she called. Daisy held the pose. "That'll do. Come here."

Daisy mounted the stairs. Not out of breath, Kitty noticed. Stamina there! And no doubt about it, without physical stamina nobody got very far.

"Did you enjoy it?" That was all that mattered for the moment. In doing something with the aim to please,

Daisy was capable of losing sight of all other considerations. When she danced or sang or mimicked she seemed to become another person, somebody *outside* Daisy Holt. Even in the gloomy kitchen at Number 6 Park Drive, imitating Mrs Westcott, she could momentarily be transported, and now given a chance to perform in space, in lovely surroundings, she had ceased to wonder about that bed for the night, or the job as maid, or where the next meal was coming from.

"You have a certain talent," Kitty said. "We'll talk about that later. Are you hungry?"

They generally were.

Disregarding nursery breakfast — porridge and bread and butter — the coffee stall orgy, and the whelks, Daisy said, "Yes, I am. I could eat an old woman on a horse . . ." The cliché should have run "harness and all," but she stopped, realising that she shouldn't even have said "old woman" to an old woman. And the very words which might have served earlier in the day, "I'm sorry," now came, quick and easy.

"I'm sorry," she said. "We all get old if we live long enough."

"That is true," Mrs Hammond said, amiable, unoffended. "I know my age. You may sit down. I have something to attend to." From the table beside the chair which looked like a throne she lifted and rang a silver bell. Daisy, unaware of the honour being bestowed upon her in being invited to sit by a woman who enjoyed keeping dukes and earls on their feet, sat and watched while page boys came running and the croaky voice issued orders. Kitty said: "I want this; send for; see to it; pick your feet up", and Daisy sat in the chair, not asleep but, as always happened, and she was accustomed to it after any performance, however trivial, terribly tired as though that other person who wasn't plain Daisy Holt had drained her. It was not until a woman, the very image of the housekeeper at the Hall — keys and all — said, "If you will come with me . . ." that she roused herself and realised that this had been, what with one thing and another, a long and tiring day.

"Go with Esther," Kitty said. "She'll see that you are comfortable." Daisy went with Esther and was made very comfortable indeed. She had not even noticed the mention of the name which was to mean so much. Amongst her many orders, Kitty had said, "Fetch Jack Skelton here, drunk or sober I don't care. Carry him if you must."

CHAPTER
FIVE

Kitty was not much given to charity and her name did not figure on the lists of the grand ladies who were. The very respectable ones barely knew of her existence and in any case there was enough prejudice against her trade to make her money appear tainted, likely to do harm rather than good even to a Foundlings' Home. A few of her gentlemen customers, kindly though raffish, knew that she was good for a fiver if properly approached and convinced that the cause was good — she never contributed to anything even remotely connected with religion. But, considering her wealth, her offerings were meagre, since, as she put it, she preferred to see something for her money. In a spasmodic, haphazard fashion she adopted protegées, and she operated a rough-and-ready Robin Hood scheme for making the rich subsidise the poor. Young men, living on expectations, or with no expectations at all, were charged — provided they were civil and likeable — far, far less than men of known wealth.

Jack Skelton had drifted into her orbit five or six years earlier when she was having the big supper room redecorated and had a hankering for something rich and strange like the frescoes in Pompeii, about which she had read. She would not, she knew, get any accredited artist to do such work, in such a place, but nobody knew better than Kitty how much untapped talent there was being hawked about. She dropped a word here and there and presently Jack had turned up, looking starved — which he was.

"You ever seen this place — Pompeii?"

"No. I've heard about the frescoes, seen some drawings. I can do better."

"You've got a good opinion of yourself, young man."

"Yes. I am in the minority. Of one."

"How d'you mean?"

"Well, I believe I'm a better portrait painter than Romney — or Gainsborough, come to that. But I paint people as they are, not as they'd like to be. Certain recipe for failure." The planes of his lean face shifted into a kind of grin.

He was not the only applicant for the job — there were plenty of poor artists about; and Kitty suggested to him, as she had to others, that he should go home, prepare a fair sample of the kind of thing she wanted and bring it back for her inspection.

"That wouldn't do."

"Why not."

"A fresco is meant to be looked at, on a wall. It should be tried out on a wall."

"Not here!" Kitty said sharply. "You might make a muck of it or I mightn't like it. I know. Come this way."

She was fat even then, but less cumbersome than she was to become. She led the way to a passage, one of her secret entrances — or exits. It had none of the luxury which distinguished most of the rest of the house.

"Try on that," she said, pointing to some bare whitewashed wall directly below the grating which gave what light there was. He, unlike the others, had brought the tools of his trade with him, in a rush bag like those carried by carpenters.

"Give me three hours," he said.

His last certain work had been painting inn-signs; a shilling a time and a meal, a job which was conducive to swift work and bold strokes, bold colours. When, after the stipulated time, Kitty came down to inspect, she was astonished. The dull, lowly passage was transfigured; all one side and half the other glowed with colour and with movement.

"You've covered a lot of ground."

"Yes. I let myself get carried away a bit . . . It's rough, of course."

"Dead right, though. Yes, I like it."

She was an ignorant woman, her mind a rag-bag of bits and pieces casually picked up and yet carefully hoarded because you never knew when something might come in useful. The one thing she knew about what was called the Ancient World was that its people were not smug about sex or ashamed of their bodies. Look at the statues! And this fellow had hit it off exactly. The most rigid puritan — if such a person should by accident come in — eating a good supper and looking at pictures like these could hardly fail to get what Kitty called ideas.

"You got the job. Now, how about a bite of dinner?" She could tell from the way his eyes lit up that he was hungry as well as hungry-looking.

Since then he had done other jobs for her and she had tried to forward his career by getting him commissions for portraits. They were never a success and Kitty had been obliged to speak bluntly.

"All this painting people how you think they look, not like they think they do'd be all very nice if you was a dillytanty, doing it for a hobby, but you've got your way to make and you ain't gonna be young for ever. Now this is what you do; you go to Sir Charles and tell him you're sorry he don't like what you did of his daughter and you'll do him another. He say you made her nose four inches long."

"I didn't. God did."

"All right, so she's plain, like I'm fat. But what good do it do to go rubbing it in? You should be sorry for the pore girl. Do her again, Jacky, with a nose like a pug dog's." She could see by his face that he was not going to accept this well-meant suggestion. "In addition to all else what sorta bloody fool do it make of me? Praising you up to the skies then you go and offend people? I tell you straight, 'nless you do Miss Clifford again I shan't recommend you no more."

"Suits me."

Alongside his unwillingness to tell what he called pretty lies on canvas, there was another obstacle to success. He drank. Not moderately and regularly and what he could afford, but in fits and starts; sober for a month and then blind, sodden drunk for a week or ten days. Kitty knew because although she had not recommended him again as a portraitist she had put other jobs in his way. Her supper-room frescoes, the cloud-and-cherub ceilings in two of her most expensive bedrooms were much admired and some people wanted their places similarly decorated. You'd have thought that was the sort of work he couldn't muck up. Yet he did, time and again. He'd begin, get so far and then go on the booze.

Kitty believed that the coincidence between the good, paying jobs and the drunken fits was due to the fact that he had money. She was quite wrong. He'd begin, get so far and then the feeling would sweep over him. Here am I, the best painter in the world, able to paint people's souls as well as their faces, and I'm painting God-damned cherubs on bloody ceilings! The only way of escape was to drink.

Why she hadn't long ago given him up as hopeless, Kitty never could understand, but somehow she never had. Something about him appealed to something in her and if too long elapsed before he exercised the right of entry, the right to eat and drink whatever he liked, free of charge, she'd send somebody round to the dreadful-sounding place where he lived, an attic over a green-grocer's shop in Soho.

Now, thanks to a girl so rightly, yet so wrongly, named Daisy, she could send for him and offer him a job, which by God he couldn't muck up or dodge away from, for he'd be under her eye all the time. And that would be a short time.

Jacky came on call. He was sober, though Kitty's experienced eye could tell that the drunken fit was not far in the past; eyes still a bit bleary, hands not too steady. He was, however, clean and well-groomed and wearing the formal black and white that constituted the dinner wear of a gentleman. He *was* a gentleman, Kitty knew; she could always tell by the voice, but his clothing was apt to be erratic.

"Very smart," she said. "And you ain't all dressed up to call on *me*! You ain't had time."

"No. I was getting ready to dine with Alderman Smithers and a few of his confrères . . . Kit, I've had to give in. No man can fight against Fate for ever. I think that if I use my knives and forks correctly and say 'Sir' every time I open my mouth, I may have the privilege of painting twelve City aldermen, in their robes. For reasons best known to themselves they crave immortality."

"So you've come to your senses. I'm glad. Awkward for me, though. I had a little job I wanted done in a hurry. Forty-eight hours, in fact."

"You know me, Kit. I'm your liegeman. Let the immortals wait. What is it? Another ceiling?"

"No. It's a hoax. A lark. I wanted some statues painted to look like life; and a girl made to look like a statue. But *you* know *me*, Jacky. I'd be the last to interfere if you're after a promising job. I'll find somebody."

"Landseer?"

"Joking aside, you get along. Eddy Saunders can slap a bit of colour on my statues."

"Not like I could. Look, I'll keep this appointment and be back. In fact, if they're to be looked at in artificial light, they'll be better painted by it."

CHAPTER
SIX

Daisy Holt and Jack Skelton first met in Kitty's bedroom, which served as reception room and office as well. That Kitty spent most of the day in bed was the general belief, but one which everyone employed by her knew to be only partially true. Clad in dressing-gown and slippers she was up and about very early in the morning to inspect what her porters had brought in from markets and shops — and woe betide anyone who came back with less than the best. For years she had done her own buying, even after she became prosperous, but the obesity — a disease, not the result of over-indulgence — had put a stop to that. However, she still knew the best from the second-best. Nowadays that small effort exhausted her and she went back to bed where she drank lemon tea while conferring with her cooks and arranged the menus. After that she rested a little before seeing Esther, her right-hand woman where anything concerning the main business of the house — the girls — was concerned. Up to a point she trusted people, believing herself to be a good judge of character, and in some cases knowing that those she employed had good reason to feel indebted to her, or to fear loss of their jobs; but beyond that certain point she

43

trusted nobody, and driving her dropsical bulk by sheer power of will, she would heave herself up and go her rounds, deliberately irregular. Everybody knew that at any minute she could be anywhere.

She was in bed, talking to Jack Skelton about the finer details of the hoax, when he said, "If you want the marble girls to look like her, I'd better have a look at her. Mind you, Kitty, I thought this whole thing over while I ate a meal so square as to be oblong, and I don't think it could work. The eyes alone would defeat me."

"You can buy glass eyes. Think of dolls."

"It would mean scooping out the sockets."

"Then scoop 'em out."

"Kitty, on four of the five you collected for me to look at, I'd do it without a second's hesitation. They're the work of memorial masons. But the Medusa is a genuine work of art, I wouldn't touch it for a pension."

"That one with the snakes? I know. That was a present to me years ago. With a back-handed compliment chucked in. Forget all that. Attend to the business in hand. You can paint her in some eyes . . . I'll send for the girl so you can look her over. One thing I will say, she ain't shy. What eggsackly she is I don't yet know, but she ain't shy."

She was breathtakingly beautiful; undoubtedly the most beautiful girl Skelton had ever seen; but it was the artist in him, rather than the man that responded to this unique combination of shape and colour. He did not want to jump into bed with her — he wanted to paint her. And here he was, conferring with old Kitty how to make her part of a joke, something to entertain bored, idle men. Really, life was hell!

Daisy came in, buoyant and confident. She'd had a wonderful supper, a sound night's sleep, a wonderful breakfast and a *bath*! She'd seen nobody except Esther who had been extremely kind, though very untalkative. When Daisy, astounded by what she considered to be the grandeur of the room assigned her, said naively, "I didn't think maids or lodgers had rooms like this!" Esther gave her a funny quick look, but said nothing. In the morning, she served breakfast — and what a breakfast! — in bed, and, again astounded, Daisy said, "I don't know what I am to do in return for all this." Esther said, "Madam has something in mind for you, I don't doubt." She spoke primly, discouragingly. And she looked like a housekeeper. At the Hall the housekeeper had been held in great awe. Daisy asked no questions. Then came the miracle of a bath, not a bath brought into the bedroom and filled from cans, of which Daisy had carried hundreds and hundreds in her time, but a fixed bath, in a room all by itself and fitted with taps. Then soon after that, Esther came and conducted her to Madam's bedroom, where there was a man.

"Daisy, this is Mr Skelton. Jack, Daisy Holt." He gave a slight bow, and he stared; not quite the staring which she was accustomed to get from men. Far more serious; more as though she were something in a shop window and he wondered whether it was worth the price. Then he said, "I see what you mean, Kit. A unique blend of the classic and the romantic. You've set me the hell of a task, you know. Amongst your gimcrack collection she'd stand out like a bird of Paradise in a flock of crows."

"You ain't seen half yet. Daisy, you remember how you stood yesterday when I told you to stop."

"Like this?" It was a movement in a square dance, one hand held high in that of the partner under whose arm you had just ducked, the other held out to the next, ready for the twirl. Daisy assumed the posture with ease.

"Thass it. Hold it. Now, see what I mean?"

Mr Skelton studied her even more intently and then addressed her for the first time.

"How long could you hold that pose, Daisy?"

"I dunno. I never tried. Say half an hour."

"Not likely. Most people find difficulty in just sitting for ten minutes."

"I'm strong," Daisy said and gave him one of her entrancing smiles — safe to do so, indoors, with Kitty watching. And what she said was true; her life so far had been calculated to produce good muscles. Long before she went into service she had worked, in the house, in the fields; and at the Hall, as the most menial of servants, she had been put upon shamelessly. Even being a nursemaid at Number 6 had called for strength. The perambulator was kept in the basement and had to be hauled up the area steps before each outing, and down again afterwards; the baby had to be carried up and down from the very top of the house.

The remarkable thing was that this man was the first person in all her life who had given even a second's consideration about what she could or could not do. People on the whole had been kind to her, but there was work to be done and servants were there to do it.

"How long do you propose this raree-show to go on?" Skelton asked.

"As long as folks want it."

"I mean how long will one display last?"

"I thought about ten minutes. Once an hour. And Jack, I been thinking about what you said last night about eyes. Applies to hair, too. Wigs. At least two, blonde and brunette — she's sorta copper colour, you'll notice. Shakund ah song goot as the French say. I thought about breathing, too. She can't hold her breath for ten minutes. But a lot can be done with sequins and a good draught with some fluttery stuff. I laid here in bed and I could *see* it. I did think of black velvet, but thass a bit gloomy so we'll have scarlet. I'm talking about the background."

"So I gathered. And what you just said about sequins provokes a thought in my mind, too. The Medusa — the only one comparable — could have a head-dress to hide the snakes. It might as well be a thorough fake."

"What I like about you, Jack, is you never mince words. Fake it is. Tell me what ain't. The whole thing's a fake. You admitted as much yourself yestiddy, only you said Fate. Fate you said, just afore you went off to get round the aldermen and make them immortal, like that Dutchie made some night-watchmen. See? We all come to it. In the end. We're all diddled from the start and the trick is to get your diddle in first. Which this will do."

The conversation went on. Much of it was incomprehensible to Daisy and seemed not concerned with her; and presently she ceased even to listen and concentrated upon holding the pose, something which grew more difficult every minute. The upstretched arm seemed to sag, to quiver, to go half numb. At last she said, with a little gasp, "I over-rated myself! I'm beat."

That drew their attention and she smiled, this time in apology.

Mr Skelton said, "As I thought. Never mind, we can find something less exacting."

"I just suggested that as a sample. She got what I call a *fluid* body. Tell you what, Jack, I don't want her *seen*. Might give the game away. And it'd be a dull old day for her, shut up. Take her along. Let her help. Explain to her whass it all about."

"If you want this ready for tomorrow night, I can do with some help. Come along, Daisy."

"Meet anybody on the way," said the old perfectionist on the bed, "make out you're sneezing or something so your face ain't seen."

It wasn't far, in the same building, a fairly large room empty save for a table and a number of life-size statues. At the Hall there had been two and towards the end of her time there Daisy had been entrusted with the task of washing them well with soap and water and a brush. As the formidable housekeeper had said, they were dust collectors and particular attention must be paid to their

48

fingers, toes and ears. Now she was actually allowed to paint one black all over!

She was given other, fascinating, jobs, too. Mr Skelton actually didn't explain much, but she gathered that it was a joke of some sort, centred about herself; some kind of show in which she must play a leading part. She was not yet sufficiently egocentric to understand fully the enormity of the compliment being paid her, in an indirect way. She just entered into the spirit of the thing and had the time of her life.

Now and again he interrupted her in what she was doing to say, "Come here. I want to have a look at you." He made particular mention of her complexion. "Milk and roses? Peaches and cream? I'd say apple-blossom." It was a kind of compliment, she realised, but he didn't sound as though it was praise; just a fact that he was noticing. In this his manner resembled Kitty's; treating her as though she wasn't human, or wasn't there. She did not recognise as compliments his groans and expressions of dissatisfaction with his work, which was to make all the faces — except the black one — resemble her as far as possible. "God! Who could do it?" "That old devil thought this one out to torment me." Things of that sort.

He was very considerate and sensible about human needs.

"There's a water closet just along the passage," he said, half-way through the morning. "Remember not to be seen."

When she'd finished blacking the statue, he set her other tasks and in no time at all there were sounds, footsteps, voices and the rattle of crockery.

"Duck down behind one of them," he said and himself went to the door and took in two trays. Wonderful food again. Daisy set about it with gusto. Skelton watched her.

"How old are you?"

"I was fifteen on St Bartholomew's Day."

"That's very young." For some reason he made it sound as though being young was rather sad. Or wrong.

"That's what Mrs Westcott said when Lady Langton named me for nursemaid. Maybe she was right." She laughed. "If I'd bin older I shouldn't have got the sack."

"How's that?" She reported the doings of yesterday morning and laughed even more. "But then I should never have come to this nice place, should I?"

Nice place! he thought. That part of him which life had not corrupted and made cynical felt sad again. He knew that by all moral standards it was his duty to tell her exactly what this nice place was; urge her to escape, to go anywhere, do anything. But that was ridiculous; compared with the lives led by most poor girls, life in Kitty Hammond's place was Heaven, at least from a material point of view. It was Kitty's boast that she never kept a girl against her will — they were all free to come and go as they pleased. She had no difficulty in getting and keeping girls; rather her problem was in excluding them. It was part of Sam's duty to turn unwanted ones away.

"Can you eat this? I can't. I over-ate last night."

50

He was referring to the pudding which wasn't really a pudding as Daisy understood it; feather-light sponge and cream and strawberry jam.

"I *could*. Whether I ought is another matter. I don't wanta get fat."

"I don't think that need bother you for, say, fifteen years."

"All right then. I'll take the risk. Then you drink the rest of the wine. I do get drunk so easy."

That seemed to amuse him. "When were you last drunk?"

"At Mr Rooke's Harvest Horky, last September that was. I don't remember very much about it but they said I danced and sang and went round kissing people. Wasn't that shocking? And in the morning I felt truly awful and I said to myself, Daisy, drinking don't suit you; be careful in future. And I hev been. Even Christmas. The funny thing is . . . Maybe it wasn't the cider all to blame; it could've been the dancing. Sometimes, like last night, when I was dancing and singing; showing off, you might say, I've sorta had the same feeling. Like being drunk at the beginning, if you know what I mean."

"I know. Well, back to work."

He pushed the trays outside the door and brought back a bundle which by Kitty's instructions had been left there. Several wigs — all of the best quality — scarves and feathers, and many fascinating things. The element of secrecy and of make-believe about the whole proceeding delighted Daisy, whose childhood had been brief and largely bereft of playfulness, and whose only experience of beauty had been that provided by Nature. But this was a very special and memorable day for another reason. By the end of it she had fallen in love.

She was not ignorant about sex — no child reared in the country in an unsheltered way and in possession of all its senses could be — and she had been told, in coarse terms, by her stepmother about how careful a girl must be — especially a girl with some looks. In Talbot St Agnes, small village though it was, there were examples of what happened to girls who let men take liberties. Not that the result was always the one warned against: the Rector said that at least half the village brides were pregnant when they came to the altar. There was a general feeling however that a girl should be pretty certain of a man before taking such a risk. Daisy never had, not because she was more moral than others, and not because of her stepmother's warnings, but for the simple reason that she had never seen anybody she favoured enough. And for all her sweet looks she had a sharp tongue and the capacity for pungent speech; one rebuff was sufficient for most boys anxious to take liberties. It was because she was not one to take walks alone with a boy, or loiter about behind stacks that she was regarded as modest and fit to be a nursemaid.

Now, in the course of a single day, all was changed, the taking of liberties, far from being repulsive and a thing to avoid, wore another face, and had Jack Skelton wished to kiss her, he'd have been welcome. Perversely, the fact that the idea never seemed to occur to him, made him more desirable in her eyes. That night she dreamed about him — the first dream of many. Intermittently he was to haunt her dreams all her life.

CHAPTER
SEVEN

Next day, in the afternoon, the display was ready. Kitty herself supervised the setting of the stage in what was known as the concert room. Backdrop, the stage itself, the six low plinths and the curtains were all of brilliant scarlet; three white pedestals held seven-branched candlesticks; the front of the stage was banked with white flowers and green ferns.

Skelton, assisted by old Tom the Penman, brought in the statues one by one on a little wheeled cart and lifted them into place. Tom could be trusted, for he was one of the wrecks whom Kitty had befriended, and he must already know something, because he had lettered the cards. He was a good penman, equally at home with the Gothic, the Italianate and the Copperplate; before he grew old he had taught his art to private pupils and in schools; but he had lost custom with age; girls learned better from young men whom they were anxious to please than from snuffly, ill-kempt old men whom they despised. When Kitty discovered him, Tom was addressing envelopes and circulars and making notices for shopkeepers, all at starvation wages. He now occupied an attic and was sure of food every time he went into the kitchen. He was allowed to take in any outside work he could obtain, but Kitty had first call on his time and skill. In the past eight years he had produced for her many small works of art, all as transient as the occupations and entertainments with which they were concerned.

Daisy was present and helped as much as she could with the hauling and heaving. She didn't like to see her beloved straining with the help of one feeble old man; and she wanted to show that she was, as she had claimed, strong. The plinths were numbered from the left; the one on which she would presently stand was Number 2.

Finally even Tom the Penman was banished. Kitty sat on a chair, large but rather small for her, behind a scarlet rope which would ensure that nobody came nearer the platform than twelve feet. She was breathless, partly from excitement. This might be her last spectacular show, for dropsy was a threat to the heart and "tapping" now brought her less relief than once it had done.

Three of the figures were intended to catch the eye and distract the mind. Medusa's snakes were hidden by a turban of blue and gold and she wore a blue cloak, toga-fashion, fastened on one shoulder with a diamond and sapphire brooch, Kitty's own. "Nothing like real stones for catching the light," Kitty said. The sequins on the Nubian girl's breasts and pelvic region caught the light, too, and gave, as Kitty had foreseen, the illusion of movement, of breathing. So did the peacock feathers in the head-dress and fan of the third outstanding figure; they quivered in the current of moving air caused by the candles' heat. The two other statues were identical, a pair made to match and designed to hold lamps in their outstretched hands; one was now rigged to offer a basket of fruit, the other a flagon of wine. Daisy, in the same placatory, inviting pose, was to hold a wreath of flowers. Her face was coloured and her body whitened. The two marble girls wore the minimum of clothing, a kind of loincloth; she wore white linen, so stiffly starched and carefully folded that it resembled stone. Kitty herself had arranged it and added a touch here and there to her face to make it look artificial. It struck Daisy as funny that Jack Skelton had spent so much time and trouble making them look like her, and then Kitty had to spend an hour making her look like them. "And for God's sake, mind your eyes. They could give the whole game away. The statues gotta fixed stare. You find something to look at and just stare. See?"

"I must blink."

"Don't think about it. Once you think you'll blink more. Bear in mind there's a lot to look at besides you. Nobody can look at everything at once — and if my name's Kitty Hammond it's the black girl will hold the eye."

While Tom had been present and while Daisy had been arranging the wigs and generally helping around, she had worn a dressing-gown. Now she must throw it off and her feelings were mixed. She had not baulked at the idea of displaying her beautiful body — at the safe distance of twelve feet, and in a crowd — to a number

56

of strange men. Now something came over her. In a second she'd stand bare-breasted before *him*.

Kitty noticed the momentary hesitation and said with a viciousness all the more appalling for being so quiet, "Don't you act shy on me at the last minute! I laid out over a hundred pound on this show. You fail me now and Sam'll chuck you back in the gutter with a face your own mother wouldn't reccernise. Get on that stand!"

For a second it was literally touch-and-go. In Daisy fear, real fear, struck, but courage rushed up to meet it.

"Don't talk to me like that! I ain't your slave! I don't care if you spent a thousand blasted pounds!"

Then Skelton, on the platform, absorbed in the last finishing touches and feeling more and more imperatively the need for a drink, called, "Come along, Daisy."

Well, if he could be so matter of fact about it, so could she! She dropped the dressing-gown, climbed onto her plinth, took up her wreath and stood. The significance of the abrupt change of attitude was not lost on Kitty.

Skelton jumped down and went behind the rope barrier and, standing by the old woman, viewed his work with a certain satisfaction, and with utter disgust.

No denying it was something to look at. Knowing that it was to be mounted in scarlet, he had used no red at all; even the red apple from the basket of wax fruit, the poppy from Daisy's wreath, had been removed. It was beautiful; and it was seductive; even the balance of nudity and a kind of modesty had been preserved. The

Medusa looked so dignified and yet so tantalising that the urge to twitch her toga away would assail any man; the Nubian girl, stark naked except for sequins, most erotically placed, was a plain invitation to lechery; and the three cool nymphs, neither naked nor clad, struck a kind of middle note. And really did look singularly alike.

"You did a good job, Jack. I'm satisfied."

"That augurs well for my new start in life."

"Well, I bin telling you long enough — you could please if you wanted to. I'm glad I changed my mind about the wigs. They do look more alike with the same colour." She had abandoned the idea of having one blonde, one brunette to set off Daisy's red-gold and the two stone nymphs had hair as nearly like Daisy's as could be obtained.

"Which would you say; if you didn't know?"

"But I do," he said irritably. "And I want a drink."

"No lack of that in this house. Tell you what, Jack. You go and hev a drink — or two. Then come back for another look. Fifteen minutes say. You'll feel better then."

Her body was nothing but a burden but her mind was sharp and she had just had the idea of a hoax within a hoax.

"You can let go now, Daisy," she called and as he made his way to the door he spared a thought; I'm glad she had that much consideration for the child.

The door closed behind him and Kitty heaved herself to her feet, waddled around the rope barrier and to the platform.

"Help me up, you thass such a Samson! Now listen, we gotta work fast. Mr Skelton want some changes. Number four in your place, you in hers, her with the flowers, you with the fruit."

Not an easy exchange to make with only the help of a lumbering old woman who grunted and puffed, but if that was what he wanted Daisy was prepared to move mountains.

"Give me a hand down. Then stand like a rock. This'll be the *real* test."

Kitty went back to her chair and dropped into it, thinking, You old fool. Kill yourself for a bit of a joke! But how better to die, when you'd had your time and your own body was a burden?

"Now look," she said when Skelton returned. "Lotsa things look better through the bottom of a glass. Take a card. Pretend you're just anybody."

The cards were gilt-edged and beautifully written; and their message was brief. Kitty knew her clientele. Gentlemen couldn't be bothered with a lot of words. The same consideration had led her to give the plinths numbers rather than fancy names.

"Pay a guinea. Win fifty. Pick the living girl. Write her number and your own name."

Skelton glanced at one of the cards and then, with an unassuaged sense of self-contempt, looked at his handiwork which seemed just as he had left it. Then the truth burst upon him and he roared with laughter.

"You old stoat! You switched the nymphs! And I'm damned if I . . . Wait a minute. The prettiest! Number four."

Inside her coating of cosmetic Daisy blushed with joy. He'd called her the prettiest. Yet he wasn't paying much attention.

"How much do you reckon to make by this masquerade?"

"Tonight? What with the cost and the prize I might just break even. But wait till tomorrer! Wait till the word get about!" Between their puffy lids her eyes glinted, not so much because of the money. She had all she wanted or ever could want; but the thought of the stir, the excitement, people saying, Old Kitty's done it again! She nudged Skelton with her elbow — it was like being hit by a cushion — and said, "You're another stoat! Wondering what to charge me for two days' playing about. Well, less say twenty guineas down and see how it go. You'll get your share. And Jack, a word in your ear. You got any drinking to do, get it done afore you start on the aldermen. Twelve men grousing could do a lot of damage."

"I'd better start now, then," he said, and went off. Not a word of farewell. Not a glance.

"Put this back on and get to your room. Careful how you go and don't muck up your paint. Esther'll bring your supper. The first show'll be at half-past nine; be here at quarter past."

Kitty spoke coldly. She remembered the moment of defiance. It had not displeased her, merely shown her the necessity for getting the upper hand. The girl was a find; might be a treasure; but the most spirited horse was worthless until it was broken in.

★　★　★

The prediction of breaking even had been an underestimation. Every man who came to Kitty's that evening saw the display once, some twice, some three times. Even Lord St Berners, who was practically blind, could not resist the gamble and made a guess, choosing 5, which he considered to be his lucky number. At one point an attendant hurried up to Kitty and asked whether any gentleman might have more than one card at a time.

"Twenty, so long as he pay."

That enterprising young gentleman marked his five cards in five different ways and felt reasonably certain that the fifty guineas was his. He was disappointed because as the attendant who handed out the cards and pencils at one door, and the attendant who collected the cards at another, were careful to explain, it was the *first* correct card taken out of the bag into which they were dropped that secured the prize.

There were four showings, the first at half-past nine, the last at half-past twelve. To each winner Kitty said, "Now I rely upon you not to go and divulge what you know. Word of honour?" They all promised and on the whole she knew they would keep their word, for hers was a select, expensive house and most of her clients were men who regarded anything in the gambling line as sacrosanct. They might owe vast sums to the people who supplied them with the necessities of life but gambling debts were scrupulously paid. Still, she found it wise to add, with elephantine good humour, "Anybody go blabbing'll get on my black list."

She kept one — not large, but very rigid. It was headed by a duke who had been what Kitty euphemistically described as over-rough with one of the girls. Naturally nobody regarded girls in brothels as being made of Dresden china and men did sometimes get a bit excited, but treatment that incapacitated a girl for a fortnight was not to be tolerated here. Bad economics and — almost worse — bad style. His Grace must be a trifle mad; he felt his exclusion keenly and was once rash enough to try to force his way past Sam and when denied admittance, struck out. At Sam! Whose face had not been flattened by a mangle but by fists in prize fights.

Excluded also were a few men who had cheated in the card room and a Member of Parliament — another madman, very handsome, exquisitely dressed, who had conceived the idea that his mission in life was to reclaim prostitutes. He'd fooled even Kitty who was not easily fooled. He'd seemed so ordinary, so much of a type, coming in, taking supper, taking part in whatever was going on, going upstairs with the girl of his choice, and there preaching sedition. The wages of sin is Death and why-not-repent-and-take-a-decent-job? Naturally the silly girls had misunderstood and thought the decent job meant being his mistress; one had actually left and come to her senses when she found what the decent job was — looking after a rheumatic old lady out at Hampstead . . . Comic that was!

Beside the extraction of word of honour, and the threat of black-listing anybody who gave the game away, Kitty had other protective devices; the three nymphs could be switched around. One evening there might be two Medusas or two girls with feathers.

At the end of a very lucrative night — all extra to the ordinary business of the house — Kitty had all the cards carried up to her room and made a rough analysis of the results. It gratified and amused her to find that eight out of ten votes had been cast for the black girl with the sequins. Just as she had thought. Kitty knew men.

CHAPTER
EIGHT

For Daisy the long night had been a see-saw between something she had never experienced before — agonising boredom — and a frenzied excitement. Behind the curtain she waited, with five dummies and Tom the Penman — the one to whom Kitty had entrusted the office, since it called for discretion and not much strength — while beyond the red folds the sounds of voices and laughter steadily mounted. Then Tom said, "Ready?" and pulled the cord that made the curtains swish open. There was a burst of applause, a tribute to the spectacle; then the hubbub began again.

Was he there, watching? Surely he must be. Come back to see the result of all that hard work. She mustn't look. She mustn't move her eyes. She stared at the thing she had chosen to stare at, sensibly choosing something that did not flicker or shimmer amongst so many flickering and shimmering things — the bare black foot of the figure she had painted. Mustn't blink; mustn't think about blinking. Think of something else. Think about him, out there, seeing how good she was.

Ten minutes, in the ordinary way no time at all, stretched out. But at least *he* had chosen a pose easy to hold; and presently the curtains swished together, and there she was, alone with the dummies and Tom.

"Was Mr Skelton there?" she asked of the old man who, sitting on a stool just behind the curtain, must have had a view of some sort.

"Not so far as I know."

To an extent Tom had a fellow feeling for Skelton, feeling that they were both artists, unappreciated, born in the wrong time. Tom felt that he would have done better, been happier, plying his craft in the scriptorium of a monastery, before printing was known, before time was measured — except by bells. And Jack Skelton would have been happier, done better if he had lived before this rage for prettification set in. Wasn't it Cromwell who demanded that when he was painted the portrait should show his warts?

Never very fond of females — parents and teachers had always said, "Well, at least Mr Burton can be trusted" — Tom had, over the years, developed a positive distaste for them. Old Kitty was all right, though inclined to ask miracles of him. To charm of person or personality he reckoned himself to be impervious and when, obeying Kitty's orders, he took Daisy to a little room behind and to one side of the platform and she looked about and said, "What are we supposed to do now?" he replied, "I don't know about you, except you must stay here, out of sight. I'm going to get a breath of air."

So she was alone again, in a small, windowless room, just within hearing of the life going on all around her, but utterly cut off. The room was comfortably furnished — Kitty believed that even transient entertainers should be well accommodated — and there was a huge looking-glass on one wall. Daisy studied her reflection with attention and thoughtfulness and approval. Mr Skelton was an artist; artists loved pretty things . . . There were sandwiches and a jug of lemonade on a sofa-table. She ate and drank with less than her usual gusto, thinking wistfully of the meals they had shared while the statues were being made ready. Oh, if only he were here now . . .

The little dressing room had a WC of its own. Daisy made use of it and came back and there was still an endless time to go before the rest hour ended. Tom came back in good time.

"Whass it like out there?" Daisy asked as though she were a long-term prisoner asking news of a lost world.

"Busy," he said. He was as bad as Esther. Then when she was in place and he was ready to pull the cord, she said softly, "Keep an eye open for Mr Skelton."

Easy enough to see what ailed her! Tom felt no pity though he was reasonably sure that she was out of luck. All the pity Tom was capable of feeling was for himself, doing such beautiful work, so utterly unappreciated.

When the curtain closed for the last time and she asked again, he broke through taciturnity for a moment and said, "He wouldn't want to come and gape. He's seen enough of this by now. Besides, he's got to get drunk enough to face the aldermen."

"Who're they?"

"People he's paid to paint."

66

"Like these?"

"More or less."

"Daisy Holt is asking if she can go out," Esther said.

"No, she may not just at present. She'd go talking to somebody. On the other hand she can't . . . I know. She can go in the shop. You take her through, Esther, and tell Mrs Bruce to give her something to do, out of sight. And tell her not to talk. And, Esther, say, I don't want her worked hard, just kept amused."

The shop was one of Kitty's subsidiaries. At first designed purely as a cover for the house of assignation, it had, under Mrs Bruce's capable management, developed into a profitable business in its own right. It had begun as a shop selling beauty preparations of cheap quality and trinkets; a place to be passed through. A place where the most respectable lady could spend an idle morning, a leisurely afternoon, where any gentleman could drop in to buy a fan or a flask of perfume or an artificial flower.

Respectable ladies — even great ladies — were so seldom free in the evenings what with the dinners, the concerts, the opera, the theatre, the balls; and they lived lives which, if not deliberately supervised, lacked privacy and made an illicit love affair extremely difficult to conduct. Kitty had made the whole thing easy. The most respectable lady could direct her coachman to the Beauty Shop; the gentleman with the most impeccable reputation — so far as women of his own kind were concerned — could look in and buy something for his wife, sister, even mother. Then upstairs! And nobody the wiser.

Once the whole affair had been run by one of Kitty's superannuated girls. For, facts must be faced, there came a time when the term *girl* no longer applied. What then? Except the streets? And even the streets getting narrower, darker, frequented by men who could not afford to be too choosy. Then, when that failed, some menial job for which they were entirely unsuited, or the workhouse.

All very sad; and Kitty Hammond, who had escaped such a fate by her wits, had a curious fellow-feeling for those who had no wits, only bodies and pretty faces. For those who had a modicum of sense she did what she could. Esther and several other women who held fairly responsible posts in her various departments had once been among her girls. Mrs Bruce had come from outside.

Esther used one of her keys and unlocked a door, led the way along a short passage and into a plainly furnished room that incongruously smelt like a hundred flower gardens. The woman seated at the table, writing in a book, looked up with a faint expression of surprise and said, "Oh, it's you, Esther."

Even with Mrs Bruce, plainly important, Esther was as short-spoken as ever.

"Yes, ma'am. Madam says will you find something for this girl — Daisy Holt — to do. Out of sight. Light work. And explain about not talking."

"I'll do my best."

Here again was that way of talking about and around her that Daisy was beginning to resent. But the feeling vanished when she realised that Mrs Bruce was regarding her with interest, even with admiration. The interest was mutual for Mrs Bruce was unlike anybody Daisy had ever seen before. On the small side; no figure at all; absolutely black hair, so straight and so shiny that it reminded Daisy of the paint she had put on the black statue. Before it dried. Enormous, completely black eyes, made to look larger, Daisy thought, by applied shadows on the upper lids and below the eyes. Mrs Bruce was pale, but it was a pallor more creamy than white. Daisy was in fact taking her first look at a woman who had more Indian blood than she cared to acknowledge. Mrs Bruce, whose looks gave her little choice in the matter, did admit to having an Indian great-grandmother. A Rajput princess. The link was actually closer than that, but who could know? What she had, alongside her mixed heritage, was the determination to exploit it to the full.

"You're very beautiful," she said to Daisy, seeing in her all the enviable things; youth; blue eyes; red-gold hair; a bust, pronounced but not gross.

"So they say," Daisy said. "But you ain't so bad yourself. You're . . . you're *smart*." Black could be smart, but with that hair and those eyes, almost any other colour would have been more becoming.

Mrs Bruce's discreetly tinted lips curved in a half smile; the dark melancholy of her eyes never changed.

"And what have you been up to to be sent over here?"

"Me? I ain't done nothing except do what I was told — and damned well too."

"And what were you told to do?"

Warming under this, the first friendliness, Daisy said, "Well, I hev to . . . No, sorry, I can't tell you. It's a bit of a secret."

"You have mastered the first lesson," Mrs Bruce said approvingly. "*Everything* in this place is secret." She rose, "Come with me and I will find you a light, pleasant occupation."

She led the way to the source of the beautiful smell. It was midway between a kitchen and an apothecary's shop. Dozens, hundreds, of bottles and jars on shelves, and at a big white scrubbed table a woman, aproned like a cook, ladling something from a huge bowl into some pretty little jars.

"Leave that now, Ella. Go to the front and check the stock."

Ella obeyed gladly, removing her apron. The shop was vastly more interesting than the work-room.

Mrs Bruce went to the bowl, dipped in a finger and then rubbed it over the back of her hand, sniffed it; seemed dissatisfied.

"I am glad that I came in when I did," she said, and went to a shelf, lifted down a large flask, tipped some of its contents into the big bowl and stirred it vigorously.

"Few perfumes are stable," she said and Daisy wondered why she should say that. Stable meant to her a place where horses were kept and anything less like . . .

70

"Fill the jars. Give the mixture a stir from time to time. When they are all filled, stick on the labels."

The labels lay, together with a bowl of flour paste, just beyond the ranged jars. They were very pretty; blue and white. The blue was the sky, far bluer than any sky Daisy had ever seen, and standing against it a dead white building of curious shape but undoubted beauty.

"How pretty," Daisy said.

"Yes. An artist called Jack Skelton designed it, from drawings I gave him. It is the Taj Mahal. In India."

Ignoring all else, Daisy said, "Do you know him?"

"We worked together."

"Ain't he *nice*?"

"He was agreeable to work with."

"Thass what I thought. And did he really make all those labels?" Daisy eyed them, eagerly; prepared, if he had so little as touched them, to handle them with reverence.

"No. He reduced the pictures I drew to the bare essentials and made, I think it is called a woodcut, so that the picture could be reproduced easily and cheaply. I must go now. The shop begins to be busy at this hour."

Into the shop, where her function was to advise and connive rather than to serve, Mrs Bruce carried with her the memory of a time which now seemed very distant, though the intervening years were not, after all, so many. It was the difference between being only just past one's first youth and being on the brink of middle age which made a few years seem so long. That and some disappointed hopes. England had always seemed to her to be the Promised Land, and when at last she reached it, travelling as a kind of companion to a wealthy widow, she had achieved one of her ambitions. Thirty-one years old, but looking much younger, thanks to Aunt Lali's recipes, she had expected to find, hoped to find, a second husband, *really* English. That had not come about. The caste system in England was as rigid as in India; the kind of man she had visualised as a husband simply did not marry young women with no background, no dowry. The young ones were prepared for a liaison of a temporary nature, the older ones on the lookout for a mistress. While she was still hopeful she was unprepared to compromise and — she now saw — had missed her chance. Aunt Lali's lotions and unguents could do something to enhance youth and to prolong it a little, but, they could not stall off what happened to the bones, the very structure of a quarter-Indian face.

She had drifted, quite by chance, into Kitty Hammond's Beauty Shop and saw in it a chance of another form of success.

One interview with Kitty, when it was at last attained, promised a great deal. Kitty was always ready to take a chance; and Aunt Lali's preparations which could keep black hair black, and skin deceptively smooth, were worth a little gamble.

Under its new name — the Taj Mahal — the shop flourished and gradually became less what it had once been, a front for a place of assignation, than a very prosperous place in its own right. And Mrs Bruce felt that she should have been taken into partnership. Kitty thought otherwise.

"I never had a partner in my life and I ain't starting now."

"Then I must leave you and take my secrets elsewhere."

"You do that and I wish you good luck. Which you won't get, let me tell you. I gotta lotta influence, one way and another. With customers *and* with landlords. You *might* get a place in Soho. All amongst the Italians who don't care what their women look like so long as they're in pod every twelvemonth. And carriage folk don't go there. Too much garlic!"

"I also may have influence," Mrs Bruce said. "With people who frequent the shop — not to buy."

"Really, I gave you credit for more sense. You think they use their own names? And even if they did . . . You try that on and it'd be blackmail. Then you would cop it."

Kitty had won, of course; in the battle of wills, in the deployment of force. Like any failed rebel, Mrs Bruce settled down.

Daisy filled all the waiting jars. In the bowl there was a smear left, not enough to fill another jar, so she experimented with it, rubbing it into her hands first, just to try, then on her face. The label, under the picture with a funny name said simply Beauty Cream. The only stuff even approaching such a thing that she had ever known was goose-grease for winter-chapped lips and chilblains. This was different. It smelt lovely and it wasn't greasy.

After that she stuck on labels. And that new feeling of boredom, of just waiting for time to pass, for something to happen, grew and grew. Like last night in the little dressing-room; just waiting.

Still, there was the night to look forward to. Surely, surely, having made such a beautiful scene, he'd want to come back and see how people liked it, and hear the clapping, the words of appreciation. But that night passed and the next and the next. Tom grew tired of the inevitable question and almost snarled at her.

"Quit bothering me. If I see him, I'll tell you."

By the fourth day Daisy had decided that she couldn't live like this any more. By day the loneliness and boredom of the room behind the shop; at night the loneliness and boredom of life behind the curtain. Something must change or she'd go off her head.

"I've gotta see Madam," she burst out when Esther brought her breakfast.

"Madam wishes to see you. You know the way. Go as soon as you are ready."

Kitty knew men; and there wasn't much she didn't know about girls. She was even willing to admit that while they were much alike in many ways, they were unalike in others and allowances must be made. And there was a fairly sound rule; after the stick, the carrot.

She offered it.

"I got something to say to you," she began in an amiable way.

74

"And *I* got something to say to *you*. I can't go on like this. Shut off, like I was in gaol. Nobody to speak to all day and all night. I'm going daft. And I ain't going to go daft."

"People that go daft, Daisy, are the last to know. Now if you'll let me get a word in, I want to talk about your future. I got great plans for you. Fact is you're wasted, pretending to be a statue. You got talent, as well as being pretty." Kitty could flatter when flattery was called for. "We'll give this show till the end of next week. No good overdoing a good thing. By that time, if you shape up properly, you can have the stage all to yourself. You can sing and dance and strike attitudes; do more or less what you like. You'll *be* the show. How would that suit you?"

"I'd like that. But not if I gotta go on living as though I'd done something dreadful and the police was after me. Thass what I can't bear. And I won't either."

The curious speck in the beautiful blue eye seemed to flicker. Leaning back on her heaped pillows, Kitty asked, dangerously silky, "And how're you going to remedy it?"

"Go mad. Jump up one night and tell all the gentlemen I'm the one thass alive and ask one of them to help me. Somebody would."

Intractable, Kitty thought. And really all the more interesting for so being.

"Somebody *might*," she said, visualising the scene; damsel in distress, chivalry coming out in somebody like young Lord Chalfont or old Judge Wilkinson. "But

75

that wouldn't get you far. Out, but not far. And you'd be doing Jack Skelton out of another nice little job."

"What job?"

"Oh, I'd ask him to set the stage for you. Design your costumes. Like he did for this show. And of course, when this thing is over there'd be no need for you to keep out of sight. 'Fact the more you was seen the better. You could go in the ballroom, in the supper-room. Anywhere you like."

"All right then. I'll try." There was the double lure. Being able to show off, being herself; but — far more powerful — the certainty, this way, of seeing Mr Skelton again.

Then another thought struck her. Wages. Since she'd been in London she'd been bad, not sending money home. It'd be nice to surprise her father. She was mildly fond of him; to her stepmother she was indifferent; for the children she had a feeling of obligation, slight yet persistent and all in a way concerned with food. She'd had, she realised, a comparatively good start in life; for five years the only child, with a good mother; always enough to eat. The other poor little wretches weren't even sure of that.

"And do I get paid?"

"You do indeed. This week a guinea. And next. After that we'll see."

Kitty's swollen hands moved about amongst the clutter on the wide bed. She produced a guinea, and then another.

"You can hev next week's in advance if you like."

"Oh, I would." The childish, ingenuous streak came uppermost as Daisy thought, How surprised Father'll be.

"We gotta think about names, too," Kitty said. "Daisy Holt is all right. I'm not saying it ain't, but it won't do. It ain't graceful enough. We'll hev to ask Mr Skelton about that, too. He's a man of edjercation."

CHAPTER
NINE

"I despair of you, Jack. I really do. Good chance like that. Chucked away in a fit of temper."

"It was not a fit of temper. It was the sheer bloody impossibility of ever getting anything done. No collaboration. They asked for a group, but they're all so busy and important, one day a fortnight is the most they could all be together. My time didn't matter. And their helpful suggestions. Christ! Smithers actually said couldn't I work by gaslight? And . . . Oh, why go on? They were driving me to drink!"

He wasn't meaning that as a joke.

"Not a long drive, if you ask me," the old woman said caustically. He looked very poorly, she thought. Been drinking like a fish and not eating properly. She did not tell him that if he had not dropped in pretty soon she intended to send for him and ask him to spare a little time from the aldermen — if he hadn't finished them. Her rule was let the other person make the petition, if possible.

"You look as though you could do with a square meal. Ring that bell. Order what you like. I'm heving the sole myself."

She always had her simple but choice meal early in the evening, before the rush started.

"Did they pay you?"

"Fifty guineas was the price. Sweated labour at that. Ten I took as a retainer like a fool and that gave them the idea they could walk on my neck from here to Milford Haven. If I'd been in a position to look down my nose at a thousand and could wait till Judgement Day for it, they wouldn't have behaved as they did."

"Thass the way the world is, Jacky boy. And you bin around in it long enough to know."

"Rub in the salt!"

"Well, now that you are here and at a loose end, so to speak, I might hev another little job for you. The sort you despise."

"I despise all forms of *job*. What is it?"

She told him, briefly but comprehensively.

"Funny. I've been making plans for her, too. I was going to ask you if I could borrow her."

"Oh?"

"As a model. Now, I could paint *her* without any falsification. And that's the kind of thing Pitt and Wade like to put on show. Have you any objection?"

"How could I hev? I don't own her. She once up and told me so herself. 'I ain't your slave,' she said. Made me laugh. Inside, of course."

"She was wrong. Sooner or later you get your hooks into anybody within a mile . . . Well, can I have her, just for a couple of hours in the middle of the day? It wouldn't give the show away. I mean I wouldn't paint her as a nymph, recognisable."

"That wouldn't matter. I'm taking that show off at the end of the week."

"Why? Didn't it go well?"

"It went like a train. You never saw such crowds. But the trick is to leave 'em wanting more. It'll go back on in the autumn. They'll all be agog then. Meantime we got time to get this other thing going — if you want the job, that is. And, boy, the two things could work in together. You paint her and we'll put it on show in the entry. That'll make a stir. Oh, and we need a new name for her. I told her Daisy Holt just won't do. Daisy, little humble field flower and a nuisance in lawns; and Holt; too much like colt. Give your mind to that for a minute."

He gave what remained of his mind. He ate his sole and began to feel better. It was absurd and he knew it, to go on trying this and that, being hopeful, industrious in patches, always chasing the will-o'-wisp which for some reason always eluded him.

He tried names over in his mind.

"I thought of painting her as Hebe, cupbearer to the gods. I think the idea came to me while we were arranging the nymphs. I thought then that she should be the one with the wine . . . Yes, Hebe."

"Easy to remember," Kitty said, trying it over in her mind, "but it ain't a Christian name."

"Nor is Diana, Daphne or come to that Catherine from which your own name is derived. In Greek it means pure!"

"So it should," Kitty said obliquely. "Well, thass settled then. She'll need a surname. Hebe what?"

80

"Something flowery. After all we're doing away with Daisy, aren't we? Wait a minute . . . Once when she was chatting away, she said something about a wood, near her village. I think it was Waywood. How would that be? Hebe Waywood."

Kitty tried it over. "Not bad. D'you ever see her dance? There's nothing so special about it. Village green stuff, but very pretty, with her doing it."

"Yes. I'd say whatever she did, it'd be pretty." A kind of distant appreciation sounded in his voice, no real interest.

"About that, I ain't all that sure," Kitty said thoughtfully. "When she ain't very pleased, she don't look so good."

"Then we must endeavour to please, must we not?"

Daisy was easy to please, and anxious to please. It all seemed too wonderful to be true. Here *he* was again; and here she was, being herself again, working with him again, and this time the centre of his whole attention.

"Hebe, when you and the other girls danced round the maypole in your village, did you wear any special clothes?"

Talbot St Agnes now seemed half a world away, but she thought back.

"Some did. I never. Till I was five I was too little and then we was too poor."

"Can you describe the clothes?"

"I can do better than that. I can dror them for you . . ."

With amazing, innate skill, she sketched what he recognised to be the basic peasant dress, once almost a uniform for high days and holidays, now only to be seen in out-of-the-way places. Full, rather short skirt; blouse with short, puffed sleeves and a low neckline gathered on a cord; a kind of waistcoat.

"The best was velvet," Hebe said, scribbling to show that the waistcoat should be black, "but sateen would do. Laced down the front. See? The laces should be the same colour as the skirts. Them? Oh, any colour — except yellow. In the country they don't favour yellow for some reason. Maybe because there's so much of it about, crocuses and daffodils and dandelions and mustard fields. I like it myself."

For the Maypole Dance she could not, of course, have a proper maypole — that needed at least six people. Instead she was to have a pole closely set with roses and at the end of the dance she was to take six or seven roses and toss them to some of the watching gentlemen. "*Not*," Kitty ordered, "any ones in particular, we don't want favouritism. Except with the very old. See some old fellow, one foot in the grave, and make sure he gets one, see?"

Encouraging men who were past using the house for its usual purpose was good policy. Men tended to become richer as they aged; and lonelier. Kitty and one or two of her girls had actually been left nice little legacies by ancient gentlemen who had found in her house the one place where the years seemed to fall away for an hour or two.

There was to be the Maypole Dance, and one with veils, all different colours, so that Daisy, wearing almost nothing, seemed to be whirling in a rainbow. In another

82

she was to be a nymph taking a bath under a fountain. In a third, hardly a dance at all, except that each step was a skip or a prance, she was to appear fully, even primly dressed, and then discard one garment after another. Kitty thought the disrobing should be thorough so that Daisy ended as naked as the Nubian girl, but at that Daisy demurred and Skelton said, "I think she's right. Some element of mystery should be retained." Then Kitty improvised again.

"Can you turn a somersault?"

"I use to do. Less see." She turned several in succession.

"In short, frilly skirts and little flesh-coloured drawers," Kitty said. "Very tantalising."

Now and again, Kitty spared a moment to instruct Daisy about conduct off-stage. She could move about in the ballroom and the supper-room, but not too frequently and not for long at a time. "You don't want to go making yourself cheap. Understand? In the supper-room you can go to tables, when invited, which you will be. Be careful about wine, you ain't used to it; and nothing but champagne, bear that in mind. And don't go eating like a horse, or they'll say I starve you." She was not to sit on any gentleman's knee, and there was the same old warning about letting men take liberties. In the ball-room she could dance just a few times, never twice with the same gentleman.

"You behave like I say and I'll get you some singing lessons. Yore voice is all right but a bit of training'd improve it."

When Kitty said things like that, Daisy found herself almost liking her; but there were other times . . .

Kitty could not forget how eye-drawing the Nubian girl was. Night after night the vast majority of men cast their vote for her. Silly on the face of it, for they were all familiar with naked statues; but she worked it out. They *wanted* to think that the naked girl was the real girl. And Kitty wanted Daisy to be naked at some point in the programme. Over the disrobing dance she had been defeated; over the nymph bathing she had a good argument.

"Even a nymph — whatever that may be — wouldn't go in the water with clothes on."

"Women wear bathing dresses," Skelton said.

"And fine sights they look," said Kitty who had seen some at Brighton. "And Hebe ain't a woman taking a dip in the briny; she's a nymph. And I want her bare."

Mr Skelton had supported Daisy before and it sounded as though he would do so again. Daisy cast him an eloquent look, and then, when he did not immediately respond, said, "Mr Skelton should decide. He's the artist."

Kitty showed no sign of displeasure. She said, "That'll do for today. You go, Jack, and see about them palm trees; and get that fountain rigged up."

The stage in the concert-room was still occupied by the statues — that show had two nights yet to run; so the rehearsals, the trying out of ideas took place in Kitty's bedroom.

"Tell the plumber he gotta work Sunday. Daisy, I mean Hebe, I want a word with you." She spoke amiably and Daisy was taken completely by surprise when, as soon as Mr Skelton had gone, Kitty said, "You ever do that again and I wash my hands of you."

"Why? What hev I done?"

"*Mister* Skelton! *Mister* Skelton," Kitty said venomously. "He's the artist. And you making calves' eyes at him. He's an *artist* all right. One that can't sell a picture or please people to save his life. Glad to take any silly little job I chuck his way. *Hired*, like you and everybody else in this house. *I'm* the one with the say *here*, my girl. Get that through your thick head. I know what people want and I supply it. I know what I want, and I get it. And I ain't gonna be argued with, not by you nor your Mister Skelton."

Kitty paused for breath. Anger and emphatic speech always worsened her condition. She managed a gasp or two and then spoke again.

"I know whass in your mind. All this saving yourself for him and him alone. Lotta rot!" That shot went home. Hot colour flamed in Daisy's face. Kitty, in her curious way, quite liked Jack Skelton, but that did not blind her to his faults, or prevent her decrying him.

"Even if he didn't drink like a fish he'd be no good to you, nor any girl. Got no heart — except for hisself and his genius what the world is too dull to appreciate. According to *him*. He may hev been all right once; I never knew him as a young man. Time I knew him he was getting sour and he gets worse. Rotting from the inside, thass Jack Skelton. And you go getting soft over him, you're asking for trouble." She pulled herself up sharply, aware that she had side-tracked herself. "And

85

you go getting uppity with me, you *got* trouble. You may be too daft to realise it but I'm giving you the chance of a lifetime. God help us, there's hundreds of girls not a stone's throw from here would give their ears for such a chance. And there's you mewing and puking about showing your bare arse. And all on account of that wastrel."

Excitement was bad for an over-burdened heart and as a rule Kitty avoided it. She rather wondered why she had let such a small thing upset her so much. It was just that mutiny must be quenched in the bud; and that despite the remark about hundreds of girls being available, she knew that there wasn't, in the whole of London, a girl to hold a candle with this one now standing before her, still only partially tamed. You could tell by the eyes.

"Now, we'll hev no more nonsense. I say what you wear or don't wear and if that don't suit, sling your hook and for next week I'll fix something to bridge over till I get an amenable girl."

Over the years Kitty had picked up a wide vocabulary; it was necessary when dealing with gentlefolk. About grammar and pronunciation she never bothered because she was shrewd enough to know that the people with whom she dealt, at all levels, liked her talk just the way it was.

Daisy was beginning to acquire the art of understanding words she never used herself and she guessed what amenable meant. Doing just what you were told. In her heart she was anything but amenable. She would have liked to answer back; to say, Go to hell!

86

Or even worse things. She would have liked to slap Kitty's fat face and walk out. But where to?

What has happened to me? she wondered. I cheeked Mrs Westcott and walked away without giving thought for the future. I didn't even know where I'd find a bed. I'm changed. That's what being in love does for you! And living soft! That day I said I'd sleep in a park. I wouldn't say that now.

She said, "All right, then." Still a bit grudging, Kitty thought, but coming round; coming round . . .

"So thass settled. Now about this picshure. We ain't got much time. You'd better go to his place, he'll hev all the stuff there and the light to his liking."

CHAPTER
TEN

Daisy's suspicion that living soft had softened her was confirmed when she saw how and where *he* lived. The place had a pretty name, Springfield Lane, but it was awful, far more smelly and littered than the market where she had ended her day of freedom. The market people did, in their own interest, clear up from time to time; nobody cleaned up in Springfield Lane.

She was not unduly sensitive to smells; in the country there were manure heaps, untended, brimming-over privies and chamber pots. Even in Park Drive the baby had not always smelt like a bed of roses. But here the stench was frightful; held in between the two rows of houses and emanating from them. How anybody could live here! Him least of all.

She had never given any consideration to his background. She reckoned she knew a gentleman when she saw one, and he *was*, no matter what Kitty might say about being drunk and a failure. In any case she could not have imagined Springfield Lane because a London slum was totally outside her experience.

The houses were tall, and so substantially built that they had survived more than a century of neglect and maltreatment. They had once been occupied by people of substance, now every room housed a family, sometimes two; and some served as business premises as well. The houses had been built before shortage of space had made basements necessary, as in Park Drive, but they had cellars, now occupied. In the house where Skelton lived the larger cellar served as a doss house, the smaller one as a collecting place for dog's dung which served a special purpose in the tanning of some kinds of leather. Little boys ran about collecting dogs' droppings; a ha'penny for a full bucket. When there was enough to justify the hiring of a donkey cart it was removed. Sometimes the man who ran the doss house complained of the smell and the dog-dung buyer always had the answer ready; his heap didn't smell as bad as the doss house customers, and had the advantage of not being lousy.

On the ground floor there was a cookshop, exuding the mingled odours of onions and rancid fat. Across the hall a green-grocer's. Skelton led the way up, past the floor where on one side a man and two pallid apprentices stitched trousers, and opposite a woman with three pallid children made artificial flowers of great delicacy and beauty. One room on this floor was occupied by a prostitute and her pimp, another by a man who made a desultory living by stealing dogs and returning them if a reward were offered. If the owner didn't care enough to offer a reward within a week, a crack on the head and into the Thames. More stairs and at their head a locked door. Skelton opened it and said, "Welcome!" in a voice that mocked the word.

At least up here the air smelt clean. But what a poor place! Even by Daisy's standards it was poor and bare and completely unworthy. Her own home had contained some solid, good furniture, handed down through generations; the servants' quarters at the Hall had been almost lavishly furnished since successive mistresses of the place had wanted new, fashionable things and relegated the old to the attics. Even her bedroom at Park Drive, bleak as it was, had a bit of carpet on the floor, a quilt on the bed and curtains at the window. None of that here. The bleak cold light — though the day was warm — came through a huge window and showed a small, hollow-backed bed covered with a grey blanket, a long trestle table with some crockery at one end, some painting stuff at the other and a lop-sided armchair. Mr Skelton did not even have a cupboard; his clothes hung on pegs near the door. Yet, despite the starkness there was something of neatness about the place. No muck, no muddle and nothing that was not needed for the business of living and of painting.

"Now," he said, "we've no time to waste. This is Saturday and Kitty wants the picture on display early on Monday evening. Skip into your things."

She was to wear, over the little flesh-coloured drawers in which she turned somersaults, a dress of filmy material, girded high under the bosom by a blue ribbon. The skirt wasn't really a skirt at all, being slit up one side, and the sleeves weren't sleeves; more like limp drooping wings falling from her shoulders. A band of blue ribbon held her hair back from her forehead, but the rest of it fell free.

He was pressed for time — had the picture been destined, as he had thought, for the display in Pitt and Wade's show room he could have spent, would have spent, more time on it. But Kitty had convinced him that there it would merely be one amongst several, in her foyer it would stand alone, and if Daisy's performance was half as good as it promised to be, the picture connected with it would fetch a wonderful price and bring him some of the recognition he craved. He took time and trouble over arranging the folds of the filmy stuff, and her hair.

He then gave her a silver cup with two handles. Where had that come from?

"Now, hold it out to me, as though you were offering me a drink. Put on an inviting expression . . . That's good! That's marvellous! Can you hold it?"

"Easy." She was, after all, offering him nothing less than her heart.

Occasionally he stared at her intently, and sometimes it was only a glance. She looked at him, more closely, more avidly than ever before. While the statues were being prepared she had had work to do, and their other meetings had been in Kitty's presence. Even now, when she could gaze her fill, she could not decide whether he was handsome or not. His face was lined; deep grooves from nose to the mouth corners, scowl marks between the eyes, a furrowed forehead. Not, Daisy decided, a happy face, though she had seen his eyes sparkle and his mouth curve in a kind of wry amusement. His eyes were clear grey, light, rather cool-looking in a face whose colour was difficult to name, faintly tanned, yet not as country faces were. Her gaze lingered on his mouth; wide and thin-lipped. It looked hard. Often in the past, in games or in dances with plenty of people about and no danger of further liberties being taken, she had been kissed by boys and wondered that the lips of even rough-looking boys should be so soft. A kiss from Mr Skelton would not be soft. The very thought sent such a thrill through her, to her very finger tips, that the bowl sagged.

"Tired? Rest if you are."

"I'm all right."

She transferred her stare to the window. It stood high enough to be merciful. The incredible squalor of the rear of Springfield Lane was invisible; all she could see were some treetops and a church spire.

The slightly off-hand consideration which had so instantly endeared him to her was still there. He asked twice if she were tired and at the third negative, said, "You must be. Take a rest." He stretched and took a few paces to and fro. "I suppose I ought to offer you a cup of tea, but it means taking the kettle down to the cobbler's place."

"I ain't thirsty."

Just as well, he thought; for tea tended to run through people, and here there was no WC just across the way; only the disgusting communal privy in the backyard. Following, briefly, that line of thought, he said, "Maybe I should have brought my gear and painted you at Kitty's place."

92

"I don't think so," Daisy said with a positiveness that was incongruous with her ethereal appearance. "She'd have come poking about and interfering. Like she did once or twice with the statues. You remember?"

He said "Yes," but his attention was elsewhere. On the time. Kitty had been as arbitrary as ever; she wanted the picture for display on Monday; but Daisy, late to bed, mustn't be roused too early in the morning; he had been allowed to pick her up at eleven; and she must be back at four, in order to run through her dances again, and then rest before the final statue show.

"We'll go on now, if you're ready." Daisy jumped up willingly. He re-arranged her draperies and her hair again. Oh, if only his hands were moving in caresses, instead of being so businesslike!

They worked until one o'clock; then he said, "I'm hungry — and if I know you, you are too."

She thrilled again to this trivial recognition of her as a person.

"I am. I could eat an old woman on a horse, with the harness. D'you know, I almost said that to *her*, first time we met. At least, I stopped just before I said harness. Wasn't that shocking?"

His face lightened into the expression that was not quite a smile and then darkened again as Daisy, anxious to be helpful, went to the domestic end of the table. There was a cheap pottery cheese dish with a cover. Inside it was a small portion of cheese which had contrived to go mouldy and dry at the same time. Wrapped in a cloth was about half a loaf of very stale bread. She regarded the fare without dismay; she had eaten worse in her time.

He said, "I'm sorry. I didn't think. And even if I had . . . Until Kitty pays me, I'm broke."

She had actually given him another five pounds for the work on the statues; he'd had the original payment, and ten pounds from the aldermen, all in a comparatively short space of time; but there had been loans to pay back, his rent was in arrears, and although nobody seemed to give it a thought, canvas and paint cost money.

"I've got two shillings," Daisy said eagerly. She wished now that she had not sent two pounds home, though at the time she had enjoyed the thought of her father's pleasure and surprise. "I'll run out and get us something." She snatched up her poor little home-made reticule from the chairback where it lay over her clothes. "What would you like?"

"Oh, anything. Not from the shop just below." It was a common belief in Springfield Lane that some of the unclaimed dogs went into the cook-shop's pies and stews.

"You can't go out like that!" She was dashing off just as she was.

"N'more I can," she said with a dazzling smile. She took one of his jackets from the pegs near the door and huddled into it. The shoulder seams were almost to her elbows and her hands were lost. Suddenly he saw her in another guise, nothing to do with nymphs and classic draperies. A bitterly poor girl, in horrible rags, offering, not wine to the gods on Olympus, but matches, or wilted flowers to any passer-by. In reality offering herself . . . What a picture that would be!

Daisy ran out barefoot. No new experience for her. Until she was five she'd had shoes; the only child of a man in steady employment and a careful, loving mother, she had been better off than many village children. Then had come the change and when her last pair of shoes really hurt she had gone barefoot until she went to the Hall where shoes, like everything else, were provided and bought full large to allow for growth. As a result her feet were shapely, with straight toes and high arches.

Skelton spent a moment in thinking how completely unselfconscious she was. Then he was back to work, painting in the silver cup which did not need her presence; but his mind had moved on and he was thinking about the next picture, and remembering how easily this unusual girl could adopt any pose, any attitude, do anything that was asked of her.

She was back, a trifle breathless, a trifle flushed. She held between her hands a pile of sandwiches from which tiny threads of steam emerged.

"Look what I found! *Hot* salt beef sandwiches! I ran like a hare to get 'em back before they cooled off."

"I'll make it right with you," he said. "By this time tomorrow I should get some money out of that old skinflint."

"Don't fret yourself about that," Daisy said. "Thass a pleasure. And you done a lot for me. Eat up while they're warm."

The bread was fresh and spongy, the salt beef just as it should be, but to Skelton the good sandwiches tasted like chaff; the bread of humiliation. Here he was — the best painter of his time — who simply because he couldn't paint to order was reduced to eating food bought with money taken from a reticule made out of a square of cloth drawn up into the shape of a bag by a bit of ribbon threaded through some very roughly made buttonholes. Well, the Prodigal Son in the Bible had eaten pig-food!

The afternoon passed even more quickly than the morning. Skelton seemed to grow more and more cross and cursed to himself. Finally he took out his watch and said, "Blast! We must be off."

She looked at the watch with surprise. She'd never seen it before; and she could tell that it was an expensive one; the dead spit of Sir Alfred's. It seemed funny in this bare room in the possession of a man who, but for her, would have lunched on stale bread and mouldy cheese. Not that he wasn't every bit as much of a gentleman as Sir Alfred; not that he didn't deserve the best. For the first time in her life she wished for riches so that she could lavish beautiful things on him.

"Thass nice," she said, "is it new?"

"No. Old. I clung on to it because it's handy to pawn."

She looked blank. "Whass that?" There were no pawnshops in villages; and although one resident in Park Drive owned a profitable pawnshop in Greenwich, the word was never mentioned there.

"Bless you, child! Long may you remain in ignorance! Get dressed now."

He did as he had done in the morning, went back behind his easel while she changed.

"I can go back by myself. No need for you to come." That was real self-sacrifice, since every moment of his company was precious.

"Kitty'd never forgive me. I promised to collect you and see you safely home."

He paused to lock the door. Then they went down the stairs into the region of stinks and noise. In the lane she said, abruptly, and with vehemence, "I don't like it. This being handed about like I was a *thing*. I don't belong to her, to be lent about. I walked into her place thinking she let beds for the night . . . And ever since, I ain't really been me. Do this, don't do the other. Even my name changed. And tell you the truth, I don't fancy Waywood much. It ain't lucky."

"I thought of it. You once said something about gathering bluebells or blackberries . . .'"

"Well, if you chose it! Thass different! All the same, Waywood ain't a lucky place — not after dark."

"Why not?"

Tripping alongside him, she repeated and expanded the hodgepodge of fact and folklore that made up the history of Waywood. Like most woods it had its share of children abandoned; their ghosts wailed. There was a pool in which a girl had been drowned, and she floated on the surface every time the moon was full. There were wolves there still — Daisy knew a man who had seen one; and she herself had seen the little house where once upon a time there had lived an old woman who could turn herself into a wolf.

"So you see," she said, as they turned out of Leicester Square, "why I don't think thass a lucky name."

"I'm afraid it's too late to change it now. Tom'll have started on the placards announcing the great new attraction — Hebe Waywood."

At the door, guarded by Sam, she said, "You coming in?"

"No, I must get back. I can work on the background."

"Then take this." She pressed something into his hand and whisked in before he could protest.

He stood for a second or two staring at the shilling. It was warm from her clutch. She had taken it out while he locked the door. She wanted to have it ready, in case he should not come into Kitty's where he could be sure of a meal.

The gesture touched him and roused a number of emotions; shame that it should have been necessary; gratitude; the determination to repay her — not only in coin; and the wish to protect her. All genuine, valid emotions, but no match for Daisy's passionate infatuation. Of that he was incapable.

CHAPTER
ELEVEN

The picture, vastly admired, stood in Kitty's foyer. In the concert room the real Hebe Waywood gave her performance, even more admired. This latest show was even more successful than the statues, and brought in new customers — men who in the ordinary way did not frequent places like Kitty's. They came to see the picture which was the talk of the town, and once inside felt compelled to see the girl dance. Then having enjoyed a free entertainment it seemed uncivil to leave without spending a substantial sum on food and wine.

Of these newcomers there were some who viewed the performance with slight disapproval. The lascivious touches upon which Kitty had insisted went ill with the peculiarly ethereal, virginal quality of the picture. The Duke of Sudbury expressed his feeling — and that of others — when he said, "Damme, it's blasphemous! Like making the Virgin Mary act like a tart and a hoyden."

To those who missed the quality in the picture, but appreciated the performance, Hebe herself was a disappointment. "Prim as a dish," said Lord Kendall. Daisy, who liked people and doted on adulation, took advantage of Kitty's permission to mingle, but she behaved with the utmost circumspection, less because she had been told to do so than because she was so absorbed, so wrapped about in her love for John Skelton that she found it impossible to be even mildly flirtatious with other men; as to sitting on their knees or allowing the slightest liberty, the thought was utterly repugnant. Between performances she would go into the ballroom and dance, once or twice. In the supper room she'd flit from table to table, taking a dainty bite here, a sip of champagne there. There were men to whom such behaviour was a deterrent, others to whom it was the ultimate stimulus.

Always, all the time, she received fulsome compliments upon her beauty, congratulations upon her performance. And always she managed to bring in the beloved's name; often with a subtlety which did not match either the picture or the performance.

"Do you really think I'm as pretty as the picture? Mr Skelton painted it, you know." Or she'd say, with a modesty, not completely false, "I think Mr Skelton flattered me. Don't you?"

Say the name often enough and it stuck. Just as Hebe had stuck. Within a few days people who considered themselves knowledgeable in such matters were asking about John Skelton. Who was he? Why had they never heard of him before? A few people — Sir Charles Clifford among them — had heard of him and nothing to his credit. "I know Charlotte is no raving beauty," Sir Charles said, speaking of his daughter, "but when old Kitty persuaded me to commission him to paint her, damme if he didn't give her a nose four inches long!

Twenty-five guineas wasted. We had to get Hobson to do her. He charged double, but he made her look human." It had been necessary that Miss Clifford's good points should be emphasised and her bad ones modified, for the portrait had been intended as bait. Sir Charles had relatives in India and if they received a picture of a likely-looking girl, there were plenty of men about who might admire the painted girl and wish to see the real one. And the India-based Cliffords could hardly invite Charlotte and then send her back unmarried. Out there they'd find somebody, probably not young or handsome, but somebody. The chances of matrimony in England were, for poor Charlotte, remote.

The Duke of Sudbury, a widower for thirteen years, had recently married a girl less than half his age, and pretty enough. He wanted a portrait of her to hang in the family picture gallery, but he thought she should have some say in the choice of artist, he thought she should see Skelton's *Hebe*; but it was, of course, unthinkable that she should set foot in Kitty Hammond's house, or know that he had done so. Resourceful as well as forthright, he arranged to borrow the picture, just for an hour or two during the daytime. He sent a closed carriage for it. His young duchess was enchanted and swore that John Skelton was the artist for her. She showed a slightly inconvenient curiosity as to where dear Horace had seen the picture. The Duke had turned more tricky corners than that. "In the house of an old friend. In mourning at the moment. And she cannot bear to be parted from the picture for more than an hour or two." The young Duchess, who shared the morbid romanticism that was fashionable at the moment, instantly assumed that Horace's bereaved friend was mourning the loss of a beautiful daughter and began composing a poem about it; loveliness cut off in the bud; oh, cruel fate . . . The Duke made a mental note that John Skelton, whoever he was, must be warned to keep his mouth shut.

Kitty said, "That would be the making of you, Jack. He's so rich. You could charge what you like; and from what I hear Her Grace is a nice-looking girl. You wouldn't hev the trouble with her you had with pore Miss Clifford."

Skelton thought for a moment, ambition pulling one way, something else in another.

"Very well. I'll do it. But not till next week. You're the go-between, Kit. Tell His Grace I'll be in Portman Square, ready and willing, next Monday."

"They," Kitty said, speaking from experience of the lordly ones, "don't like to be kept waiting. Why can't you start tomorrow? You're only at work now painting Daisy — I must remember to call her Hebe — as a beggar girl. Sounds awful to me . . . And what is more, you're dead wrong. I wouldn't say it to her face, but nobody looking like she do would be out in the street selling half-dead flowers for more than five minutes. You must know that as well as I do. She'd be whipped up in no time. Did you ever see a real pretty girl begging?"

"I must admit, no. But, having usually so little to give, I tend to look away."

"Thass what I mean. A picture like what you're doing now is sheer waste of time. It ain't true to life. And nobody's gonna buy it. Rags ain't nice to look at and people don't like being reminded about the pore. You oughta nip round to Portman Square tomorrer morning. 'Bout eleven."

She could see by the look on his face that he had no intention of doing so. Wondering why she bothered with such an awkward, unrewarding fellow, she decided to have a word with Daisy, who could be awkward but was certainly not unrewarding.

She began with some muted praise. It didn't do to let people get swelled heads.

"You're doing pretty well, so far. Keep it up and I shan't complain. Now . . . You like Jack Skelton, don't you?" Daisy blushed wildly. "There's something you could do for him. Real important." She explained. "So you say you can't go for two or three days. Make out you're tired. That'd give him time to make a start and get settled in to this new job. See what I mean?"

Daisy's heart plummeted. She had so greatly enjoyed the last few days. On this picture he was not working against time, so there'd been a chance to talk and an almost festive atmosphere. Kitty had paid him for the Hebe picture and his help with the stage and the costumes. He'd been prudent enough to pay two months' rent in advance, but had plenty left over for food and some kind of wine. They lunched at leisure and she was able to entertain him, chatter about the past, mimic the people she had met overnight, and Kitty herself.

"You have a great talent," he once told her. "When you imitate old Kit you really *look* fat."

Now these happy sessions were to be suspended. He'd be giving his attention to this great lady, maybe even arranging her clothes and her hair. Almost unbearable thought!

"All right," she said unwillingly. "If thass for his own good, I wouldn't stand in his way."

"It will be. Can you write?"

"A bit. There was a cook in my first place learned me a little."

"Then you sit right down and write a little note and I'll send it round first thing tomorrer morning."

That she could write a bit was no modest understatement. The cook, who believed that everybody should be able to read and write, had gone to another post before the lessons had advanced very far. Daisy's spelling was mainly phonetic and her punctuation practically non-existent.

"Deer Mister Skelton I cant cum for the next few days I am two tarred I look foreward to seeing you soon."

How to end? She pondered and then finding — as other people had done — that it was easier to write a thing than to say it, added, "with love daisy".

The appeal of this piteous little screed was lost upon Skelton who saw that Kitty had outwitted him again. He thought, Blast that old fox! Just because she can run a successful whorehouse she thinks she can run everything and everybody! He had half a mind not to go, but thought better of it. He'd charge for this interruption . . .

The Duchess was as bad a sitter as Daisy was good. To begin with she could spare only one hour a day and she was incapable of sitting still or staying silent for more than five minutes at a time; she was also extremely self-conscious and rank-conscious. She had not been a duchess long enough to wear her dignity naturally; when she wasn't fidgeting or chattering, she assumed a look of such portentous dignity that she looked wooden. At the end of each trying hour, she insisted upon seeing what had been done and gradually dissatisfaction crept in. After all, she was pretty enough to have made an outstandingly successful marriage and here she was, being perpetuated for ever in a picture not one half as beautiful as the sample of Skelton's work which she had admired.

She never told Skelton outright that she was dissatisfied; something about him prevented that; but she could complain to Horace, who was compelled to agree that it wasn't quite pretty enough, though he had seen her looking exactly as she was portrayed; his pet name for her — Kitten — always seemed singularly inappropriate at such moments.

"*And* I do not like his manner," the Duchess said, at the end of yet another complaint.

"You're not saying that he dares to be familiar?"

"Oh, no. But gruff and uncivil. Sometimes he does not even bother to reply to a remark. He just grunts."

"I must say he did not take it well when I said I thought he had not quite done you justice. Shall we sack him and try somebody else?"

Skelton took his dismissal and his one hundred and fifty guineas and went off quite cheerfully to resume painting his flower-seller. He'd had the last word when he advised His Grace to hold on to the picture even though he disliked it and it was not quite finished. "In fifty years it'll be of more value than twenty Hobsons." His Grace could hardly hope to live to see that day, but studying the portrait again he had an idea that the conceited fellow might be right; he hadn't caught the best in Kitten, but there was something about the stiff, wooden face, even a hint of prescience. If Kitten lived another fifty years, as she well might do, that could be her usual, not her occasional, expression.

Skelton dropped in at Kitty's, to tell her that he'd finished at Portman Square.

"And it took long enough," Kitty said. Which was true, because working only one hour a day, with a fidgety sitter, the job had taken more than the few days he had intended to devote to it. "And work piling up for you here."

"What work?"

"Copies! You're always on about not being appreciated and you see once you give your mind to it and turn out a pretty picture, you're appreciated all right. I could've sold that *Hebe* over and over, if I'd been so minded. Lord Chalfont offered me five hundred pounds, believe it or not. I said it wasn't for sale just now, but copies would be as soon as you make 'em."

"When Hell freezes I'll make copies."

"All right. Be awkward then. Somebody else will."

"You can't do that to me. It's my picture."

"Thass news to me! You *did* it, granted; to go in with the show. But I paid you for it, Jack Skelton, and don't you forget it. Thass *my* picture, and if I want a hundred copies made, I'll hev them."

"You make me sick!" The buoyant mood, money in his pocket, freedom to do what he wanted, collapsed. He knew that he was helpless. Any clown could make a copy of any picture and sell it; well within the law so long as he didn't try to pass it off as an original.

"You gotta bilious nature," Kitty said placidly. "There's no harm in a copy, labelled as such. You oughta be grateful. Think how they'll spread your name about. Think of the pleasure they'll give."

Just at the moment he could not afford to quarrel with her. She might retaliate by refusing to lend him Daisy any more; and he already had another idea to try out when *The Flower Girl* was finished.

"Have your own way. You usually do. How's Daisy?"

"Hebe! All the rage." Kitty brooded for a moment. "The depths to which people'll sink! Night before last a chap come in here; stranger, but dressed like a toff and not on my list; so he was welcome. Sat through two shows, arst her to take wine with him, and then what d'you think? Offered her a job in Paris — he was a Frog, naturally. Called hisself an impresario! And it was an offer! 'Quivalent to three hundred pounds a week according to Freddie Chalfont. *He* was the one warned me; he come here to me and he said, 'Kit, somebody's trying to steal our Hebe.' Mind you, from here where I sit, I see most of whass going on, but naturally I can't hear. Freddie says 'What you gonna do?' Know what I did? I said, 'If you don't mind soiling your hands, dear boy, chuck him out. Get Lord Kendall to lend a hand. That'll show him how we stick together. Better than sending for Sam.' Lots've others joined in and he weren't such a toff when he went out as he was when he come in, believe me. Boys'll be boys, even when they're peers."

"How did Dai . . . Hebe take it?"

"In the right spirit, thank God! She don't want no Paris. And as I explained to her, after, she's better off here. Look what I've done for her already. And I aim to do more. She's starting singing lessons tomorrer. With that Italian fellow, Luigi Mazoni. He give her a test yesterday and he said she had a wonderful voice but no ear. That he could rectify in no time, he said. And I said to him there was no time to waste. The way people flock in to *see* her, I reckon what she do now'll go another fortnight. Then it'll be high summer, a dead loss in this business. When we start up again she'll sing as well as dance and do antics . . ."

"What time is her lesson tomorrow?"

Kitty grinned, remembering how Hebe had dug in her heels over the timing. She'd said she couldn't take lessons in Mr Skelton's time; he'd want her again any day now.

"Six o'clock."

"Well, if she can come back with me now we can do half a day's work . . ."

Daisy behaved exactly like a puppy greeting a beloved master. Tripping alongside him she said, "My God, that ain't half seemed a long time. I began to think you'd forgot all about me." It would have been heaven, of course, had he replied that the time had seemed long to him, too; and that he could never forget her. But he just wasn't the sort to say such things, and she thought none the less of him. She gave her account of the Frenchman's offer. "D'you know, I couldn't hardly understand him. His English was awful. Kept talking about franks — I thought he meant boys, but it was money. Lord Chalfont heard him. And then there *was* a rumpus. Him and Lord Kendall and Mr Seymour set about him and chucked him out." She cast Skelton a sidelong glance and went on, "Looks like they don't want to lose me, don't it?"

His response to that was to say, "Just for once they were right. You do put on a good act, but it's not worth three hundred pounds a week. He was trying to buy *you*."

"What? Like slaves? Do they have them in France?"

Really, he thought, her innocence or her stupidity was inconceivable.

"We'll cut through the market and buy some food. What would you like?"

"Oh, whelks!" She gave a little skip of joy. "Oh, what a wonderful day! You're back. And whelks!"

109

She recognised the market as the one where she had bought her hat. The atmosphere was quieter now and only the food stalls were busy.

"You having whelks, too?"

"I think not."

"You don't know what you're missing." The man who sold whelks and those who were eating them laughed. Skelton felt conspicuous and irritable. Then there was an argument. People either ate their whelks on the spot or brought something to put them into.

"Can't afford to give paper bags away, the price I charge."

Skelton thought of offering his hat, or his handkerchief, but the look of the shellfish repelled him. He said, "Wait a minute" and went to another stall and spent threepence on a basket.

"Here you are." She realised that he was cross. But why? Not with her? He couldn't be; she hadn't done or said anything, surely. But somehow she felt reproved and did not, as she had intended to do, demand a double helping. In a chastened voice she said, "What are you going to have?"

"A sandwich." And then he saw another stall and forgot everything for a moment. A crudely lettered sign said, "Genuine Indian." The stall sold shawls, of a texture so fine that they could be pulled through a ring only very slightly larger than a wedding ring. The stall-holder gave proof of this by showing one, half-way through a brass ring. Some of the colours were harsh, a glaring scarlet, bright orange, crude green, but the blue one . . . What a blue, soft without being wishy-washy, real Mary blue.

"How much?"

That largely depended upon the customer.

"To you, sir, two guineas," the man said as though granting a great favour. "And cheap at the price. Match the lydy's eyes a treat that will."

"So I thought," Skelton said and handed over the money without a haggle. The seller wished he had asked more.

"D'you mean that is for me?" Daisy asked, awed not by the price but at the thought that *he*, was buying something for her.

"It's for you. Come along, we're wasting time."

Up through the stink and the noise, into the quiet of the neat bare attic room.

"Oh, I can't tell you how lovely it is to be back here. And everything just the same!" She made one of her indescribable gestures, as though embracing the whole room; more, the whole world. And then instantly changed to the very element of remorse.

"God help us! We never got your sandwich. Shall I nip along?"

"No. There's something there if I want it. And I've been over-eating lately. The crumbs that fall from the rich man's table are very rich indeed. Get into your rags . . . Can you remember how you stood and how you looked?"

"I gotta good memory . . . 'Nother thing we went and forgot was the flowers . . . Shall I nip . . .?"

"No. I could paint them when you weren't here. And some of the rags . . . It was the expression . . ."

"Right you are. Here I am. I got some half-dead flowers to sell. And if you don't buy 'em, just to chuck away, me and my pore little children will starve. Ain't that right?"

Even after the lapse of time which had seemed so long to both of them, her fluid body and her mobile face were back exactly as they had been before the interruption. He gave a few of the grunts of which the Duchess had complained and swore once or twice. Then he said, with triumph, "Got it!" Perfecting the achievement — a soul for sale, fixed for ever, took about ten minutes. Then he flung down his brush and said, "I'm a selfish brute. You never ate your whelks."

"They'll be just as good cold. What about you?"

"I could eat an old woman on a horse, harness and all."

She laughed. "So you remembered that?"

They sat down together in complete amity, she with her whelks and he with what was under the cover and in the cloth — the seemingly identical stale bread and cheese.

Then he said, "Daisy, are you religious?"

"You mean about God and all that? I dunno. Thass all such a muddle. My mother — that is, my real mother, she was a great one for it. Church every Sunday and me with her. I could say the Creed and the Lord's Prayer's soon as I could say anything. Then — I was about five — she got ill and I prayed, so did my father. She suffered something awful . . . The doctor

112

come and said she was bound to die. Cancer he said. So then my father prayed different: let her die! And that din't work, neither. I ain't bin much for praying since then. Mind you, I go by the commandments. I don't steal nor nothing like that. Why?"

"I wondered if you would object to pretending to pray. Like this . . ."

He folded the blue shawl into a triangle and dropped it over her head. Instantly she closed her eyes and placed her beautiful hands together, fingers pointed upwards.

"No. I want your eyes open. Upcast. That's it! Wonderful!"

It was wonderful how she had somehow changed from the Flower Girl, pleading for some material benefit, to a girl asking for some spiritual consolation. It was also wonderful how having her hair totally hidden did not detract from her loveliness; if anything it emphasised the clear cameo profile. *The Prayer* would be started as soon as *The Flower Girl* was finished.

And with that thought his mind reverted to the vexed business of the copies of *Hebe*. A solution occurred to him and presently he said, "There's something you could do for me, Daisy. Not stealing exactly, but sly."

"There ain't a thing in the world I wouldn't do for you. For you, I'd . . ." She broke off and in an instant changed from earnest sincerity to laughter. "Know what I was just gonna say? I was just gonna say I'd dance naked in the street for you — but then I dance naked every night, don't I? What is it?"

He told her.

Only cleaners and underlings were astir early in Kitty's house and it was the woman whose morning duty it was to wash the black and white marble floor in the foyer who first noticed that the ornate gilded frame on the gilded easel was empty. She missed it because she had liked it. She was a country girl who had ended in a place very similar to Springfield Lane, and although she would have said that the girl in the picture was all right, it was not the girl who had attracted her moribund nostalgia. It was the daisies in the grass under the girl's bare feet and the single spray of apple blossom over her head. Skelton had added these touches partly because there was a direct connection between Daisy's complexion and the pink and white of the apple blossom, and partly because the sky needed lightening. He had avoided blue because there was blue enough, and painted in a rather thunderous, dull purple sky, a splendid background for Hebe but sombre. The flowering branch redeemed it; and the daisies had come naturally, daisies grew in grass.

Emma Hawkes missed the picture but its absence did not concern her. Nor for some time, anybody else: there were a dozen explanations. Only Kitty, with her customary acumen hit on the right one. Jack Skelton hadn't wanted it to be copied, so he'd stolen it. She issued orders that when Mr Skelton came just before eleven o'clock to fetch Miss Waywood, he was to be brought straight to her.

"So!" she said, rearing herself into a more upright position, "You thought you could fool me! Lotsa men

— women too — hev thought that. And been wrong. You go fetch that picture straight back."

"What picture? Not the *Hebe*!"

He sounded shocked and outraged and innocent, but she knew how deceptive people could be.

"What other picture would I care about? You din't want copies made so you took it. You bring it back or you and me are gonna fall out."

"Kitty, I assure you, since I put the picture there, I have not laid a finger on it."

"Where was you last night, or early this morning? It was *there*, Sam saw it, at two o'clock this morning. And gone at seven. Where was you at that time?"

"I question your right to ask, Kit. But if you must know, I'll tell you. I brought Daisy back; then I went to Jessop's and hired a rig and drove down to Wichfield — that's in Surrey. I have a cousin there — the only member of my family with whom I am still on speaking terms. Some time back he lent me twenty pounds and I went to pay him back. I stayed the night. We got a bit drunk together . . . I brought the horse back — all the better I may say, for the rest and a full manger, and was at Jessop's at about half-past nine this morning."

"Thass a good alibi," Kitty admitted dubiously. "Whass the name of this cousin of yours?"

"If you must know, Charles Overton. Sir Charles. When he was younger he was a Member of Parliament; he's still a Justice of the Peace. Send and ask, if you like."

Kitty had always suspected that Skelton was well connected, though until this moment he had never referred to his family, they had, in fact, been a bit of a mystery.

"All right; I take it you was out of town. Did you *hire* somebody to steal my picture?"

"That is a very offensive suggestion, Kit. I'd have thought you knew me well enough by now to know that if I meant to steal it I'd have taken it myself — after we had the argument about copies. And whom could I have hired — in the time? I came here, collected Daisy, went straight back and painted through the afternoon. Brought her back, went, as I said, to Jessop's. And what hired thief, even if I had had time to hire one, would have got past Sam? And how? With a picture that size."

"Well, if it wasn't you . . ." She sounded anything but convinced. "I gotta do a bit of thinking. I've had some good offers for that picture. It could be somebody I'd said no to, and was determined to hev it. Most likely one who stayed the night. Upstairs. Sam saw it when he knocked off — two o'clock. Then there's only Joseph to let out the late-stayers and he ain't all that bright. Somebody might hev got past *him*. Somebody who wanted it and was here part of the night . . ."

"That is sound reasoning. Now, if I may have Daisy, I have work to do."

Kitty then did a thing she rarely did; she apologised.

"I'm sorry if I wronged you, Jacky. You seemed, as the perlice say, the natural suspect."

"I shall be interested to know what you work out; I still think of it as *my* picture."

She knew she had angered him. They'd had disputes before and had called each other names, but always

116

with a kind of goodwill at the back of it all. Not cold and distant, like this. For a moment she felt slightly depressed; then she set about the business of finding out exactly who had gone upstairs last night and whether one of those who had was one who had made an offer for the picture ... Chalfont, Kendall, Seymour, Wilkinson, Lee, Turnberry.

CHAPTER
TWELVE

Daisy was waiting in the foyer, the blue shawl over her arm. She gave him one of those eloquent glances which said all. It's all right; I did it! But they did not speak of the picture until they were well away from the house and out into the rattle and clatter of traffic. Then he said, "Good girl! Where is it?"

"Where she'll never think of looking," Daisy said happily. "In the shop. You know. The Taj Mahal. There're a lotta pictures there. Mrs Bruce'll take any picture that looks a bit Indian. She told me. Now and again she'll put one in the shop, but most of 'em are just waiting . . . So I thought . . . I mean, I could've put it under my bed. But *she*'ll look there. Judging by the cobwebs most of them Indian pictures been there for years. I pushed ours well to the back."

"That was very clever of you."

She basked in his approval and in self-approval. For she had not merely been clever, in her own estimation she'd been extremely brave, since she had a fear — completely silly, she'd be the first to admit — of emptiness, loneliness, after dark. In order to do what *he* wanted, which sounded so simple — take the picture out of its frame and put it somewhere where it would

be safe until this demand for copies had died down —
she had forced herself to overcome a fear none the less
real for being silly. Waiting on the stairs, above the
lobby, a well of darkness faintly lit by one candle;
waiting until the boy, Joseph, snatched a sleep;
removing the canvas, running back to her own
bedroom; thinking, Under my bed? Thinking, No,
come on, Daisy Holt, you can do better than that!
Thinking of the perfect hiding place and then carrying
the picture and her own candle through what seemed
miles of deserted passageways. Somewhere in the house
itself there were people, mostly asleep by this time; but
the shop and the rooms above it were silent and empty.

"Thass a funny thing," she told Skelton, "but a place
thass generally full of people can be emptier than a
churchyard when they've gone. I was fit to jump out of
my skin with fright, specially in the shop."

"You were very brave. I'm going to buy you a
present."

"But I had one yesterday." She smoothed the blue
shawl lovingly.

"That was really for the picture. Something for
yourself. What would you like?"

Discounting the handed-down clothing, she had only
received one present in her life and was at a loss.

"Oh, anything," she said, in what sounded a careless
way, but was meant to imply that anything he gave her
would be cherished for ever.

"Then how about a new reticule?" He was pandering
to himself in that suggestion. He could never see that

119

poor homemade thing without being reminded of the day when he hadn't a penny.

"I dunno . . . That cook — the one I told you about, the one that learned me to read and write — *she* made this for me. One Christmas. But I tell you what. If you got me one a bit bigger, I could keep this one inside it, couldn't I? That wouldn't be like chucking it away."

"I'll get you one when I take *The Flower Girl* to Pitt and Wade's. The shops around there are very smart."

Mr Wade — Mr Pitt had been dead for some time — regarded *The Flower Girl* with approval. He did not share Kitty's opinion that pictured poverty made the rich feel uncomfortable.

"Now that, Skelton, is what I call a picture. Yes, indeed. Such colour, such contrast, such moral content. I always knew that you'd make your mark as soon as you found your proper *métier*. With this you have. My congratulations!"

Mr Wade was not given to easy enthusiasm; pessimism and discouragement were more in his line. Skelton felt a brief glow of pleasure but no surprise; he had never underrated his talent and when in the past Mr Wade had refused either to buy or display his work he had put it down to the man's damned ignorance and bad taste. In that he was partly right, for although Mr Wade had been in the art-dealing business for many years, he had little real knowledge, except about what would sell, and even about that he was not invariably right because public taste was not only perverse but

120

dangerously subject to fleeting fashion — as bad as clothes.

He ran his business on three distinct levels. He sold genuinely old pictures by relatively unknown artists which had come on to the market by mischance — the break up of an old house, the end of an ancient family. Many of these found their way into the houses of newly rich men in search of ancestors. The more anonymous the subject of a portrait, the less known the artist, the better; but the subject must be aristocratic looking, a simpering fine lady with a rose or a pug dog, a Tudor gentleman in a ruff, a Cavalier. Once or twice, buying for this market, Mr Wade had hit upon genuine finds, pictures by men destined for fame but at the time prepared to, glad to, work for a few pounds and board and lodging.

Then there was the modern side. No new house could be considered properly furnished without a picture or two. When Mr Wade was offered a picture which could hardly fail to please those who were buying pictures as they bought chairs and tables, he bought it outright and put it in his window and usually sold it, sometimes at about eight hundred per cent profit. Mr Wade saw nothing unfair in this; he had his overhead expenses; rent, rate and insurance, wages for assistants.

Then, because he did not fully trust his own judgement and was aware of how quickly public demand changed, Mr Wade had his third department in which he displayed pictures which he was not prepared to buy, but which might catch somebody's fancy. There they hung, properly displayed in the wide entry through which every customer must pass. A month, Mr Wade judged was the limit; if a picture had not attracted some attention in that time, take it away. If it sold, Mr Wade, having invested nothing, was content with fifty per cent.

Nothing that Skelton had produced so far had been judged worthy of display even in the lobby, a fact which rankled in his mind even now when Mr Wade was lavishing praise and offering fifty pounds down. "And a place in the window, on its own. That is worth money. It can establish a name. Your name."

That was true.

"I thought seventy."

"It is part of the artistic temperament to over-rate itself and to think that pictures accost customers and say, Buy me! Believe me it is not so. But . . ." Mr Wade took another look at the picture and weakened because the appeal of it was so great — to women the rags and the faded flowers, to men the other more vibrant thing. This was a picture which did accost and say, Buy me. "I will split the difference. Say sixty."

"All right."

"Come into my office," Mr Wade said. "It so happens that I have something further to discuss with you. I am hearing about you in a curious connection . . . May I offer you sherry?"

Not for the first time Skelton reflected that Mr Wade was not quite as English as his name.

"Thank you. In what connection?"

"A picture that has been stolen. I have been offered stolen pictures in my time. I have even bought one or

122

two — but never knowingly. No permanent good can come of such trade. The gentleman who came to inquire if I had seen or heard anything of John Skelton's *Hebe* said he was most anxious to buy it and had offered Mrs Hammond, from whose house it was stolen, a good price for it. And if it was as beautiful as your girl with the dead flowers, that is easily understandable."

"Thank you," Skelton said with no gratitude in his voice.

"You used the same girl?"

"The same model, yes."

"What I was thinking," Mr Wade said, coming at last to his point, "if *Hebe* aroused so much interest, something similar would be very saleable. *The Flower Girl* is saleable but gentlemen incline towards the classical."

"Nudity?"

"More or less. And no lack of subjects. Aphrodite rising from the sea . . ."

"Daphne turning into a laurel bush? Leda and the Swan?"

"Exactly. For such a picture I would pay not sixty but a hundred pounds. Half in advance, should you wish."

"At the moment I am painting her, fully clad and with a shawl over her head. And that will be better than either of the others. After that . . . Who knows? Something will strike . . . We'll see. I can't promise anything."

No, Mr Wade thought with a tinge of regret; no real artist ever could. God, in bestowing one gift upon them, seemed to have withheld others, most of which made for success; they made appointments and turned up late, or not at all; they had no idea of the real value of money, overestimated the value of their own work and when in funds spent like drunken sailors. A hopeless, contrary breed and in the final count less profitable than the good craftsmen to whom the word *commission* meant more than *inspiration*.

"Well, remember, when this work is completed, I shall be greatly interested."

"Thanks — for the sherry," Skelton said and went away to buy Daisy a reticule.

When she unwrapped it she said, "Ooh . . ." a long drawn-out sound of awe and appreciation. "Ain't it the most beautiful thing you ever seen?"

"It's pretty." Amazing, he thought, that she who faced the perfection of beauty every time she looked in a glass should say such a thing about a merely pleasing arrangement of blue and white beads. Beads were all the rage just then; bodices and capes so thickly encrusted as to be stiff and heavy, almost like armour.

"I shall keep it for ever. And think of you every time I look at it. Thank you. Thank you a million times." She had an impulse to throw her arms around him and kiss him. Something deterred her. The knowledge that he didn't feel about her as she felt about him; her wish not to give him the impression that she was easy.

"I'm glad you like it," he said and went to the easel. "Ready?"

This picture took no preparation time, she simply had to throw the shawl over her head and arrange her hands.

Presently he said, "Any news of the great picture hunt?"

Daisy giggled. "Lucky I din't leave it under my bed! Kitty been mad as a March hare. First she made sure nobody took it out. Sam swore it was there when he went to bed and Joseph swore he never dozed off — which he did, but I ain't in a position to contradict, am I? Anyway, only one man who wanted it real bad spent the night in the house, and, you know what? He walked straight out into the bailiffs' arms. Two of them tracked him down and took him off for debt. Turnberry his name is." Her expression changed to bewilderment. "What I can't understand is a man owing hundreds of pounds, wanting to buy a picture. Can you?"

"Easily. If Kitty had agreed to sell it he'd have asked her to wait for the money a day or two, and then he'd have sold it to somebody who really wanted it, and made a bit of profit. Enough to keep his creditors at bay for a week or two."

"I see. I never thought of that. Well, anyhow, she then thought it must be *in* the house and she had the whole place combed through. Even the kitchens. Even the shop! Lucky I put it in the middle and didn't disturb the cobwebs much."

"Very lucky. Very clever."

"I know whass got Kitty on the raw. For once in her life she been outwitted. That ain't happened to her often. And it took *me* to do it!" Oh dear, how cocky that sounded! She hastened to say, "But *you* thought of it."

He accepted that tribute with a kind of grunt and put on what Daisy called his painting face and it was not until they were feasting again — cold roast fowl and the sweet wine she preferred — that she said, "Whass gonna happen to *her* now? *Hebe*, I mean?"

"I haven't really thought. It is Kitty's picture. I was only anxious that she didn't have cheap copies made. That idea was intolerable and if ever I do her another picture we must have a clear understanding. She can show it or burn it, do what she likes, but no copies."

"She's gonna want another picture. She said so. To Signor Mazoni. Did you know Italians shouldn't be called Mister? Well, I din't, till he told me. There ain't gonna be no shows like I do in August or the beginning of September. Then I'm gonna sing as well and I heard Kitty say something about a girl that was turned into a nightingale. You ever hear of her, Philo something?"

"Philomel?"

"Thass it. You ain't half clever!"

Skelton thought briefly of the impossibility of painting a girl singing. Even Daisy, mouth wide open, would be unattractive. But as herself, gazing entranced at a singing bird in a flowery bough . . . Yearning, a little envious, poised, ready to be transformed. She could express all that and he could paint it.

CHAPTER
THIRTEEN

It was an exceptionally hot August, and dry. Splendid harvest weather for the country, but bad in London and other places where filth and congestion invited diseases, cholera the most fatal of them, diphtheria a close runner-up. Kitty, who had lived through many epidemics of what she comprehensively called plagues, was almost morbidly concerned for the health of her girls and of the younger servants. She reckoned that anybody over thirty was a veteran like herself, and likely to survive. After due thought she sent all the girls to the coast — not to Brighton but to a quiet little fishing village much like Brighton had been before it became fashionable. The house was officially closed; what shopping was necessary was done by older servants; young ones splashed about with whitewash in which Kitty had faith as a preventive of infection.

Daisy could have gone to the seaside, with, but not quite of, the girls. Daisy had slipped into place — a peculiar place, even Kitty admitted — in the very mixed house. She was not yet a prostitute, she was not a servant. At first, while the statue show was on she had lived apart and often, Kitty thought, in ignorance of what went on around her. Then, on show as herself, she had mingled, in the ballroom and the supper-room, with Kitty's clients and with the other girls. At that point Kitty had expected some unpleasantness, girls being so prone to jealousy, and she was prepared to deal with it firmly, but none came. The girl had the knack of getting on with people, and the young women whose talents were confined to the bedchamber appeared willing to admire and accept her as one who had special talent, special looks and who did not put on any fine airs. All Kitty's girls were chosen for their looks, all had their measure of vanity, but beauty like Hebe's — they all knew her by that name — came only once in a generation and the pretty ones' acceptance was a kind of tribute. Also in her favour was that she was not in competition with them. She never took a man upstairs; on the contrary, her performance on the stage, deliberately designed to rouse sensual desires, and her behaviour between shows, nicely arranged to keep such desires alive but not satisfied, tended to keep the upstairs custom brisk.

Neither Kitty nor anybody else had bothered to explain the character of the house to Daisy. The truth had dawned upon her gradually and once realised, affected her behaviour to the girls — not through contempt, but through pity. Pampered and privileged as they undoubtedly were, they were of that class known as unfortunate, the kind so earnestly described by Mrs Bell. They were young now, and employed by the best night house in England, but what would become of them *after*? Seeing them in the evening, in silk and brocade, wearing jewels, some fake, some real —

gentlemen could be very generous — it was difficult to imagine them grown old and noseless, but the threat was there. All the more reason for being nice to them.

About her own future beyond tomorrow, she gave hardly any thought at all. She was congenitally incapable of taking a long view; she had always felt that something wonderful awaited her, and now she was unable to think of the future, or the something wonderful, without bringing Mr Skelton into it. And once she thought of him, everything stopped short at tomorrow ... At the same time the view was not bounded by the bleak, neat attic which he called a studio; it was vaguely set against a background of comfort and beauty, not necessarily of luxury. Just nice and clean and pretty, with him and her together.

Offered the opportunity to go with the other girls to the seaside, she refused, though she had never seen the sea and would have liked to do so. Kitty then dealt a smashing blow.

"Please yourself, but if you think I'm gonna hev you going backward and forward betwixt Springfield Lane and here, you're making a mistake. Thass a plague hole at the best of times. Jack Skelton want to paint you he can come here."

And that wouldn't be the same at all. However, direct defiance was out of the question.

"Am I not to go out at all?" Daisy asked.

"I din't say that. You stay in in the heat of the day and then take a nice little drive in Hyde Park in the cool of the evening. Thass the thing to do this weather, if you gotta be in London."

Skelton had already decided to move. Not very willingly. The attic and his way of life suited him in a fashion. The surroundings and the approach were disgusting, but after a time disgust expended itself. Once the door at the foot of the last flight of stairs was closed, the stinks and the noise ceased to exist. And five shillings a week was cheap for so much well-lighted space. Up to a point he was indifferent to money, was disinclined to earn it in any way distasteful to him; but his very indifference made him careful of taking on any commitment which might threaten his independence. Keeping up any kind of household would have tied him down.

However, he could now afford something better and while he was thinking about it the dog-stealer died of cholera, the three dogs he was keeping died of hunger and to accustomed stenches there was added the foulness of corruption.

Wade had sold *The Flower Girl*. Daisy in the attitude of prayer was in the shop window — in solitary splendour and being mistaken every day for the Virgin Mary. Skelton's star was in the ascendant, and he could afford decent accommodation; but although he had a firm belief in his genius he had lost confidence in his luck, so when offered what seemed to be exactly what he wanted, a chance too good to be missed, he did not give up the attic in Springfield Lane. "It'll always be there to fall back on," he told Daisy.

She was inclined to be sentimental about the attic. "We had some happy times there, din't we?" But she was enchanted with the new place, part of a large house

130

which had been subdivided in Well House Close, just off the north side of the Strand, through a dull-looking archway.

"Fancy! You could walk past a hundred times and never know it was there, couldn't you? Ooh, and ain't it pretty? Just like the country!"

The old houses stood around an irregular-shaped patch of grass, green even in this torrid weather, because at some time in the past the old well had been converted into a fountain. There were two rowan trees, their berries just reddening, and every one of the eight houses had window boxes, bright with geraniums.

The half house which Skelton had hired consisted of a kitchen with a studio built on to it on the ground floor; one large room and three smaller ones above. It was fully furnished.

"Down to the last spoon!" Daisy said. "Fancy being able to walk away and leave all this!"

"Mr Christopher Foley had a shrewd eye for the market," Skelton said with the savagery with which he often spoke of fellow artists. "The moment Landseer made animals the fashion, Foley painted pets — with or without owner . . . Give Landseer his due, he can *draw*. Foley can't, but he can *paint*; boy with wolfhound, girl with kitten . . . That kind of thing. And not a good bone in the lot. Still *he* hit *his* target. He can afford to drop all this as one would an old overcoat and buy a palace just outside Florence."

"Well, that was lucky for us. Kitty'll let me come here. You can finish the one of me making lace . . . You know, every time I think of that I laugh. Me, fiddling about with all them pins! Back home there was an old woman made lace; I used to watch her. Like magic it was. Now me, pretending! Who'd believe it? Ooh, and I forgot. Kitty said, remind you about the nightingale girl. She wants that in not less than a fortnight. And nobody's gonna steal that one. Thass gonna be nailed to the wall."

"And how are the singing lessons going?"

"Not very good. I do *try*. But what I do don't seem to please Signor Mazoni. I mean, I just get going and he'll rap with that little black stick and stop me. I hit a wrong note or something. I can't sing that way. I *can* sing, give me half a chance, but not his way. Understand what I mean?"

"Only too well!"

He knew. Wade had practically commissioned him to paint Daisy in classical myth style. Instead he had gone from the girl praying to the girl making lace — a logical process, for the prayerful hands were so lovely that a picture making the most of them seemed the only thing to do. Perhaps after that, and after the nightingale girl he'd try to meet Wade's demands.

The new house gave Daisy a chance to show another talent; with a kitchen to use, she could cook. Once it had been her modest ambition to become a cook and at the Hall she had watched very carefully and listened and often been allowed to help in the preparation of simpler dishes.

"We needn't always have bought stuff now," she said happily. "I can make us a proper meal."

132

"We can't spare the time."

"Oh yes, we can. With no work at night there's no need for me to lay abed in the morning. I can come early, do a bit of shopping on the way, and then we can start early and make time for cooking later on." Now that Daisy could reach Skelton's studio without passing through notorious slums, Kitty no longer insisted upon her being escorted to and fro. She would have preferred that Daisy should have held to the programme she had outlined at the beginning of the plague time — young, country-bred people were the likeliest victims; but she wanted the nightingale picture ready for the opening night and Skelton, awkward as usual, refused to leave his studio, so there was no choice.

One morning, early in September, with just that touch of change in the air and the rowan berries as red as the geraniums, Daisy arrived, straight from Covent Garden market bearing a bunch of dark grapes, so freshly cut, so little handled, that the bloom was intact.

"Ain't they lovely?" She held them up for him to see, and he saw something over and beyond; just for once he could please himself and Wade's public at the same time. A Bacchante!

Always, so far, he had seen her in terms of pictures or some other form of display. He was aware that she gave him a dog-like devotion, sometimes amusing, sometimes pathetic, always useful. He never did or said anything to encourage her and rarely thought about it; when he did, he was certain that it would pass, die down from sheer inanition. Almost all he had of emotional drive was absorbed by his work.

That afternoon, preparing to leave after a lovely, most satisfactory day, she said, "Oh blast Signor Mazoni! But for him I could stay another hour. Why don't he never want a holiday? Or give me up in disgust, like he sometimes says he will? I swear I'll do so bad and be so stupid this afternoon, he will. Or hev a stroke or something. Then I can sing as I like."

But that afternoon Mazoni did not come. One of the numerous female relatives whom he worked so hard to support brought a message; Luigi didn't feel well today, but would be better tomorrow.

"Fancy that," Daisy said to Skelton next morning. "Just when I wished something'd happen to give me another hour in the afternoon. Now today I shan't go rushing back. He kept me waiting yesterday, I'll keep him waiting today. Turn about is fair play, ain't it?"

She cooked, as was now usual. Skelton, his mind filled with the nightingale girl — and after that the Bacchante, and after that who knew what? — did not notice that she ate hardly anything. But they'd hardly begun the afternoon's work when she said, "I'm sorry. I feel awful. I'll have to sit down for a minnit."

Immediately he was all concern. She must lie down. In this studio there was a couch as well as several comfortable chairs.

"It's the heat," he assured her. After the sparkling morning the day had turned sultry. He went into the kitchen and made tea. She sat up to drink it and felt dizzy and was frightened, wondering if this was how people felt just before they fainted. The worst thing she had ever suffered in her life was a really bad cold and the worst of colds had never made her feel like this. All she knew about fainting was seeing people do it.

"Better?" She knew that he wanted her to say yes, and get up to resume her pose, and she was anxious as always to please him, so she made an effort. The whole studio swung crazily and she fell back.

"I think . . . I might . . . faint."

"Brandy," he said and ran upstairs to the living-room. She'd never drunk brandy before and didn't like it; but she forced it down, felt worse instead of better and then endured the ultimate humiliation of being sick; right there, under his very eyes; right there on the polished floor. To the water which the violent vomiting had brought to her eyes, were added tears of mortification. In a low, humble voice, she said, "I'm sorry! I'm sorry. I'll clean up in a minnit."

"Don't give it a thought."

She lay back for a little, thinking how awful. Even in the old studio he'd always been so neat and so tidy so . . . fastidious was the word she wanted but did not know . . . so particular. And now in his lovely new place she'd gone and made such a mess.

"I think I'd better get home to bed."

"That might be best. I'll get a cab."

That took a little time, just at the hour in the early afternoon when after the lunch-time rush cabmen fed themselves and their horses. Skelton had to walk quite a distance before he secured one, jumped into it and said, "Well House Close."

When he was back he saw a change in Daisy. The flush which had made him think that the heat was responsible for her condition had died away, leaving a ghastly pallor and her eyes had turned glassy. Unknowing. Could one miss what one had never appreciated — that glad, welcoming look?

"Too many stairs," she said. And even her voice had changed in some indefinable way. Gone flat and a trifle hoarse.

"No stairs, Daisy. Come along, I'll help you."

"So they say. Can't believe all you hear."

This was delirium, which implied a fever of some kind. He knew that cholera and diphtheria were raging and that both could take a number of forms. Of contagion he had no fear at all; like so many other actual things, it hardly impinged upon his consciousness; nothing to do with him! His business was to get Daisy to bed and to hope that within, at most, forty-eight hours, she'd be better. He held her, gently but supportingly, and made soothing, nonsensical answers to the few rambling things she said during the brief journey.

The odds were a hundred to one against Kitty being on the ground floor, let alone in the foyer at this or any other hour, but she was. She had people she could trust absolutely, but some things she liked to see for herself, and the refurbishing of the entry was one of them. The foyer had not been whitewashed, but painted — rose pink; gentlemen liked pink, and now, before the crimson carpet was replaced, she must make sure that the two colours did not kill each other. That was the kind of thing which no lieutenant could decide. She was already in a very bad temper. It was a hot afternoon and although, since Daisy Holt's arrival and the concomitant schemes and excitements, she had on the whole felt better — even the stolen picture had been a stimulus — her body was still a load to cart about. And the colours did clash, which meant either new paint on the walls or new carpet on the floor where the black and white marble ended. Another cause of irritation was a letter from Esther, received that morning. Of all the ungrateful, difficult creatures in the world, girls were the worst. Esther wrote that in her opinion the girls should come back; they were bored with Seaforth where there was nothing to do but eat and sleep, bathe and loll — and quarrel. The quarrelling had reached such a point, Esther wrote, that she had been obliged to use force.

Now, on top of it all, there was a cab and Skelton hauling out of it the girl now called Hebe. Whiter than a sheet, staring-eyed and sounding like a ventriloquist's dummy. Talking in a strange voice, rubbish.

She'd been all right that very morning and Kitty had a kind of rule-of-thumb measure; the quicker the onset, the quicker the death. Even the doctors held that view. In any plague the smitten people who complained of aches and pains and were ill in a mild kind of way usually recovered; those stricken down suddenly were marked for death — and in death the victim of any kind of plague was even more infectious than in life; or so many people, including Kitty, believed.

With the house re-opening in just under a fortnight and all the other girls coming back tomorrow, Kitty chose what seemed to be the only sensible course.

"Stay where you are," she said to Skelton, who had reached the doorway with Daisy just managing to walk with a great deal of support. "I'm not having her in here."

"You must! Where else can I take her?"

"Thass for you to decide. And don't you must me, Jack Skelton. Try the Bermondsey nuns."

"It's too far. She should be in bed now. She needs a doctor."

"Sam, shut the door."

The cabman had watched and listened with great interest and now as Skelton turned back to the cab, made his contribution.

"Bermondsey and all such places are full to the doors, guvnor."

"Back to Well House Close, then," Skelton snapped, lifting Daisy in. The cabman was glad of the short journey and whipped his horse into a show of liveliness; he didn't want the girl to die in his cab.

Kitty set herself to the immense task of getting upstairs and, that accomplished, gave her mind to some entertainment with which to replace Daisy's performance. She had no hope of the girl's recovery, no pity for her plight — in fact when you come to think about it, the silly bitch was largely to blame, galloping about in the plague-infested streets; if she had refused to go to Skelton, Skelton would have been obliged to come here and this need never have happened. Now she must get her spies out to go round the agencies and the halls in search of talent. She had regarded the Frenchman's action in trying to collar Hebe as infamous, yet she had no hesitation in using the same tactics. And there was that good old saying about there being as good fish in the sea as ever came out . . . But every rule had its exceptions and she doubted if she would look on Daisy's like again.

Skelton's door — once the kitchen door of a larger house — lay to the side, and the cab could not get near it. Daisy was by this time unconscious and Skelton was obliged to carry her in; slender as she was, she seemed to weigh heavy and he decided against taking her upstairs for the moment. He laid her on the studio couch, went out and paid the cabman. As he did so he remembered with relief that one of the houses was inhabited by a doctor. He went and rapped vigorously with the well-polished knocker. He was fortunate, Doctor Burgess was at home; he believed in a rest after lunch, especially in warm weather.

"The young lady whose portrait I was painting, collapsed a short while ago," he explained, careful not to mention what he feared since doctors too had been known to fight shy of raging infections.

Unlike Springfield Lane where everybody minded his own business to such an extent that murder could be — and was — committed practically on the doorstep without rousing any interest at all, Well House Close was inhabited by people who were aware of their neighbours and on the whole liked to be friendly. The eight houses now provided middle-sized homes for eleven families, all of the professional class. They had looked slightly askance at Mr Christopher Foley when he first moved in to what was the cheapest and meanest result of sub-division — just a kitchen and some rooms which had once been servants' quarters. But he had built a first-class studio, which proved that he was not a poor artist, a potential sponger; and then he rapidly became successful, even famous. Definitely an asset to the small, slightly ingrown community. His behaviour had been impeccable, and a spare man was so useful at dinner parties. Everybody was sorry when he decided to go abroad. Everybody had been half-prepared to welcome this other artist to whom he had let his house.

But Skelton was different; though more of a gentleman — and the people in Well House Close were acutely aware of social distinctions — Skelton in the first few days had shown himself no substitute for Foley. He refused invitations bluntly; too busy, he said. And then, in no time at all, there had been That Girl coming and going. Very pretty of course, but no class at all, tripping in each morning, laden with meat, fish, vegetables, fruit. The fact that she left quite early — her movements were closely observed — did not lull suspicion. Alongside the most intense respectability ran a powerful prurient streak . . . Fornication could be committed during the daytime.

Doctor Burgess who represented the Well House Close ethic so closely that he might have been born there, though he had only attained to it in his fortieth year, looked down at Daisy whose attitudes had always been somehow controlled by something other than her consciousness. Now, deeply unconscious, deathly pale, her eyes closed with the lashes, slightly darker than her hair, making crescents, she looked very beautiful, and very dead. A girl carved in alabaster. The couch on which she lay was low, and one slim but shapely arm had fallen over the edge of it, so that her hand, the palm short and faintly pink, the fingers white, pointed, slightly in-curled, lay on the floor. He lifted the arm, felt for her pulse and found it. Feeble, but fairly steady. Surprising. Temperature low. Symptoms inconsistent with the two current plagues, cholera and diphtheria.

Doctor Burgess was puzzled, but no doctor of reputation was prepared to admit to being puzzled. Assuming a learned and critical expression, he said, "Tell me what happened, exactly." Skelton could speak of the turning dizzy, the being sick, the brief delirium. The hurried journey in the cab, the rebuff at Kitty's house were, he thought, irrelevant. The cab had, however, been seen and taken notice of since cabs were somewhat of a rarity in the Close where few people were dependent upon hired transport.

"Did she go to the dentist?"

"The dentist? No. Why d'you ask that?"

"I was considering the possibility of her being in a state of shock. As the result of a tooth extraction or . . ."

"A quick visit to a back-street abortionist?"

Plainly, despite his voice and his bearing, no gentleman!

"The thought had occurred to me."

"Vile! Utterly disgusting!"

But that, Doctor Burgess knew, could be typical upperclass bluff. The born gentry thought they could get away with anything. He'd once been called to attend a lady of title suffering from puerperal fever who denied that she had borne a child. And men were as bad; sufferers from syphilis almost invariably accused some comparatively innocent complaint such as measles gone slightly wrong.

"It will be necessary for me to make a full examination."

"If that's the best you can do; do it."

"And I would like a responsible matron to be present."

"Please yourself," Skelton said.

He'd done his best; tried to get the poor girl home and into bed, been defeated by Kitty, brought her back, fetched the doctor. What more could he do?

Make a few rapid sketches of Daisy as she lay, seemingly dead. Spare a thought of regret that life-size memorials in marble and alabaster were now hopelessly out-dated; look on the grey couch as a grey sea, bringing a drowned dead girl back to land, *Beautiful in Death* or some such title. Then the truth hit him. If she died their rewarding and happy association would be no more. All the pictures he had planned to paint with her as their focus would never be made. The premonition of irreparable loss came upon him, and something else, too. She'd been a wonderful companion as well as the best possible model. Amenable, amusing, devoted, so easily pleased. Poor little girl! He was still far from reciprocating her feeling for him, but in that moment a tiny crack breached his monstrous egoism.

Doctor Burgess was not long away. The responsible woman lived above the mews at the rear of the Close, so he had only to cross his own garden. She was a midwife and nurse of little training but vast experience. To most people her manner was pleasantly dictatorial but to Doctor Burgess she was sycophantic. Most of her jobs came through him, or his recommendation.

"I need a little help, Mrs Paske. It won't take ten minutes."

"Then I can do it, and glad to. I'm due back at Mrs Lawson's at half-past three."

"How are they?"

"Both doing well."

"I must try to look in some time today." He always pretended that he was severely overworked. His family and Mrs Paske encouraged him in this harmless fantasy, and now Mrs Paske said exactly what was expected.

"I'm sure I don't know how you get through all that you do, Doctor."

Going back through the garden he told her of his suspicion and what he wanted her to do.

"That was very clever of you, Doctor. With so much illness about a lot of doctors wouldn't have thought of *that*!"

Less than ten minutes was enough to prove Doctor Burgess's suspicion to be unfounded. In fact if Mrs Paske knew anything — and she thought she knew almost everything — the girl on the couch was a virgin. Surprising! Also surprising was Mrs Paske's response to Daisy — and to a lesser degree to Skelton. Daisy, even in her present poor state, was very pretty and Mrs Paske was one of those plain women capable of an ungrudging admiration for beauty in others. As for Mr Skelton, bad-tempered and curt as he was, she found him attractive, too. And he had good reason for being angry. Poor old Doctor Burgess had made another mistake! But he was not going to be confronted with it by Mrs Paske. Oh no! On the contrary she was going to help him out.

"I understand what made you suspicious, Doctor. These low summer fevers do resemble shock and haemorrhage."

"I thought it wise to make certain. Thank you very much, Mrs Paske."

"I could lend a hand with the nursing here, if wished. The monthly nurse Mrs Lawson engaged seems quite a sensible creature."

Mrs Paske did not take on the duties of monthly nurse for a number of reasons — it called for no skill, and it meant living in for longer than she was willing to be away from the mews where she lived with her brother Jim and his hopelessly inefficient wife, Effie. The only thing that Effie could do — and that she did very well — was to drift through a day without doing anything. She couldn't or wouldn't cook, or clean, or sew. Sent out to shop she forgot things, or bought the wrong ones, and invariably came back with the wrong change. She was, in fact, an amiable half-wit and ever since Mrs Paske had been left a childless widow and come to make her home with her brother, she had kept the place going. She was fond of her brother Jim and tolerant, in a contemptuous way, of Effie to whom for some strange reason Jim seemed devoted, treating her rather as he would have done a child, had he had one. But in order to keep the mews flat in any kind of order, food on the table, clothes and furniture and floors clean it was necessary that Mrs Paske should take jobs of short duration only; midwifery, nursing through a crisis, even laying out, a most necessary, though despised job.

A job right here, on her very doorstep, suited her well and Skelton, determined to do his best for Daisy, but utterly ignorant, was only too glad to employ her.

The puzzling and originally negative symptoms gave way to those of a classic case of diphtheria. High fever, prolonged delirium, and the deadly membrane in the throat. With that Doctor Burgess was equipped to deal and at the end of six weeks Daisy had recovered her hold on life. But she had changed. Bone thin — good feeding could cure that — but her voice had altered irrevocably. When she spoke the clear almost childish treble which had made mispronunciations and faulty grammar almost acceptable, had become deeper, rather husky and infinitely more seductive; her singing voice had gone. She could still sing but no longer with any carrying quality. Pleasant in an ordinary-sized room, useless on a stage. Her beauty was temporarily in eclipse, hollows where curves had been and at first a kind of stiffness, a loss of the marvellous fluidity that had been one of her distinguishing gifts. Even had she gone back to Kitty Hammond as soon as she was able, Kitty would have found no use for her now. Not that she wanted to; not that Skelton wished, or intended her to. Kitty's behaviour on that hot afternoon had disgusted him and he was a man capable of cherishing a grudge.

PART TWO

CHAPTER
ONE

All through that autumn Skelton's pattern of life — work, get some money, get drunk, resume work — had been interrupted. Mrs Paske said there was many a legally married husband who might well take a lesson from him. Certainly he made her work very easy since he never went out except to shop — which he did very badly until she took him in hand — so she was free to pop in, as she called it, at the mews half a dozen times a day. Certainly he was genuinely anxious in the time of critical danger, and really most upset when told that sometimes diphtheria could take the form of what Doctor Burgess called pustules, as permanently disfiguring as those of smallpox. "God, no! She'd be better dead!" he exclaimed. And Mrs Paske did not take that amiss because she had no notion of the feeling behind the exclamation; and did in fact almost share his concern that such beauty should not be ruined.

Mrs Paske did not think it strange that Skelton never used an endearment; her work took her into the inmost core of many married lives and she knew that *darling* and *my dearest, my love* and *sweetheart* could be all too easily said by men who, having said them, felt free to go off to the office, the business, or even to parties.

She thought of Skelton as a very quiet gentleman; one who did not wear his heart on his sleeve. And she was particularly impressed when, Daisy recovering and with the ravenous but precarious appetite of convalescence, Mr Skelton went out and bought whelks. Enough to feed half a dozen cabmen.

St Luke's little summer, due in October, came late that year; well into November and it coincided with Daisy's full recovery. Skelton hired an open carriage and took her for drives in the unseasonably warm afternoon sunshine. And he walked her, lending his arm, around the patch of green in the centre of Well House Close. Little, weak, tottering steps at first; but then her splendid constitution re-asserted itself.

Mrs Paske had not been the only one to be deluded by Skelton's behaviour. Daisy, hitherto humbly aware that she was the one who loved and he the one content to be loved, now thought she knew differently.

She'd been through Hell; what the well-known psalm called the valley of the shadow of death. She could remember being sick on the studio floor, and after that nothing much, except feeling very ill and having terrible dreams. The Westcott baby weighed a ton and the stairs from basement to nursery were as high as St Paul's. She was lost in Waywood and beset by wolves. She was at Kitty's, on the stage, stark naked and supposed to do something, but what? No idea what, just standing there, inviting rape and two hundred men, with rape in mind, surging forward. She was ravenously hungry and there was delicious food which she could not swallow because something had stuck in her throat, a sharp bone. Once her mother had come to her rescue. Quite unmistakable; square plain face and white apron. She'd said, "Mother! Oh, thank you. Thank you. They told me you were dead." That had touched the maternal streak in Mrs Paske and led to the inevitable conclusion — the girl had obviously had a good mother. But, weaving in and out of the delirium, the semi-consciousness, and finally the full return to her senses, there was Mr Skelton, elusive as the will-o'-the-wisp over Wardship Marshes yet as fixed as Monday morning.

She struggled out of the confusion; knew where she was and who she was — though her first glance at herself in the glass seemed to deny her identity; even her hair had gone dull and thin and her face was that of an old woman. Daisy knew all the fairy stories; there was that princess who pricked her finger and went to sleep for a hundred years, in a castle surrounded by a thorn bush; but in the story she had remained young and beautiful and a prince had forced his way through the thorns and wakened her with a kiss.

That was a fairy tale; this, to which she was wakening, was real life. And good enough with Mr Skelton so kind and attentive, proving every day that he did, after all, regard her as a person, not simply as a useful model. He was consideration itself, even now when she looked so ugly. He'd even thought about her clothes. She had fallen ill on a very hot day, and winter had arrived while she was abed. All she had was a summer dress and the blue shawl which she took with her everywhere; on hot days she carried it, folded, in her basket. When she began to recover, though the weather was exceptionally warm for the time of year, she needed more than that.

He asked first had she left any clothes at Kitty's, and when she told him just another summer frock, some underclothes and a spare pair of shoes, he said they were not worth bothering about. He then went out and spent what must have been a great deal of money buying everything a girl could possibly need. Mrs Paske called it quite a trousseau. What Daisy looked best in, now that her hair was in such a poor way, was a cape, with a hood all edged with pale golden-brown fur. In it she looked pretty again, her thin cheeks flushed with pleasure. In no time at all, he decided, she would be paintable again.

Mrs Paske, who had always believed it to be beneath her dignity to do any housework in a house where she entered as midwife or nurse, abandoned her theory for once and still came to cook and clean, insisting that Daisy must not exert herself too soon or too much. The proximity of the mews and the studio made managing very easy; sometimes Mrs Paske cooked for five in Effie's kitchen and ran round with a meal for Daisy and Mr Skelton in a covered dish; sometimes she reversed the process. Alongside her cynicism was a romantic streak to which this unusual pair made a great appeal. She hoped — almost expected to hear — that they were to be married; and when this did not come about, invented reasons. Perhaps Mr Skelton was married already, to a lunatic wife or one so disagreeable that she was impossible to live with. That would explain his melancholy expression and rather offhand manner. But how to explain why he did not sleep with the girl of whom his actions, if not his words, proved him to be so fond? Was it because of some blood kinship? Half-brother and sister? There was some mystery about the girl's name; she was Daisy Holt, she'd said so herself; yet the parcels of clothes had been addressed to Miss Hebe Waywood. All very interesting to a woman whose own life had been dull; there was some drama in childbeds and deathbeds — twins where only one baby was expected, a breech presentation, a will made at the last moment, relatives at each other's throats; but custom staled even such things while the studio life retained a kind of mystery.

Once, Mrs Paske, doing a quiet, cooking job in the kitchen, overheard an interesting snippet of conversation. It was now almost Christmas time and Daisy was able to sit while Skelton put the final touches to *The Lacemaker*.

". . . so little left to do. Couldn't you have finished without me?"

"I made one attempt. Hopeless. I always thought Romney was a complete fool, painting Emma Hamilton thirty times when he could charge God knows what for a portrait. I understand better now. I'm going to paint you fifty times . . . Look down at that damned lace."

"We don't have to do the nightingale now, do we?"

(She could not really remember going back to Kitty's place and being turned away; she'd felt too ill to notice anything; but Skelton had described what happened, in furious terms. Kitty's behaviour, even for her, had been abominable: "I always deluded myself that somewhere

153

inside that ton of blubber there was a heart the size of a pea; but I was wrong and I shall never go near her again. And nor will you!"

"Yes, we shall do it. But not for old Kit. I'm not altogether pleased with this. Looking down, your eyes don't show to advantage. In the nightingale thing you'll look up . . . But that can wait. I want to paint you in that furred hood . . . Not quite to Wade's taste perhaps, but to mine. After that, who knows?"

A number of things conspired together to alter a state of affairs which Skelton found quite satisfactory. Things Mrs Paske had said to Daisy; Daisy's return to health but not yet to full nervous stability; an invitation for Skelton to spend Christmas at Wichfield; alcohol.

They were having supper at the gate-legged table near the fire in the studio and Daisy, who as yet had no palate for wine, was dutifully drinking her share of the claret. Doctor Burgess had antiquated views about the value of red meat and red wine. She was better, wonderfully better, but still subject, as she had never been before, to moods. Sometimes she cried for no particular reason. So far she had always managed to do so in private and since she was one of those fortunate women who could cry without getting red eyes or a swollen nose, nobody knew.

Skelton said, in his usual casual manner, "My cousin Charles wants me to spend Christmas with him. I think I'd better go."

"Then I'll be alone. At Christmas!"

154

"Mrs Paske will look in. She'd sleep here if you asked her to. In fact I'm sure she would — and be glad to. Didn't she say that with what's-her-name's family coming like a flock of vultures they'd be sleeping on the floor?"

Yes, Mrs Paske had said that and Daisy had half offered Mrs Paske the spare bed. All very sensible and matter of fact, even pleasant. Now something tipped in her mind and she said, "I can't bear it. I just can't bear it. I often think I'd be better dead. I've tried and tried . . . I loved you from the first go. I done just what you wanted. I never been a bother. And you treat me like I wasn't human. Like I didn't hev any feelings when all the time I love you so much I could die of it. Oh Jack, just for once, just for one night, love me."

It was exactly the kind of emotional situation which he had tried most sedulously to avoid. The third — and unwanted — son of a loveless marriage of convenience he had been unfortunate in not finding, as so many deprived children did, a substitute in a good nurse, a tutor, or, at Eton, a friend. He'd carried about with him two qualities fatal to human relationships; self-sufficiency and the certainty that he was a genius, something slightly apart. He'd had the traditional calf-love affair with an older woman, the wife of one of his superior officers during his two years in the army, and simultaneously, a kind of understanding with the daughter of a neighbour, a pretty girl with a respectable dowry, but when he decided that soldiering was not for him, she had shared his family's shock and disgust and dismissed him summarily. Since then he had been

155

celibate for long periods, though women found him attractive. When the mood was on him there were always places like Kitty's. He had never mixed work with sexual activity and even now was reluctant to do so. But he had some feeling for Daisy; the resentment he felt against Kitty for the way she had behaved proved that, so did his concern for her health, his wish to please her and to protect her. In all it did not amount to an overwhelming, world-shaking passion, nor the concealed romance which Mrs Paske had imagined. But it was enough for Daisy who was so innocent, and who had ardour enough for a dozen — once she let herself go.

Mrs Paske, of course, sensed the change the moment she set foot in the house next morning and took full credit for it, for it was she who had told Daisy over and over that Mr Skelton must be in love with her to behave as he did, better than most husbands; and that sometimes a girl should make the first move, especially when the gentleman was so quiet. Daisy's outburst at table had been genuine enough but she would not have dared to indulge in such outspokenness without, at the very back of her mind, a glimmer of hope, planted there by Mrs Paske; the hope that what she said would be contradicted. As it was.

CHAPTER
TWO

Sir Charles Overton was disappointed and slightly annoyed when Skelton excused himself for Christmas. He enjoyed John's company. Despite the difference in age, rather more than twenty years, they were congenial to one another, shared the same sense of humour, the same cynicism, and to some extent the same artistic temperament. Sir Charles was the only member of the family who had any sympathy with Skelton's choice of career and when other relatives had done some symbolic hand-washing — Go your way, then; starve in a garret; but don't expect help from us! — Charles Overton had seen himself making loans, fostering talent, being kind and understanding and dependable, a patron in the old style. That situation had never come about because Skelton would not be patronised and lacked what cousin Charles had in abundance — the proper respect for money. All through his years of penury he had borrowed only once, and then only twenty pounds, promptly repaid, and he had never shown the slightest interest in how Charles intended to dispose of his considerable wealth. This attitude the elder man found at once admirable and deplorable. But it was different. Sir Charles had other cousins, nephews

157

and nieces who angled for his favour, inviting him to weddings and christenings, or mere visits; he'd lost count of the babies who had been brought to Wichfield to exercise their infantile charms. He was generous but never extravagant on such occasions.

He had been married twice and the old adage about lightning never striking twice in the same place was plainly refuted by his history; both his wives had died in childbed; something to do with the Overton big head which he himself had not inherited — in looks he was a Skelton — but which apparently he had transmitted. His first wife, a delicate, frail-boned creature, had died, and the child with her, during a prolonged and horrifying labour; his second, deliberately chosen for her sturdy build — good peasant blood somewhere — had suffered the same trouble and died of childbed fever, after a forcible delivery by forceps which had crushed the baby's skull. After that he had given up. He was a warmer-natured man than John Skelton and had been fond of both his wives and had no intention of suffering the same hurt and loss for a third time. He contented himself with mistresses, carefully chosen to be beyond child-bearing age.

He attributed John's refusal of the invitation to his improved circumstances; the change of address was significant, and so was the gossip of a near neighbour, Mr Salcombe who owned *The Morning Observer*, a paper dedicated to views still called Tory, but with a difference. Conservatives bought it for its sound news and leading articles; Liberals liked the pages devoted to literary and musical reviews, and people who could just

158

read bought it for the sake of the running serial on the back page. The hacks who worked for Mr Salcombe knew the recipe exactly; each short daily instalment must concern a character called Sam Blower — every man's mythical Everyman who must, each day, meet with an adventure, face some danger overcome in the last few lines; and wherever Sam Blower found himself, digging for gold in California, marooned on a desert island, exploring darkest Africa, his story must be told in words of two syllables, no more. Mr Salcombe even distrusted the word *several*. "Keep it simple. Say *a few* or *a lot* as the case may be." It was a good formula in that it worked. Unkind people might call the paper *The Daily Blower*, but it was the only print to find its way into humble homes and the never-ageing Sam Blower cheered many a deadly dull workaday life.

Mr Salcombe, who had met Skelton at Wichfield Place and who visited his paper's office in Fleet Street at least once a week, when he also went to his club and heard everything, had passed on the news about the success of the new kind of picture, all inspired by the same exceptionally beautiful girl. Sir Charles had assumed that she was Skelton's mistress, an assumption slightly premature, but in the end justified. Shortly after Christmas he wrote a letter in which reproaches were only half-playful. "Even married men," he wrote, "sometimes spare a little time for their poor old lonely relatives." And, "If you really cannot tear yourself away from your inamorata, bring her with you, to celebrate my birthday. I shall be sixty-five." Then he added,

159

"Seriously, John, I need a little help with Plenrerith and my gout is monstrous this year."

Had such an invitation, combined with such an appeal, come to Skelton before he was fully committed to Daisy — a thing which had resulted directly from the Christmas invitation in which no mention was made of her — Skelton would have accepted it easily as one might an invitation to come and bring your dog or your pet parrot. But now things were changed and he was as much in love with Daisy as he was capable of being. Not very profoundly, but sufficiently to make him sensitive to her position and aware of her complete lack of worldliness.

She was now his mistress; and in Well House Close the whole thing was comparatively easy. That they were, in the current term, living in sin had been accepted almost from the first and although ladies might give Skelton a cold bow of recognition if they came face to face, and gentlemen would exchange the time of day with him, Daisy was ostracised and seemed not to notice. Mrs Paske was the only one who mattered, and she was as friendly and helpful as ever. At Wichfield Place, however, things would be different and far more complicated, for Sir Charles was far from being the lonely old man he called himself in his letter; he was the keystone of a close-knit little community, the local big-wig, and since his gout prevented him from moving about much he entertained a good deal. There were still women around who indulged in sporadic bouts of match-making for him. In such a household a mistress must observe certain rules and keep to her well-defined place. Skelton doubted Daisy's ability to do so. Also something in him made him shrink from explaining such things. However, he made the effort. He began by telling her why he felt it incumbent upon him to go to Wichfield at all.

"My cousin isn't exactly pitiable, but I feel under some obligation to him. He's always been kind to me. I had splendid holidays at Wichfield when I was a boy and later on he was the one person who understood why I left the army and didn't behave as though I'd broken all the commandments in the course of half an hour . . ."

Daisy, with her fingers linked and her chin propped on them, might have been posing for a picture called *The Listener*. Skelton paused, trying for the thousandth time to define to himself what exactly it was which gave her every move, her every expression so much extra value. Then he explained about Plenrerith.

"Plenrerith is a property in Cornwall and it's been a bother to him ever since he inherited it. The uncle who left it to him had some very grandiose ideas about turning a quiet fishing village into a holiday resort. Something like Brighton, but more picturesque and with a warmer climate. He'd spent a small fortune on it when he died, leaving it half-finished. Charles thought the only thing to do was to go on with the place, but even when he was more active than he is now he couldn't devote much time to it, so he had agents; all either incompetent or dishonest."

"I expect he would like you to look after it."

"He did once suggest it. I couldn't quite see myself . . . I think that *now* all he wants is to talk it over. He's rather vain. He wouldn't like to admit to anyone else that he'd been made a fool of. Also, I have no doubt he wishes to see *you*. But . . ."

That part of him which could never bear to be tied down, to accept responsibility for anyone but himself, or for anything but his work, made its first wriggle of rebellion. He'd allowed pity for the girl who had served him so well — and fury with Kitty — to make him responsible for her during her illness; he had then compounded his error by allowing a gust of passion to make him take her as his mistress. With this result; he must either persuade her to let him go to Wichfield alone for at least two days, or take her with him after explaining the position of a mistress when other women, damn them, were present; as they would be, for Sir Charles always kept his birthday in style.

His dislike for having to say such things — and for the situation in which he found himself; and for the complete falsity of the convention that held that a decently married woman, or a girl hoping for marriage, might be irrevocably compromised by sitting at the same table with a female of uncertain status — made him sound almost unfriendly as he said, "Well, there you are. You can stay here, with Mrs Paske for company, or come with me, bearing in mind what I have just said."

"I heard. I shan't cause no trouble. I'd sooner go with you than stay behind. January is the snow month.

162

You might get there and not get back and I'd eat my heart out. I'll pretend I ain't there — except when told otherwise."

Her instant understanding, her meek acceptance did not soothe Skelton. It merely pointed up something which he did not care to face and he said irritably, "I wish you wouldn't say ain't."

"Oh," she said, startled. "Why?"

"For one thing there is no such word. And it makes you sound like Kitty Hammond."

It was the first time anyone had ever criticised her speech. Even Mrs Westcott, while deploring it, had accepted it, merely stipulating no swearing in front of the children. To correct the errors of grammar and pronunciation would have been too formidable a task and a nursemaid straight from the country must have allowances made for her.

"I wouldn't want to sound like *her*," Daisy said, completely unresentful. "Tell you what, every time I say something wrong, you tell me. I'm a quick learner. You learn me."

God! What an uphill, what a tedious task! Demanding patience, of which he had none, except where his work was concerned. And what did it matter except on this one occasion when, going to Wichfield for a day or two, if only she'd been better-spoken there'd have been no problem about her status; she could have been passed off as a young relative, one of Charles's numerous godchildren or something equally ordinary?

★ ★ ★

Sir Charles knew all about mistresses and their place in a household; he'd had three, none very young and, though comely, of no great beauty. They had all acted as and enjoyed the status of housekeeper. One had married, with his blessing and a hundred pounds as a wedding present, his head gamekeeper. One had died, very neatly and expeditiously while shopping in Barsham on a very hot day. She had, naturally, a gig at her disposal, and all she had to do was to tell the driver to rap on the window of the grocer's shop with his whip and somebody would have come running to take her order. But something had gone slightly wrong the previous week and she, good conscientious woman, had insisted upon climbing down from the gig and taking the matter up with the proprietor. While she was railing at him she broke off, clutched at her bosom and dropped dead. The third was, to borrow a phrase, still in office, wielding immense authority, holding the keys and moving by gradual but apparently irrevocable stages from being housekeeper and mistress to housekeeper and nurse. Writing to John Skelton that his gout had been monstrous this year, Sir Charles had been truthful.

Cousin John's mistress, who was also his model, would certainly be young and pretty and lower class, so in order to spare everybody's feelings Sir Charles decided to reserve his hospitality — even his birthday party — to men only, giving his gout and grumpiness as an excuse. To his obliging and tolerant housekeeper, Mrs Warren, he explained that his young cousin was bringing a young lady friend with him. The only just

164

perceptible pause before "friend" told Mrs Warren all she needed to know and she gave orders for the Park Suite to be prepared. Two bedrooms separated from, or linked to, each other by a small dressing-room.

Daisy had feared, from Skelton's lecture upon discreet behaviour in a mistress, that it might mean sleeping apart, so the arrangement was a joyful surprise and she could gloat over the beauty and luxury of her room without any reserve. The room had been furnished by Sir Charles's father in order to serve exactly the purpose it was now serving; and since every woman looked her best in pink, to be there was like being in the heart of a rose.

Daisy had been comfortably housed at Kitty's and she loved her little room above the studio; she had seen the family rooms at the Hall at Talbot St Agnes, but never, never anything like this. Yet, oddly enough, standing there in the midst of such beauty and richness, she felt that she had known it all along — something wonderful awaiting her, the details not precise, but its coming certain. The certainty had brought comfort in low moments, contributed to the gaiety and good humour which had endeared her even to fellow servants and accounted for her fecklessness. Now the wonderful thing had happened; it was *now*! The last shreds of her post-diphtheria moodiness fell away, her spirits rushed upwards; she could have kissed everything in the pretty room. Sir Charles declared afterwards that when he took her hand for the first time he received an electric shock which had a magic effect upon his gouty foot. Certainly on the day of Daisy's arrival he could hardly hobble, had not been able to greet his guests at the door, as was his amiable habit, and sat in his library with the afflicted foot on a stool, wearing soft velvet slippers, the left one slashed for comfort. By next day, his birthday, the pain and the puffiness had subsided; he was up and properly dressed.

Despite all that Skelton had said to Daisy about keeping in the background, he had visualised the possibility of her dining at least on one of the evenings he was prepared to spend at Wichfield at her host's table, so he had provided her with an evening dress. It was blue — everything he had bought her so far was blue — made of velvet, the low bodice encircled with a fall of creamy lace; more lace edging the short but enormous sleeves, and frothing about the voluminous skirts. It was her first evening dress, for though at Kitty's all the girls were thus provided, chiefly with dresses of provocative design and colour, black or poppy-coloured, Daisy, even when mingling, had not been so equipped. For her Kitty had decided that the keynote must be simplicity. Contrast had a value all its own. When Daisy told Skelton that all she owned in Kitty's house was one summer dress, some underclothes and a pair of shoes, she had told the truth. All the other white muslin dresses, sashed with blue or lavender or rose, had been part of the stage equipment. The one spare dress, so lightly abandoned, was Daisy's own, bought with money she had earned, what was left over after she had sent the bulk of her earnings home. Now and again it worried her slightly that since she left Kitty's she had had no money of her own; but she had written to explain that she had been ill, lost her job and was better, but not yet earning, so her father would know and not fret. She didn't fret either, just thought about it now and then at odd moments. One such moment came on her first evening at Wichfield when in the heart-of-a-rose bedroom, helped or hindered by a prim and silent maid, she donned the elegant gown. She thought, Oh dear; here I am, wearing a dress that must have cost at least ten pounds and I haven't sent a penny home for months! But that was a butterfly thought, quickly diverted. She had more serious things to think of, and being careful not to say *ain't* was one of them. She must not, simply must not, shame her lover in front of his grand, rich cousin. She said to herself, Daisy Holt, keep your mouth shut; say yes and no if asked a question, and smile, smile, smile.

To smile at Sir Charles was an easy thing to do; he was so like John. Older, of course — his hair was silvery and he carried more flesh — and he seemed slightly more like some of the men at Kitty's place, ready to be pleased and eager to please; but in the nicest, most dignified way. On this first evening there were only three of them at table, and she sat on Sir Charles's right, the guest of honour. Because of her determination to restrict her speech, he thought she was shy and exerted himself to put her at ease. With the sudden cessation of the pain in his foot, his spirits were rising and he was able to view his sixty-fifth birthday less as an affliction than a triumph. Soon he had broken down the barrier of what he considered shyness — somewhat unusual in a girl so exceptionally beautiful.

Earlier Skelton had suggested that she should retire soon after dinner. "There's something he wants to talk over with me and I'd like to get it out of the way." He felt reasonably sure that Charles was about to repeat his request that he should go and take charge of things at Plenrerith, he knew that he had no intention of doing so, and if, as result of his refusal, some coolness occurred, better this evening than on the birthday itself.

Sir Charles showed no haste to get down to business.

"My congratulations, dear boy. What a charmer. Where did you find her?"

"At Kitty Hammond's. Not, I hasten to inform you, as one of the girls. She was an entertainer."

"In what way?"

"Singing; dancing; striking attitudes."

"Talented too, eh? Do you think she would perform for our small company tomorrow evening?"

"She'd be delighted. Her voice isn't what it was." He explained why and how it had come about that Daisy had ended under his roof.

"It is rather difficult to imagine you playing the Good Samaritan; but I imagine even a bad one would have done just what you did."

"You think I'm heartless because I don't dance attendance on you, Charles, flattering and fawning and thinking of benefits to come."

"Ah!" Sir Charles's expression of face, tone of voice changed. "Maybe that is why I respect you and turn to you in a dilemma." His expression changed again, into a grimace of pain. "Damn it! It's back! Definitely a twinge. McGibbon, who is my friend as well as my physician, gives me most unpalatable advice about diet. I told him frankly that *poor* men have gout, so why blame red meat and red wine? It is Plenrerith which provokes my gout."

"Yes? What of Plenrerith?"

"As you know, agents didn't work — or worked only for themselves. So I tried Overtons — fair enough, the damned place came to me from the Overton side. I was honest with them both, Max and Algie. Did you ever meet? No? You've missed nothing! I told them, try to get the thing going, get it finished and it will be to your ultimate advantage . . . I intended to will it to them, once it was worth something and not the dead loss and the expense it has been to me ever since I inherited it. And I grant you, Cornishmen have been awkward since Trelawney's time; they think of themselves as people apart. Oddly, on the only two occasions when I was active and had time to visit the place, I got on with them not too badly. Max had nothing but quarrels, and Algie provoked a riot." A spasm of pain, mental or physical, crossed Sir Charles's face. "The hotel, which was practically completed, was badly damaged, so were several houses." With a kind of glee he added, "Algie suffered some slight injury. Some misguided fellow tried to brain him with a shovel — an obvious exercise in futility."

Skelton made a sound of commiseration.

"The question now is what to do? Cut my losses and let the place go back to holdings the size of a pocket handkerchief — and lobster-fishing? Or press on?" He half answered himself. "A shame after the thousands, literally thousands, I've poured into the blasted place. What do *you* think?"

"Surely that depends upon the amount of damage done."

"Exactly. And how, from this distance, can I possibly assess *that*?" He waited, and still Skelton did not offer.

"I know you refused to go and take charge when the last agent proved to be such a swindling rogue. All I'm asking you to do now, John is to go down, look at the damage, consider the possibilities and then report to me."

"I'm not qualified to judge, Charles, any more than I am qualified to overlook building operations and order workmen about. I told you so at the time."

"I remember. Too much responsibility, you said. You know, dear boy, this reluctance to accept responsibility is a failing."

"Maybe. I'm responsible for my own work. So far that has been enough."

"So far. Just at the moment, I am given to understand, you are enjoying some success. Long may it last, I say. Do you never think of the future? Tastes change, fashions change."

"I know. I'm prepared for that. I even — this may surprise you — kept the tenancy of my attic. I've failed in the past, I may fail again. Then back to Springfield Lane!"

170

Sir Charles reflected that one of the qualities he had always admired in John was his honesty, even with himself.

"Look," he said, "will you, as a favour to an old, ailing and worried man, go to Plenrerith just for a few days, no more than a week at the outside, and use your eyes. Not your judgement. Take no responsibility. I'll make a list of the things I specifically need to know. Merely report."

"All right," Skelton said after a brief hesitation. "I'll do that. And in return, you can look after Hebe for me. She'd be lonely in London. You know how it is. She's never been alone and there's only a middle-aged, working woman for company."

"It will be a pleasure," Sir Charles said. He reflected that John *had* changed a little; showing some consideration for his young mistress. Women kept openly were bound to be lonely. He had managed better with his, who while sharing his bed, in secret, had never been lifted out of, divorced from, their own setting.

Daisy was not the first woman to lie between the pink silk sheets, under the pink curtained canopy and say, "I love you! I love you! I'd be glad to die now." When Sir Charles's father had arranged and furnished that suite, a Royal Duke, ostensibly faithful to his acknowledged and accepted mistress, had taken an inordinate fancy to a married woman of unblemished reputation and just at a time when any scandal could have had the most unfortunate political repercussions. It had been a vagrant infatuation, easily assuaged. Since then there had been others indulged in this relatively unimportant house and attracting little of the undesirable public attention which was the drawback to visits to greater houses and more important people.

Skelton did not wish to spoil this night of love by telling Daisy that on the day after tomorrow he was to go to Cornwall for a week and leave her at Wichfield. He thought, Better tomorrow, when she has sung and danced and charmed everybody and is feeling ebullient. He still held in his mind that outburst sparked off by his proposal to leave her for a mere two days, the emotional eruption which had engulfed him. Not entirely against his will, nor could he actively regret, but almost from the first waking moment next morning he had known that he had behaved out of character, acted on impulse and put himself in a false position. He was not fitted for participation in a permanent love affair. Daisy was the sweetest, the most ardent bedfellow he had ever known and he wanted her to be happy. But . . . Well, he'd felt obliged to bring her to Wichfield, and he rather dreaded having to tell her that he was leaving her there for a week. Already a faint feeling of being burdened was in the offing.

"What would you like me to do?" Daisy asked when he told her that Charles would like her to entertain his guests.

"Sing a little; dance a little. Anything. They'll be easy to entertain. Most of them will be happy just to *look* at you."

172

Any man with a drop of blood left in his veins would be.

"All I have is my blue shawl." She clung to that and to the beaded reticule, like a child to its first toys.

"You charmed old Kit with nothing," he reminded her.

"Yes. But that was ages ago; afore — I mean before — I knew better. And my frock was short, well above my ankles. My new, *beautiful* one is long. Suppose I tripped!"

"They'd love it! They're all oldish . . ." He was about to say "unsophisticated" but realised just in time that the word was outside her range, ". . . pretty simple men; out for an evening without their wives. Pleased with anything."

"I want *you* to be pleased, my dearest dear."

Skelton felt the burden of obligation, inseparable from being the loved one, increase slightly, and for the first time he thought of going to Cornwall with a degree of something near pleasure and then with a jerk of remorse.

"Whatever you do will please me. Not the somersaults, though."

"Oh no! They was — were — old Kit's idea. I'll dance decent and sing decent; in that May Day song only one verse is a bit bawdy. I'll leave that out, and the same with the girl going with the gypsies. Funny. I musta sung that a hundred times without knowing what the girl was giving up. Now I do know; and I feel just what she did. I *would* follow you barefoot."

That was the kind of statement which, he knew, other men would have found flattering. He found it troublesome because the most submissive was in the end the most possessive. It was the meek who would inherit the earth!

The birthday evening was a triumph for Daisy. Except to test her voice and her agility occasionally she had neither sung nor danced since her illness and an audience stimulated her. She had regained her ease and fluidity of movement and what her voice had lost in carrying quality it had gained in allure. With the help of the prim maid, who proved to be an excellent needlewoman, she had solved the problem of what to wear, making from a fine linen sheet a kind of tunic with a cross-over bodice which emphasised the shape of her breasts; it had no sleeves, and the skirt stopped short at the knee with a slit half-way up the thigh on one side. She wore it under her elegant dinner dress so that no time was lost in changing. Sir Charles had provided a plethora of scarves and veils. Earlier in the day Daisy had said, "I'm afraid I have only one shawl to perform with." A word to Annie, the maid, and there for Daisy's approval and selection were wonderful things, veils and scarves which two Lady Overtons had worn over their heads and shoulders when going out in the evening, or over their hats when being driven in high gigs. Some had threads of gold or silver, some were sequinned. These and many other relics had been preserved, at first through sentiment, now outgrown, and later because they had been forgotten.

Before dinner Sir Charles said, "Now I must not be selfish, my dear. I have had and shall have, the pleasure of your company, so you must sit at the end of the table, with a specially favoured guest on each side."

On this evening, he noticed, she was not at all shy. There was a great deal of laughter at that end of the table. Once the thought flashed through Sir Charles's mind that Hebe's greater animation might be the result of the slight distance between her and John. Poor little thing, perhaps she had been told to be on her best behaviour. He liked and respected his cousin, even admired him for his break with conventionality — something Charles Overton would have liked to do himself — but he had always thought of John Skelton as a bit of a cold fish and even in the short time he had had for observation it had been made plain to him that Hebe was head over heels in love and that John was not. A man in love would have wanted to take his loved one to Cornwall with him. There were other little signs, too . . . Oh, well, nothing to do with him, except that he wanted to make the pretty little thing happy during the week John would be away.

Ordinarily, when entertaining only male guests, Sir Charles used his library rather than the drawing-room which was larger and grander but far less comfortable; even its sofas and so-called easy chairs were not conducive to lolling. It had been a matter of principle with the first Lady Overton that one should sit upright with a space between one's spine and the back of whatever one sat upon. Other ladies felt the same. But Hebe needed space for her performance and the library, though large, was well filled by a huge desk, some free-standing bookcases, a map table as well as several really easy chairs. Sir Charles had decided upon a compromise; most of the spindly gilt, or lacquer chairs from the drawing-room moved into an anteroom and some comfortable chairs brought in, to make, with the one relatively comfortable sofa, seating accommodation for nine men. The drawing-room had two fireplaces; one warmed the end where his male guests would sit, the other the end where Hebe would perform, the carpet removed to reveal the shining parquet floor.

Skelton had dismissed them all as simple, happy to be out without their wives and ready to be pleased with almost anything, but he underestimated them. Apart from Doctor McGibbon and Mr Salcombe who owned a newspaper, they were all country squires, largely conforming to type, concerned with rents, the price of corn, the upkeep of property. Doctor McGibbon at fifty-one was the youngest present; Lord Fenstanton, nudging eighty, the oldest; but they had all once been young and frisky and there was something about Daisy's performance at once so artless and so seductive which made dead or dying embers glow. Even Doctor McGibbon, slightly puritanical by nature, felt it and had to remind himself fiercely that his wife was an excellent woman, well-connected and possessor of property worth four hundred pounds a year; that she was plain of face and had never been otherwise was not her fault. Lord Fenstanton, once a rake, was reminded of a fascinating little Creole he had known and enjoyed in Paris, sixty years ago; good God, before the Revolution! He could have wept for lost youth and lost potency, but he feared to look senile; there had been a few disquieting signs lately, little lapses of memory, a tendency to fall asleep at odd times and in odd places. Another member of the audience, Mr Ackroyd, when Daisy put the blue shawl over her head, and adopted exactly the pose of a girl at prayer, remembered that he was born and bred a Roman Catholic and had lapsed. Thank God, it was never too late to make one's peace with Him; Holy Mary, pray for us sinners . . .

Skelton watched and listened, aware that every man in the room envied him. Aware, too, that he should be either proud or jealous. Neither feeling touched him; he was satisfied because she performed so well and so discreetly, judging her audience so exactly; but he was not proud of her as he was proud of the moments when he had caught her beauty so exactly on canvas, and he was not jealous because he knew that she belonged to him so absolutely. So absolutely that when, later on, he must break it to her that he was going away for a week and she must stay here, there would be another scene, more tears, more protests. The kind of thing which had led to his undoing just before Christmas. He was right.

"Why can't I come with you?"

"Because it is a tedious journey. Beyond Salisbury the inns are bad. And I don't know what I am going to find in Plenrerith. From what I gather conditions may be rather rough."

"I wouldn't mind. Just so long as I was with you . . . You know, looking at all those poor old men . . . John, I felt how precious every single minute is. Let's not waste a whole week. Darling, you know I'm strong; any old lodging would do for me. So long as we was together. Oh, please let me come."

Why not agree and have done with it? He was tempted, but the inmost core of him which had prevented him from being dependent upon anybody and had — up till now — kept him from allowing anybody to be dependent upon him, held out, all the more assertive because it was in danger of weakening.

"You'll be far more comfortable here. You like Charles, don't you? And he was delighted at the thought of having your company."

"He've managed without it so far!" That was one rather disconcerting thing about her, the sudden flash of shrewdness, the touch of tartness.

"Daisy, that is neither here nor there. Everything is arranged." Now he was sounding gruff, so he offered a crumb of explanation. "For one thing, it is more than likely that I shall have to complete the journey on horseback; and you don't ride."

"No, thass true." There and then she determined to learn, immediately; during this blank week at Wichfield. If only the weather stayed kind. Then if in future John had to go to Plenrerith again — or anywhere else where horse-riding was necessary — she could go too.

CHAPTER
THREE

Sir Charles, freed of his gout, entranced with his companion, felt positively rejuvenated, and was delighted when she asked him to allow her to ride. "Nothing easier, my dear. But you'll need a riding habit." Once again his first wife's wardrobe was raided and Daisy had the choice of three outfits, dark green, grey and tan. They all fitted well enough for Daisy to have worn them as they were, but Annie was a perfectionist and insisted upon making minute alterations. The tan habit, which Daisy chose because she thought it went best with her hair, had been made at a time when all things military were the rage; it had a good deal of braid, a good many gilt buttons. With it went a rather severe little shako-like hat with a cockade of tawny-yellow feathers; gloves with gauntlets, also be-braided and a pair of soft tan boots, which, like most footwear passed on to her, were just slightly too big; but only slightly and since she was to ride, not walk in them, it didn't matter.

With her hair knotted up and partially hidden by the hat, Daisy looked immensely attractive in a different fashion. Like a pretty boy, Sir Charles thought. He said, "John should paint you like that."

"Perhaps he will. He once said he would paint me fifty times."

Beginners started on sedate steeds and with a leading rein held at first, by a groom on foot and then, presently, mounted on another quiet animal. Sir Charles, in the saddle for the first time in three months, sat on his tall dapple grey, Hern the Hunter, and oversaw the process. He was surprised and pleased to see that Hebe, or Daisy — Skelton used both names for her, but he himself preferred Hebe — came to the business as though born to it; superb balance; excellent hands, and something more subtle, a good relationship with the horse.

"And you really have never ridden before?"

"Well, only carthorses now and again. That was when I was young. It was a treat, but no pleasure. They look so wide and flat — at least when they have enough to eat — but even then they do hev sharp backbones."

"You come from the country?"

"Yes. Place called Talbot St Agnes. Up in Suffolk."

"The name reminds me of something. Langham?"

"Langton is the name of the family. My father is their carpenter."

"And a very good one, I am sure."

"He can do most things. He likes mending furniture best. Once there was a chair, got woodworm and a leg fell off. My father made a new one and Sir Alfred hisself said nobody not even him could tell which was which."

Of her past she had never talked much: she had mentioned Waywood to Skelton and also her mother's

180

religious tendency and death and the cook who taught her to read. Actually she found Sir Charles easier to talk to. He was more interested in little things so she rattled on, one thing leading to another; how she had come to London, had the sack, landed at Kitty's, what she had done there and incidentally what Skelton had done in the way of arranging scenery and costumes.

"But I'm glad thass over. Waste of his time, really. He is so clever . . . How long would a letter take to get to Cornwall?"

"Two days, if the weather holds."

"Then I oughta write straight away."

"You do that, my dear, and we'll send it to catch the mail coach at Barsham this afternoon."

Everybody at Wichfield Place knew that the master took a little rest in the afternoon, but this concession to increasing age was never acknowledged as such; he retired to his library, ostensibly to read or look over his accounts, and, guarded from any disturbance, dozed in a chair until roused for afternoon tea.

Daisy wrote to Skelton. "My deerest, deerest deer, you hev been gone only a few houres but how lonely I feel I carn't tell you. Last night we was lovers, tonight I must sleep alone. I miss you every minnit. I long for you so extreemly I could die of it this morning I did some riding it was easy and sir Charles said I was a natteral rider. How I would enjoy it if only you was heer this week will be longer than any yeer I ever lived thro. I never knew annybody could love somebody like I love you my darling John sometimes I think of all the peeple there is in london and how we mite hev missed each other it is like thinking how it would be not to be born at all I dont think I was ever propperly alive till we met. And even then it was not till you kist me. I send you 1000 kisses with this and all the love in my heart. I love you and love you and love you. Your ever loving Daisy."

It was the longest piece of writing she had ever engaged upon and when she read it through the only fault of which she was conscious was that it did not convey the full strength of her feeling for him. Yet, frowning at it, she wondered what more she could say; she had said it all, and it was not enough. Love needed more than ink marks on paper.

By the evening she had thought of another thing she might learn during John's absence. Conversation at dinner had gone well. Sir Charles mentioned her two names and asked why Skelton called her sometimes by one and sometimes by the other.

"Well, really I'm Daisy Holt. My father's name is Benjamin Holt and I was born when them big daisies was in full blow. Some people call them margareets, some say bull-daisies. Kitty Hammond didn't like it. I mean it didn't matter when I was just a statue — what is the word? Anonymous? Later when I did much the same as I did last night, all on my own, I needed a different name and John settled for Hebe and Waywood. Why Hebe I don't quite know, but Waywood because it was a place I once talked to him about. Acherly I don't think thass a very lucky place."

"And which name do you yourself prefer?"

"Well, I'm getting used to Hebe now, though John sometimes forgets and says Daisy. But I like Hebe because in a way it was over Hebe I could first do something for him. Thass rather a long tale. And secret. If I told you you wouldn't tell nobody, would you?" Her eyes sparkled, her lips curved.

"Of course not."

The story of the picture of which so many people wanted a copy and how she had stolen it and where she had hidden it lost nothing in the telling. She was not only a natural rider, she was a natural actress; when she said, "Oh, I was scared," she looked extremely frightened; when she described the slipping of a picture into a pile of others in a way which would not disturb the cobwebs, she gestured with her beautiful hands . . . Absolutely entrancing!

"You have entertained me splendidly. Now what can I do to entertain you? Do you play cards?"

"You mean like whist? No. I do know Beggar My Neighbour, but you can't play that with only two."

"There are card games which two can play. I would very gladly teach you."

"You could do something better than that, if only you would. I know I talk countryfied and John don't like it. I did master *ain't*. John said it made me sound like Kitty Hammond, the last thing I'd want to be! But when I said to him *learn me* he looked . . . well, sort of daunted and I never said that again. But if you could, and would . . . I can learn. I know Signor Mazoni said I had no ear — but that was for music, *his* way. Words I could do better with. I'm sure I could."

Turning school-master at sixty-five! Sir Charles thought. And he thought of the constant, niggling corrections and of how most children hated their tutors; how he'd hated all but one of his and how that well-liked one had come so close to spoiling his whole life, inspiring him with the desire to be, not a country squire, Member of Parliament, Justice of the Peace and all the other orthodox things, but a carefree, footfree archaeologist, digging about in Greece, or Crete, or Rhodes. That would have been the life he would have chosen, had he been free to choose, and that was one reason why he liked his cousin John who had broken free, defied tradition, been pretty near starvation at times, but won through. At least temporarily. For just as one swallow did not make the spring, the fleeting success of a few pictures did not establish an artist's success or guarantee a certain income for the rest of his life.

Letting his thoughts wander in this way, he had delayed his reply and Daisy said, "No, I can see. Thass too much to arst. Don't you worry. P'raps one day I can hire somebody to learn me, like Signor Mazoni did with music."

"I'd most willingly teach you, my dear. That is, if you don't mind being corrected frequently."

"Oh, you are kind! I shan't mind being told I'm wrong." She looked at him with such glowing gratitude that had Sir Charles not known how deeply she was in love with John, he might have been misled. "Less start now."

"Let us," Sir Charles corrected, setting out on his new role with enthusiasm.

★   ★   ★

184

"There's something very odd about this, Mr Bridges," Mrs Warren said, stirring her nightcap of hot whisky toddy. "When Sir Charles ordered the Park Suite for Mr Skelton and a lady friend, I took it to mean just what it meant, though I didn't expect just a common little actress. I suppose you heard Annie's description of what she anticked about in the night before last."

"I did, Mrs Warren, I did indeed. In fact I advised Annie not to *enlarge*. I never encourage gossip."

They were sitting before a blazing fire in the housekeeper's snug room, enjoying the nightly ritual which varied only with seasons; in hot weather they sat by the window and took their whisky cold. Both within their own spheres were discreet; even the understanding between them was tacit. The butler at forty-three, Mrs Warren at forty-five had every hope and intention of outliving Sir Charles. There would be legacies, which pooled, and added to savings, would bring them independence; an apartment house in London: rooms let to young single gentlemen who would have their own men-servants to do the fetching and carrying. Love did not enter into their calculations, mutual trust and esteem did.

"I suppose there was good reason for Miss Waywood remaining here. I understand that Mr Skelton has gone to Cornwall. A long journey in winter and conditions somewhat unsettled."

"What I don't like," Mrs Warren said, fixing upon a minor grievance as a whipping boy, "is this using the poor dead lady's things." She had never known the first Lady Overton and had indeed often cursed the hoarded clothes which served no purpose and necessitated constant watchfulness to guard them from moth damage. "First the scarves and things, then the riding clothes. It'll be the furs next." The furs were rather a sore point; once in a cold winter some time back when her intimacy with her master had been in full flower, she'd dropped a hint or two and had received, not the hoped-for permission to wear the sleek sable or the curly astrakhan, but a brand new fur jacket — of rabbit skin; warm enough but of little value.

"Well, they do say there's no fool like an old fool. Still, we must not despair. I don't think Mr Skelton would part all that easily. She is very pretty."

"Money has a good loud voice, Mr Bridges."

"There's no gainsaying that. What I'm a bit worried about is this red wine. I know Doctor McGibbon said no claret, no burgundy. Sir Charles told me so himself."

"And red meat only once a week, if that."

"The birthday was an exception. Now it's every meal. And port wine worst of all. It seems that Miss Waywood has a liking for port wine; the sweeter the better."

"And not a twinge," Mrs Warren said with resentment. "Of course, when she leaves, *if* she leaves, he'll suffer for it, collapse like a pricked balloon; and I shall be the sufferer. Up and down all night; hot plasters, cold water bandages and nothing but groans for thanks." She managed to sound disgusted by a prospect for which she secretly yearned.

★ ★ ★

186

The week which Daisy had thought would be as long as a year dragged on. The weather, though it turned colder, remained fine, so she could ride every morning; every afternoon she wrote to Skelton, saying the same things; how she loved him, how she missed him, how she was longing for his return; every evening except one was spent in conversation with Sir Charles who proved to be an excellent tutor, ready to correct, but equally ready to praise, and willing to laugh at an error. The whole process demanded less patience than he had expected; she was indeed, as she herself had said, a quick learner, mastering even that besetting fault, the double negative. "Think Daisy. If you say, I don't know nothing it sounds as though you knew something. Either you know nothing; or you don't know anything. Do you understand?"

"Less — I mean let us see. Suppose you offer me more wine . . . If I say, I don't want no more . . . that empty glass is no more. If I don't want that, I mean I want a full one."

"Exactly. And a full one you shall have, my dear."

The exceptional evening was the direct result of Lady Fenstanton's curiosity and Lord Fenstanton's desire to please a wife thirty years younger than himself. The significance of Sir Charles's "men only" invitation had not escaped her notice and on the morning after the birthday she asked in her rallying, hearty way what on earth all the naughty boys had been up to.

"That cousin of Overton's was staying at Wichfield and he'd brought along a dancing girl who gave a performance."

"Highly indecent, I suppose."

"On the contrary. Quite modest and rather touching."

"So touching that mere females must be excluded for fear of wounding their susceptibilities?"

He liked her astringent manner of speech; he thought it witty.

"The performance in itself was harmless, but . . . Well, the girl was at table with us."

"And occupying the Park Suite? I *see*. People make such an inordinate fuss about this breaking of bread together. Had there been a theatre in Barsham, and she were dancing there, even the most straitlaced lady could have watched and remained virtuous."

"I didn't make the rules," he said. "And very few women have your tolerance." Her ladyship, an earl's daughter, an earl's wife, a woman of impeccable character who had actually reformed an ageing rake, could afford an unorthodox action occasionally.

"I'm so tolerant I propose to invite them all to dinner and then ask the girl, as a favour to me, to show her pretty paces."

"I think Skelton was off somewhere. Either I didn't catch, or I've forgotten."

"Then we shall be a foursome. Very cosy. I'll send a note at once."

"Not for tonight, Veronica. Two such evenings in succession . . . Rather much. I intend to have an easy

188

day and an early night. And . . . perhaps it would be as well to indicate that you expected . . . hoped . . . for a performance, so that she may be . . . prepared."

"With fans? Peacock feathers? Once, when Papa had some sort of fearfully important appointment in Paris, Stella and I stole out all alone and went to a place called *le Paradis*. We wore veils, of course. The girls there had fans and peacock feathers. I thought then, and I have never changed my opinion, that such half-measures are more suggestive than plain nudity."

"There is nothing of that kind about Miss Waywood. She wore a kind of shift, with scarves and a blue shawl."

"How disappointing for you all."

Privately Sir Charles detected a smack of high-handedness about the invitation; but he, like everyone else in the area, was accustomed to allowing Lady Fenstanton to indulge her whims. And it would be an outing for Hebe. He conveyed the request tactfully.

"Lord Fenstanton — you remember him — the eldest of my guests the other evening, was so impressed by your performance, my dear, and praised you so highly to his wife that she wishes to see you. We are invited to dine at the Castle and she wondered if you would sing and dance for her after dinner."

"Of course I will."

"Her ladyship leads a rather dull life these days. She is a good deal younger than her husband and once upon a time she was very gay, in Paris and Vienna. Then she had three children, two of whom died very young. By the time that was over, poor Fenstanton's age was telling and they live very quietly. It will be a treat for her to see you. And Wichmore Castle is worth seeing. Very grand indeed."

"Grander than this?"

"There is no comparison, my dear. Mine is a modest, though I hope comfortable, country house, Wichmore is stately."

"Well, it'll be a treat for me to give somebody else a treat; I've had so many myself lately."

He thought what an admirable, what an unusual attitude for the girl to take towards an invitation which, though somewhat arrogant, even he recognised as an honour. He was no more a snob than the next man but he was aware of social differences, fine as the graduations of the spectrum were. He began to think about the six-mile drive and the increasing cold.

"What did I say, Mr Bridges?"

"Concerning what, Mrs Warren?"

"Furs! Didn't I say it'll be the poor dead lady's furs next? It's come about. Annie had her orders this morning to get out the sable cloak and see it was well aired."

"Not surprising, Mrs Warren. Sir Charles and Miss Waywood are dining at the Castle tomorrow. And if Annie's judgement is to be trusted all Miss Waywood's clothes, though pretty and suitable for most occasions, are cheap."

"Like her!"

190

"Just so. And Sir Charles has always been one for keeping up appearances." By a tone of voice, a look in the eye, Mr Bridges managed to convey the words, *As we know!*

"Suppose he takes it into his head to *marry* her."

"That," said Mr Bridges, "is something I think highly improbable and would prefer not to think about, *yet.*"

In ordering the sable cloak, lined with quilted satin and made in a day when all cloaks had voluminous hoods, out of the lavender and rosemary-scented obscurity in which it had hung for so many years, Sir Charles had given no thought to keeping up appearances; he was not that kind of snob. He had thought only of Hebe's comfort during a cold drive to Wichmore and a possibly colder one home. Her blue cloak with its edging of pale golden fur was vastly becoming, but it was only a single layer of lightweight cloth, some cotton probably interwoven with the wool. It was the same with her evening dress. There were many qualities of velvet, even more of lace, and it was a poor, pretty dress, cheap velvet, machine-made lace.

His kindly gesture was wasted. Daisy said, "Oh, how beautiful!" with such admiration that he, undecided until that moment whether to lend or to give it, decided to give. But she went on, "If you don't mind, I'd sooner wear the one what — the one *which* John gave me. I mean . . . He chose it for me and it makes me think of him."

Rather quizzically, Sir Charles said, "I do not think you need any tangible reminder."

"No. I don't. I think of him all the time. I half thought I'd hev a letter by now."

Sir Charles experienced a pang of pity. John could have scribbled just a line or two at wherever he spent the night and made certain that the missive travelled by the fastest mail coach. The way the poor girl had begun looking for the postman was really quite pathetic.

"We shall hear in due course," he said, though he expected no letter. John would inspect the damage, estimate Plenrerith's possibilities and come straight back with a verbal report.

The visit to Wichmore, a success from every point of view, gave Daisy material for another letter, written late that same evening.

"My derest, deerest deer now I hev something to tell you apart from how I love you and miss and wish you was here. This evning sir Charles and me . . ."

She halted her pen and remembered that one of her lessons had dealt with the mysteries of *I* and *me*. Sir Charles had been very clear on the point. "Hebe, you wouldn't say me went riding this morning, would you?"

"No, I'd say I went riding."

"Then you should say 'Charles and I.' Do you see?"

"Yes. I say 'John and I came to stay here.' D'you know, I think I've got that fixed. If I do it, I say I, and if somebody does it to me, it's me. Is that right?"

Sir Charles, who had not attempted to confuse her with set rules and terms, said, "Splendid!"

So now she blotted over the *me* and wrote *I*. ". . . went to Wichmore Castle to hev dinner and afterwards I danced and sung and everybody was

192

pleased with me. Did you ever go there it is very grand lord Fenstanton was a bit sleepy but Lady fenstanton said I was marvelless some things she made me do twice and at the end she took a ring of her verry own finger and put it on mine and said we was friends for life sir Charles says it is a saffar it is blew and verry valuabble. Cumming home it was verry cold and slipperry for horses so it took a long time but heer I am in my lovely bed and I wish to God you was heer. Darling, deerest, pleese dont stop in that place or if you must because of the wether send for me pleese just say cum and I will cum thro frost or snow or ennything like the girl in the song barefoot, darling I don't think you know quite how I love you just to think of your name send little shivers thro me. Please dont waist a minnit but cum back to your ever loving Daisy with a thousand kisses."

Skelton wasted no time, not because he longed for Daisy but because he wanted to get back to work and he felt there was nothing that he or anyone else could do about Plenrerith. He had promised Charles a week of his time and should not have been back before Wednesday, but on Tuesday, just as Sir Charles and Daisy returned from their morning ride, there he was in the hall, being helped out of his topcoat by a footman.

She had often spoken of swooning from joy or sorrow but she had never done it until now. She said, "Darling!" in a half-incredulous voice and fell into his arms. When she came to she was on the sofa in the library.

"It was the surprise. Everything went black," she said apologetically. Sir Charles fussed about with brandy, another cushion behind her head, a light cover over her legs. He was impressed — almost made uneasy — by such violence of emotion. He'd loved, and been loved in his day, but nothing like this. Of course some females swooned, or pretended to for almost no reason at all, but Hebe's had been a genuine faint and quite out of keeping with her look of health and vitality. He feared for her.

Skelton seemed rather put about, embarrassed by the display and presently glanced at his watch.

"I thought that if I told you what there is to tell before lunch, we could leave immediately after and be in London before dark."

"Hebe may not feel fit to travel."

"Of course she will."

"Very well, then. I am all ears. What did you find?"

"Chaos. If you ask me, Algie was lucky to escape with his life. Two imported workers — foreigners as they call them — were not so lucky; and more would have been heard about *that* but for a Mr Tresize. I'll come to him in a minute. Bad feelings run so high that I couldn't obtain a bed in Plenrerith itself, I had to lodge in Penston, full three miles away. The hotel is damaged, but not irrevocably, the same could be said of most of the new houses."

"What of the harbour? My uncle had spent a fortune on making it suitable for yachts and other pleasure craft. In fact Plenrerith is only easily accessible by water."

194

"Some fanatics rolled a few rocks into the water and damaged the jetty. But there again, not irretrievably. The real problem is, Charles, that neither you nor any outsider will ever get the work done. And that brings me to Mr Tresize. He worked in the tin mines at Penston, thought he'd try his luck in California and struck it rich, very rich indeed. He's back now, with a finger in every pie and he has made an offer for Plenrerith, as it stands. Three thousand pounds."

"It sounds a lot of money; but it is a fleabite to what has been spent already, first by my uncle who conceived the idea, and then by me, fool that I was! John, what would you do?"

"I think you said yourself. Cut your losses and consider yourself well rid of an incubus."

Sir Charles looked pained and Daisy, remembering how kind he had been, thought, Poor old man, all alone, with nothing to love but his possessions.

"Don't be sad," she said, "money isn't everything."

"I know, my dear. It isn't the money so much as the thought of the waste. A well-intentioned idea brought to nothing . . ." But even as he spoke from the surface of his mind, his thoughts were running in another direction. It had been a long time since anyone had been enough in tune with him to notice a passing expression and he realised that he loved her and believed that but for her infatuation with John — completely unworthy of her — she might love him. A dangerous thought to entertain at the age of sixty-five.

CHAPTER
FOUR

In later years, Daisy, looking back, thought of the years as beads on a string, some dull, some shining. The most shining year of all was the one which began at Wichfield with John's return and ended so badly . . .

During that year Skelton painted assiduously and well; not the fifty pictures of which he had once spoken, but twenty, all of Daisy, in differing guises and poses, mainly classical and all saleable. Domestic life ran smoothly, largely thanks to Mrs Paske who continued to do most of the cleaning and cooking, and continued to speculate about Mr Skelton's reason for not marrying Miss Waywood. It couldn't be because his family objected, for Sir Charles had not only had them to stay with him, but early in March when the worst of the winter was over, came to spend two nights with them. And a nicer gentleman it would be hard to find.

It was on this visit that Daisy asked Sir Charles's help in a little matter which, though it did not bother her unduly, did cause intermittent concern — money.

"I don't like to look grasping," she explained. "John is so generous to me. Anything I want for shopping and five shillings a week for Mrs Paske, to spare my hands. And two new dresses since Christmas . . . I've tried to screw a little out of the shopping money, but I've never managed, prices go up and up and whenever I see something nice I think, John'd like that! Mind, I enjoy eating too. But I really do need some money to send to my father. I always did, when I was earning. And really, I am earning now . . . Oh dear! That sounds awful! I don't mean it that way. I enjoy just being with him while he's painting. It's not work to me. What I'd like best would be for Mrs Paske not to come so much and have three shillings a week and me cook more and have two shillings. If you'd just say that to John. And no more dresses till I ask."

"But you could say that yourself, my dear. And it would come much better from you. I'm afraid John might consider that I was interfering."

She was disappointed, and as always with her, the slightest emotion was reflected and exaggerated in her expression. She looked extremely distressed.

"Somehow I just *can't*. Time and again I've nearly brought myself to it and I never could. John is funny about money. He don't think much about it himself and don't think other people should."

It was a true observation; but Sir Charles, who had always respected his cousin for his attitude towards money, his lack of sycophancy towards a richer relative, now took another view and thought, despite being an artist he lacks imagination.

"I'll see if I can slip in a word," he said. Daisy gave him another swimming look of gratitude and again he thought that if only she could be detached from John . . . At the moment the chance seemed remote, but one never knew. Here, sharing their life briefly, Sir Charles had observed several things, small in themselves, but in the aggregate significant, which confirmed his feeling that the love was a very one-sided affair. For instance, John had suggested that on his first evening in town Charles should take Hebe to the opera. "You're both musical," he said. That could have been taken as a considerate gesture to both of them, but not the way he said it, with just that shade of contempt for a taste he did not share.

Hebe said, "But then you'll be alone, darling."

"I can bear that," and again his voice betrayed him; it said that being alone was a luxury seldom enjoyed. And although they had enjoyed the opera and momentarily lived in the world of make-believe, Hebe said once, "I wonder what John is doing." And then, "I do hope he hasn't got drunk. I've only left him alone once before. Mrs Paske's brother had a birthday and I went to the party she'd arranged for him. And John was quite drunk when I got back."

He was quite drunk at the end of that evening, too. Sodden drunk and asleep on the couch in the studio. Hebe covered him warmly and said, "Oh dear. He'll have a thick head and shaky hands tomorrow. I ought not to have left him."

"There is no need to blame yourself, my dear. He was a hard drinker when you were in your cradle."

Skelton had in fact taken to alcohol for comfort, during the break with family tradition, during the years of failure. Oblivion in a glass! No need for it now, but the habit had been formed and it did not fit with the domestic way of life into which he had stumbled. He was not wildly in love with Daisy but he was still fond enough of her not to wish to upset her. Even Sir Charles, jealously watchful, could not think that.

The next day was a busy one for an elderly gentleman up from the country for the first time in more than a year; and not on the whole a very reassuring one. Nobody actually *said*, "Overton! By Jove, I thought you were dead!" They said, "Oh, Overton! Nice to see you. How's the gout?" Surprised to see him; rather proud of remembering what he had ailed. Things moved on; a year was a long time; and though Wickfield was within easy distance of London it was a bit off the beaten track and neither it nor its owner were important enough to be visited by busy men. Since his retirement from Parliament, three years earlier, he had been virtually forgotten even in the two clubs to which he still belonged. Somebody, well intentioned, said, "You don't look a day older!" and that made him feel very old indeed, for it was a remark made only to those who had noticeably aged.

In the afternoon he had an appointment with a lawyer — the ostensible reason for his visit. He had a perfectly good lawyer in Barsham, but the transfer of that ill-fated Plenrerith demanded a more specific service than Mr Copeland felt able to provide. So here Sir Charles was, at three o'clock in the afternoon, facing a stranger, young, lithe, earnest, who said, "Sir Charles, I assure you, there was no need for you to make the journey. I would most willingly have come to you." Civil, but quite uncalled for!

Feeling old and in need of comfort he went along to his tailor and bespoke a new suit of clothes. It was gratifying to be told that his measurements had not changed by an inch since last time — but he knew that already. He also knew that tailors were not above practising innocent deceptions.

It was truly comforting, in a way, to go back to Well House Close, to the half-house with only the one entry, the kitchen door, and there to find Hebe, dressed in her best and wearing a ridiculous little apron, basting a couple of ducks.

"I wanted to make you a lovely dinner, all by myself," she said.

Through the rich scent of roasting duck came the sharp, pungent aroma of sliced oranges. Just as, through her obvious desire to please, shot the appeal. He remembered that he had promised to slip in a word and had not yet done so. He'd had no chance.

And when the chance came it was difficult. After a dinner that could not have been bettered so far as the food went, though the wine left a good deal to be desired, Hebe said, "I'm sure you have a lot to talk over. And I'm tired; so if you will excuse me . . ."

Hell's afire; how am I to tell that insensitive lump that his mistress wants two shillings a week to send to her hungry family and is afraid to ask for it?

He thought about it for a while and then said, "Curiosity is said to be vulgar, I know, but do you make her an allowance?"

"No. Why?"

"I just wondered what an ideal model *and* a good cook was worth."

"It never occurred to me to pay her. She gets her keep. I buy her clothes from time to time. And I'm putting money away for her — a thing she'd never do for herself. For a girl of her class she's most inept about money."

"Oh, in what way?"

"Extravagant. Vague. And generous. She can't pass a beggar. I may not be very businesslike myself but I always *attempted* to live within my means. Hand to mouth, borrow, even pawn when times were bad. Hebe just has no idea." He could not well mention to his guest who had just enjoyed a splendid meal, that Hebe invariably bought the most expensive food available. Ducks might be common enough, cheap enough in the country, in London they were a luxury; so were oranges at this time of the year; and cream.

"So you're saving *for* her?" It struck Sir Charles that this was unlike John, always so indifferent to money; but he had seen it happen before. People who affected to despise the stuff when they had none, coming into possession of a little, suddenly turned thrifty or miserly.

"Well, I feel responsible for her. But for me she'd either be dead or still at Kitty's place. If she'd done what the old hag ordered, she'd have been responsible . . . And she is young, good possibly for another seven years in the song and dance business, and ten . . . upstairs. You could say that I've been her ruin, poor child. And none of it intentional. It was the *last* thing I wanted."

"I never quite knew what you did want." Sir Charles forced himself to speak with his usual geniality but it was difficult; he liked his cousin much less than he once had done.

"Simple enough," Skelton said. "To succeed in my own line, in my own way."

"And that you are doing."

"I doubt it. The trap was well disguised, but it was a trap and I walked into it, with my eyes wide open."

"How do you mean?"

"Oh God, must I explain? Can't you see? I meant to paint portraits, real people, plain if they were plain, even ugly. I failed. Then I fell in with what you call the ideal model. So she is . . . At least twice a day, painting her in one pose, I see another . . . Another beautiful picture that Wade can sell. That is *not* what I set out to do. I may have been her ruin, but she's been mine . . . Unless I cut and run. In the end I must. I've been . . . bewitched, if that is not too fanciful a term."

"And where would you run?"

"We all have our dreams. Egypt. Java. Tahiti. Far more likely it will be back to Springfield Lane. Absurd as it may sound, that was more my milieu than this." He looked, with a marked lack of appreciation, around the comfortable room, furnished to Foley's taste, belonging to Foley, the successful man. Skelton was now enjoying success of a sort. It was not the sort he wanted and was beginning to pall. "But first I must make some provision for Hebe."

"Before you abandon her."

202

"That is a contradiction in terms, Charles. To provide for is hardly to abandon, is it? With a certain sum of money — more of a dowry than most girls of her kind can hope for — she'd marry some decent, respectable fellow."

Sir Charles wanted to say, "When you decide to get rid of her I should be glad to offer her a home." But the time was not ripe. Give the situation a little longer and the chances were that Hebe would see John for what he was — a cold-blooded, self-centred fellow.

"Very worthy, I'm sure. Meantime, may I make a suggestion. Let her learn to manage money by allowing her some of her own, however little. That is the only way."

There! He had done it, and, he thought, tactfully.

Sir Charles went home to Wichfield to wait; not too impatiently. His gout had vanished and did not return, as he half feared it might, when warmer weather came, so his feeling of being rejuvenated continued. But he was sixty-five and his sexual drive, never strong enough to be troublesome, was almost dormant. He was in love with Hebe in his own fashion, a mixture of possessiveness, paternalism, and lust of the eye. He had always loved beautiful things and was a collector in a modest way.

"Shopping money; Mrs Paske's wages," Skelton said laying out the coins. "And this is yours, Hebe, to do exactly what you like with."

"Five shillings. Ooh, the most I'd hoped for was two."

Hoped for! Skelton remembered that his cousin had started that conversation by asking about her allowance — completely out of character.

"Did you talk to Charles about money?"

"Well . . . Yes, in a way."

"And what does that mean?" He sounded nasty and some shred that remained of the old Daisy half-reared, ready with a sharp retort. Daisy, however, was eclipsed, made weak by love, and she said, "I only just mentioned that lately I hadn't sent anything home and was a bit worried."

"Then why not ask *me*?"

"I don't know. I just couldn't bring myself . . . Please, darling, don't be cross. I wasn't complaining, honest I wasn't. I only just mentioned . . ."

His growing dissatisfaction with himself, with his work found vent in this absurd, irrational outlet.

"You went behind my back," he said, "knowing perfectly well that you had only to ask."

"I didn't mean it that way." She began to cry. And of course she cried, as she did most things, beautifully. Tears gathered and stood in her eyes, making them seem larger, deepening their colour, then they spilled over, hung on her lashes like diamonds, dampened her cheeks like dew. Most men would have hurried to embrace her, kiss away the tears, apologise for a moment's irritation, say that it didn't matter. Skelton was differently geared; he thought, What a picture! He wondered how to paint tears and whether anyone would believe that a woman could cry without making herself ugly.

Actually he painted the tears superbly well and in later years *The Penitent* was reckoned to be his finest picture. His reputation was made by the handful of paintings of Daisy in non-classical roles, a portrait or two which had pleased nobody at the time and the unfinished one of the Duchess of Sudbury. The series of pictures which Wade had so gladly bought and so profitably sold were dubbed minor by a generation that saw no beauty in near-nudity.

CHAPTER
FIVE

The days passed, uneventfully and for Daisy happily. She was sending home only a pound a month, but at least she was doing it regularly. John got drunk from time to time, but she made little of that, quite unaware that her face betrayed her, translating mild dismay into distress, and that solicitude, meant with all the goodwill in the world, could be tiresome. It was May Day again and she said, "Just think! It's a year since Mrs Westcott sacked me. And what a year!"

Then it was June and one morning John said, "We are invited to Wichfield again. Would you like to go?"

"Oh, I would." She clasped her hands together, almost, not quite in the attitude of the girl praying; the difference was very subtle but it did not escape his eye. "Meadows full of daisies and the wild roses. And I should love it — but not . . . not if you wouldn't. I mean, if it interfered with your work."

Damn it, *you* interfere with my work! All the time. Every attitude you strike is paintable. I'm becoming as repetitive as Foley! I shall end being able to paint nothing else.

"I should welcome a holiday," he said.

Once again Sir Charles set himself to charm — this time with deliberate purpose, but with decreasing hope. It was plain that though John's never very ardent feeling for Hebe had cooled still further she was as infatuated as ever; it showed in tiny things.

"Well, and what would you like to do today?" Sir Charles would ask.

Invariably Hebe looked at John and waited for him to suggest something, a ride, a drive, a walk. Almost as invariably he said, "The object of a holiday is to do nothing."

"Then we'll *do* nothing," Hebe said. Yet although he had elected to do nothing except to sit or lie about in the garden, he seemed bored, discontented, or slightly ill at ease. Once or twice, when he and Sir Charles were alone, he seemed to be on the brink of saying something of more importance than their usual exchange of chatter, but nothing was said until the visit, planned to last for a fortnight, was half-way through.

It was a Friday, the first day of a small, two-day agricultural show, held annually in the grounds of Wichmore Castle. The event had been mentioned during the week, and Sir Charles knew that Hebe was looking forward to it. She said she hoped this lovely weather would last; she planned what to wear; she said there had been such a show each June near Talbot St Agnes but that she'd never managed to go much as she would have liked to. Skelton had never indicated that he had no intention of going until the morning of the day itself — a morning of slight haze that promised a fine hot day. Then Skelton said, "Count me out."

Hebe's face took on that look of distress and she said, "Oh, why? Darling, do you feel ill?"

"No. Do I have to be ill in order to avoid a noisy stinking crowd?"

Sir Charles had once — and only once — visited Springfield Lane, and now stung by the contempt in John's voice and even more by the lack of kindliness, said sharply, "Your nose has become sensitive all of a sudden! As a matter of fact, those who attend on the first day are largely patrons who subscribe three guineas a year, or people who can afford five shillings for a ticket. And even the people who come on Saturday are washed and dressed in their best."

Sir Charles was defending one aspect of the life which he had adopted with slight unwillingness and now thought the best possible; he was a convert to squirearchy, and spoke with fervour. He was a patron of the show and one of the judges in the three cattle classes. Last year, with his summer gout at its worst, he had none the less managed to hobble about and do his duty. By comparison, this year he was sprightly.

"Well, I prefer not to go," Skelton said with an air of dropping the subject. "It need not affect anyone else."

"It affects *me* very much. I shall be much engaged all day. I have to judge the cattle, have lunch with the other judges and take a Farmers' Tea with the prizewinners. I cannot possibly do that and escort Hebe at the same time."

"Oh, please," Daisy said, "don't worry about me. If John wishes not to go, I'll stay at home with him."

"But you said how much you were looking forward to it," Sir Charles protested.

"Hebe can walk around unescorted," Skelton said. A rational statement; she went shopping alone in London, a far more dangerous place than a Wichmore meadow frequented by the patrons and people who had paid a swingeing entrance fee.

"That is not the point!" Sir Charles was thoroughly ruffled. He'd taken tickets for them, for entry and for luncheon in the public marquee; he'd actually timed his invitation to include this event. He looked at his cousin angrily and then searchingly as though by staring he could learn the answer to the riddle of this puzzling behaviour. Under the scrutiny Skelton moved restively.

"What a coil about nothing! I have something to think over and I'd welcome the chance of an hour or two alone in order to do so. Is that so extraordinary? But of course, if Hebe can't walk, in broad daylight in such respectable company, alone, I'll come."

Daisy, on the verge of tears, said, "Of course not. I'll stay here, but I won't disturb you."

"You said you particularly wished to go."

"Yes. And so you shall," Sir Charles said, taking a sudden decision. He'd forego the luncheon with his fellow judges and the tea with the prize winners. He was bound to act as judge, but in the stand, with the crowd, a woman unaccompanied would not be conspicuous, all eyes would be on the animals. "Get your hat, my dear. It's time we made a start."

"Now I don't know what to do!" Daisy looked from one to another of them.

"You go," Skelton said. "And enjoy yourself."

"Come along, Hebe. I'll see that you do."

Planning for two passengers, Sir Charles had ordered the dog-cart, capable of seating four and with accommodation for dogs as well; as it was he could drive his gig, actually more to his liking.

"I think John is hatching," Daisy said, as they bowled along. "He is often moody when he is planning a picture."

Sir Charles wanted to say that John was a selfish swine, but the time for that was not yet.

"I suppose one must make allowances for the artistic temperament."

"That's just it! And I *do*. That's one reason why we get on so well together. I couldn't draw a picture to save my life. I can kind of sketch, scribble, you know, when words don't seem enough. But I do understand, so if he wants to talk, I listen and let him talk, just putting in a word here and there. But when he has a dumb spell, then I go dumb, too. I found that the best way. Like today. If I'd stayed there, he didn't want to talk so what was the use?"

"Exactly! We must see if we can manage without his company, just for one day."

He spoke lightly and, adjusting herself to his mood, Daisy said, "Can only try."

They both enjoyed themselves. Sir Charles was not obliged to sacrifice his judges' luncheon or his prize-winners' tea, for hardly had they entered the show-ground before Lady Fenstanton bore down upon them, greeting Daisy as Heaven-sent.

"Doctor McGibbon absolutely *forbade* my husband to make the slightest effort on such a hot day; said he would not be responsible. As though anyone had asked him to be! However . . . Poor man, he is feeling rather *morbid* about it. The mere sight of you, my dear, would cheer him immensely. So if Sir Charles can spare you . . ." She whisked Daisy away to the Castle itself, to a kind of terrace, part of an ancient battlement, shaded by a striped awning under whose shade Lord Fenstanton lay on a *chaise longue*. The view from that height was splendid and when his lordship had a wakeful spell he would recognise Hebe and realise that for her he need make no effort. Since Lady Fenstanton must, for the first time, do double duty and be here, there and everywhere, nothing could have been more fortuitous.

"I had the best view of all," Daisy said as they drove back to Wichfield. "And I was so glad your cow won. I clapped as hard as I could. You probably couldn't hear, but I did."

Sir Charles had entered a cow with her calf, in a class for which he was not acting as judge and had won a guinea and the coveted red rosette.

They talked of this and of their respective meals.

"Did you have a nice lunch? What was it?"

"It never varies. Cold roast beef, jam puffs and beer."

"Then I did better. Lobster salad, strawberries and cream, and champagne. Lord Fenstanton went to sleep

211

in the middle of it. He has gone downhill in six months."

"Yes. Towards the end of life, as at the beginning, six months can bring great change."

I am now half-way towards being sixty-six; the change in me has been for the better, but I am vulnerable and I have no time to waste. I have done nothing towards attaining what I want; but what can I do except wait for her to come to her senses?

"I do hope John hasn't felt lonely and got drunk." Daisy said.

CHAPTER
SIX

When Sir Charles found and read the note that awaited him, propped up against the looking-glass on his dressing-table, he turned pale under the ruddy tan to which this hot day had added. He thought of the old proverb about being careful of what one asked of the gods because one might get it and not like it. He did not like this at all! Certainly he'd wanted Hebe for himself, but he had hoped that his desire would be gratified in a natural way, a painless transference of her affection from John, so plainly unworthy of it, to himself. This was a different thing. This was an amputation. And it was typical of John Skelton to have performed it in so callous a manner. He read the note again.

"Dear Charles, I did not want a scene so I am taking this opportunity of slipping away. I know that Hebe will be safe with you and I know that you will understand why I must get away from a situation which daily becomes more intolerable. Hebe has every virtue, every grace, but routine and domesticity are smothering me, both as man and artist. I must away. I cannot say where because I do not know. It will not be London. I know you will break it to her gently and I wish you both happy. J."

Very slowly and rather jerkily, Sir Charles went about the business of washing and changing for dinner, a meal deliberately belated because a man being sociable with prizewinners, eating substantial sandwiches, sausage rolls and plum cake, drinking more beer, or very strong sweet tea, could not be expected to feel much appetite before nine o'clock. Now he would have no appetite at all! What on earth was he going to tell the poor child? How could such news be broken gently? Why should he be the one who must face a scene?

He was tempted to defer the bad moment; go to bed, saying he was tired; walk across to Ackroyd's place, say he'd come for a nightcap and linger over it until it was so late that Hebe must at least have suspected something. Either course would be cowardly and would mean leaving her alone to face her suspicions, then her certainty. Was she already aware of the empty silence in the adjoining room? Oh dear! For half a minute he wished he'd never set eyes on the girl. But that wish came from the surface of his troubled mind, not from his heart.

He disapproved of spirit-drinking before a meal, but he needed more support than a glass of sherry or madeira could give, so he hurried down, ahead of the gong, and poured a stiff brandy and drank it like medicine. It had little effect. Repeat the dose? Before he could do so the gong boomed. Then he noticed the table, laid for three and hastily ordered the third place cleared. Hebe was a little late and came in quickly, swept a glance around the room and said, "Oh! I rather hoped . . . I can't find John. I've looked everywhere, asked everybody. I thought the gong might . . ." Then she saw the table, set for two. "Did you know?" She looked slightly less agitated.

"I knew we should be alone for dinner. We are late."

"Of course. I didn't think of that. I was afraid . . . You know . . . What I said on the way back." She was conscious of the presence of the butler and the footman.

"Nothing like *that*," Sir Charles said, meaning that John was not lying dead drunk somewhere. "Everything is all right. I'll explain later. He's all right."

He thought sourly, Yes he's all right, damn him!

What had been a delectable meal, carefully planned, light and mainly cool — even the soup had been jellied, iced consommé — was eaten without appreciation, Daisy waiting for the moment when the servants withdrew and Sir Charles could speak freely, Sir Charles waiting, dreading the moment when he must deliver the blow.

"Now," she said, when at last they were alone, "tell me. Or shall I tell you? He's gone back to London. I've felt this brewing up. The country don't mean to him what it does to me. He only came to please me. I felt that at the time. I knew I was being selfish, yapping about wild roses and bull daisies. Poor John, bored to death and all my fault. You see, he even wouldn't tell me, thinking I'd cut my holiday short, which I would have, if only he'd told me. So he went slinking off and not a crumb in the house and Mrs Paske thinking we'd be away till Saturday. Really, he is silly sometimes. Still, I'll be there tomorrow."

Cut to the heart, the note in his pocket burning into his side, Sir Charles reached out and filled her glass with the port wine she loved, and Daisy, thinking, Might as well make the best of it, drank it down.

That should fortify her a bit, he thought. The brandy which had seemed so useless was now making itself felt with him. He thought, Amputations should be swift. And complete. Let her know the worst. Get it over.

"Hebe, my dear, John has not gone to London. He has simply gone away."

"Away? Where to? What do you mean, gone away?"

"Hebe, he has left you."

"I don't believe it. We was like this," she linked her fingers and held them out. "He never looked at another woman. I never looked at another man. We never had a cross word. I can't believe he's gone and left me. I just can't." But Sir Charles could see that she was believing it. Even her lips were turning white. He prepared to deal with another swoon. She put the clasped hands, symbol of unity, on the table and leaning forward rested her forehead on them.

"God! God, I can't bear it. He is my life. I can't live without him." She began to cry, not in the hysterical way that Sir Charles expected and feared, but deep racking sobs. He sat silent, still, waiting, watching her whole slender body shake and thinking that such violence of grief could not last long; it must bring exhaustion; but presently he could bear it no longer, and reaching out laid a hand on her heaving shoulder.

216

"Don't, my dear. You'll shake yourself to pieces . . . And it distresses me beyond words."

By accident he had hit on the right approach. He could see her gulping, fighting for control. When she raised her face it was bleached and stricken, the face of one who has received a lethal wound.

"I know. It ain't very nice for you, either. How could he do it to us? How could he?" Shock had caused such dilation of her pupils that her eyes were no longer blue, just deep, dark pits of misery.

Sir Charles wanted to rail against his cousin; to say he was not worth a single tear, a thoroughly heartless, selfish rogue. Instead he found himself saying the opposite.

"He showed some consideration in his timing, Hebe. He knew that you would be safe with me. I'll take good care of you. I'll make it my business to see that you are happy. It is a sorry blow *now*, but you are young . . ."

"Young. Happy. I shall never be that again. This has about done for me."

"Don't say that. Time does heal, you know. And you have all your life ahead of you." He knew that he sounded trite, but what else could he say?

Having fought for control, Daisy held on to it. She brooded for a moment and then asked in an ordinary voice, "Did he tell you he was going, or leave a note?"

"A note."

"And he didn't say where?"

"Simply that he was not going to London."

"Could I see it? I mean I might read something between the lines."

217

He had carried it downstairs with him in case she should refuse to believe him; then he would have shown it, despite the hurtful sentences. But she had believed him.

"I'm sorry. I was momentarily so upset that I tore it to pieces. My waste-paper basket will have been emptied by now. Actually there was nothing of a revealing nature, simply that he was leaving, not for London, and asking me to tell you."

"It could be Egypt," she said. "He met a man at Wade's; an . . . you know the word . . . digging up old things . . ."

"Archaeologist."

"Yes. He was wanting a painter to join his team. You know, that should have warned me. The fact that John thought about it, even for a moment. It wasn't his sort of work. But he . . . Well, neither was what he's been doing lately, not really. I mean, painting me over and over. I could see he was getting fidgety. But he could of painted somebody else; I wouldn't of minded. I said so once."

There was something indescribably touching about that. Such beauty and such humility. Every virtue, every grace. A nature as lovely as her physical being. And all tossed away like an outworn glove. Sir Charles thought: I'll make it up to her. I'll . . . I'll marry her!

It had not been his intention. He'd wanted her as his mistress, a pampered pet. He'd seen from the first how things were between her and John, imagining the one-sided affair flagging and failing and Hebe being transferred from one owner to another, as dogs were,

218

and horses. Now, curiously, he felt ashamed of regarding her so lightly; he wished to give her all he had to give and that included a title. He carried his easily, regarding an old baronetcy as superior to a new peerage, and considering that in a way he had paid for what he had inherited by the sacrifice of his personal ambition. To women, he knew, a title of any kind had great value — all the endeavours to lure him into marriage proved that. And it was within his power to bestow a title on this sweet girl, once the wound had healed. There'd be some talk, of course, but with Lady Fenstanton already so much on Hebe's side, the outcome was assured; where Lady Fenstanton led all would follow.

"I think, my dear, that you should go to bed now. A good night's sleep acts as a buffer. Everything will seem different tomorrow. I have some pills, prescribed for me by Doctor McGibbon when gout made me restless at night. They are effective and quite harmless. Best taken with a glass of warm milk. I'll tell Mrs Warren."

Mrs Warren and Mr Bridges had already decided that something odd was afoot. It was unusual for a guest simply to disappear as Mr Skelton had done. Sir Charles was a considerate employer and when he said there would be three for dinner, he meant three. Plainly he had not known that his cousin was leaving.

"He didn't seem quite like himself just before dinner," the butler said. "He'd been at the brandy, and he *looked* a bit upset. If I hadn't known different I'd have thought Wichfield Witch hadn't won. But she did.

And all through dinner there was what I call atmosphere. Holding back, you know."

"He'd have read his letter by then. In fact James saw him reading it when he took the hot water."

"And he was a bit sharp about having the extra place cleared. What mystifies me is how Mr Skelton *went*. I made a few discreet inquiries in the yard. He must have gone on foot. Apart from the gig not a vehicle, not a horse has stirred all day."

"And the nearest coach stop three miles away. Yet no row that we *know* of."

"If there was, it was at breakfast. Sir Charles *had* ordered the dog-cart and then changed to the gig. Yet he expected Mr Skelton for dinner. All highly peculiar. And there goes *your* bell."

The housekeeper's bell rang in the housekeeper's room, a light-toned soprano tinkle, not to be confused with the bass which summoned Mr Bridges, or the jangle which demanded unspecified service. Mr Bridges noted with satisfaction that Marion was still agile, light on her feet. She hastened away and was gone for quite a time. When she came back she sat down by the open window and took a sip of her cold toddy before speaking.

"And that was funny, too," she said. "Warm milk and gout pills for Miss Waywood."

"On a warm evening like this!"

"That was what he wanted. I heated the milk myself and there he was putting the pills down and saying they should help her to sleep. And she looked as though she'd been hit on the head with a hammer. Stunned like."

"Well, we shall see what we shall see."

"I think I can see all now, Mr Bridges. Second sight I cannot lay claim to — though my old granny had it and they say it misses a generation, but from the first, back to just after Christmas, that time she came here with her antics, I knew he'd gone soft. And she young enough to be his granddaughter!"

Pills designed to ease pain and bring sleep worked for a bit; but when Daisy woke she was crying and had obviously been crying in her sleep; her pillow was tear-soaked. She continued to cry after she was awake, washing away something of youth, of resilience, and the challenge that she had brought to life. In the pre-dawn chorus, the beginning of another day, she faced the truth. John Skelton had never loved her as she had loved him. He'd liked her, been sorry for her, found her useful as a model and enjoyed being her lover, but only briefly. He never was one to stick to one thing. He'd tired of her, both as mistress and as model and he'd simply walked away. Within his rights. She thought, Give him his due; he never promised me anything, never pretended, and he had, as Sir Charles said, timed his desertion with consideration; he had not left her alone to fend for herself; he'd left her here . . . And but for one thing it would have been a very neat arrangement. She had some idea of how Sir Charles felt towards her, kindly — probably a bit of lechery, in so old a man content with a pat, a kiss, a smile, perhaps now and then a fumbling attempt at intimacy — and since she herself now felt older than Eve, finished with love, and grateful for kindness, no doubt they'd get along very well, except for one thing . . .

Sir Charles was relieved to see that a night's rest had restored her composure, if not her colour, and was delighted when she asked if they should go riding that morning. He thought her a plucky little thing and was pleased to think that today of all days Barsham, usually so dull, offered some form of diversion.

"We'll go into Barsham and drink coffee in the Priory Garden."

Like any other concourse of people — even for a public hanging — the agricultural show attracted hangers on, people with wares or entertainment to offer; but Lord Fenstanton took the show seriously and would not allow anything not directly connected with agriculture to enter the Castle Meadow. Harness, farm tools, even baskets, bulbs and seeds were permitted, what his lordship called pedlars' trash and dancing dogs were barred. Of this situation the landlord of the Angel inn at Barsham was swift to take advantage. The inn had once been the monks' hostelry, and to the rear of it was a space of about three acres, useless for husbandry because of the ruins, some standing starkly above ground, more silted over. To this rather desolate area the landlord laid claim, paid sixpence a year in an ancient tax called a farm-fee, and hired it out for a variety of purposes. All the people who but for Lord Fenstanton's prejudice would have been in or near the

Castle Meadow, set up their booths on the Priory Rough. Then the landlord introduced another innovation; he realised that many people of the better class while being willing to be entertained, did not wish to mingle, so he trimmed up his somewhat neglected garden which overlooked the Rough and there served coffee and other liquid refreshments, sandwiches, cakes and ice-cream.

Daisy ate her ice-cream in such a slow, languid manner that it half-melted on the glass plate. From time to time people approached the low fence which divided the garden from the Rough. A woman offered gay ribbons and lace that she declared was handmade; Sir Charles looked inquiringly at Daisy who shook her head. "It's her livelihood," he said, and bought lavishly, little fairings for his female staff. An Italian, with a monkey dressed as a sailor, sang *Rule Britannia*, and received sixpence. Another man brought a performing dog. "Send him away," Daisy said. "I don't like animals doing tricks." In fact the dog had only one trick which was to stand on his hindlegs and bring his right front paw up into a gesture of salute and personally Sir Charles saw little difference between that and a dog being trained to retrieve a pheasant, or to walk at heel. However, he made a gesture of dismissal. Poor Hebe, he thought, she *is* in low spirits. "How about a glass of wine?"

"Not now, thank you. Perhaps after . . . There's something I must tell you." She looked straight at him and he saw that though her eyes were blue again, the sparkle had left them.

223

"Tell me," he said, gently.

"John seemed to think — and you spoke — as though I was going to stay with you."

"I'm sure that was his intention. It is certainly my fervent hope."

"I'm going to have a baby."

"Oh!" He looked and sounded dismayed. "Did John know?"

"No. As soon as I was sure I meant to tell him, but it was like the money, I never could bring myself . . . He didn't like children. He never would paint one."

She was so sure that a child would be unwelcome that she'd tried to get rid of it. She swore Mrs Paske to secrecy and asked her advice. Mrs Paske said, "You tell him, love. Men feel different when it's their own. And now he ought to marry you. I've said so all along." Then finding this line of thought unproductive she offered advice of a more practical kind — but nothing dangerous. About that she was most insistent; she was very fond of Daisy and had her own standards. Too many so-called midwives dabbled in other things. They got the profession a bad name. A pint of hot ale with a whole nutmeg grated into it; as much gin as could be taken at a sitting, a single dose of pennyroyal. What these would not shift God obviously intended not to be shifted, and to go further was to invite disaster. "You get up to any tricks unbeknownst to me, miss, and I shall tell him and call him a murderer, which would be true." Nothing had availed and seeing Daisy off to Wichfield, Mrs Paske had offered a final, very sensible piece of advice. "You tell him while you're there. Sir

Charles is a gentleman. He'll stand up for you and you'll come back married."

Now Sir Charles knew. His colour had gone patchy and he looked distressed. He turned in his chair and beckoned a waiter, ordered port wine for her, brandy for himself. His mind was racing. One thing he must know.

"When?"

"Mrs Paske thought late December."

Six months! Too little time to carry out the first plan that shot through his mind — marrying her immediately and passing the child off as his; born somewhat prematurely. Even that would have been rather difficult; once a man was sixty people were all too ready to question a child's paternity, there were endless jokes about it, but given eight, or even seven months he might have risked it.

"You told Mrs Paske? Who else?"

"Not a soul. And she swore. I trust her. Not that it matters now."

"Of course it matters." He spoke rather harshly, for through his muddled feelings one, quite unexpected, had struggled to the surface — a distaste for pregnancy and everything concerned with it. It was a feeling grafted on by his experience; two happy marriages ended by childbirth. He had not realised until now how deeply his revulsion cut, how sedulously he had avoided pregnant women. A tenant would say, gladly or morosely, "We look to hev a young 'un in the spring," or whatever season. Sir Charles would not go near that house. Once the child was born, Sir Charles had been ready with his congratulations, his guinea christening gift, his willingness to stand as godfather.

Now here he was, facing Hebe, three months pregnant and looking as virginal as a snowdrop.

She sensed his withdrawal. She said, "Don't you bother. I'll go back to London, get a job of some sort." She sat up straighter in the little white-painted wicker chair and placed one of her slender hands on each side of her still slender waist. "It won't show for months yet. When it does, well, maybe I can get a job as fat woman in a pantomime."

"That is silly talk. No. No. We'll think of something better than that." He thought, Apart from all else, this child will be a Skelton. Skeltons and Overtons had not always seen eye to eye; but Sir Charles had loved his mother, a Miss Skelton, and badly as John had behaved, he felt an obligation, almost a family responsibility. Nevertheless he felt all the aggrievedness of a man who had behaved impeccably and been landed with a problem not of his own making, and one which he could not well discuss with anyone.

"I think we should go now," he said. In the stableyard, helping Daisy to mount, he remembered something and once they were on the road, said, "I believe riding is considered unwise for ladies in . . . in your condition." Embarrassment made him sound stiff and pompous; Daisy stole a glance at him and thought he looked grumpy.

"It wasn't a condition I wanted to get into," she said. "Far from it. But as my stepmother used to say: Children don't wait to be invited. I knew John would be angry, but I don't see why you should be. Like I said, I'll go away. You can forget all about it.'

"That would be quite impossible. And I am not angry. I am trying to work out what best to do." However, the fond glance was missing and he did not say *Hebe*, or *my dear*, as was his habit, and after a minute her crushed spirit managed a momentary recovery and she made, all unwittingly, a statement which had a great effect on Sir Charles.

"What I *don't* want is you treating me as though I was a pickpocket. All I done was fall in love. Granted, I didn't stick out for a wedding ring — I'd never hev got it and I knew that. So now I'm left to face the music and I'd sooner do it my own way than be . . . well, treated as though I'd done wrong and been half-forgiven."

Courage was a quality that he had always admired. That in her situation, abandoned, penniless, pregnant, she could muster enough of it to sound defiant, tipped his mood, made him forget that pregnancy was a most undesirable condition.

"Nobody is going to treat you like that! Trust me. Everything will work out all right, if we are very careful. Very careful, my dear." The old kindliness was back in his voice, the old fond look in his eyes.

What did not return so quickly was his determination to marry her, and sometimes he reflected that that idea had been a mere flash in the pan, the result of emotion; it might recur, it might not; in any case there was no need to think about it yet. What demanded immediate attention was some sort of plan covering the next six months. Whether, at the end of that period, Hebe became his mistress or his wife the fact that she was to be a mother, must, he thought, be concealed. He realised that he could all too easily be made to look like a fool, a silly old man, taking over, or even marrying, his cousin's pregnant, discarded mistress. Secrecy was essential.

One person already shared the secret — Mrs Paske. He tried to recall what he had noticed about her during his visit to Well House Close; it was very little. He remembered vaguely a stoutish, middle-aged woman with what he called a superior working-class manner.

He toyed with the idea of sending Hebe back to Well House Close with Mrs Paske to take charge, but a tentative inquiry, made through his London lawyer, revealed that though John Skelton had abandoned the place in much the same hasty way as he had abandoned Hebe, he had written — from Dover — and cancelled his tenancy. The Studio was already re-let.

By the time he received this information Sir Charles's mood had swung again and he had decided that he did not wish to lose Hebe's company for longer than necessary. She was still entrancing to look at and good company. She'd lost something, a kind of bouncing ebullience, but to Sir Charles that was no loss, it made her more suitable for him. And the pregnancy was so far from being evident that occasionally he wondered if she could not be mistaken. None of the things which he hated as presages of disaster seemed to afflict her; no morning sickness, no whims and fancies about food, no darker pigmentation around the eyes, no swollen ankles, and no bulges. It was as though it were not happening, but all the time he knew that it was and that something must be done about it; and the more he thought, the more his thoughts centred about Mrs Paske, the only other person to whom the secret was no secret.

"I don't think she would come," Daisy said, when he first mentioned his tentative plan. "She is so greatly attached to her brother who has a pretty useless wife. Martha thinks she keeps his family going — and she is right."

"Suppose you wrote and invited her — just for a holiday and we'd see how things worked out."

Daisy's letter reached Mrs Paske a few days after she had received a bit of a shock. She had promised to keep an eye on the Studio — she had her own key. She looked in twice during the first week and on the Friday of the second went round early to get the place really spick and span for Daisy's return. She was polishing the studio floor when she heard the kitchen door open and close. They had come back a day early! She went to greet them gladly, for she had missed Daisy. She admired Mr Skelton far less than she had done, but her affection for Daisy had increased. In the kitchen were two strange men, depositing bundles on the freshly scrubbed table, and outside the door was a cab, laden with luggage. Since the houses in the Close were so much divided and sub-divided, Mrs Paske's first thought was that the strangers had come to the wrong address. They were both respectable looking and did

229

not act like intruders; slightly surprised to see her but no more.

"This the Studio. Mr Skelton's house."

"It *was*," the elder of the two said pleasantly. "It is ours now. This is Mr Pryce. My name is Forbes. Did you work for Mr Skelton?"

He had intended to suggest that she should work for them, but hesitated, thinking that she looked simple-minded.

"Then where's Mr Skelton? Where's Miss Hebe?"

"I understood from the agent that Mr Skelton had gone abroad. I know nothing of the lady."

"I don't understand it. I just don't understand. They were coming back tomorrow and here I was getting the place ready."

The cabman staggered in, a heavy bag in either hand. "Upstairs, please," Mr Forbes said.

"But you can't. All their clothes are there. They only went away for a fortnight. There must be some mistake. This is the Studio, Well House Close."

"We know that. It belongs to Mr Foley who let it to Mr Skelton, who relinquished his tenancy and handed in the key."

"When?"

"My good woman, how should I know? The house agent knew that it was exactly what we were looking for. We came on Tuesday and had a look. Now we are moving in."

"I just can't believe it." Mrs Paske was slowly realising that the bottom had fallen out of her world. Ever since that hot day in the previous summer her attention, her interest, her affection had centred about this place. She'd cut down on other activities, accepting only a few jobs that promised to be brief and which were within easy reach. She'd disappointed Doctor Burgess so often that he had ceased to call upon her.

Mr Forbes's pleasant manner changed; he grew impatient, and his tone sharpened.

"Whether you believe it or not, it is so."

"This on top of everything else," Mrs Paske said with seeming inconsequence.

Everything else meant the monstrous ingratitude shown by Effie and Jim's even more unforgivable disloyalty. She'd shared their mews flat for many years, contributed towards expenses, kept the place going, planned ahead before going to a job, come home to wash and mend and clear up. Then Effie's own sister, newly widowed and homeless, had wanted to move in. Effie, of course, wanted Flora, and Jim, *Jim*, had sided with her, pointing out to Martha that *she* could always get a job with bed and board thrown in. Mrs Paske had intended, as soon as Miss Hebe returned, to ask whether she could live in here. Now this! Not that it was so serious, for what Jim said was true. She could always get a job, dancing attendance to some old ailing person — just the kind of job she had avoided because she must look after Jim. Ungrateful hound!

"Can you cook?" That was Mr Pryce, trying to take defensive action. He and Brian Forbes had shared rooms and studios for some years, and in the intervals when hired help was not available housework and cooking fell to him.

"I'm not a cook. I was just making the place nice for Miss Hebe. And now . . ."

Miss Hebe was gone. She might never see her again. Had she been a crying woman, Mrs Paske would have cried then. As it was her face merely twisted and her eyes blinked as she unfastened her apron, put her key on the table and walked out.

"I was going to suggest . . ." Mr Pryce said.

"My dear, I know. So was I until I realised that the woman was dim-witted."

"The place is very clean," Mr Pryce said, rather wistfully.

Mrs Paske's notions of abroad were extremely vague; foreign parts. That might mean anywhere. And none of it to be trusted. And Miss Hebe going to have a baby. Who'd look after her? There could be little hope that the poor girl would have stayed in England; where Mr Skelton went she would go, even on her hands and knees; she was as daft about him as ever, despite his peculiar behaviour. Mrs Paske did not hold it against him that he hadn't married Hebe, she still thought there might be some explanation of that; it was more his general behaviour and the fact that Miss Hebe didn't dare tell him about the baby.

For three days Mrs Paske was so preoccupied by the thought of that sweet girl going through her ordeal tended only by some black creatures with rings through their noses that she hadn't the heart to begin to look for a job though Flora was definitely coming.

232

Then the letter arrived and all the bells of Heaven rang. She read it again, just to make sure that it was not a dream, and then said cuttingly, "There'll be no question of who will sleep on the parlour floor. Sir Charles Overton has invited me to his place in the country. For a holiday." Like many other seemingly unlikely statements, it was strictly true.

Daisy had written, "Come as sune as you can I cant wate to see you," and a glance at the fob watch which she wore on her bodice informed Mrs Paske that she could pack, walk to the coaching inn just along the Strand and be in Surrey by lunch-time.

Her arrival, her appearance, everything about her added to the mystification in the servants' hall and in the housekeeper's room. James, the footman who was sedulously copying Mr Bridges's voice and manner, was the first to see her.

He reported. "She came to the *front* door and when I opened it she said, 'Miss Waywood is expecting me.' I'd had no information so I showed her into the ante-room and fetched Miss Waywood who was in the garden. Oh, I'd asked her name of course. It's Paske, Mrs Paske. Miss Waywood seemed surprised but very pleased and when they met they were both near crying. Mrs Paske said, 'My dear, you don't know what agonies I've been through!' and Miss Waywood said, 'Oh Martha, how good of you to come at once.' I just heard that and was half across the hall when Miss Waywood called and said there'd be two for lunch and Mrs Paske would have the room next to hers in the Park Suite."

"Sir Charles made no mention of a guest when he told me he would be out for lunch," Mrs Warren said. "But he has been a bit absent-minded lately." It suited Mrs Warren to pretend that Sir Charles was growing senile. He'd ceased to be interested in her as bed partner, and there the failing was in him, not her; and although it might look as though she had been supplanted by the girl, all the evidence was against it. Miss Waywood was alone — very much alone, since Mr Skelton's departure — in the remote Park Suite and Sir Charles held to his own room at the other end of the house. Nobody, not even Mrs Warren, lynx-eared and in a room nearby, had ever heard a sound in the night, no comings, no goings; and there were none of the other signs of which Mrs Warren had once been so acutely aware. That Sir Charles was fond of the pretty girl was obvious, but fond in the rather silly way of old men with pretty daughters.

CHAPTER
SEVEN

Mrs Paske settled in well. She regarded herself as a professional woman; she had actually taken a brief course in the art of midwifery; she had been the confidante and assistant to Doctor Burgess and others; she had done some nursing unconnected with her special line. And always she had been a person slightly apart; not a servant, not quite one of the family, even when she took meals with them. For Jim, whom she loved, she had been willing to cook, clean and mend; for Daisy, whom she loved, she had been willing to cook and scour, but here, at Wichfield by invitation, she moved into a special place, one that seemed almost predesigned for her. Towards Daisy she was friendly, but never — after that one cry of greeting — familiar; towards Sir Charles she was respectful but not servile, and she had the right attitude towards such servants as came into contact with her, amiable, impersonal, a trifle distant. In no time she had made herself completely at home.

Sir Charles found it a comfort to have someone who knew, and with whom he could discuss the future, or at least as much of it as the pregnancy would cover; beyond that he had no very clear view himself.

Sometimes he thought that if all went well, by which he meant that the birth was kept secret, he might marry Hebe; sometimes he thought better of it and reverted to his intention of making her his mistress — that was if by the time the whole bothersome thing was over, he needed a mistress; there were even times, rare but not to be ignored, when he wished he had never set eyes on the girl and felt himself to be a kind of victim, unwillingly involved in a muddle not of his own making. At such moments it was a great comfort to have Mrs Paske to whom he could talk very freely about his feelings for his cousin; feelings which Mrs Paske shared, even outmatched. Very cursory questioning had revealed to her that there had been no impediment to Mr Skelton doing the right thing by Hebe and she was very bitter about it.

"When she was so ill last summer, I was impressed by the way he acted and the concern he showed. I was deceived. I see now that all he thought about was painting her; he was afraid of losing a good model — and cheap. And she so much in love with him." Mrs Paske was on the very brink of saying, "Still is," when her common sense halted her. No point in making Sir Charles jealous.

"He is a thoroughly selfish fellow. Always has been. His break with family tradition was a great blow to his parents. I was stupid enough to admire what I thought was independence of spirit . . . For his treatment of that sweet girl there is no excuse." Often Sir Charles's anger with his cousin heightened his feeling towards Hebe.

236

"One thing is certain, even had he married her she would have been very miserable."

"Yes, I realise now that he was not a man to make any woman happy; leave alone such a tender-hearted young lady, with such a capacity for affection."

"All we can do, Mrs Paske, is to do *our* utmost to make her happy. And to smooth her path . . ."

That kind of remark was always the cue for discussion of the future, talk about how the time just before the birth, the birth and the time immediately after could best be arranged.

Mrs Paske was worldly-wise enough to understand Sir Charles's desire for secrecy; he was a gentleman with a reputation to maintain. And if Mrs Paske's secret hope was ever to materialise it was necessary that Hebe's reputation should appear to be unblemished. Mrs Paske had quickly seen that the best thing in the world would be for Hebe — now as dear to her as a daughter — to become Lady Overton. She resolutely refused to admit that Daisy was pining for her lost lover; low spirits, lack of appetite, even that sad look in the eyes could all be attributed to her condition.

Between them Sir Charles and Mrs Paske hatched out what seemed to be a satisfactory scheme. As soon as the pregnancy began to show, she and Hebe, posing as mother and daughter, both widowed, would go to some quiet comfortable lodging in Margate. In a town accustomed to visitors, even in winter, since the air there was supposedly so health-restoring, they would attract little attention. They would use assumed names. When the child was born, Mrs Paske, reverting to her own name and role, would take the baby to a reliable woman who earned her living by acting as foster mother.

"And when do you think it will be necessary to . . . start the holiday?" Sir Charles asked, meaning when would it show?

"Possibly not before October. She is so young and strong muscled, and I insist on a good walk each day. Lolling about on sofas is responsible for a lot of flabbiness — and some troubles afterwards."

"It is so comforting to think that she is in such good hands," Sir Charles said, making up his mind that as soon as there was the slightest nip in the air he would present Mrs Paske with a fur muff and tippet.

But despite the favourable way in which things were shaping, that autumn saw the return of his gout. Perhaps his half-mystical notion that Hebe's sheer vitality had healed him had had some validity, for now her vitality was low — or diverted. Perhaps his more realistic idea that worry over Plenrerith had given him gout was also valid; worry about Hebe had taken its place. She was young, she was healthy, she would bear a Skelton, not an Overton baby, she would have the best of care; but his induced horror of childbirth would not be assuaged by such sustaining thoughts and by mid-September the gout had struck.

He turned, naturally, but tactlessly, to Mrs Paske, who was a nurse. Mrs Warren, who had accepted Mrs Paske's presence as a sop to convention — a young, pretty girl needed a chaperone of some kind — was much offended, especially when some of the intruder's methods and theories did not coincide with her own.

"I'm not given to language, as you know, Mr Bridges, but that woman is an *interfering bitch*. I always carried out Doctor McGibbon's instructions and she had the sauce to say they were old-fashioned! I don't know about *you*, but sometimes I've had enough of new brooms."

"I'm not subject to interference," Mr Bridges said. "What I find irksome is waiting on people of that class. With the girl — and just for a holiday — it was perhaps understandable. I mean Sir Charles's friends understood. Gentlemen are allowed their little fancies. But to bring in the old woman and treat them both as family, even to having them at table *with other guests*, that I find mortifying. And I think I know where it is leading."

"Marriage?" Mrs Warren voiced a suspicion that had been troubling her ever since she decided that Daisy was not Sir Charles's mistress.

The pair exchanged a long, meaningful look. Their plan for the future had tacitly assumed the death of an elderly, failing man, likely to remember them handsomely in his will, since he had no wife and no children. Last year, with Sir Charles house-bound and not very cheerful, the goal seemed almost in sight. Now things had changed and if he did intend to marry . . .

"I sometimes think," Mr Bridges said slowly, "that if one intends to strike out it should be done before one is *too* decrepit."

"I entirely agree. And this is the time of year when property is most easily come by."

"There need be no ill feeling. I came here as second footman twenty-three years ago. Your service, Mrs Warren, though less long, has been devoted. I think that if we explain to Sir Charles, he might think of a parting present of a, hmmm . . . a substantial nature."

Ordinarily he would have done so, but now, worried about Daisy and greatly distressed by the return of his old affliction, Sir Charles took entirely the wrong attitude, looked upon their giving in of notice as a form of desertion and said, "Go tomorrow if you want to," in a manner which Mr Bridges called peevish and Mrs Warren thought distinctly ungrateful. Bad feeling was engendered.

It was easy enough to replace Mr Bridges; James had been understudying for that part. A good housekeeper was more difficult to find just at this time of the year, but Mrs Paske said, "Don't worry, Sir Charles, and don't try to make a replacement in a hurry. If I can't run this house just as well and more thriftily, my name's not Martha Paske."

"But you have only a limited time."

"A good month, at least." She was keeping her eyes open, Daisy's waistline a matter of constant concern, and so far marvellously satisfactory. She was reminded of a story which, had it not happened under her very nose, she might have regarded as impossible. In a house where she was nursing an old man who had slipped and broken his thigh, a sixteen-year-old maid had gestated, given birth and never missed a duty. Nobody knew, nobody would have known, had she not attempted to smuggle the baby out in a basket which the cook suspected of containing stuff stolen from the storeroom and insisted upon searching. That story had had a happy ending; everybody had been so astounded by the girl's fortitude that she was allowed to stay, with her baby.

Mrs Paske had thought at the time that everybody must have been very blind — not to the girl's figure but to the lack of something in the laundry. She had guarded against such a lack rousing suspicion at Wichfield; she was forty-two and the change had not come to her yet; so a substitution was easy.

So far as the two laundrymaids at Wichfield were concerned, Miss Waywood was regular as the clock and Mrs Paske was over the hump.

All Soul's; All Saints'; St Hubert's Day. Sir Charles, a stickler for observing ancient customs, was this year, as last, able only to hobble out on to a nearby balcony and look down on the members of the local hunt enjoying his cherry brandy. Thanks to Mrs Paske's ingenuity he was able to put up a good show, raising a glass of harmless raspberry syrup, but he felt very low. Hebe was at last beginning to thicken and the departure to Margate could not be long deferred. His left foot was swollen and very painful, his right suspiciously puffy. No adequate replacement for Mrs Warren had yet been found, and soon he would be alone, worrying about Hebe at Margate. Waiting for news . . .

Then something happened to distract his thoughts from himself. From his sitting position on the balcony he had only a limited view, but Hebe, her figure concealed by the sable cloak, on one side of him, and

Mrs Paske wrapped and muffed on the other, emitted little cries and there were calls, shouts from below, only one sound really distinguishable, somebody called, "McGibbon! McGibbon!"

"What is happening?" Sir Charles asked, craning forward as far as his posture allowed.

"A slight accident," Mrs Paske said.

"There's a horse down. Kicking. Oh, I never could bear to see . . ." Daisy put her hands to her face.

"Now don't be silly," Mrs Paske said. "Look, it's all right. It's up. But the rider . . . Hebe, my dear, help Sir Charles back. I think I may be needed."

Needed in three places. In the room to which the young man who had been riding a nervous, untried horse lay suffering what Doctor McGibbon said was a mild concussion; in Sir Charles's room where the commotion had caused the right foot to inflame so that it was almost as bad as the left. And in Hebe's room, where a premature — yes, surely premature — labour was in progress.

Mrs Paske was equal to what she must face; she could delegate authority. James to look after Sir Charles, Richard, lately second, now first footman, to look after the stranger and his mother who arrived in a hysterical state saying that she had warned Frank a dozen times and had a prophetic dream only last night . . .

In the midst of the hubbub, Mrs Paske remained calm, concentrating upon the one thing that mattered — her darling's safe delivery. A premature labour was always a tricky business; when it was also the first it was

242

doubly tricky and this one had another disadvantage. Mrs Paske was accustomed to say, "Scream out. It helps." Though the Park Suite was fairly isolated, and the whole house in an uproar, she dared hardly say that now. And to add to the difficulties was the fact that Hebe was so unwilling.

Mrs Paske had intended, once they were in Margate, to talk to Hebe and explain that childbirth was a natural process, very painful, soon over; that one must give way, go along with it, not fight against it. Now there was no time, the poor child was unprepared, quite unresigned. Attitude mattered in these things, the experienced midwife knew, and mothers could be roughly divided into two classes; those who looked forward to a first child, or after a daughter, to a son, after a son to a daughter, or to a living child to replace a dead one; willing votaries; and those who approached the business in a matter-of-fact way — here we go again! Every case she had dealt with had been an open confinement after an openly recognised pregnancy, welcome or unwelcome. Poor Hebe had all these months been pretending and the reality was like a smack in the face.

"My dear, my darling, you must help yourself," Mrs Paske said. "No, don't crush my hands, I need them. Pull on this," she pushed into Daisy's hands the end of a towel she had fixed to the foot of the beautiful bed. "Pull and then let go inside yourself."

Eight o'clock, and nine and ten. At Wichfield there was no escaping the steady tread of the hours. One might avoid the watch, the clock, but the clock over the stables chimed each relentless hour. Boom, boom. Eleven now, and the labour twelve hours old, with Hebe, poor darling, weakening, and Mrs Paske beginning to despair and reduced to trying one of the oldest, least credited of tricks.

She had told everybody that Miss Waywood had been upset by the accident and would lunch and dine in her own room; trays had been carried up; Hebe had eaten one mouthful, Mrs Paske had eaten two or three and had prudently scattered some of the food on to the windowsill where some birds had happily disposed of it; but outside, on the landing, on a dumb waiter, some things which need not be carried up and down for each meal stood ready. Shortly after eleven o'clock, Mrs Paske in desperation reached out and took up a pepperpot. Two minutes later Daisy gave a violent sneeze and that did the trick; the little girl, small but certainly not premature, shot out into the world, into Mrs Paske's receptive hands.

Among all her preoccupations, Mrs Paske had managed to have ready some wine in one of those jugs made with a little hollow at its base in which a stub of candle would burn, keeping the contents warm for a few hours. She poured a cup, said, "Drink this, my dear. Then try to sleep." She had already carried the baby into her own room. Babies, she knew, were quiescent for a few hours, as though they, like their mothers, were exhausted by the birth-struggle. Then they recovered and were hungry. She had only a short time.

244

She went back and bundled together everything that might rouse suspicion. She was a neat, expert worker and there was the minimum of what she called mess. The soiled things could be burnt in the fire hole under the copper in the wash-house. Bundle in one hand, candlestick in the other, she was ready to go when Hebe said, in a weak, drowsy voice, "May I see her?"

"Better not." Mrs Paske knew all about maternal instinct. Many women, ranging from the unfortunate girls who resorted to the Refuge for Fallen Women where she had done part of her training, to the respectable who, pregnant again at a time when they thought their family was completed, were often resentful; but . . . In nine cases out of ten, something happened once the child was born. Even the unmarried mothers would often go to extraordinary lengths to keep the baby which could be nothing but a burden; in families the latecomer was generally the Benjamin. The sight of the infant brought a change, and feeding it generally clinched it. Since Hebe was doomed to separation from her child, better that she should not see it. "You go to sleep and forget all about it."

To reach the wash-house Mrs Paske was bound to go through the kitchen. It was a shock to find somebody there. The mother of the young man whose horse had thrown him was busy at the stove, frying eggs and bacon.

"Frank came round and said he wanted his breakfast. I didn't like to disturb anybody at this time of night." The boom of the stable clock, twelve, underlined her understandable reluctance. "Did I wake

245

you?" Tenderly she basted an egg. "If so, I'm sorry." She was not at all sorry. Seeing Frank wake from what looked like death, hearing him speak, had emboldened her to face far worse things than disturbing a strange household and find her way about a strange kitchen and larder where every article seemed to be in the wrong place.

"I merely wondered," Mrs Paske said. "I am glad your son has recovered." She backed away, holding her bundle unobtrusively. That could be disposed of at any time. The baby was a different matter.

She was absolutely opposed to any drugging of babies. Some people believed that a little gin was harmless and induced sleep so that others could sleep; they were ignorant people and only slightly less ignorant were those who bought soothing syrups which contained opium, heavily disguised. Yet here she was concocting a soothing syrup of her own, warm heavily sweetened milk and a few drops of Sir Charles's painkilling medicine. She was ready with it when the baby gave its first hunger wail.

Most babies were not very pretty — except to their mothers — for a day or two, but there were exceptions and this was one. Not at all reddish and crumpled and bald, more resembling somebody at the end of life than somebody at the beginning. This baby had hair, a darkish fluff which would rub off, of course, and grow again almost any colour; it also had the slate-blue, unfocused eyes of the newborn, but larger and better shaped than most. This scrap already held the promise of being as beautiful as her mother, to whom beauty had so far brought little good. But Mrs Paske hoped for better things in the future.

She went along to Sir Charles's room very early and roused him from his drugged sleep. He had not been told what was actually happening to Hebe and it took him a few seconds to realise what Mrs Paske meant when she said, "It is all over, Sir Charles. Hebe and the child are both well. I shall take it to London as soon as it is light. My excuse will be that I am going to consult a doctor who knows a great deal about gout and to bring you other medicine."

"Oh. Oh, yes, of course. Boy or girl?"

"Girl."

"And Hebe is all right?"

"Right as a trivet. How do *you* feel this morning?"

"I have hardly had time . . . Better, yes, decidedly better."

"She must stay in bed, of course."

"I shall go along and see her presently."

"That would be nice. I shall be back as soon as I can."

She was gone before he was sufficiently awake to ask how she intended to get the baby out of the house. Worrying about that increased his gout pangs.

CHAPTER
EIGHT

"Set me down at the next corner," Mrs Paske directed. "Drive on to the White Hart and wait for me there. I should not be more than an hour."

She alighted; a well-dressed, eminently respectable woman, shielded against the chill of a November morning by a sealskin tippet and a huge muff. The corner site was occupied by an apothecary's shop which boasted two entrances, one on Piccadilly the other on Hay Lane. Mrs Paske passed through. At the end of a slight slope Hay Lane branched, to the left another street devoted to small and rather exclusive shops, to the right to one of those still almost rural vicinities, a cluster of small houses centred about the church dedicated to St Luke and called St Luke's Street.

At Number 8 St Luke's Street lived a respectable widow, Mrs Shillitoe, with whom, given time, Mrs Paske would have made contact in order to ascertain whether she had room for another baby. Should this not be the case, Mrs Paske knew other women engaged in the same trade, but Mrs Shillitoe was her first choice. As she plied the knocker she hoped very much that there would be a vacancy.

248

Mrs Shillitoe opened the door and for a second did not recognise her old acquaintance. Months of luxurious living had plumped out Mrs Paske's face and the furs gave her an opulent look.

"Why, it's Mrs Paske! I have not seen you for a long time. Come in."

"I have been out of London for some time," Mrs Paske explained as she stepped into a cosy room where, on a rug before the fire — well-guarded — two young children were engaged in some game. A much older child was carefully dusting the sideboard. She was Mrs Shillitoe's own daughter, mentally and physically retarded; at the age of fifteen she was no taller than an eight-year-old and had the understanding of a child two years younger.

"Sit down," Mrs Shillitoe said, edging a chair forward an inch. "It's a raw morning." But you are well dressed to face it, Mrs Shillitoe added to herself. Mrs Paske had always been as well-dressed as her budget would allow, but never befurred like this.

"Hattie," Mrs Shillitoe said, speaking with great distinctness, "take Peter and Margery into the kitchen. And then see if you can make a pot of tea. Don't bring the tray, just call me when it is ready."

With people like poor Hattie one could not be too careful, sometimes they understood more than they appeared to, sometimes less; and they could not be trusted not to talk.

"It's this," Mrs Paske said, and from inside her capacious muff she produced Hebe's child, wrapped in a small shawl.

Providing a layette for the baby had been rather a problem to two women who were, if anything, over-careful. Hebe had never stitched or knitted a single tiny garment, and Mrs Paske only a few, doing about the amount of work that any woman of her age might be expected to do for grandchildren, nephews or nieces. The real work was planned to begin at Margate. Still, there had been enough to equip the child for a short time. And all of the best quality.

"Asleep?"

"Very mildly drugged." Explanations were not necessary, but, as on two former occasions when Mrs Paske had made use of Mrs Shillitoe, she offered a watertight story which like all the best fabrications was a near version of the truth.

"A young lady of position," she said, "due to be married at Christmas to a most respectable and eligible man who would of course have repudiated her. She and I have spent the last few months in seclusion. And I undertook . . ."

"I see. I'll have a look, if you have no objection."

"None. She's a fine, healthy child."

Mrs Shillitoe never accepted a baby defective in any way. People called the service she rendered baby farming and regarded it with well-justified suspicion. Farmed-out babies died all too readily. She had never lost one yet. Two of her charges were now in their own homes; a girl had been formally adopted by her mother when her marriage proved sterile; a boy had been claimed by his father as soon as his wife was dead. Others went, at the age of six, to rather expensive schools. Mrs Shillitoe never kept more than three children at a time — that was why her charge was so high — and she never kept one after the age of six; they ceased to be babies, needed exercise, and lessons and God knew what.

She examined this child of a one-sided love, found no fault, even a word of praise.

"Well developed. And bonny, too. Born when?"

"Last night."

"You're early." Mrs Shillitoe seldom asked a direct question, but she liked to know as much as possible."

"Born within easy walking distance," Mrs Paske said, now laying a false trail.

Hattie called. Mrs Shillitoe handed back the baby and went into the kitchen for the tray. In her mind she was already arranging for a wet-nurse; like Mrs Paske she knew exactly where to find what she wanted. Poor women were extremely prolific and usually good milkers. She never employed a known drunkard or a consumptive.

"I suppose Simon went to school," Mrs Paske said conversationally as she sipped her tea.

"Yes; he went to Manchester in September. This child has a name?"

"She is to be called Margaret. Margaret Walpole. Mother, Elizabeth, father, John. India merchant."

By this Mrs Shillitoe understood that the child was to be christened, as others had been, at St Luke's. People were very peculiar. Most of them were prepared to hand a child over, never see it, but they wanted everything done in order and they were prepared to pay

— that is the people with whom she did business; there were others, of course. *Pay!*

"I have been obliged to raise my charge, Mrs Paske. Costs rise all the time. Twenty-five shillings a week, paid in advance. And clothing provided."

Clothing was a source of revenue; children grew so quickly that their clothes were outgrown before they were outworn. Very few new garments were ever needed at 8 St Luke's Street. Mrs Shillitoe was not a shark, but she had the future to think of — especially Hattie's future, which worried her a great deal.

Mrs Paske's muff was the kind which precluded the necessity of carrying a reticule; it had a purse inside the lining; she unsnapped it and counted out the shining coins that would buy two months' expert care.

"I shall probably look in from time to time myself," she said. "Whether I can or not, the money will be paid."

"I know. And I assure you, every care will be taken."

Looking down at the apparently sleeping child, Mrs Paske felt a touch of sentiment, transferred from Hebe to her offspring.

"I hope that Margaret may in due time be adopted, as little Adelaide was."

Out into the street again. Into the apothecary's, this time to buy. Except for colichine — another name for saffron — there was no known specific, but instant cures for gout were widely advertised and sold. She bought all on offer and, carrying the package prominently, walked along to the White Hart and was

252

driven back to Wichfield. And there the medicine was not needed. Sir Charles had hobbled along to Hebe's room and found her all right; rather languid and pale, as was only to be expected, but safely delivered and back on the road to health. A flood of relief washed away the pain; exuberance took over and his determination to marry her revived.

CHAPTER
NINE

Daisy could not, of course, be allowed the time in bed which followed childbirth with all but working-class women. Two days recovering from the shock which had put her to bed; then downstairs for lunch; a little rest; another appearance at dinner; a walk in the garden on a suddenly mild day. In gentle stages Mrs Paske tried to edge her back into life and sometimes, not so gently, to make her see where her real duty lay.

"Sir Charles has been very good to you, Hebe. It is a poor reward to him to see you going about like a week of wet Sundays."

"I know. I simply don't understand myself. Something seems to have happened to me. I've gone all contrary. I didn't want that baby, now I do. I know it sounds fanciful but I think, Martha, I honestly think that the baby kept me going after . . . after John abandoned me. I dunno, I didn't think about it — at least not like that — at the time. But something stopped me from chucking myself into the lake. And now I've lost the baby, too. I feel like a Hallows Eve turnip, all scooped out, empty, but with a sort of face."

She knew that Martha disliked all mention of Skelton. She had dismissed him summarily, passing judgement; "Not the gentleman I took him for." She had dismissed the baby, too. "She is safe and well cared for. I saw to that. And she is costing Sir Charles twenty-five shillings a week. Surely for that, at least, he deserves a smile."

"Like this?" She made a smile, the actress in her, the quality which had made her the perfect model, still operating well. A beautiful smile; but heart-breaking, too.

The astonishing thing was, Mrs Paske thought, that though Hebe's beauty had seemed perfect, not to be improved upon, it was even greater now.

"Yes. Like that. Look, my dear, he's old, and he has had sadnesses in his life. He's good and kind and generous. A smile or two and a little interest in his plans for Christmas would cost you nothing and mean a lot to him."

"All right. I'll try. For your sake, too. You've been very good to me, Martha."

After all, Daisy thought, when the Hallows Eve turnip was scooped out, left hollow, the face which it would expose to the world, when the nub of candle was lighted within it, could be merry or glum; the slit mouth could curve upwards in a grin, or downwards in a grimace. To please two kind people who had been infinitely good to her she must pull herself together and act cheerful, not think about last Christmas! Not wonder where he was or what she had done, or failed to do that had made her so lightly discarded.

★   ★   ★

With Sir Charles Mrs Paske's manner and speech were more astringent. He now felt that he could discuss anything with her; he could even tell her what she already knew.

"I love Hebe. I think now, looking back, that I fell in love at first sight. Ridiculous at my age."

"Sixty-five is no age at all. Age is not a matter of counting birthdays, Sir Charles. I've known men old at forty, and young at near eighty."

So had he. The relative who had bequeathed him Plenrerith had been young enough to embark on such an undertaking in his seventies. But now age had another problem for him, something which he had not considered before, and what an oversight! In January he would be sixty-six. Still capable of fathering a child? There again potency varied as much as health of body and liveliness of mind. If he took Hebe to bed, as wife, as mistress, would he be endangering her life? Courting yet another bereavement.

Even of this he could speak to this sensible woman.

"Rubbish," Mrs Paske said. "If I may say so, Sir Charles, you are morbid where that subject is concerned. Understandable, of course, with your unhappy experiences. But both your wives died of a first parturition. Hebe has had her first baby. Second confinements are both easier and safer."

"I hadn't thought of that."

"I wonder," she said, "if you have thought of another thing . . ." She paused to lend force to her next words. "Would it not be wonderful to have a son of your own?"

256

"Of course, Mrs Paske. But I resigned myself so long ago . . ."

"There are exceptions, of course," Mrs Paske pressed home her argument, "but when a woman has a daughter, the chances are more than even that her second child will be a son."

Upon that thought she left him.

True love is not hungry for gratitude, but Mrs Paske was disappointed by Hebe's reception of the news that Sir Charles had been given something to think about.

"I suppose it would be the best thing. But I don't want to marry him, or anybody else. I know you think it's silly, but I'm still in love with John. Oh, I know, I know he was selfish and heartless and never loved me, but I loved him and I can't seem to get over it."

"You will, in time."

"So you say. But I even think about the baby now. In a different way. John's baby. And I never even saw her. Is she like him?"

"Not in the least. And for that you should be thankful, for her sake. Girls who resemble their fathers are generally very plain. Margaret is like you, my dear."

"I wish I could see her."

"Well, who knows? If you play your cards right, give Sir Charles a son of his own, he's more than likely to let you have her here. We could say she was an orphan in whom *I* took an interest."

In a lackadaisical fashion Daisy played her cards rightly. Sir Charles, free of gout, again wonderfully

257

rejuvenated, gave his usual big pre-Christmas party and at it announced his engagement.

There was a great deal of talk, some of it malicious but more of it cordial and tolerant, for Sir Charles was popular. And although nothing was known of Daisy's origins the only positive thing known against her was that she had once been a dancer. She had come to Wichfield first apparently as Skelton's mistress, but who could be certain even of that? In her favour Lady Fenstanton's attitude carried great weight. When the announcement was made, Lady Fenstanton, quite the most important woman within a radius of fifty miles, had embraced Miss Waywood and said in her loud, carrying voice, "My dear, I am so glad! I wish you every happiness." She had also congratulated Sir Charles most warmly and given a back-handed slap to those who over the years had tried in vain to bait the matrimonial trap.

"Now we know what you were waiting for — the loveliest girl in the world. But then, as I always said, your taste is faultless."

After that what could lesser mortals say?

Lord Fenstanton, who no longer went out and was very seldom awake, did rouse up when told the news and said, "This'll be the *third* time I've had to give Charlie Overton a wedding present."

"Darling, I believe you are jealous," Lady Fenstanton said.

Daisy, of course, made a most beautiful bride. Could Skelton have seen her he would have been side-tracked

258

again; a picture called simply, *The Bride*. But he was not there, except in the bride's thoughts; rather bitterly.

I always felt something lovely waited for me just round the next corner. I was right. I had it. But that corner is a thing of the past now.

She had known about half a year of what seemed to her perfect happiness and felt that she would never be happy again.

When the daisies whitened the meadows again, she would be seventeen.

CHAPTER
TEN

Very gradually, and with some steps backwards as well as forwards, resignation came. Daisy set herself, conscientiously, to make Sir Charles happy, and since he was over-susceptible to her mood and could only be happy if she appeared to be happy her histrionic talent was well exercised. Looking happy, behaving lightly, even frivolously became almost natural to her. She even became capricious because indulging her most vagrant whim gave him such obvious pleasure. In the three years immediately following their marriage he was obdurate over one thing only, and that was about bringing Margaret to live at Wichfield.

"Really, dear," Mrs Paske said, "you shouldn't press him. Remember he is old, the mere mention of the child upsets him and at his age any kind of disturbance is bad. I see her once a month, I assure you she couldn't be better cared for." Mrs Paske could have said, but did not, that even without disputes marriage to a young woman had finished off many elderly gentlemen. Not, she imagined, that Hebe was sexually demanding, rather the reverse.

"I absolutely hate it. Don't look so shocked. After all you were married, Martha. How would you have felt if soon after your husband . . . soon after you became a widow, some other man was . . . well, you know, pawing you about?"

Mrs Paske's marriage had been brief and joyless, and made for practical reasons which had proved worthless; she had long since ceased to think about it and for Daisy to ask her to compare feelings was quite futile.

"It seems a small price to pay — for all this," she said placidly. "All this" was luxury and spoiling and doting which just stopped short at one point.

It was out of bed that Hebe was demanding; she wanted to give a party or go to a party as often as possible. Any excuse would do. Her own entertainments introduced a new element into the stodgy routine of the countryside. *A fancy dress ball*. ("But of course," Lady Fenstanton said when asked if she meant to attend. "I have already picked my character. A woman I most whole-heartedly admire." That kept everybody guessing. And Lady Fenstanton made a wonderful Lady Hester Stanhope in Arabian dress.)

Another innovation, ideal for a summer evening, was a treasure hunt through the Wichfield grounds. Sir Charles himself printed the cards which gave the clues — he wrote better than either Hebe or Mrs Paske and he derived great pleasure in making them puzzling enough to tantalise, yet not so puzzling as to make people give up and go and sit in the house.

Then there were Daisy's own shows. They were resumed by accident. One day Lord Fenstanton woke for a bit and said, "Am I right in saying that Charlie

Overton married that girl who danced? Didn't we send him a pair of candelabra?"

"We did."

"Then why doesn't she dance for us? And sing? And do attitudes? Fair play between gentlemen I always held." He relapsed into slumber but he had given his wife the idea for *her* very original party, centred about Hebe who this time performed in the gallery built for minstrels centuries ago. And that gave Sir Charles a chance to indulge Hebe by making a room at Wichfield Place designed expressly for her performances.

So it went on.

But the hoped-for child never came, and the years did, each one a little heavier than the last; but the gout held off and, as he had told Mrs Paske, he had resigned himself to being childless years ago. In a way — a way which increased with his impotence — Sir Charles looked upon Daisy as his daughter, pampered, wilful, dear. And that made the thought of her daughter, growing up in London, the more repulsive to him.

In three years Daisy saw Margaret twice. The first time was just before Christmas when the child was about thirteen months old. Mrs Paske had given way and said, "Well, if you must, you must. I think it unwise, but I'm tired of arguing with you. We'll go shopping for Christmas, and you shall see her."

What happened was dramatic in a small way. The little girl, very forward for her age, even allowing for the fact that girls were more precocious than boys, and some girls more precocious than others, was now able to take steps, firm, purposeful. She saw Mrs Shillitoe every day, many times a day; she saw Mrs Paske once a month; she had never seen Hebe. But brought in, she went straight towards her, clutched at her skirts at the end of the run to steady herself and then held up her arms, wanting to be lifted. In any child such a gesture was appealing, and Margaret was beautiful, all pink and white and golden and blue — just the kind of child whose portraits had made John Skelton mock. Daisy hugged her and showered her with kisses, dressed her in the blue velvet frock which Mrs Paske had made. Both the elder women thought that it was like watching a child playing with a new doll. But the parting was painful and Daisy cried all the way home.

That visit was made openly and as they neared Wichfield Mrs Paske said, "Now, my dear, control yourself, if you can. If Sir Charles sees that the visit has upset you, he will not be in favour of your going again."

Daisy said, almost sullenly, "It is all his fault. Why shouldn't she live with me?"

"You know why, Hebe. And now in addition to all the other reasons there is this marked resemblance. Nobody, seeing you together, could doubt for a moment."

Daisy still thought that she could get her own way with her doting old husband, and although she controlled herself through dinner, afterwards she cried in the library and Sir Charles reacted exactly as Mrs Paske had anticipated.

Speaking with unaccustomed coldness, he said, "Since seeing the child upsets you so greatly I suggest that you do not go again."

Daisy would have ignored that, but Mrs Shillitoe wrote to Mrs Paske that Margaret had cried, refused to eat her supper and worked up a slight fever. "She is a very wilful little girl over some things and I should prefer you to make visits alone in future. Strangers upset her." Even in a letter Mrs Shillitoe was discreet.

Mother and daughter did not meet again until the summer when Margaret was two years and nine months old, and this was different altogether.

Mrs Paske, Sir Charles and Doctor McGibbon, in that order, became concerned about Daisy's physical condition. She was losing weight, had a cough at times, was alternately frenziedly gay or unreasonably depressed. The ethereal quality of her beauty became emphasised. Mrs Paske, who would have enjoyed letting seams out — and should surely by now have been doing it — was instead taking little tucks in. Doctor McGibbon distrusted the apple-blossom complexion, so often the hallmark of a consumptive. A month's holiday at Margate, no excitement, no late nights, a rest every afternoon and of course, sea-bathing, was what he advised. In fact it proved to be a very exciting holiday indeed, and very seldom did Daisy rest in the afternoon.

"You're simply making things harder for yourself," Mrs Paske said, when Daisy first mentioned her plan. "And it is a risk. Who knows who may be at Margate at this time of the year? And you've only to be seen with her once . . ."

264

"That is the beauty of it; if we are seen together — with Mrs Shillitoe *and* Hattie *and* Peter *and* Margery, I shall say that I was attracted by the likeness."

Mrs Paske could not deny Hebe anything that was within her power to supply; so when the Wichfield party moved into the best accommodation which the best hotel could offer, Mrs Shillitoe moved into humbler, but still comfortable lodgings on the landward side of the town. It was not only the first time that Mrs Shillitoe had seen the sea, it was the first time in her adult life that she had eaten food cooked by other hands. She was inclined to look upon Daisy, whom she knew as Mrs Johnson, as a fairy godmother.

The weather was kind. Daisy devoted the mornings to Sir Charles — leaving him only for her ritual bathe; they walked or sat in the sun, struck up a holiday acquaintance with their fellow guests, drank coffee at the open-air cafés, watched entertainers on the beach. Sir Charles still said that afternoon rests were for the elderly and delicate, so in the afternoons he went to the sitting-room, read the papers, dealt with correspondence, and if he dozed a little attributed drowsiness to the effect of the strong sea air. Daisy went to her bedroom and then slipped out by a side entry which Mrs Paske had looked for and found. Then she actually ran to the trysting place at an unfashionable part of the beach where she was welcomed rapturously by all the children — poor Hattie was really still a child — because she bought sweets and fancy cakes, and any toys offered by itinerant sellers. She would play with all the children for a while, and then Mrs Shillitoe would suggest some game or pursuit which would occupy the elder children so that Mrs Johnson could have her little girl to herself. She had known many mothers, official and unofficial, but she had never seen anything like the link between this mother and daughter; the nearest thing to it was her own link with the retarded Hattie. And that was strong enough to make her indulge in a little trickery . . .

Plainly Mrs Johnson had plenty of money and absolutely no idea of how to handle it. It seemed harmless enough to say that on their way to the beach one of the children had seen something in a shop window and coveted it. Blissfully happy herself, Daisy wished everybody to be happy. "Buy it, Mrs Shillitoe. Buy them all something." It was a theme capable of elaboration. Of all things Mrs Shillitoe most enjoyed a cup of tea early in the morning. "I'm used to it, you see. First thing every morning I have a cup of tea to start the day with. But at our lodgings early tea is extra."

"How much?"

"It sounds a lot — a shilling a day. A shilling for a pot of tea!"

"Well, I suppose this is their harvest time," Daisy said, opening her reticule. And Mrs Shillitoe could do without morning tea; she could do without many things if a minute sum could be added to what she was saving for poor Hattie.

Certain other small things proved to be extra, too. It was perfectly true that at the lodgings anybody who preferred cream to custard, or was greedy enough to want two eggs for breakfast, must pay a little more.

"I find that I am eating like a horse, too, Mrs Shillitoe. Pray see that they all have cream and as many eggs as they can eat."

Two hours went by in the blink of the eye; she must be back at the hotel for four o'clock tea. After that a drive in the carriage, dinner, the long, dead evening. It seemed long and dead even if there were a concert; even if they played whist. Facing such an evening, Daisy had to say, "Goodbye, darling. I'll see you tomorrow."

"Don't forget."

"I shan't forget. Goodbye Hattie, Peter, Margery. Goodbye Mrs Shillitoe."

Often there was a scene. Margaret held on to Daisy, "I want to come with you."

"I'm sorry, darling, I can't take you with me. But I'll be here tomorrow." Margaret began to wail and her clutch on Daisy's skirt tightened.

"Now, now! None of that," Mrs Shillitoe said. Nobody, not even Daisy, could complain of the tone of voice, or the way in which Mrs Shillitoe's hands dealt with Margaret's clinging ones; but both were firm. Well, of course a woman with four to deal with had to be firm, but the memory of Margaret's tearful face, her louder wails, the tug which detached the little dimpled hands, stayed with Daisy as she sped home and made herself look like a woman who had spent the afternoon resting. Is there sand in my hair? My skirt is wet from paddling . . .

One of the people with whom Daisy and Sir Charles sometimes played whist was a widow, Mrs Hamilton-Hope, still sprightly at forty, well-preserved, and with a manner towards all men, young or old, which Sir Charles decried as skittish. He was old-fashioned enough to disapprove of her staying alone at a hotel; every decent woman should have some female relative or hired companion. "I think she probably couldn't afford it," Daisy said. "Nothing she owns is very good in quality."

"Then she should have taken accommodation for herself and a companion at some cheaper establishment." He was also quite certain that her hair was dyed; almost certain that she was on the look-out for a husband. No harm in *that*, but no decent woman would be so brash about it. He was therefore something short of delighted to discover that they were distantly related, Mrs Hamilton-Hope's grandmother having been a Skelton, first cousin to Sir Charles's mother. He rather hoped that stiff questioning would reveal some flaw in this claim of kinship, but Mrs Hamilton-Hope was word perfect even when he basely tried to trick her. "I always wondered what became of Augustus."

She repeated the name, looking puzzled. "Had he another name perhaps. Or was he one of the Shropshire family? I never knew an Augustus. There was Philip, and Roger — he died in India, and Arthur who went to Virginia . . ."

Sir Charles then veered about and decided that something must be done for this distant relative, such as inviting her to make a fourth at their table, share the

268

afternoon drives. Duty, rather than liking, dictated his behaviour and he was positively angry when one day, relentlessly pursuing the intricate pathways of family connections, she mentioned John Skelton.

"I never knew him myself, but Cousin Agatha once said she was so sorry for her Uncle Thomas when he threw up his army career and took to — was it painting?"

"It was. And the less said about him the better."

He had seen Hebe, taken unaware, stiffen to attention and then look stricken. He never mentioned John's name to her and imagined that Mrs Paske, being such a sensible woman, had been equally reticent. He hoped that Hebe had forgotten; she *should* have forgotten! The look on her face told him otherwise; it hurt him, but at the same time made him impatient with her. Really, he'd done his best, pandered to every whim; considered her in every possible way. Take this holiday, for instance, just at the time of harvest when he'd have been far more happily engaged riding round his estate. Not that he grudged anything. And certainly he was delighted to see that with the holiday only half spent she looked so much better.

Two evenings later they were settling down to after-dinner whist; Sir Charles, Hebe, Mrs Hamilton-Hope — now, because of the relationship, on first name terms — and a Colonel Spencer upon whom Frances had her predatory eye. Mrs Paske could play, indeed played rather well, but she always tactfully withdrew when a fourth player was available.

Innocently, Frances said as Sir Charles shuffled the cards, "Hebe, dear, who is that exquisite child?"

Daisy was not quite caught as she had been by the casual mention of Skelton, because she never ran out of the hotel and along the promenade towards where Mrs Shillitoe and the children waited without being aware that she was taking a risk. Not perhaps a very great one, but a risk.

"What child, Frances? I'm afraid I don't quite . . ."

"But the other three are so plain, so ordinary looking, and she is so beautiful."

"Who is?"

"The little girl with whom you were playing this afternoon. At the other end of the beach."

"Me? You must be mistaken, Frances. I never go to that end. And I rest in the afternoon."

"Doctor's orders," Sir Charles said, passing the cards to Colonel Spencer who was completely oblivious and didn't care who played with what children so long as he was not called upon to do so.

The game pursued its usual course but it was a short session. Sir Charles said something about the soporific effect of the Margate air and said he intended to have an early night. The suggestion was welcomed by Frances Hamilton-Hope — it left her alone with Colonel Spencer; and although he did not particularly welcome *that* and meant to avoid it, he was glad to be rid of Lady Overton as a partner; she never played well and this evening was worse than usual. Beautiful as an angel, of course . . .

★ ★ ★

270

"Now, tell me the truth." There was an ominous note.

"You know it already. I've seen Margaret every afternoon. She's my child. I love her and she loves me. We've done nobody any harm."

"You deceived me."

"I had to. It was my only chance of getting to know her."

"And you have damaged yourself. That odious woman mentioned her looks. She's now putting two and two together and making five. If you can't imagine what she will be writing all over the place, I can. I've gone to considerable trouble — and expense — to protect your reputation, and now by your incredibly indiscreet behaviour you may have wrecked the whole thing."

He had never spoken to her, looked at her, in such a way. Something of her old spirit stirred and she wanted to say, "I don't care." But she mustn't anger him more.

"If you could only see her, Charles. She is such a darling. Not only pretty, but so amiable and so intelligent. I know you'd love her."

"I should *not*! In any case I do not propose to put it to the test. I really am displeased with you, Hebe. I can't think how you could be so thoughtless. Frances Hamilton-Hope may not have been the only person to notice. Does Mrs Paske know how you spent the afternoons?"

"No. The blame is all mine."

"I should have known that she would have better sense." He did not like to think of the two women conniving against him. Nevertheless he mentioned the business to Mrs Paske who made one of her rare mistakes.

"How ridiculous! But I can see what happened. You may not have noticed, Sir Charles, but I have. From the first, Lady Overton has been *copied.* They copy her clothes, the way she does her hair . . . They paint their faces pink and white. It was an imitation that Mrs Hamilton-Hope saw."

Sir Charles subjected Mrs Paske to a long, cold look.

"Very plausible! Very ingenious! It happens that Lady Overton has admitted everything."

Mrs Paske flushed — a dusky, unbecoming crimson.

"I do not think she should be judged too harshly. It was unwise. But neither you nor I are capable of understanding a mother's feelings."

The remark did nothing to soothe Sir Charles's feelings. The two of them *had* connived against him! At the thought a pang shot through his vulnerable left foot. The upset had started his blasted gout again.

"We leave for home in an hour," he said.

The conversation had taken place at the breakfast table, to which Daisy had not yet come. Mrs Paske rose.

"I had better start packing," she said and went swiftly away.

The gout had not improved overnight; but to set against it was his pleasure at the thought of getting home and seeing something of the harvest after all. And something Mrs Paske had said had reached its mark; he thought: No, I never had a child. I do not understand.

Then Daisy's behaviour hardened his attitude again.

272

"Not me! I can't. I can't go today. She's expecting me. I promised. It'd break her poor little heart and that I wouldn't do for all the tea in China. Punish me, if you like, but not her. Please, Charles, please. Tomorrow. I'll go tomorrow."

"You'll come today."

She became hysterical. Lost her head completely.

"I shan't. And you can't make me. I'm going to see Margaret and take her the doll I promised and say goodbye properly if it's the last thing I do. I've been let down by somebody I trusted. I know how it feels. Go on, go home if you like . . . I'll stay here. I'll wash dishes. No, I'll sing and dance on the beach . . ."

She was doing two dangerous things: reducing a rather vain old man in his own estimation by making so light of the position he had conferred upon her; Lady Overton washing dishes indeed! And she was challenging a proud, hardy old man. He had no doubt that she was capable of carrying out her threat — about joining entertainers on the beach. How the gaping crowds would flock!

A hundred malicious imps with red-hot needles stabbed his foot. Others, equally malicious but differently armed, attacked his mind, placing little darts which rankled. The question of *class* which in his infatuation he had chosen to ignore. Face it now! Both his beautiful Hebe and his sensible Mrs Paske were of a class to whom honour meant nothing.

Peasants. Sneaking off behind his back, thinking themselves clever, probably laughing at the ease with which they deceived him.

Then there was jealousy. Hebe had loved — still loved — John; she loved the child sufficiently to be recklessly silly in order to enjoy two hours of her company while for himself she obviously had not a shred of consideration.

There was an even darker thought. What of the future? Suppose, just suppose, that Hebe should conceive an infatuation for another man. She well might. Not yet twenty! She would be utterly unscrupulous and Mrs Paske would aid and abet her.

Angered and disillusioned, he was yet forced to compromise.

"You know where Margaret is staying?"

"Yes. But I have never been there. I thought the beach was safer. Less conspicuous."

"You know perfectly well that you would be conspicuous anywhere!" His tone was not complimentary. "I will defer our departure for an hour. Go and buy the doll and take it to her and say goodbye."

For this concession she was insufficiently grateful. The wild notion of remaining in Margate, moving into the back-street lodgings, seeing Margaret all day, every day was still with her and very attractive. It even extended to deserting Sir Charles altogether. She would go back to London . . .

It took Mrs Paske's cold common sense to dispose of that madcap scheme.

"It does sometimes seem to me, Hebe, that you can't see beyond your nose. Don't you want the best for your little girl? What could you give her — however hard you worked, however well you did — compared with what

Sir Charles can do for her? He's paying for the best care for her now. Presently there'll be schooling . . ."

"I'm thinking of *now*."

"That is what I mean by being short-sighted. And if you can't look far ahead, look near. Close on seventy, bear in mind, and nobody lives for ever. The day may well come when you can have Margaret at Wichfield. Wait a bit, anyway."

Mrs Shillitoe was glad that Mrs Johnson's holiday had ended so soon. Granted she was very generous and treated all the children the same as far as little gifts and treats went, but the fuss after each leave-taking! You could hardly blame the child for being fond of her mother — Mrs Shillitoe had never for one instant been deceived — but often Mrs Johnson went away in the afternoon, Margaret set up a hullabaloo and Hattie cried because Margaret cried, and often Peter and Margery joined in. Mrs Shillitoe found it embarrassing to be out on the open beach with four woeful children. People stared!

Mrs Hamilton-Hope was very sorry to see her kinsman go. The connection had lent her status. Given time, she felt that she might have worked her way towards an invitation to Wichfield, very welcome, should her stay at the Grand Hotel prove unproductive. She was observant and up to a point imaginative without being sensitive. She had a nose for anything curious and intriguing. She was *positive* that she had seen Hebe playing on the beach with a very beautiful little girl; Hebe had denied being there. Then Hebe had played very badly, even for her, and Charles had cut short the session. Now they were gone, though she knew that their suite was booked for a month. Curious? Curious!

On the previous afternoon she had seen Hebe on the beach while she herself was on what, at this end, passed as a promenade, merely a footpath. She walked so far, either in one direction or the other, because exercise was necessary. The Grand's charges were high and she liked to get her money's worth, so she ate well, and might all too easily become fat.

This afternoon she went again and there was the drab unnoticeable woman, the one positively ugly child, the two plain ones and the beauty. Mrs Hamilton-Hope, lifting her skirts, stepped down on to the beach and approached Mrs Shillitoe who looked up from her knitting.

"Good afternoon. I rather wondered if I might find Lady Overton here. She was here yesterday."

"Not Lady Overton. Who is she? I never heard of her. I'm sorry."

The beautiful little girl, cuddling an obviously expensive doll, could only be blood kin to Hebe. An absolute replica in miniature.

Hattie, afflicted poor dear, but now and then showing signs of flickering intelligence, said, "Mamma. The Pretty Lady."

"Yes, darling. But that wasn't Lady Overton. That was Mrs Johnson." Mrs Shillitoe turned a bleak, blank look upon Mrs Hamilton-Hope. "She was a lady who had a fancy for children and liked giving presents."

Peter, who had he been born on the right side of the blanket would have been heir to a dukedom, said, "Mrs Johnson gave me this." A model of a locomotive which did not travel well on the beach. Margery displayed a toy kitten which, pressed in the right place, made a squeaking miaow. Hattie, not to be outdone, exhibited a string of pink coral beads. They were all hoping for sweets, for Daisy had been lavish with those, too, and to them one well-dressed, sweet-smelling lady was the same as another. Only the exquisite child held aloof. Just for a second, hearing the rustle of silk, smelling the eau-de-cologne, she had looked up hopefully and then, disappointed, withdrawn. This lady was not her Pretty Lady and even had she come laden with chocolate drops or peppermint balls, Margaret wanted none of them. She turned to the doll which the Pretty Lady had given her that morning, with kisses, saying goodbye.

Mrs Hamilton-Hope said, "How nice. How kind of her. You have a very happy little family, Mrs . . .?"

"I like to think so." Mrs Shillitoe had recovered from the slight shock and remembered that secrecy was her business; she did not supply her name. "Hattie, you may paddle now. Just at the edge and all holding hands." Peter and Margery went willingly; Margaret refused to move. "Let her do as she likes," Mrs Shillitoe said.

"Your youngest is a very beautiful child."

Mrs Shillitoe made a cautionary gesture. "So people say, but she's old enough to take notice now. I don't want her to grow up vain. Her Papa is inclined to spoil her quite enough." Mrs Shillitoe was aiming to establish an ordinary family background. She sensed something. This was not the kind of lady to step off the promenade and take such interest. There was some reason.

"Yes, she is . . . what you said. Strange when you look at *me*. It's in the family, though. I had an aunt, and I have a sister, quite lovely. Hattie, keep to the edge!"

CHAPTER
ELEVEN

Mrs Paske re-established herself in Sir Charles's good graces some time before Daisy did. She was a good nurse and while this untimely attack lasted he was dependent upon her. She was sympathetic which Doctor McGibbon was not. McGibbon blamed over-indulgence in food and drink. Mrs Paske blamed herself.

"I made a grave mistake," she said frankly. "I thought that if you knew about the child and Hebe's seeing her every day, you might get upset and suffer a mild attack. Then we were discovered and you took it, if I may say so, far too seriously. With this result. I'm very sorry. So is she."

"I see no evidence of that."

"Well, some allowance must be made. At the moment she is so sorry for herself . . . And, I think, ashamed — like a little girl caught out in some misdemeanour."

No one ever had a better advocate.

With Daisy Mrs Paske was brisk.

"You're making too much of it, too. You must see that he's just a silly jealous old man who needs pampering. And, my dear, being cold and dignified does not suit you at all. Say you're sorry, make a fuss of him and everything will be all right again."

Over-optimistic. Daisy, who had hated the poisonous atmosphere engendered by disapproval, did apologise, did fuss, did shed a few beautiful tears; was ostensibly forgiven and restored to favour. But damage had been done. Sir Charles felt that she had betrayed his trust — granted in only a small matter; he saw that now, but he still felt that anyone deceitful in a small matter was likely to be deceitful in larger ones. Daisy thought that in tearing her away from her child he was being spiteful. She forgot his many kindnesses.

They did not resume their marital relationship. Sir Charles, with his worry gout merging into his winter gout, was past all sexual desire and Daisy, who had accepted his embraces as a duty to be performed, with, at first, some slight hope of motherhood again, was now content to let the matter go.

But Margaret she would not let go; and just before the child's birthday she said in a way new to her, "Charles, Margaret will be three the day after tomorrow. I wish to keep her birthday with her. I thought I had better tell you so that you cannot again accuse me of being deceitful."

"Very considerate. The carriage is at your disposal. I suppose I can rely upon you not to drive up to the very door. Watson is an observant fellow."

PART THREE

CHAPTER
ONE

Two years passed; periods of dull ordinary life, with here and there some event standing out like a molehill on a flat lawn. Sir Charles's gout became almost chronic, the intermissions growing shorter and shorter; both feet, both hands and finally his eyes were affected. There were times when even the light indoors increased the pain and he sat or lay in a darkened room. Mrs Paske tended him well, Daisy, by the light of a heavily shaded lamp placed at the far side of the room, read to him by the hour, his friends made visits; but it was a melancholy way of life and suffering did not improve his temper. And for the first time since the death of his second wife he began to give a great deal of thought as to what would happen when he was dead.

As he had once said, he had long been resigned to heirlessness. He had known that with him the baronetcy would end; the big-headed Overtons had never bred well and so far as he or anybody else knew, he was the last of them. He accepted this with a curious lack of sentiment, probably because he had not been reared to the role, and had never wanted the title during those years when youthful aspirations formed character. Some of the estate — about five hundred acres — was subject to entail and by the process of escheatment would revert to the Crown. The house would not. The original Wichfield Place had been much damaged in the Civil War and was now no more than humps in a pasture known as Place Pound. The Overton of the day had built the new Wichfield Place on land he had bought for the purpose. Overtons had on the whole been thrifty and shrewd; they had bought land when it was cheap and held on to it. It was in Sir Charles's power to dispose of four good farms, several smallholdings, a dozen rented houses as well as the house and a considerable sum of money, safely invested. To all this John Skelton could have succeeded; Sir Charles had always thought of him as his heir rather than the Skelton boys, and their ineptitude over Plenrerith had put them out of the running. There were other Skeltons, a good many of them, for unlike the Overtons they were prolific, and there was one about whom Sir Charles knew nothing and of whom, therefore, he could not disapprove.

A few preliminary inquiries offered promise; first cousin to Max and Algie, he sounded to be of a different breed. Born to a poor and obscure branch of the family, he was a working farmer, growing potatoes in the rich reclaimed fenland of Lincolnshire. Thirty-two years old, married with two sons, George Skelton sounded what Sir Charles called likely. Anyway, he'd better have a look at him.

From his letter in response to an invitation to Wichfield in November, Sir Charles judged him to be an educated man. He thanked Sir Charles for his

284

invitation which was timely, since the last potatoes had been harvested. His wife would come with him, a treat for her, she'd never been farther south than Cambridge.

For Mrs Paske the whole exercise had the taste of dust and ashes. If *only* Hebe, who in an illicit affair had bred such a beautiful child, could have produced a son! Little hope, or none, of that, now. Then why not leave everything to Hebe? Mrs Paske understood the law of entail, but she also saw, all around, widows left in full charge. Not that Hebe was capable of that — but Mrs Paske was. The climactic had passed with her, soon after the return from Margate; she'd had a bad change, severe headaches and for a time a shakiness which she had diagnosed as a benign tremor which *might* be palsy. However, ignored, both symptoms had receded and left Mrs Paske twice the woman she had been. She now had energy enough to act as nurse, oversee the household and supply what supervision the estate needed.

She had tried to put her view to Sir Charles, but he was difficult to reason with these days. He easily became upset and that exacerbated his gout.

"So, let the potato farmer and his wife come," Mrs Paske said almost viciously to Daisy. "Sir Charles is still in his right mind and will see that his plan is unworkable."

"I don't want a fortune," Daisy said. "Just enough for a little house where you and I and Margaret could live together in peace."

"You may think so, my dear; but you'd have to alter your ways."

That was true. Daisy had steadily become more and more extravagant. She spent a great deal of money on clothes, on entertainment. It was usual now for most parties at Wichfield to include some of her performances and the stage settings she devised for herself were often costly. Her dances had become more sophisticated; an Indian dance demanded palm trees — real ones; a Spanish dance needed orange trees. Many of her poses were embellished with jewellery, not, to Mrs Paske's regret, real stuff which would keep its value, but fake, pinchbeck and coloured glass, good for an evening's spectacle and then good for nothing. But Daisy did not spend money only on herself; the family at Talbot St Agnes benefited greatly; comfort in the home, and outside of it a boy receiving the education needed for a doctor, two girls being apprenticed, one to a dressmaker, one to a milliner. Also, since Daisy could never go to St Luke's Street without taking lavish presents for *all* the children and always leaving at least a couple of sovereigns for Mrs Shillitoe to add to Hattie's fund, she usually exceeded her allowance and had to appeal to Sir Charles, saying as she had once done to John, "I don't know; everything seems to cost more every day. And money slips through my fingers."

He continued to be generous, partly because he was generous by nature and partly because now and again he had a slight feeling of guilt about his change of feeling towards her. He had not given her a child to replace the one she loved so dearly, and whom he would not accept. He had not given her, since Margate, the blind, devoted affection that a young, beautiful woman, married to an old man, should expect. Such thoughts usually occurred to him in the middle of the night when he woke, very clear-minded. Doctor McGibbon, once he was absolutely certain that his old friend's gout was not the result of over-indulgence — that certainty following a fortnight of practically prison diet, with no resultant improvement — had been generous with palliatives, all opium derivatives. Mrs Paske measured the doses; the last one ensured some hours' sleep and then, at three o'clock, four o'clock, the dead hours of early morning, Sir Charles would wake, instantly lucid and more clear-headed than at any other time of the night or day. Then the pain, or a new pain, would start up and in order to escape both the pain and the clear thinking, he'd reach for the pills left by Mrs Paske, "just in case". Then he would sleep again.

George Skelton, slow moving, slow spoken, an amiable giant of a man, with some of the Skelton good looks and a full share of their curious unworldliness, arrived late on a November afternoon, driving a horse, its worth and stamina well disguised under ill-bred lines and a rough coat, harnessed to the kind of vehicle which prosperous farmers had discarded, a utilitarian cart with room in it at the back for several sacks of potatoes, or a pig or a young calf under a net. There was an unupholstered seat, a mere board for driver and passengers; and in the back a sack of potatoes. Almost the first words the putative heir said to his putative benefactor after greeting, were, "I've brought you some Champion potatoes to try. I don't mean champion in the ordinary way. Champion is their name. It's a breed."

He had also brought his champion wife.

Lucy Skelton alighted from the mud-splashed cart as neat and clean as a wasp; self-possessed, a match for anybody on earth, or, if necessary, God or the Devil. Before her marriage she had been a governess, feared not only by her pupils but by their parents, and that at a time when governesses were a meek and largely despised breed. There was a gypsy strain in her; it showed in her colouring, black hair, black eyes and a swarthy skin; it showed in her disposition; If I don't suit you, I'll move on and bad luck to you! She had moved on, always leaving her mark behind her — none of her pupils remembered her kindly, but they could all read by the age of four. Her method was simple and direct. C-A-T spells cat. C-A-T; what does it spell? Get it wrong and you had a sound smack. What does C-A-T spell? Most of them had it right the second time. She had whisked in and out of four or five different households before she met George Skelton and realised that something could be made of him.

With deliberate spite, in order to show the potato farmer as the hobbledehoy that he was, Mrs Paske had planned an elaborate dinner necessitating a formidable array of cutlery, calculated to confuse. Let Sir Charles see! George Skelton eyed the display and said easily, "This is where I must keep my eye on Lucy."

Lucy, equally at ease, said, "We live very simply. With only one maid and four in family it is necessary to cut down on the washing-up. I do the cooking myself."

"Lucy's a marvel," said her husband.

"Not at all," she said in her matter-of-fact way. "Anyone with the use of their faculties and able to read can cook. When I was at Windlemoor the cook had a fit on the evening of a dinner party. I cooked. His Grace said it was as good a meal as he had ever eaten. He gave me this brooch as a memento." She indicated, without pride, and also without modesty, a large amethyst encircled with tiny diamonds which decorated her otherwise plain plum-coloured dress. An afternoon dress, Sunday wear.

Somehow, she managed, without saying a word or even giving a disparaging look, to imply that the elaborate dinner was not the perfect example of culinary art.

She spoke of her sons. Young George was already at Oundle and Richard would follow him there next September.

"There's just a year and a week between them. Having children is such a handicap to a busy woman. I thought it best to get it over and done with."

"I thought Providence arranged such matters," Mrs Paske said. Lucy gave her a glance which reproved indelicacy and asked had she any family.

The pair were invulnerable because they had no pretensions. Sir Charles liked this distant relative and felt that Wichfield would be safe in his hands. Lucy he could not actually *like*, but was bound to admire — she made all her own dresses; she could cook; she could make butter; she was, according to her husband, the accountant of the family; she seemed to find time for reading and for keeping in practice with the piano. Nobody could say she was conceited; self-satisfied, yes, and, he sensed, domineering. And so plain! Not that that was her fault, any more than it was his that he couldn't feel warmly towards dark women. She was obviously a good wife and mother.

Next day, braving a cold easterly wind, Sir Charles took George on a tour of the estate, part of which he might one day inherit. George seemed to be impressed not by the extent of it, but by the fact that Sir Charles was obviously such a good landlord.

"Up North," he said in his laconic way, "most landlords are absentees, spending the money they wring out of tenants in London. There are exceptions, of course . . . And maybe some excuse. Lincolnshire is plain ugly, all fenland is. I have planted a tree or two, near the house, but they don't seem to thrive. You can drive ten miles and not see anything higher than a potato plant or a head of celery. I must say, you've got a beautiful place here."

"It's older country. And I will say I've tried to be a good custodian. Whenever a tree has to be felled I plant another. Do you shoot?"

"Off and on. Vermin mostly. Pheasants and partridges like hedges to nest in and trees to roost in, so they're rare around us. Wild duck for a few days in the spring. I shoot then and Lucy gets busy. Boiled, and pounded, given a good seal of mutton fat, it'll last the year round."

"I'll arrange for a few friends to come shooting on Thursday," Sir Charles said. He would have liked to think that he could make one of the party, but already, though he had pulled his hat low and had chosen the carriage to ride around in, his eyes were stinging and sore.

"Oh, I must be home by Thursday," the putative heir said with a gentle smile.

"But you said you had harvested your potatoes."

"So I have. But there's stock. I have a hired man, but he's not very bright so it's a bit of a responsibility for the boy."

Sir Charles thought, This is a responsible man; the kind praised in the Bible, "diligent about his business". Anything more unlike Max or Algie could hardly be imagined.

Later in the day his opinion of Lucy improved a little. She knew nothing of gout, she admitted, but she knew a good lotion for sore eyes.

"Have you ever tried it? A solution of salt and bicarbonate of soda."

"Sir Charles's eyes are already sore," Mrs Paske said. "Surely salt would worsen them?"

"Tears are salt," Mrs Skelton commented, "and a good cry never hurt eyes yet."

"They redden them."

"Mine," Sir Charles said, "are already red. It would do no harm."

The remedy was ineffectual, but the solicitude pleased him. Lucy prepared the lotion with her own hands. "I've no doubt you have good servants," she said in a tone which denied the content of the words, "but I've lived in great houses and I know how jobs get handed down to the lowest kitchen maid."

That night, in the connubial bedchamber, George and Lucy Skelton had a talk which would have surprised Sir Charles, and Mrs Paske. On the previous evening, tired by their journey which had included a hasty look at London while the horse had a rest, they had gone to bed almost in silence. Now, stepping out of her outmost petticoat, a good black taffeta one, Lucy said, "Well?"

"It's a good property; about eight hundred acres — apart from the entailed section. There's a lot of waste, of course, especially around the Home Farm. That's more or less a show place."

"We'd soon cure that! It's a good house, too, I got the girl to show me over. There are spare bedrooms better than this."

"This is all right," George said, glancing around the room which, if not one usually assigned to honoured guests, was luxurious by his standards.

"Eventually it could house three families quite easily."

"Yes, it'd be nice to be all together without living in each other's pockets." George slipped his nightshirt over his head. "And I've been thinking about that entail. You say it'll go back to the Crown. Then it'd need a tenant. Why not Richard — when the time comes?"

They stood for a moment, wrapped, as so often before, in a communal dream. George and Young George working the eight hundred acres and Richard working the rest; all together, but in separate establishments, under the one roof. And Lucy the real ruler of all. A small kingdom under a matriarch.

"At the same time, we have to consider that girl. No child yet and I'd say he was past it. But . . ."

"But what?"

"She's very quiet and the quiet ones are the craftiest. And there's no denying she's pretty . . . I think she's set her heart on a baby. You wouldn't notice, but I did. Whenever mention was made of our boys a look came over her face. Like . . . like a hungry person would look when food was talked about."

Years of marriage to Lucy had shown her husband that she was both quicker in the uptake and more far-sighted than he was himself. He'd often thought that had she lived in earlier times she'd have burned for a witch.

"There's not much she can do about that."

"No? I only know what I should do, in her place. Get me a baby by some other man. *He* couldn't make a fuss without looking a fool and a child born in wedlock and not denied from the start counts as legal. *Then* where should we be?"

"Well . . . No worse off than we were before," George said in his imperturbable way.

"It would irk *me*, having seen all this. I'm thinking of the boys. *Our* sort of farming is all very well, but it's hard work. And penny-pinching all the time to set Richard up on his own." She began to brush her sleek black hair.

"She didn't strike me as the flighty sort." George was more intent upon calming Lucy's fears than in defending Daisy.

"Girls as pretty as she is can get away with anything, even murder. And I'm not saying that she *is* flighty. I'm only saying that I understand her. She wants a baby; Sir Charles needs an heir: and there *is* a simple solution."

"If I didn't know you were sound as a rock talk like that would set me thinking," he said teasingly.

"It's more a question of knowing that I have all I want, *in that way*."

It was true. George was still a fond lover and she had her boys.

Lucy Skelton, with all she wanted *in that way*, had been largely responsible for Daisy's quiet, wistful mood. Every time George looked at his wife with that doglike devotion, or referred to her with such praise, Daisy experienced a pang. This very plain, matter-of-fact woman seemed to have everything that was desirable, while she had so little that she valued — and would soon have less. For Mrs Shillitoe had decided that Margaret was ready for school. Intelligent, precocious, well-grown, more than a little spoilt and very wilful, she no longer fitted easily into the household in St Luke's Street, where Peter and Margery had been replaced by two infants.

Margaret, fortunate in having Mrs Shillitoe as foster mother, was about to be privileged again. The Misses Reade ran a very good school, specialising in children whose parentage was obscure and who had no homes to which to go for holidays. The Misses Reade held that the sins of the parents should not be visited on the children; on the contrary it was a Christian's duty to try to make up for the deprivation. The fees were high, one hundred and twenty pounds a year, but the girls were well fed and well housed and well taught. Some, when ready to leave, found posts as governesses, or companions to lonely old ladies. Many had modest dowries and made respectable marriages to farmers and clergymen and missionaries. Lucy Skelton was herself an ex-pupil of the school.

The place had only one drawback. It was in Manchester, so a day visit was impossible, and Sir Charles, growing daily more self-centred, was unlikely to agree to a longer absence. Daisy had reason to envy Lucy Skelton and to look wistful when she spoke of her boys.

CHAPTER
TWO

The next event in a life becoming more and more governed by the waxing and waning of gout and the resultant moods was the arrival of a letter from Mrs Hamilton-Hope. There was nothing extraordinary in that, for in the two years since the meeting at Margate she had kept loosely in touch, greetings for Sir Charles's birthday and at Christmas, and the expressed hope that one day they would meet again. She wrote from various places — all rather grand. Sir Charles did not issue the hoped-for invitation. Sir Charles had disliked her, then relented and acted as a kinsman should, and been how rewarded? The woman by a few words — admittedly innocent — had led to his first quarrel with Hebe. It had been lived down, but it was like a drop of ink in a jugful of water; disillusionment and distrust had remained.

Yet the appeal in the letter was irresistible. By a combination of unfortunate circumstances, Mrs Hamilton-Hope found herself with nowhere to go for Christmas. She had accepted an invitation to Kent, refusing several others, but her host and hostess had been called to Scotland where their daughter was dangerously ill. Another establishment where she was always welcome

296

at the shortest notice was smitten with influenza. She could, of course, go to Westmorland but it was a long journey to take in winter, she being in London, preparatory to going to Kent; so she thought that she would take advantage of Charles's oft-repeated invitation to Wichfield, that was, if it would cause no inconvenience. If it did, only the slightest, she would face a lonely Christmas in London since no one was in Town over the festive season.

"I never *invited* her," Sir Charles said grumpily, "but I suppose we must have her." Obviously she hadn't found a second husband, still had no home of her own. Women and spinsters in that state were inclined to move in and stay for ever — he'd known several cases. He did not intend to have that happen; he'd word his reply saying that Frances would be welcome until New Year. Now he must find an extra man for his dinner party on the twenty-seventh. How about Roger Stokes, a fairly near neighbour whose wife had died at Michaelmas and who was, in theory, still in mourning but who might be willing to behave unconventionally in order to oblige an old friend? And he just hoped to God that Frances wouldn't make such an obvious dead set at him as she had at Colonel Spencer.

"Arrange for her to have the red room," he instructed Mrs Paske. "It's small, but on the warmer side of the house."

Daisy had no thought beyond her Christmas visit to St Luke's Street, her last visit there since Margaret was due to go to Manchester on the first of January. Some schools of the better kind demanded a kind of uniform but the Misses Reade asked only that pupils should be well provided for in the matter of clothes, warm for winter, cool for summer, sensible for ordinary wear and something pretty for occasions. Between them Mrs Paske and Mrs Shillitoe were making ready the necessities; Daisy planned a shopping spree with Margaret at Hawksley's, a shop which from humble beginnings had advanced to such magnitude that it boasted that it could provide anything from a needle to an elephant.

Sir Charles, generous in all but one direction, had given Daisy as much money as any woman bent upon shopping for Christmas and extras to a school outfit could possibly need. At three o'clock, December days being short, the carriage was to await both Lady Overton and Mrs Hamilton-Hope at Clark's Hotel in Piccadilly, the place where Mrs Hamilton-Hope was staying.

That they should meet earlier, in the restaurant which Hawksley's — well ahead of its contemporaries — provided for lady customers, was fortuitous, and in the circumstances inevitable. Two lean, peripatetic years had taken toll of Mrs Hamilton-Hope's wardrobe, always more showy than substantial, and she wished to do Cousin Charles credit. A new evening dress was essential, and so were certain items of underwear. After that, lunch.

Daisy had bought Margaret not one, but three pretty dresses and then — wanton extravagance — a small fur coat. Hawksley's knew their market, and the little fur coats, rabbit made to look like ermine, were well to the fore, ideal Christmas gifts for pampered little girls. After that, lunch. The restaurant was crowded and the harassed waitress, doing her duty, said, "If Madam doesn't mind sharing a table . . ." and led Daisy and Margaret to the only partially occupied table. Well, fancy. Fancy meeting here. What could be more pleasant? What could be more awkward? Not that anyone at one of the close-packed neighbouring tables could have seen anything wrong.

"I have a new coat," Margaret said, stroking it. "Mrs Johnson, my Pretty Lady, bought it for me just now. Isn't it lovely?"

Margaret was in great spirits and garrulous; Mrs Hamilton-Hope was attentive and ready with a leading question now and then. The chance encounter did not please Daisy who would have liked to have her child to herself for this, the last meal they would have together for an unknown period of time. She saw no actual danger in this meeting; Charles knew where she was, he could not accuse her of being deceitful or indiscreet; the use of the name Johnson proved how careful she had been. It might be puzzling to Frances, but she could think up some plausible explanation for that. She cut the meal short. "We must go to the toy department, Margaret."

"I'd like a doll. Margery broke the other."

"A doll you shall have. Say goodbye to Mrs Hamilton-Hope, dear." To Frances she said, "I shall see you at three o'clock. Watson is very punctual."

On her way out of the store Mrs Hamilton-Hope noticed that the smallest white fur coat cost twelve pounds and that ones in Margaret's size were fifteen or eighteen. Hebe was obviously not short of pocket money . . .

Watson was punctual. Mrs Hamilton-Hope's baggage — all that she owned in the world — was stowed; the two ladies warmly wrapped in a great fur rug. Daisy was straight from, her nerves raw from, one of the scenes which Mrs Shillitoe so much deplored. This time there was not even the poor consolation of being able to say, "I'll see you soon, darling." The child clutched and cried, said, "Stay here. There's room in my bed." And, "Why can't I come with you?" It had been most painful and even Mrs Shillitoe, who understood and sympathised, was compelled to say, "Mrs Johnson, try to control yourself. You make her worse."

At first the streets were crowded. No one of sufficient consequence to mean anything to Mrs Hamilton-Hope might be in London over the festive season but the countless others would be and everyone who could afford it meant to eat well; wagons full of produce, animals on foot, filled the streets and the noise made conversation impossible. Then they were out of it, and Watson, observant and weatherwise, knew that it would soon freeze; once into the open country he urged the horses on.

"I did not realise, Hebe, that you had been married before."

"I wasn't."

"The child called you Mrs Johnson."

"She has always known me by that name. She is an orphan in whom Mrs Paske — you remember Martha — took *some* interest, not quite enough to my mind. I don't blame her, she has enough to do, looking after the house and acting as nurse. So lately I have made the visits. And it is a fact that anybody with a title is always charged more. So I simply called myself Mrs Johnson."

Yes, and not only lately! More than two years ago.

"She is, as I have said before, an exquisite child. With no intention to flatter, extremely like you."

"You *do* flatter me! I think she is beautiful. At best I am pretty. I do find her endearing and that may account, of course, for my taking over where Mrs Paske left off. Little treats, little presents. I've tried to make up to the poor little thing for having no parents."

"How admirable! You speak so feelingly — were you yourself an orphan?"

"Far from it! At least, I had a mother until I was five. She died and I missed her. My father is still alive, married again . . ."

And, God! If I did what I wanted to do when Margaret was crying, cut loose and gone to Manchester, scrubbed floors if I couldn't find a better job, what would happen to my half-brother, my two half-sisters? Even to my father who has grown accustomed to having a little more than he earns?

CHAPTER
THREE

Mrs Hamilton-Hope began by borrowing. "Hebe, dear, I did not realise that in the South the weather could be so cold. Could you lend me a wrap?" "Hebe, I foolishly bought a crimson dress with which my garnets would have been perfect. But I did not pack them. Have you anything which would look well on crimson?"

"Diamonds go with any colour," Daisy said and lent a brooch in the shape of a true lovers' knot.

Mrs Paske said, "If you ask me she never had any garnets — or if she did they're sold. You get your stuff back."

Sir Charles knew nothing about the lending; what he did observe, with deep disapproval, was Frances's attempt to be flirtatious with poor Stokes; and that after he had warned her that the man was still in mourning. She said she understood, only too well, what bereavement meant and then proceeded to act like a silly girl and yet with purpose, angling for an invitation.

"I seem to remember hearing about what a beautiful, historic home you have, Mr Stokes. Ashfield Abbey, is it not? Old buildings absolutely entrance me. Dear Charles, I am not decrying Wichfield, it is beautiful, but it has not the patina which only age can give."

Mr Stokes knowing what he should say, but not intending to say it, looked uncomfortable and was rescued by Lady Fenstanton. Lord Fenstanton had slept his way to death, a most enviable end. His wife had mourned him with all proper ceremony and had never for a moment been that awkward thing, a spare woman, for her son, twenty-two years old and extremely handsome, had hurried home from one of his ill-defined journeys as soon as he knew that his father was dead. He had never got on well with his father, being more or less in love with his mother, the most competent, outspoken, and yet towards him indulgent woman he was ever likely to encounter. He would be her escort, her right-hand man until he was nearing thirty, then she would tell him that he had a duty to posterity and must marry Daphne, Alexandra, Rosalind or whomever she had chosen.

Hearing some reference made to Ashfield Abbey by this extremely coarse woman whom Sir Charles had introduced as a relative, Lady Fenstanton said, "If age in buildings attracts you, Mrs Hamilton-Hope, you should come to Wichmore. Our castle was old when Ashfield Abbey was being built. Come to tea, tomorrow."

Both worldly women knew what an invitation to tea meant. A concession: a snub. Near equals were invited to lunch, equals to dinner.

Mrs Hamilton-Hope gave the correct answer, "How extremely unfortunate. I am engaged tomorrow afternoon."

★　★　★

Mrs Paske had been right in saying that if Frances Hamilton-Hope had ever had anything of value it had been sold. She now had nothing to sell and was desperate. Even when her husband — dead these eight years — had been alive they'd lived from hand to mouth, trying this, trying that; breeding horses, breeding dogs, venturing into the wine trade, the one kind of business which a gentleman could engage in without losing caste; all hopeless. Yet, when she was widowed, she'd had enough to live on, in a cottage with perhaps one little maid-of-all-work; a living death and she had rejected it, staking all not on one throw but on a series of throws of which Wichfield was the last.

Sir Charles, suffering the aftermath of his party, was immune to all hints. He had done his duty, asked her to stay for Christmas and until the New Year and he made it horribly plain that he expected her to leave on the second of January. A little pressure must be applied, and in the right quarter, for even Frances realised the frailty of her lever.

She went about the business with the same lack of subtlety as she showed in her efforts to interest men. She caught Daisy in the act of writing to Margaret. The child, like most of Mrs Shillitoe's charges, knew her alphabet and could count a little, but reading was an art yet to be acquired; however, some teacher would read the missive and Margaret would know that she was not forgotten. "Darling childe, I hope you are hapy and setling down now what name did you give yore doll, it is cold weather here Rap up well when you go out . . ."

For Daisy herself writing was an exercise in concentration and she looked up with a little frown of annoyance at the interruption.

"I'm writing to that little orphan girl. She goes to school the day after tomorrow. I don't quite know how long a letter takes to get to Manchester, but I want to be on the safe side."

"You have ample time. I've been wondering why you did not have her here for Christmas."

"Charles is rather too old to appreciate young company."

"I should have thought her resemblance to you would have endeared her to him."

"He has never seen her." That was the pity of it. Daisy was convinced that if he could once bring himself to meet Margaret face to face, he would succumb to her charm and that would have been a happy-ever-after ending to the troubled story.

"He knows of her existence?"

"Of course. She is — what exactly is the word? — his protegée as well as Mrs Paske's and mine. He made himself responsible for her maintenance."

"Indeed, how very generous! One would hardly have credited him . . ."

Frankly she did not believe it. She remembered Margate.

"I must remember to tell him what a lovely little girl she is, and with such charming manners."

"Frances, I'd sooner you didn't mention her. I've learned not to. It upsets him and even Doctor

McGibbon now admits that any kind of upset makes his gout worse."

Mrs Hamilton-Hope gave a little laugh, derisive rather than amused.

"How very curious! Does it embarrass him to have his charity acknowledged?"

"It isn't that. I think that the child is connected with something . . . in the past . . . Something he doesn't like to be reminded of."

Your past you mean, my dear!

"I suppose men must have their little foibles. I must say his temper has not improved since we were all at Margate."

"He has suffered almost constant pain."

"I *had* hoped to be asked to stay on here. I have tried to explain my predicament to him. Being without a settled home, even temporarily, is extremely trying; especially in winter."

"Charles, couldn't Frances stay a little longer? I'm sure she would like to."

"I know; she's dropped hints like bricks. I just can't do with her. I was explicit; I invited her for Christmas and New Year. It isn't as though she had nowhere to go. Skeltons are thick on the ground. I never liked her, and now she makes me feel uneasy. I don't know why. I once knew a man who felt uneasy if a cat was in the room, even out of sight."

"Then, Hebe dear, can you help me? I can't very well go to a house still in the grip of influenza. But I could go to a hotel nearby and wait. Or perhaps I might venture to Westmorland after all. In either case, I need fifty pounds. As a loan, of course. Can you oblige me?"

"I think so. Oh, yes. At least I know where I can get it."

Daisy's witlessness about money, rooted in the years when she had none, or had a shilling and felt rich, had not vanished during the years of plenty. She was still improvident. Sir Charles was generous, but money simply slipped through her fingers. Mrs Paske was different, a saver, aware even on the sunniest financial day of a rainy day looming.

"Martha dear, could you possibly lend me thirty pounds? I had my allowance and my Christmas money, but I sent a lot home — and some presents. And I bought Margaret a fur coat. I've gone through all my reticules and pockets and drawers and the most I can round up is twenty pounds. She needs fifty."

"Blackmail, no less! What is she holding over you?"

"Oh, I don't know exactly. I did ask her, please not to talk about Margaret, not to say we met in Hawksley's. I know what he would say — that I should have taken her to some humble place where people like Frances don't go. Maybe I should have done, but it was such a treat for her, poor little thing, and then we were taken to her very table. And she will harp on the resemblance . . . I'm so afraid she might go and say something to upset him."

"Let her try! Hebe dear, once you give in, fifty pounds today will be a hundred next time. You take my advice, give her nothing. Tell her to do her worst and be off. And don't forget all the things she has borrowed."

"Oh, Martha, I can't . . . I feel that if I don't oblige her she'll go and *talk*, making a mystery of it. I know she thinks Margaret is mine. I mean would anybody just interested in an orphan buy her a *fur* coat? And somehow or other it'll get back to Charles and . . . Oh, it's all so hateful! She actually asked me why Margaret wasn't here for Christmas."

"And for that pretty behaviour you propose to lend her money! You think again. I did advise you at the very beginning to let the child go, not to see her. You'd have spared yourself a lot of misery. Now I advise you again. Don't let yourself be blackmailed."

"Then she'll talk."

"What guarantee have you that she won't talk even if you give her money?"

Daisy thought that over for a moment and then made one of her astonishingly shrewd statements.

"She won't, if, as you say, she intends to borrow again. Please, Martha, lend me the money."

"Then you'll fasten a clog on your foot that'll stay there as long as he lives."

"While he lives I can pay for peace. It's his money really, isn't it? And by God, once he's . . . I mean the day will come when I can take that child by the hand and say, 'This is my daughter; isn't she beautiful?' I will, too!"

Very unwillingly, because she thought it bad policy, not because she grudged Hebe anything, since she had much the same feeling for her as Hebe had for

Margaret, Mrs Paske lent thirty pounds, in her eyes a large sum. It had taken time and ingenuity to scrape together, for it had never occurred to Sir Charles to offer Mrs Paske a regular wage. She lived well, received presents, was one of the family, had anything she cared to ask for, but he regarded her as a kind of mother-in-law. The seventy or so pounds which Mrs Paske had accumulated had come partly from gifts and partly from thrifty housekeeping. She hardly knew why she was saving. It was something she had always wanted to do and never managed, Jim and his family needing so much. But the instinct held, even now, when there seemed no need for it, for Sir Charles would surely leave Wichfield to Hebe, and money to keep it up.

Mrs Hamilton-Hope, having found her milch cow, went jauntily off to Bath where apartments were cheap in dead winter. She took with her the real ermine wrap and the diamond knot brooch and a few other borrowed trifles. And presently Martha Paske had more to worry about than that.

CHAPTER
FOUR

Lady Fenstanton had taken to Hebe at first sight and had done a lot to smooth the way to social acceptance; now as time went on and Sir Charles became virtually housebound and less and less inclined to be sociable, her ladyship felt sorry for the poor girl, so beautiful, so talented, and leading such a dull, lonely life. Other county ladies had always regarded Daisy with some envy and it was easy enough for them to say, "No use asking the Overtons; he's past it, poor fellow, and if she came alone it would mean finding a spare man." Lady Fenstanton took the opposite line; for one thing she found spare men quite easy to provide; for another, she had herself experienced what it felt like to be married to an older, ailing man. Also she was unconventional enough not to break her heart if women outnumbered men at her table. She included Daisy in almost every party and was gratified to see, as an evening wore on, that rather wistful look of resignation give way to liveliness, an animation very slightly exaggerated. After dinner Daisy usually sang. Once at a party, which even Lady Fenstanton herself privately thought unusually heavy and stuffy, Daisy galvanised the dull company by acting as she had sometimes done at Kitty Hammond's.

310

"Come on! Everybody sing! What song do we all know? *Rule Britannia!* Let yourselves go!"

The gentlemen responded first, and then the tightly laced, prim-faced ladies, seeing Lady Fenstanton singing, off-key but heartily, joined in. And it didn't stop with *Rule Britannia.* The spirit of mischief took hold of Daisy and she led them through several old country songs — near bawdy and all.

Afterwards she apologised. "I'm afraid I was a little drunk."

"My dear, you converted a deadly dull party into a riot. I can't thank you enough."

Sometimes at the Castle — nowhere else — Daisy acted as well. Not too often for, as Lady Fenstanton said, nothing which could be counted upon constituted a treat. There was a kind of tacit understanding between them that such performances were reserved for Wichfield on the increasingly rare occasions when Sir Charles felt well enough to entertain a few people, and for the Castle.

Daisy's fear that on the evening of the sing-song she had been slightly drunk had been justifiable. For the emptiness of her life after Margaret's departure to Manchester she had found solace, just a slight blurring of the sense of loss, in two or three glasses of wine instead of the usual one, in a little brandy now and then, gradually becoming more now than then. Mrs Paske, ever observant, said alcohol made people fat, which was so ridiculous as to be amusing. Daisy's waist was still eighteen inches, a fraction under. Her hands, held up against light, were translucent.

One of her loves had vanished into nowhere — gone abroad; the other was no farther away than Manchester and Daisy wanted to go there, but Sir Charles and Mrs Paske and a faceless person, Florence Reade, made a powerful anti-visit combination. "If you go once, she'll expect you again and again and suffer disappointment," Sir Charles said. "And there is this business of travelling alone on the railway. A woman in your position could not possibly travel alone, and whom could you take, safely, except Martha? And I need her here."

Mrs Paske said, "A clean break is the kindest way. I said so from the first, but you would not listen. Now it's come and you should leave it alone."

Miss Florence Reade, who acted as secretary, read Daisy's ill-spelt letters and came to the logical conclusion; Mrs Johnson, c/o Lady Overton, Wichfield Place, Surrey, was clearly the mother of this exceptionally lovely child. Housekeeper? Cook? Seduced perhaps by the master or the son of the house? In perfect copperplate hand she wrote that Margaret had settled down and seemed to be happy. "It would be inadvisable for you to write often. Once a child is here the less she is reminded of the past, the better . . ."

"Hebe dear," Lady Fenstanton said on a day in April when Margaret had been gone for fourteen months, "I am planning a colossal party to celebrate three things. Freddie's birthday, his twenty-fourth and it could be his engagement party, too . . . And the Queen's birthday,

312

that is on the twenty-fourth. And I really must do something about Hugo."

"Who's he?"

"A cousin of sorts. In fact, if I hadn't produced Freddie, he'd have inherited everything — and spent it all on some madcap scheme. He's just back from the Antarctic — minus two fingers, he says. You will do a show for me, won't you?"

"For *you* I would act in a barn."

Lady Fenstanton laughed. Daisy's refusal to perform in other houses had angered hostesses and her excuse had not soothed them; only Wichfield, where Sir Charles had made the Music Room, and the Castle with its Great Hall were suitable. Mrs Ackroyd had said tartly that this was palpable nonsense; anyone who wished to act could act anywhere, even in a barn.

They put their heads together to devise a truly spectacular show. Lady Fentanton had heard about islands where girls wore skirts of grass and wreaths of flowers about their necks; Daisy, once she knew a little about Antarctica, could see herself as a Snowmaiden — a compliment to Captain Hugo Stirling and the expedition which had cost him a small fortune.

The irony was that she dreaded meeting him. She always hated any deformity or mutilation; the idea of shaking a hand lacking two fingers appalled her . . . And then . . .

"Hebe dear, Captain Stirling. Hugo, my dearest if not nearest neighbour, Lady Overton."

And if he had had an arm missing, or a wooden leg, it would have been all the same. Hand met hand, eye

313

met eye and there was an explosion. Silent, subterranean, devastating.

Hugo Stirling was forty-two. A second son, he had followed the family tradition — second sons went into the Navy. A midshipman at fifteen, he'd found the early stages of promotion easy, was Post-Captain at twenty-eight, Captain at thirty. Then his elder brother had died in a hunting accident and he had retired from the service and tried, without success, to make a poor and much neglected estate into a paying proposition. Finally he'd sold most of it, and sold it well at a time when one could hardly give away agricultural land. Birmingham was growing fast and needed room for expansion. He'd spent his money and an occasional legacy or two on what Lady Fenstanton called madcap schemes, all connected with the sea and with the heroes of his youth. Old Lord Fenstanton had left him a token legacy of a thousand pounds which had helped to finance an expedition intended to match, if not outdo, Captain Cook's exploration of Antarctica in 1772. Despite the improvements in ship-building, better knowledge of diet and medical care, and Cook's own charts as guide, nobody had yet pushed as far south. Captain Stirling had hoped to, but he had just failed. Only in one way had he bettered Cook's performance; Cook had lost only one man — an incredible record; Stirling had lost no men; only two fingers, and those his own.

In a period of relative peace — no major sea battle since Trafalgar, no land battle of consequence since Waterloo — explorers were the centre of popular attention and Hugo Stirling could have been lionised, asked to lecture, begged to write a book. In such things he had no interest. He'd gone back to Warwickshire, sold another hundred acres of land, tried and failed to make up his mind to dispose of the family house, now almost engulfed in suburban development. He hoped, during his stay at Wichmore, to cajole Lady Fenstanton or Freddie, or both, into making a loan which might well be an investment, since his next venture was to be a treasure hunt. Nobody yet had found the bulk of Henry Morgan's ill-gotten hoard.

Captain Stirling took Lady Overton in to dinner and sat beside her at the table all ashimmer with gold and silver. She saw nothing of it, could not afterwards have said who sat on her other side or directly opposite. They might have been alone on a desert island.

"Is your husband here?"

"No. He is rather old — and not in good health." She spoke jerkily, short of breath, her heart beating down to her very fingertips.

"May I see you home?" Not a request; a certainty shaped like a question.

"My carriage is here."

"Send it away. Be considerate to your coachman. Say that another carriage is going your way . . . Say anything."

"Watson would appreciate that. He also is rather old and hates late nights. Could you . . . Could you get word to him? After dinner I shall be so busy."

"What doing?"

"Wait and see." How easily the light, the butterfly touch came back. Though how she could sing, leave alone dance, with her body in such tumult and her mind in such confusion, she simply did not know.

She did it, of course, because part of her was a natural performer; she had entertained her fellow servants in kitchens, more sophisticated audiences at Kitty Hammond's; and what had her life with John Skelton been save a series of postures, attitudes adopted and held for his benefit? And her life with Sir Charles? County lady, respectable; amiable wife with only one flaw, her devotion to her child.

Curiously, making ready for this party, she'd felt old; too old for the white or blue which suited her so well, and she had chosen a dress of shot silk, like a dove's neck, grey or muted violet as the light struck; a dress for a very staid matron. Now the years fell away and she was young again. The tides of passion, abruptly dammed, diverted and then dammed again into a stagnant pool, tainted by memories and denials, suddenly burst out of the confining bounds and swept all away — even, momentarily, the child in Manchester to whom she must not write too often.

Everybody agreed that on this evening Lady Overton surpassed herself. Lord Fenstanton, whose birthday it was — and whose engagement had *not* been announced — took advantage of his position and of the occasion to kiss her, a shade too heartily for his mother's taste, and said loudly that she had made his birthday . . . Less loudly he said, "Come and drink a toast with me."

"I must change first," she said and slipped away, and she did not reappear to join the crowd in the supper room. Her absence would have troubled Lady Fenstanton, had Freddie not been there in full view. Who else was missing her ladyship neither knew nor cared.

The vehicle that waited by an unfrequented entrance was a modification of the once fashionable curricle. It was drawn by one horse, not two and had no back seat for the miniature groom called a "tiger". A one-man vehicle in which no respectable lady would have dreamed of riding unless the driver were her husband or very near relative.

Scooping her up into the narrow space beside him, Hugo said, "God! I thought you'd changed your mind."

Daisy said, short of breath again, "Those diamond icicles took some untangling. But I'm here."

"Which way?"

"Let me think. Oh, this avenue goes to the South Gate. Then left. A short stretch of road, then left again and into the woods."

He drove with his good right hand, his left, of which she had now no horror, holding her close. She could feel his heart beating as hard as her own. Two hearts that beat as one. It was true, it could happen. It was now. The wonderful thing which had always seemed to be awaiting her, which had appeared, wearing a false face, and then disappeared leaving her bereft. This time, practically swooning amongst the bluebells with their scent of honey, she said, "I always knew . . ."

"So did I — but I'd lost hope. And then there you were. A dream come true."

This, of course, amongst the bluebells, was the worst thing a woman could do. Committing adultery. A word without meaning.

It was late when she reached home, where a sleepy footman and a worried Watson were awaiting her. Carriages had been ordered for eleven, and Wichmore was only six miles' drive away; there was no fog, nothing to warrant delay. Watson had enjoyed his early night, gone to bed and then begun to fret lest he had taken his dismissal too readily. The gentleman who had told him that he could go home was a stranger; what kind of coachman had he? And what would Sir Charles have to say about such casual behaviour? Watson lighted his candle and saw that it was after one o'clock. Of course her ladyship was home now and he was worrying about nothing; but he knew he wouldn't sleep until he had made certain. He pulled on his breeches and slippers and went across the yard and around the house, to the entrance used by the family on such occasions. There was a light within and Robert waiting.

"Her ladyship is late, very late," Robert said.

"I know. I got a bit worried. But the worst I could think of was somebody's lost the way, or gone a roundabout road to drop somebody else first. Maybe I should've waited."

"You keep an eye on the door, I'll make a cup of tea."

They drank tea.

318

"Maybe I should harness up and go to look."

"Can't see what good you could do. Which way would you go? Main road or through the woods?"

"Nobody but a fool would take the wood road with a *carriage* and after dark at that. You can hardly squeeze through in daylight . . ." Watson looked even more worried. "There's a lot of fools about."

Eventually wheels, hoofbeats.

"That's no carriage. That's a gig!" Watson said. His fear that something had happened was intensified. Lady Overton, in full dinner dress, being brought home in a gig!

Robert swung open the door and Daisy stepped in, bringing with her the scent of the night, of green things, of flowers. She stood, momentarily blinded by the light; distended pupils made her eyes look black in her paper-white face.

"I'm late."

"My lady, what happened? Not . . . not an accident?"

"What a worrier you are! No, no accident. Just a slight . . . confusion. The party went on and on. But Captain Stirling saw me safely home."

It was bliss just to say his name, even if it were only to two servants, one worried, one resentful.

CHAPTER
FIVE

He'd said, "I must see you tomorrow."

"Of course. Come to lunch."

The invitation was easily explained.

"Charles, I asked Captain Stirling to lunch; I knew you would enjoy his company. He's just back from Antarctica."

"Stirling? Stirling. Oh yes, of course. Second cousin of old Hector's, looked like being the heir at one time . . . That was thoughtful of you, my dear. I remember reading something in *The Times*, and in Salcombe's *Observer*, of course. I hope you didn't invite a whole gaggle of folk."

"Indeed I did not. Conversation is impossible with more than four at table. I must talk to Martha about food. I understand that they lived for months on hard biscuit and salted stuff."

"Until McGibbon changed his mind, I lived on worse. Sheer pap. I still hold that it undermined my constitution. And in the end he admitted it. He said that if diet would cure gout I should have been cured."

That was how talk at Wichfield tended to go these days, back to the gout!

Mrs Paske, less self-concerned, less inward-looking, sensed something immediately. She had seen Hebe in much this state before. Loving Hebe, as she undoubtedly did, was a self-denying business, since Hebe was always in love with somebody else; with that rascal John Skelton, with the child, and then with melancholy itself, never mentioning Skelton, and speaking of Margaret almost as though she were dead. Mrs Paske knew nothing of poetry, but, inspired by love, she could think in poetical imagery — Hebe was like a lamp, the light within it almost extinguished by a cruel draught, then what was left of it gradually dying out for lack of fuel, now suddenly refuelled, burnished and dazzlingly bright.

"And who's Captain Stirling?" Mrs Paske asked, when informed that there would be one guest for luncheon and that it must be a very special luncheon indeed.

"Some kind of relative of the Fenstantons. He's an explorer. I thought Charles would enjoy a chat with him." It was not what she said that gave her away, it was the glow, a kind of vibration.

Neither Sir Charles, open-minded, nor Mrs Paske, already suspicious, saw anything particularly engaging in Hugo Stirling's appearance. He was tall, but too thickset to have any grace; his sandy hair, worn very short, was grizzled with grey at the temples; his eyes, blue-grey, were startlingly pale in his darkly weathered face. Sir Charles, his sore eyes seeking some family resemblance, found it in the nose — just like poor old Hector's: Mrs Paske thought that had she not known of his connections she would have applied to him that most damning of phrases — not *quite* a gentleman.

He talked well and quite modestly, but Sir Charles was past taking really wholehearted interest in outside things, however exciting. At one point he said politely, "You should write a book." He had reached the stage where he would have preferred all this in a book, he on a sofa, Hebe reading to him to spare his eyes.

"It has been suggested to me, sir; but writing is not my line. And I have so little time. I'm already preparing for what sounds like something out of a book for schoolboys, but which is actually as seaworthy as most investments."

There Sir Charles's interest dwindled to vanishing point and he began to think about his afternoon's rest, which he now took unashamedly, often helped by a dose, five drops or ten, dependent upon his condition, bringing if not actual sleep, a gentle lulling, a surcease of pain.

". . . away for about two years."

Daisy's insides, heart, lungs, stomach, suffered a fall. With her usual mental myopism she had not looked beyond today — this afternoon to be precise. Her fork, laden with one of cook's most special concoctions, went back to her plate. She couldn't swallow and she mustn't speak.

It was left for Mrs Paske to fill the silence.

"Two years! And what does your family think, Captain Stirling, of yet another long absence?"

"My family, ma'am? Apart from those over at Wichmore, I have none. I have a wife. She lives in

322

Jamaica. Fourteen, fifteen, years ago she tried England, but her health was too delicate for the climate. Also, being accustomed to slave labour, she thought English servants uncouth and uncivil."

"You live apart?"

"How else? She is happy where she is and I . . . I'm happy anywhere. It is a workable arrangement."

There, you see, my dearest, my darling, my more-to-me-than-daughter; there is no future in this, even if poor Sir Charles dropped dead tomorrow. As he well might. And *I* was the one who got that piece of information out of him!

Exhausted by the effort to take interest, and by the need to muster his resistance to seductive talk about Henry Morgan's treasure and the possibility of a thousand per cent, or no per cent at all, Sir Charles made a move towards his siesta. Captain Stirling said, "Well, if you should think better of having a hand in this wild-goose chase, let me know, sir."

"I shan't. But I wish you good hunting. My dear, I leave our guest in your hands . . ." With a guest of another kind he might have suggested some afternoon's entertainment — a ride round the estate, a visit to the Home Farm, a model place; but to this man, to whom the Antarctic was a playground and the South Seas a garden, Wichfield had nothing to offer.

Sir Charles shuffled away, to the rest, the partial oblivion, the ante-room of death. And he felt slightly querulous because Martha, always so attentive, seemed to hover over the coffee cups. A footman was good enough to lean upon, but it was Martha who measured out the doses. He called her, rather sharply, and all she had time to hear was Captain Stirling saying that now that he was here he would like to see the remains of the lost village.

"As you have probably gathered, Lady Overton, I'm a dedicated romantic. My aunt mentioned some ruins. A church old when the Castle was built. I should like to see it."

"Actually there is very little to see, Captain Stirling. I felt somewhat romantic about a lost village when I first came here. But of course, if you wish to see a few humps in a sheep-run and a bit of wall, with weeds and trees . . . I will gladly show it to you. Rather too far to walk on such a warm afternoon. We'll ride. I'll change." Daisy sounded very prim and proper.

The lost village was almost legendary. It and its little Saxon church had been deserted before the Norman Conquest. What had been hovels or houses had long been, as Daisy said, mere humps in the ground which had made ploughing difficult. So it was a natural sheep-run. Sheep, unlike goats, did not nibble at self-sown trees, so the woods had encroached again over the years; only a bit of rough but immensely sturdy wall, once the East end of the church, had survived, and on a stone plinth a Celtic cross, much weathered.

It was a remote and lonely place, not even used for sheep any longer. Sir Charles's immediate predecessor had abandoned sheep when imports of wool from Australia had made sheep-keeping uneconomic and the old man who had been his shepherd for fifty years died. Nobody came forward to fill his place, for the lost village was known to be haunted; even the tough old shepherd admitted that he had heard chanting and seen lights move about the altar.

Last night they had bedded amongst bluebells and the fronds of young bracken; today thymey grass was their bed.

Except for murmured endearments, they spoke very little. No words were necessary. It was Daisy's first experience of passion meeting equal passion. She had loved John Skelton far more than he had loved her; Sir Charles had been fond, in his way ardent, but she had merely tolerated his embraces. Now this! Wonderful beyond all imagination and doomed to end so soon.

"I suppose you *must* go," Daisy said when they lay, utterly spent at last.

He was not a man given to serious thought, or, where people were concerned, deep feeling. Easy come, easy go, had been his rule with love as well as money, but for him, too, this meeting had been cataclysmic.

"I lay awake last night — what was left of it, thinking. God, how I've wasted my life! And my substance. But then, how could I know?"

"That we'd meet?"

"That you existed."

"I feel the same. If only I'd known, oh, I would have done so different! But then, if I had, we'd never have met. Isn't life a muddle?" She saw her own past, unrolling like one of Charles's maps, no step in the progress ever consciously planned; chosen by Lady Langton as a suitable nursemaid for Mrs Westcott; sacked; ending at Kitty's; meeting John, loving John —

but what a tepid, lopsided love that now seemed — Sir Charles. Step by step, each seeming inevitable, leading somewhere, and ending in a muddle.

Hugo Stirling had had more control over his life; he'd played an active not a passive role — and ended in the same kind of muddle. Married to a pretty, petulant Creole, and though she had virtually deserted him, he still supported her; Eugénie's income from the settlement he'd made, four hundred pounds a year which made her a rich woman in Jamaica where prices were low, had taken eight thousand pounds to secure. Even now he did not grudge it; a man should provide for his wife and he had loved her — once. He'd loved other women — the silly old saying about a sailor having a lover in every port was not so far off beam.

But nothing like this.

For the hundredth time in less than twenty-four hours he reckoned his assets. *The Mermaid*, now being repaired and refitted at Plymouth, antiquated by any standard, and not the kind of craft in demand nowadays; a crumbling old house and about a hundred acres of land, let off to a tenant farmer. Some value there; building land fetched about five pounds an acre, but how long would that last? He had one skill, he could sail anything that would float, but there were scores like him, and if he hired himself and *The Mermaid* into slavery, carrying coal, carrying cattle, what a life for Hebe! Though a practised seducer, he had never actually stolen another man's wife, and he felt that if he asked a woman to abscond with him, he should at least be able to offer as much comfort as she was leaving. The more so because he could not offer honourable marriage. Eugénie refused to live in England, but she was a pious Catholic who would never divorce him, and the idea of divorcing her had not occurred to him until this moment. Did a desertion, fifteen years old and agreed to, condoned and subsidised, constitute what was known as "grounds"? Eugénie's father had been reckoned the cleverest lawyer in Jamaica, probably dead now, but her brother . . . Oh, there was no end to it!

"Look," he said at last, "I *must* make this last throw. It's *not* a wild-goose chase or something out of a tale for schoolboys. I'm not operating on some old chart produced by an old sailor on his deathbed. Nothing like that; just cool, logical deduction, but of course an element of risk . . . Darling, I said two years. I'll do it in one if I break my neck. If I'm right, and I *know* I am, I'll be the richest man since Croesus. If not, well we'd still have a roof. I'd breed pheasants or pigs."

She put her hand lightly on his mouth and said, as to a child, "Sh! Let's not spoil now with talk about the future. We may not have any."

He said, "What do you mean?" but was not interested in the answer; for at the touch desire leaped up again.

Spent once more, he said, "I have to go to London tomorrow. Make some excuse to come. We could have a night together."

Dizzying prospect!

"I can't. He hates me to be away. In the past, when I had a real errand there, he always made a fuss."

"Worth a little fuss. Or don't you think so?" His voice was heavy with suggestiveness.

"I'll try, darling. I'll try." She was incapable of thinking clearly, and merely had a vague hope that Martha would help her. True, Martha had not seemed to like Hugo much, but once she understood . . . Martha fussed and scolded, but she had never yet failed in an emergency.

He was planning. His knowledge of London was not very up-to-date, but in the past he had known hotels more renowned for their discretion than any other quality, and he had used houses of assignation — Kitty Hammond's among them. But there must be nothing sordid about this. He'd find something.

"Where do you leave your carriage when you go to London?"

"At the White Hart in Piccadilly."

"Could you be there by twelve?"

"*If* I can get away at all, oh, easily."

Talking about it like this made it at once seem urgently real and utterly impossible to achieve.

"I have an appointment at half-past ten. It shouldn't take more than an hour. I shan't let it, anyway. I'll be there by twelve."

"There's a little room to the left of the archway, reserved for ladies who are waiting. I'll be there." She thought of sitting among all the prim and proper ladies waiting for their carriages, or their husbands, while she waited for her lover. If . . . "Darling, I'll do my very best, but if I'm not there by twelve, don't wait and waste your time. If I'm coming at all, I shall be there by twelve." No mere accident should deter her, let a horse fall dead or a wheel drop off the carriage — she'd beg a lift.

She began to pin up her hair and hopelessness fell like a cloud.

"Darling, we'd better say goodbye now, just in case . . ."

Like all sailors, he was superstitious.

"Don't talk like that. It's unlucky. Look, it's hard on four o'clock now; in sixteen hours we'll be together."

"I shall think of you, every minute of the day and night. For the rest of my life."

"And I of you." He meant it. He'd never met, and would never meet, anyone like her, so beautiful, so passionate and, most important of all, with such a capacity for rousing passion in him.

Daisy rode home with resentment and rebellion seething in her mind. Why should she be so tied down? Other women, married women, often went to London — on harmless errands, poor things! Mrs. Salcombe patronised a dressmaker in Bond Street; Mrs Ackroyd an American dentist in Wimpole Street. Or they just went shopping, and attended exhibitions, no questions asked. And here was she restricted, largely because Sir Charles was so narrow-minded and so *local*. He liked Daisy to give her custom to the dressmaker in Barsham, and if she had ever needed a dentist — which, thank God, so far she had not, he would have insisted that Mr Bates was good enough.

CHAPTER
SIX

Martha was completely unhelpful — and a bit coarse with it.

"If you think I'm going to help you on the road to ruin, you're wrong. Just for once, Hebe, look ahead. Suppose you had another baby — with Charles in the state he is. Think of the scandal . . . All right, you're in love! So you were with Mr Skelton, and much good that did you. Dearie, this time wait."

"He's going to be away for a year and all I ask is this one night."

"What's a year, at your age? He's getting on, of course; old enough to know better, if you ask me, but he's hale and hearty. He'll last a year. And if he's serious he'll do something about that wife of his. God bless my soul, I knew a man whose wife just took off, back to her parents, and he divorced her. It took a bit of time, but he did it. Be guided by me, this time wait and see which way the cat jumps. Charles can't be long for this world."

"I don't want him dead. Poor old man. I just want to be in London, free, for a day and a night. Is that so much to ask?"

"Like a cat out on the tiles! I'm having nothing to do with it."

"All right. I shall go all the same! If Charles finds out and turns nasty, I'll go away for ever."

They had dinner at a table set up in the library to spare Sir Charles the exertion of going to the dining-room twice in one day. It was a dismal meal, despite Sir Charles's efforts to make conversation, mainly about their lunch-time guest and mocking. "He got nothing out of me and I doubt very much if he did better at Wichmore. Young Fenstanton is a bit of a fool but his mother has her head screwed on properly." Then, after a little thought, "Young men cook up these madcap schemes. Not that he's so young. It may surprise you both, but I was a bit silly once. I wanted to be an archaeologist."

Who cared?

Mrs Paske said, "Charles, I must ask you a question; and please answer frankly. Which of us, me or Hebe, could you better dispense with for twenty-four hours?"

What a question!

"I need you both. What are you talking about?"

"My poor brother. It's all rather complicated." More than rather, very complicated. An accident that wasn't Jim's fault, but he was threatened with dismissal, and not only the loss of his job, but of his home. There was just a chance, however, Jim's employer being only a tenant and the *real* landlord seemingly willing to put in a word, if properly approached.

"Jim's such a bad hand with a pen. And worse when it comes to talking — all stammer and stutter. He really does need somebody to put his case."

Sir Charles, confused, as he was intended to be, tried to cut through the tangle with a cogent question.

"But why, for God's sake, Martha, a day and a night? The whole thing could be settled in an hour."

Considering Jim's unhandiness with the pen he had conveyed an astonishing amount of information. The gentleman who might be disposed to speak up for him was a racing man and never available until very late in the evening. Eventually Martha repeated her question.

"Personally I don't see what good either of you could do, but . . ." He refrained from saying that Martha was now essential to his comfort while Hebe was something pretty to look at. "Hebe might make the better advocate, being unrelated."

"And a title counts, too." Mrs Paske said with satisfaction.

"Martha, you were marvellous! How can I ever thank you? What made you change your mind?"

"I didn't. I still think it's very foolish and very wrong, but you said you'd go willy-nilly. Now you can do something to please me. You only pecked at your lunch and hardly touched your dinner. You can take a swizzled egg with a good dash of brandy in it."

Nowadays it took a little time for Sir Charles to regain full consciousness in the mornings. Robert always brought the tray of tea and drew the curtains; then

332

Martha came along to pour the tea, drink a cup with him and listen to the complaints with which the day began: his neck was stiff, his eyes hurt, his foot throbbed, he could hardly get his fingers around the handle of his cup. Martha was always soothing; he'd slept with his head awkwardly on the pillow; the light was exceptionally bright; perhaps he needed a lighter blanket; should she hold his cup for him?

This morning, however, he held back the complaints and remembered that Hebe had spoken of setting out early to avoid travelling in the heat of the day. She'd mentioned half-past eight, and it was now almost nine.

"Did Hebe get off in good time?"

Mrs Paske, speaking very quietly and looking at the communicating door, said, "She didn't go. I thought better of it. It seemed unfair to bother her with my family's troubles. And she is tired. I hope she'll sleep all morning."

Instantly something stirred in his memory, undefined as yet. Somehow connected with Hebe asleep in the daytime. He looked at Mrs Paske with suspicion; what he was trying to recall had something to do with her, too. His memory was failing but he was as reluctant to admit it as he had once been to admitting having a siesta. Often, if he waited, he could catch the elusive thing. And now he had it. Margate! Hebe pretending to sleep in the afternoon, and actually cavorting about the beach with that child. But she'd needed an alibi then; not now; he'd agreed to her going.

"It doesn't make sense," he said. Mrs Paske was accustomed to some slight incoherence in the morning and merely said, "So we must be quiet."

"Once is enough. This time I am going to see for myself. Assist me to that door."

"If you wake her, Charles, I shall be very cross." Worse than cross, furious; worse than furious, defeated. And having planned so well.

With the utmost caution she opened the door with her left hand, her right arm supporting the shuffling old man. And there Hebe was, as though posing for a picture — *A Girl Asleep.* Her right arm was thrown up beside her head, her left lay outside the covers, the hand just cupped as though holding something very precious and very fragile; her hair was tumbled in rich confusion and her face wore the look of utter peace.

"Sound asleep," Sir Charles commented. "I can't understand it."

Mrs Paske closed the door very quietly, but firmly. "Hardly to be wondered at. Up more than half the night at the Castle, entertaining yesterday. She needs rest."

"Only the young can sleep like that. I had a very bad night myself."

Back to himself; the pattern of the day resumed.

By three o'clock Mrs Paske began to be worried; she had meant only to make impossible the keeping of that dangerous appointment. Perhaps she had been over-lavish with the sedative, or, more likely — for she was an experienced woman — Daisy was unduly susceptible. Anyway, she must be roused now. She went about it gently, a little shaking, a little slapping, smelling salts, a handkerchief drenched in eau-de-cologne. Nothing at all to account for the fact that the moment consciousness returned, before she knew the time or the trick that had been played upon her, she burst into crying, really heartbreaking sobs and moans. "Everything was so beautiful," she managed to gulp. "Why must I come back?"

Mrs Paske, taking up a defensive attitude, said, "Darling, I was obliged to wake you. I was frightened. Do you know the time? It's almost half-past three. You've been asleep for sixteen hours."

"What?" Daisy sat upright in the bed. The crying ceased as though a tap had been turned off. The years of gentle, cultivated speech fell away. "Why the *hell* didn't you wake me?"

"Have I not been trying?" Martha Paske asked, her eyes and voice steady.

"With a scented handkerchief! You should have stuck a bloody pin into me! And would — if you'd been my friend. Go away! Get out of my sight! You've spoiled my life."

"You and I are not going to quarrel at this late hour. You were utterly exhausted. I doubt that a pin would have wakened you — though if I'd thought of it, I would have used it."

Daisy broke down completely. "I know. I know. Martha, I'm sorry. But if you only knew what it meant to me. Now he'll think I didn't care enough. Or daren't risk it. And I . . . I don't even know where he is."

Mrs Paske said, "There! There! We'll think of something.

She offered the bosom which had never been used for the purpose for which it was made for Daisy to cry upon. She patted and made soothing noises. She suggested staying in bed for the rest of the day. She suggested tea. Daisy accepted everything meekly. Something in her had broken, for the second time; in the same place, and difficult as the first mending up had been, this was well-nigh impossible.

As soon as she had pulled herself together, Daisy rode over to the Castle. Only Lady Fenstanton could help her now. And she could hardly ask outright. Not without making a public display of the most beautiful secret in the world. She lacked all subtlety — the kind of thing which would have guided the conversation into the desired channel; nor had she the effrontery to ask outright. So it was left for Lady Fenstanton to mention — at last, at long, long last — Hugo's name. And in an ugly context.

"I do hope, my dear, that Hugo did not coax Charles into investing in this latest madcap scheme."

Really, it was awful to have so little control of one's blood. She'd been waiting to speak his name, edging it in somewhere, calling him Captain Stirling, of course; and she'd been waiting, almost praying for Veronica to say "Hugo". Yet when she did, up the red blush came, starting, it seemed, from the heart, sweeping up to the hairline.

"Oh, no," she managed to say. "In fact he hardly mentioned it. He entertained Charles with stories of

336

past exploits." Lady Fenstanton noticed the blush and thought, Ha! but went briskly on.

"I was rather afraid, having failed with Freddie and me, he might try Charles or somebody. He's a very persuasive rogue."

"Is he a rogue?" Daisy succumbed to the human craving to talk about the beloved, but she tried to speak lightly, in a gossiping way.

"Oh, definitely," said Lady Fenstanton who had introduced the word with intent. "I don't mean that he is deliberately dishonest. I think he believes in all his wild-goose chases and I know that he is willing to waste his own money — as well as other people's. I suppose when I used the word I was thinking more about his general lack of conscience. Especially where women are concerned. He behaved disgracefully to that poor girl he married."

"Well, at least he allowed her to live where she likes."

Lady Fenstanton who had — she thought — cunningly guided the talk so that the word of warning might be issued, looked slightly surprised.

"He spoke to you about her? Most unusual! As a rule he only remembers her existence when it serves his purpose. How these things get about I simply don't know, but it is common knowledge that the old Duke of Sudbury would have divorced his wife, had Hugo been in a position to marry her. He doted upon her to such an extent he wanted her to be happy. But of course, Hugo had his alibi."

To most women this would have been very disillusioning talk, but Daisy thought, We all make mistakes; we all change: look how much in love I was with Jack Skelton: we go fumbling about in search of the real thing, and until it happens we don't really know that everything else was false. I knew as soon as I met Hugo; he knew as soon as he met me. And now, just because I over-slept and Martha didn't wake me — or wouldn't — he's gone off, thinking I didn't care, thinking I was just a young woman married to an old man, easy game, ready to flirt — more than flirt — with the first willing man but not prepared to keep a rendezvous which seemed difficult. Of all the intolerable things which had happened to her — and now, looking back, it seemed that she had met with nothing but intolerable things — this was the worst. This was the end of all. Unless . . . Call up the other thing which had been, besides beauty, bestowed upon her, the ability to strike an attitude.

"This is all very interesting," she said, "but beside the point. Did you see me go beetroot red just now when you mentioned madcap schemes? I blushed with guilt, Veronica. I've rather gone behind Charles's back. I think nobody knows now that when he was young Charles had antiquarian interests. He collected maps and charts. All kept separately in the library. Useless to him, but it did occur to me that some of them might be of use to Captain Stirling. I thought of it rather belatedly and of course I could hardly mention the matter to Charles — nobody likes to be reminded of old dreams that ended on a dusty shelf. But I thought . . . I could at least send them, couldn't I? If I knew where. And Charles need never know. To me it just seemed such a waste."

A plausible story, and made easier for Lady Fenstanton to swallow because she had always thought of Hebe Overton as being rather simple — in the nicest sense of the word; open, frank, unpretentious. She overlooked the fact that there was another Hebe, the one who took charge of the performance. Admittedly, she had noticed the blush, and for dear Hebe to go hunting on dusty shelves was a betrayal of her interest in Hugo, but then any woman of whom he took the slightest notice seemed to respond extravagantly.

"His ship is *The Mermaid* and she's somewhere in Plymouth. A package would find him. Don't expect any thanks, my dear. Hugo never writes unless he *wants* something. Now, will you stay for lunch?"

"I'd love to. But I must leave directly afterwards. Charles doesn't like me to be away too long."

Throughout the meal she was gay and seemed to be sympathetic with Veronica's main preoccupation at the moment — getting Freddie married to Geraldine Bruce: a most suitable match in every way. "His trouble is that he's been infected with these new romantic notions. He says he isn't *in love*. I simply cannot make him see that love goes over — often leaving bitterness behind because it has led two utterly incompatible people into marriage." She said a good many other things in similar strain; addressing a woman who was about to take a most desperate step, and all for love.

CHAPTER
SEVEN

Wichfield lay in its afternoon hush. The master of the house was taking his siesta and Mrs Paske, though alert, was resting with her feet up, the door between her room and Sir Charles's open, the door between his room and Daisy's closed because otherwise there would be a draught. Daisy entered her own room like a thief, packed the minimum of clothing and every jewel she could lay hands on. The really valuable things were in the safe. She stole out again, leaving a note for Martha on the dressing-table.

In the stableyard the gig she had ordered when she returned from the Castle was waiting. The man holding the horse's head was amazed to see Lady Overton carrying a valise, but it was not his place to say anything, only to hurry forward and take it. And then to remind her ladyship that this horse, the one she had chosen, was inclined to shy at steamrollers. This was the time of year for road-mending.

"Thank you, Harry. I'll keep a sharp look out." She gave him one of her wonderful smiles and he wanted to say, "Let me come and drive, in case of steamrollers." But if she'd wanted him, she'd have asked.

From his siesta Sir Charles always woke as he did in the morning, with pains, with complaining. And Mrs Paske said in the usual way, "You'll feel better when you've had a cup of tea." It was ritual now for the three of them to take tea at or around four o'clock, in Sir Charles's bedroom. It was a beautiful afternoon and after tea Mrs Paske would take a walk, leaving Hebe in charge, to read to Sir Charles, or to chatter about her morning visit to the Castle which had included lunch. After that it would be the question of whether Sir Charles felt like going down to dinner, or whether the meal should be served upstairs.

The tea-tray was brought. Mrs Paske went to the door of Hebe's room and called. Then she opened the door and saw a folded paper propped up against a cut-glass, silver-topped scent bottle.

For two days she had been feeling complacent; she had *saved* Hebe. Walking towards the dressing-table, snatching up the paper, reading the brief, the terse message: "Martha dear, I have to go. I am sory, do the best you can," she felt utterly defeated. She turned dizzy and was obliged for a moment to hold onto the dressing-table for support while the room swung round her and all her inside turned topsy-turvy. Then she steadied herself, pushed the paper — a kind of death warrant — into her pocket and went back to pour tea.

Play for time. It was the only thing to do.

"She isn't back yet," she said. "I expect Lady Fenstanton asked her to stay on."

And how long would that silly excuse hold? Oh, God, why did I ever allow myself to get mixed up in all this? What can I say? What can I do? Unless I keep very calm I shall have a stroke! Then where should we be?

Then, in the irritating way of elderly people who repeat their thoughts and their words, Sir Charles began saying that even had Hebe lunched at the Castle, she should be home now. Where was she? What could she be doing? Even if she had lunched . . . Finally, since the bad moment was inevitable, Mrs Paske said, "Charles, I have to tell you something. It may anger you, but for your own sake, I beg you not to give way to spleen. Hebe has gone to Manchester. To see Margaret. The child has been ill and Hebe has been so worried . . ."

"She didn't even say goodbye."

Mrs Paske vented some of her profound inner agitation on reproaches.

"Of course not. And if you will forgive me saying so, that is your fault. You never made allowances for maternal feeling." Mrs Paske spoke with force, for she knew about maternal feeling, however misplaced; she felt it for Hebe! And felt it still, angry as she was. My child! Right or wrong to be protected.

"How do *you* know?"

"About Margaret's illness? Oh, Hebe confided in me. I knew she wished to go, and that if she suggested it you would oppose it. So she simply went. Here is her note."

It was, fortunately, vague, ambivalent. It could be shown.

342

But how long could this alibi last? A few days? A week? A fortnight?

Mrs Paske felt very much like the little Dutch boy in the story who had plugged a hole in a dyke with his thumb, then with his hand, his arm, his whole body. And failed.

She said, "I only hope the little girl wasn't suffering from cholera, or typhoid. Both very catching."

That did divert his attention for a few minutes. He said, "I hope to God not!" But he soon reverted to his grudge. Hebe had defied him; Hebe had left without saying goodbye; Hebe had always put the child first. Remember Margate.

And when Sir Charles thought of Margate he remembered that this kind, competent woman, upon whom he now relied so much, had then conspired against him. Now he held it against her and was unusually cantankerous and hard to please, far less grateful than he had been.

Mrs Paske waited. Hebe had begged for an alibi for one night and balked of that had cried and said her whole life was ruined because now she didn't know where he was. It followed that she must have found out. How? Obviously from the Castle. No questions could be asked there for fear of starting talk. Ladies were as much given to gossip among themselves as kitchen maids. Questions could be asked in the stableyard, if one pretended to some knowledge.

"Sir Charles is not quite certain which conveyance her ladyship took."

"She took the gig, and Dodger, ma'am."

"Her ladyship was called away suddenly — to a sick relative."

It sounded all right, but there was something odd about it, when the men came to talk it over. For one thing what relatives did her ladyship have? None had ever been seen at Wichfield. And why Dodger, possibly the least reliable of all the horses and one which she had not driven before? But such questions were mild compared with the inquisition which was going on in the house.

"What about money?" Sir Charles asked. "She never had any towards the end of the month. I suppose you *lent* her some."

"I did not! I sympathised with her feelings. Any woman would. But I was not in favour of her going and exposing herself to possible infection."

"How long has the child been ill?"

"I don't know exactly. Hebe knew only four or five days ago."

"I've often thought that Hebe lacked sense. This proves it. Rushing off into the blue like this. And she couldn't reach Manchester in a day. Where would she stay at night? Imagine, Lady Overton arriving at some wayside inn, alone. Not even a maid! How much luggage did she take?"

"I don't know. You speak as though I was in connivance with her."

"It wouldn't be the first time, would it?"

Ignoring this dig, Mrs Paske said, "I can find out about the luggage."

She went into Hebe's room and pried about. Only one small valise, some underclothes — and all her pretty, not very valuable trinkets were missing.

"She took so little," she reported, "that she can only have contemplated a very short stay."

That was the one, the only hope. Hebe had pleaded for just *one* night. But then why *all* her jewellery? Mrs Paske agreed with Sir Charles about Hebe's lack of sense, but surely even she, however great her infatuation, would not contemplate eloping. And with a married man.

Sir Charles, soothed by his opiate drops, slept, but Mrs Paske lay wakeful, worrying, exhorting herself not to worry, and then worrying again.

In the morning Sir Charles started on what was to be his recurrent theme for the next few days.

"Is there a letter?"

"There could hardly be. She left only yesterday."

"She could have written from wherever she stayed the night. It shows a gross lack of consideration. She must know how worried we are."

No letter by the second post that day; none next day.

Loyally, and now despairingly holding out in her lonely stronghold, Mrs Paske said, "I expect she is very busy. A sick child needs a great deal of care." She knew now that it was not just for one night. Worry was keeping her from sleep and it was having another, most disagreeable effect, too, turning her bowels to water.

Incoming post to Wichfield was never heavy. The custom had been that letters should be laid on the hall table, and Mrs Paske, always aware that there might be one addressed to Mrs Johnson c/o Lady Overton, had usually been the first to seize upon them; but now Sir Charles, prodded by anxiety, gave orders that all letters should be brought straight to him. On the third day there was a letter addressed to Hebe, and Sir Charles, defying the unwritten rule that letters addressed to other people were sacrosanct, said, "I am going to open this!"

Mrs Paske's bowels betrayed her, making her understand why people who used euphemisms called diarrhoea "the trots". When she came back, feeling eviscerated and looking very pale, Sir Charles said, "What do you make of *this*?" It was a letter from Frances Hamilton-Hope and it varied little from those which Daisy had received in the past; never regularly but often enough to explain why Hebe was almost always short of money. Mrs Hamilton-Hope's letters always said that there was something she could do, or somewhere she could go, if only she had ten, twenty, fifty pounds, and they always contained some veiled threat in the form of reference to the child. This one was no different. Mrs Hamilton-Hope had been invited to join a party, several old friends who had taken a house in Brittany for the summer, but there was the fare, and clothes and tips to be considered and she needed at least fifty pounds and then — "I hope for her sake that that exquisite little girl grows more like her mother every day."

Compared with what was happening *now*, this was trivial. Oh, if this were all! Easy enough to say, quite accusingly, "Well, there again, Charles, you have nobody but yourself to blame. This woman found out about Margaret and since you were set on secrecy, poor Hebe has been blackmailed ever since. Purely and simply because she did not wish *you* to be upset. I advised her most strongly not to yield in the first place, but she was so considerate for you."

"And damn it all, can't you see that secrecy was necessary *for her sake*? It was *her* reputation I was trying to protect. Not mine. If I'd bred a bastard it could have cavorted about here and inherited all that is not entailed. With a woman it is different. I protected her. And how has she repaid me? Gone off, without so much as a goodbye — and with a very dodgy horse! Insufferable behaviour. *This* is nothing; let the bitch whistle for her fifty pounds." He tore the letter across and across, rather fumblingly for his fingers were very swollen and he knew that he was incapable of writing the letter he wished to write. "Look here, Martha, we must know; did she get safely to Manchester, is she well? I'm in no state to sustain such anxiety."

"Nor am I," Mrs Paske said and hastened away as another pang struck. She was literally at her wits' end. She still wished with all her heart to save Hebe from the result of her folly, but she could see no way. There was something almost uncanny in writing, at Sir Charles's dictation, a letter expressing some concern, but a good deal more peevishness, a letter which Hebe would never receive; a letter which would cause some bewilderment in Manchester, and, if somebody up there used sense, would eventually be sent back here. Night and day she racked her brain to think of some explanation, something short of the deadly truth.

Doctor McGibbon, dropping in on a routine visit, was shocked by Mrs Paske's appearance, so much so that he broke his rule about not encouraging self-pity. "You don't look very well, Mrs Paske. I think you are too much tied. I did not say anything to Sir Charles; I have no wish to distress him. I'd better have a word with Lady Overton."

"She is not here. She was called away to a sick relative." Suddenly, disconcertingly, Mrs Paske's eyes filled with tears. As Doctor McGibbon had deduced, she was near breaking point — but how near and for what reason he naturally did not know. All he could do was to prescribe a tonic for Mrs Paske and suggest the hiring of a professional nurse for Sir Charles, whose condition was deteriorating.

Five days.

Six days.

A week.

Now all hope was lost. Hebe was not back from a few nights on the tiles. The Manchester alibi would no longer hold. The moment was coming, nearer with every tick of the clock, when Mrs Paske must confess, and say, "I do not know where she is."

One old tried remedy for her physical condition was port wine and brandy in equal proportions, a remedy willingly taken by even the most abstemious person in such a state. For her it did not work as a cure for "the trots", but enough of it made her bold. There were moments when she thought, When I must tell him, I can do it; and then I shall be free. What happens after will be no concern of mine . . . I can earn a living.

CHAPTER
EIGHT

Daisy reached Plymouth late in the afternoon of the day after she left Wichfield. She had chosen her horse well and at Yeovil, where they halted for a short night, Dodger had eaten better than she had and was ready to go, the high-wheeled gig light as a toy behind him, at six in the morning. In the late afternoon, the sun still high but westering, Plymouth, approached downhill and slightly from the north-west, looked much like any market town but set in the embrace of shining water. That appearance was deceptive; as she came nearer the sea Plymouth more resembled the market in Soho, except that no one was courting custom, they were all delivering things; carts, wagons, hand barrows all laden with barrels and bales were like a tide sweeping not from sea to shore but from land to sea.

Mindful of what she owed to Dodger, Daisy found an inn which said "Good Stabling" and drove in under the archway. The ostler there immediately respected her because she obviously knew about horses; saying, "Rub him down first. Then let him drink. After that, oats. I shall be back." She gave him half a crown; sixpence was regarded as a good tip. Knowledgeable, generous, and so pretty, she had his goodwill, even when she showed herself to be ignorant in other ways. Taking her bag in her hand, she said — in Plymouth — "I am looking for a ship called *The Mermaid*. Can you direct me?" It was as though he'd gone to London — he had made one visit to the city — and asked the first person he saw for direction to a house with a given name, but no street address, no district. Plymouth docks covered an area which if less large was fully as complicated as any city. With anybody else the ostler would have been impatient but with Daisy he was kind and as helpful as he could be. Was this *Mermaid* one of Her Majesty's ships? No, it was a privately owned vessel, belonging to a Captain Stirling. Well, that did at least separate the sheep from the goats and he could tell her which way to turn at the end of the street. "And then ask." Anybody, he was sure, would be helpful to *her*.

And they were. As she drew nearer and nearer her objective, passed along as it were from hand to hand, Daisy found herself at the foot of a sloping gangway up which some barrels were being trundled and her latest guide said, "There you are, lady. That's him. Captain Stirling." He pointed to a group of men who seemed to be lowering something through a hole. "Him with the hat," her guide said. It was true that one of the men wore a crushed-looking panama hat; otherwise there was nothing to distinguish between them; shirt sleeves rolled to the elbow, trouser legs rolled to the knee, canvas shoes.

Daisy stepped aboard *The Mermaid* and almost ran across the cluttered deck. There was so much commotion, both aboard this ship and those which lay on either side of her, that her first tentative call, "Captain Stirling!" went unnoticed. Before she could speak again, more loudly, though her heart was beating so hard that she was short of breath, one of the men straightened up, rubbed his hands, turned, saw her, and tapped Hugo on the shoulder. Then Hugo turned and saw her.

She remembered the moment all her life. That look of blank dismay; of astonishment with no joy in it. It passed, and as he came quickly, in long strides, towards her, he contrived to smile, but even the smile was wrong.

"Hebe! What on earth are you doing here?"

"I had to come." She dropped her valise and held her arms as though to embrace him, but he simply took her by the wrist and pulled her past some bales and barrels, down some very steep stairs and into a little room that smelt of tar and fish. There something of the old magic revived and he did embrace her, kissing her until what remained of her breath had gone and she was as limp as a rag doll. Then she seemed to drop out of his arms and was sitting, dizzy, on a kind of shelf, fixed to the cabin wall and covered with a grey blanket. His bed?

"I couldn't get to London that day," she said as soon as she had her breath back. "It was all arranged . . . I thought Martha was my friend, but now I think she put something in the drink she made me take . . . I slept all day and I knew you'd be gone . . . Hugo, I couldn't bear it. I thought you'd think I didn't care. And, darling, I do. I do. I love you so much. I can't live without you."

352

He ignored the last words; women had said them to him before — and they'd lived.

"So you felt you must come and explain. Darling, that was sweet of you; but I understood that you might find it difficult. You said twelve, I waited till one. Then I had to get back here. There was so much to do."

"I know. Thank God there was. I was so terrified that you might be gone before I could find you."

"How did you?"

"Oh, as soon as I felt well enough — that was yesterday morning — I went to the Castle and Veronica said *The Mermaid* and Plymouth, so I took the best horse and the gig and came. Darling, be glad."

She was the prettiest, the most seductive, the most attractive woman he had ever encountered and she had managed to do what no other woman had ever done — make him look to the future. He'd actually thought, during their brief encounter, of settling down, making what remained of Amblebury and the poor old *Mermaid* commercially viable. But even then in the first great impact of lust — love — call it what one wished, he'd seen the impossibility of it and, setting out for Plymouth on the day when Hebe had not kept the rendezvous at the White Hart, he had known relief as well as disappointment. Now here she was, and though desire was lively again, so was caution.

"Are you alone?"

"Of course. I couldn't bring anybody, could I?" She pushed to the back of her mind that dismayed, unwelcoming look with which he had greeted her. It was due to surprise. "I'm here. I'm alone. I'm free."

The last word rang through the cramped space. She remembered that day when Mrs Westcott sacked her and she'd been free, with something wonderful waiting around the corner; nine years ago. Now here the wonderful thing was, within reach. She took his hand and pressed it against her face.

"Where are you staying?" He had failed to notice in the shock of seeing her there that she had had her valise in her hand.

"Staying? Nowhere. I came straight to you — as soon as I'd stabled the horse."

"And where was that?"

"Oh!" Her eyes widened. "I didn't notice. It just said 'Good Stabling', and Dodger had been so good. Awkward though. He doesn't shy only at steamrollers . . . But he ran like the wind. I could find the place again. I must, mustn't I, because I must sell him, and the gig? They should fetch something. And I brought all my jewels. Veronica said you wanted people to invest in your madcap scheme, and I can. Darling, isn't it wonderful? Just you and me together, for ever and for ever!"

"Let's get out of here," he said, and pulled her to her feet.

At the head of the steep stairs, he said, "Wait here a minute," and went and spoke to the other men. Then he turned back to her, noticed her valise near the head of the gangway and picked it up. Daisy clung to his arm.

"Where are we going?"

"To a place I know. It isn't far."

354

Planning that one glorious night in London — if she could get away — he'd wanted something not sordid and he wanted the same thing now; something which was, curiously, easier to find in Plymouth than in the centre of London because in Plymouth everything was on a smaller yet on a more strictly departmentalised scale. Any man who had been at sea for any time was woman hungry; and there were places which supplied women for those who had none of their own, and there were places which supplied everything except the woman, in surroundings which outwardly at least gave no sign of being shopworn, used, degraded. All beautifully clean and fresh; smooth, newly-laundered linen on the bed, washed chintz on the chairs; even a bowl of early roses on the table. Service discreet and quiet. Everything fully up to standard, like Wichfield, but with the great difference. Here she was with the man she loved. This was Heaven; something which Daisy's mother, so long dead, had always said came after death, if you were good . . .

He had not contradicted her when she said for ever and for ever; he still loved her, she was certain of that; such supreme ecstasy in the act of love-making could only be achieved when two people felt the same passion. She had temporarily forgotten that look of dismay. The shock came when they had almost finished supper.

"How did you manage to get away?"

"I just came."

"Did you give no excuse?"

"No. I scribbled a note to Martha, saying that I must go. She would understand."

"Then what will you say when you go back?"

Her eyes widened and darkened with shock. "But, darling, I shall never go back. I've come to be with you — always."

There was a little silence. Then he said, "Darling, that is impossible. Where I'm going, no woman . . ." The rest was a jumble; he spoke of dangers, of dreadful diseases, rough seas, jungles, swamps.

"I don't care. Hugo, I *don't care*. If I could die in your arms I'd die now and be content." It was the kind of thing women said in the heat of passion. It usually didn't mean much.

"Listen, you must be reasonable. Of *course*, I want you with me, but one woman among the men I've managed to scratch together; desperados one and all, there'd be trouble in no time. There's barely one who wouldn't slit my throat for . . . a moment's gratification."

"I could cut off my hair and be one of your crew."

He said, "Oh, for God's sake, Hebe. Let's not talk romantic nonsense. And don't cry. I simply can't stand it. We've got to think, and think hard."

That kind of thought, an assessment of possibilities, a making of plans for the immediate future, had always been beyond her range. She'd run away on impulse, and there could be no going back.

He was sure that her husband would forgive her. An old, infirm man married to such a lovely girl must

356

surely understand and be lenient. Be only too glad to see her back.

"Charles isn't like that. Once before I did something — oh, such a silly little thing compared with this, and he sulked for ages. In fact I believe he never felt quite the same towards me. I can't go back. And anyway I wouldn't want to. I don't want to go back and act sorry and be in disgrace, when all I've done is follow my heart."

Spoken with real emotion the most trite phrases sounded brand new. In fact, this scene, familiar in essence though new in circumstance, cut home, and when Daisy said, "The last thing I wanted to do was be a bother. I thought you'd be *glad*," he felt as he had not felt since, aged fifteen and trying hard to be brave, he had seen his mother's coffin lowered into the grave.

At the end of it all he said, "Look. It's only for a year, Hebe. Less, if we're lucky. And if you're absolutely determined not to go back to Wichfield, you can go and wait for me at Amblebury."

"Where's that?"

"My family home — what remains of it. On the outskirts of Birmingham." And as soon as he'd said it, he regretted it, remembering how comfortable, how luxurious, even, her home at Wichfield was. God, what had he done to her? To the woman who, of all his many women, had come nearest to arousing love — as opposed to lust — in him. Later on, thinking the whole thing over, he was inclined to blame his age — getting sentimental in his middle years.

CHAPTER
NINE

At Wichfield, so comfortable, so luxurious, every hour worsened the situation. Uncertainty and agitation aggravated Sir Charles's gout, and Mrs Paske's endurance broke when the letter which he had forced her to write was returned, unopened, from Manchester. Miss Florence Reade had remembered the connection between Lady Overton and the lady who called herself Mrs Johnson.

With the letter in his hand, his eyes mere slits between their swollen lids, but glittering with suspicion and malice, Sir Charles said, "And now suppose we have the truth."

Nine days now; and confession was a relief. After this, no more worry. A swingeing good dose of the port wine and brandy and Mrs Paske could go to bed and sleep the clock round.

There was no way of breaking such news kindly; she could only beg for some understanding on his part. "She's still so young, Sir Charles . . ." They had been on Christian name terms for some years, but this was no time for familiarity. "She has such an impulsive nature. She knows so little of the world. She doesn't understand the seriousness of such an action."

358

He sat still, an old man carved in grey stone, saying nothing. Mrs Paske babbled on, loyal, even in this extremity, saying things certain to give offence. "She hasn't had much of a life, you know; not even her child to love. And she's so warm-hearted. She acted on impulse. By this time she's sorry, I'm sure . . ."

This was the thing which all old men, more particularly those married to a very attractive younger woman, most dreaded. Everybody would snigger and say: "Well, what else did he expect?" And when he thought of all he had done for Hebe! No, he must not think of that. Anger simply impaired one's judgement.

When he spoke, Mrs Paske believed that some of her pleading had reached him.

"She must be brought back. And *you* must do it."

"But . . . But I don't know where she is. I'm sure she'll come home of her own accord. She's silly, but she'll soon see through *him*."

"Ring the bell," he said. She did so and it was promptly answered.

"Tell Watson to have the carriage ready immediately." For a moment Mrs Paske thought that what she had told him had deranged him. It was months since he had ventured out of doors. His next words, however, showed sound sense.

"You," he said, "will compose yourself and dress for making a call. You will go to the Castle and say this: Sir Charles was much interested in something which Captain Stirling said the other day, and after thinking it over, is very anxious to get in touch with him. Should Lady Fenstanton ask after Hebe say that she is in

359

Manchester, with a sick relative. Get all the information you can and come away quickly. We have no time to waste."

Mrs Paske thought that he had taken it very well, shared her anxiety for Hebe, wanted her back. He would be disagreeable — as he had been after the trouble at Margate — but in the end ready to forgive. She felt that she had argued well. And her errand to the Castle was a perfectly easy, ordinary one.

She would have thought differently had she heard Sir Charles's brief talk with Mrs Salcombe, the wife of the proprietor of the *Morning Observer* who was making a round of morning calls. Sir Charles said, over the madeira and the biscuits of the same name, "I am rather worried. My wife was called away suddenly to a sick relative in Manchester. Some kind of low fever. And Doctor McGibbon once told me — in an unguarded moment — that a prolonged low fever could damage the brain."

That was the revenge he had planned, sitting there like a stone statue while Martha argued Hebe's case. Providentially, or so it seemed now, he knew more than most ordinary men did about a private asylum, not far from Tenterden. One of his great aunts, palpably mad, had lived there, a lingering death-in-life, for twenty years. It was a clean place, very different from the workhouse departments which housed poor idiots and lunatics. And if he could just get his hands once more on Hebe, to that place she would be consigned; and no matter how often she said that she was Lady Overton and absolutely of sound mind, nobody would take any notice; for there were people there who claimed that they were Napoleon, or Moses, or Christ, or that they had invented a flying machine or found the elixir of eternal youth. Once inside that place what they said counted for nothing.

Lady Fenstanton spared half a thought to the fact that Hugo must have made an impression at Wichfield; first there was Hebe wishing to help him with maps and papers, now Sir Charles was showing interest. But it was only half a thought, for she herself was just about to leave for her town house in Portman Square and was glad that Mrs Paske did not linger. She gave the name of the ship, and of the port, just as she had done to Hebe. She did not think of mentioning Amblebury; it was so long since Hugo had lived there for any length of time that she never thought of it as his home.

Sir Charles had acted on the assumption that Mrs Paske would return with the required information. He'd sent for Harry and told him that he must be prepared to drive Mrs Paske to wherever she wanted to go — not in the carriage, but in the dogcart: and that he might have to be away for a night or even two.

"Is it Manchester, sir?" Somehow word had got round that her ladyship had gone there, and Harry, always eager for a new experience, was delighted by the prospect. Pity about Dodger, there wasn't a horse in the stable to match him for speed.

"Mrs Paske will give you directions," Sir Charles said. He then ordered Daisy's maid to pack an overnight bag for Mrs Paske. The girl, who was fond of

Daisy, put her hand to her mouth. "Is it her ladyship, sir?"

"We know little as yet."

Awaiting Mrs Paske's return, Sir Charles thought of an argument which should carry weight if Hebe showed reluctance to return. He produced it when she hurried in.

"Tell her to think of the child. Unless she is amenable I shall instantly withdraw my support; and unless Captain Stirling is willing to shoulder the responsibility — which I very much doubt — it will be the poorhouse."

Mrs Paske was still suffering from the effects of insomnia but the other symptom of anxiety had completely vanished. And although Sir Charles's expression was still stern and his voice chilly, his obvious desire to have Hebe back as soon as possible was comforting. None of the she-shall-never-darken-my-doors-again which Mrs Paske had so much dreaded. Borne up by hope, feeling that now the worst was over, Mrs Paske faced the daunting task of finding and persuading Hebe with confidence.

But by the time Mrs Paske reached Plymouth, *The Mermaid* was already four days out to sea and Daisy had reached Amblebury.

PART FOUR

CHAPTER
ONE

The old house had once stood back from the world, surrounded by its park and reached through a long avenue of elms; a few had been retained to justify the calling of the street of just-detached houses Elm Avenue. The builder who had erected his houses in the immediate vicinity of the big house had built for what he thought of as superior people — not quite in the carriage class, but superior. They had not exactly relished the fact that other parts of the estate had sprouted out with vastly inferior dwellings, not the notorious back-to-back houses, but not far removed, long terraces — terraces were cheap to build since one dividing wall served for two houses. Most resented of all was the retention of the land immediately surrounding the big house as a kind of farm. When the wind blew from the south, as it tended to do in summer when the superior people liked to sit out in their gardens, there was often a whiff of piggeries, of manure, of turnip tops, and the outside leaves of cabbages which Mr Wheeler had cut off and left to rot before taking the cabbages into market. The whole thing was, as one Avenue dweller had expressed it, so out of place; farms, small-holdings, market gardens — and Mr Wheeler's activities covered all three activities — should be in the wide, open country, not channelled and funnelled in Elm Avenue. And it was not only smells; sounds carried too; Mr Wheeler's cows lowed and his cocks crowed, his five or six sheep bleated; and every morning, every morning, some of his many children went out pushing handcarts laden with produce, waking all good citizens too early. Then presently there was the wagon, iron-wheeled and drawn by a heavy, clop-clopping horse, driven by Mr Wheeler himself, taking stuff into the market. Nothing could be done about it because Mr Wheeler was, in addition to all his other activities, Captain Stirling's accredited agent. In Amblebury, despite all the changes, Stirling was still a name to conjure with, and there was some curious and most unfair thing known as right-of-way, which Captain Stirling had reserved to himself. "You get my back up," Mr Wheeler had once said to a complaining householder, "and I'll shut them gates. So think on!" Investigation had proved the man right. Captain Stirling had sold land on both sides of the Avenue, but not the Avenue itself, and the gates were there between massive stone pillars topped by carved owls. The gates were flung back, and their lower curlicues were deep in grass and nettles, but they could be closed, and would be if anybody annoyed Mr Wheeler, or failed to address him properly and correctly.

Daisy drove in towards the end of a beautiful day and immediately thought that she had been misdirected for the seventh or eighth time. Hugo had spoken of an old, rather dilapidated house, and here she was in a street of houses, all very spick and span. Getting into Birmingham had been relatively easy, but the city was full of people who had never heard of Amblebury. Most of them seemed slightly hostile, very different from the people of Plymouth or the people of London — almost like foreigners, in fact. She was not sufficiently self-conscious to take into consideration the change in herself. The pretty girl whom everybody was so willing to befriend in London, the pretty young woman who so little time ago had asked for direction in Plymouth had changed. But at last she had found somebody who knew where Amblebury was. He said it was a village and so it had been, not so long ago. Now it was street upon street, and although Hugo had mentioned the gateposts with the owls and she had, most miraculously, found them, it was only to find herself in another street, better than most, but still a street. In it, however, there was a woman, cutting flowers — lupins — in a little front garden and when Daisy reined in and asked direction once again, the woman said, "Oh, Mr Wheeler's place? It's straight ahead. You can't miss it."

It couldn't be missed because it was at the end of the road, a big, and as Hugo had said, a tumbledown house, staring bleakly out upon a world in which it had no place. Even the surface of the road had changed and the smooth street gave way to a rutted cart-track which led around to one side. There was no longer any approach to the front door. All that had once been a continuance of the elm avenue, a pleasure garden, a rose pergola, a maze of great antiquity and an elegant little tea-house in the so-called Chinese style had succumbed to Mr Wheeler's plough, hoe, spade. Young lettuces and radishes and carrots were growing — and growing well — up to the very walls, up to what had once been the steps of the porticoed entrance. Amblebury, once famous for its hospitality, could now be approached only from the back.

Daisy followed the rutted track. Dodger, once so lively, inclined to shy not only at steamrollers as Harry had warned her, but at a bit of blowing paper, or a perambulator, or a wheelbarrow or some washing on a line, was now subdued. Daisy had chosen the place in Plymouth which said "Good Stabling" and she had mentioned oats, but Dodger had had few oats since he had left Wichfield and his spirits had declined.

Mrs Wheeler, seeing the horse and gig come to a stop at the back door, said, "Well, here the woman is."

Mr Wheeler, intent upon his supper, surrounded by his family intent upon theirs, six of them, all shovelling food into their mouths as though somebody were intent upon snatching it from them, said, "Mind what I said, Bella. We've gotta house and feed her, but we ain't hired to wait on her. Bert, you go and put the horse in the stable. Betsy and Elsie, move along, make room for the lady on that bench. Ted, hand down another plate and give that stew a bit of a stir."

As soon as Daisy had given in and agreed to go — since she felt there was no alternative — to Amblebury, Hugo had written to Mr Wheeler, telling him that a friend, a lady, was coming to stay at Amblebury and he wanted her well looked after. The lady was to have whatever she wanted and Wheeler was to keep an account of what he spent, so that Captain Stirling could reimburse him when he returned — which he hoped would be before the end of a year. Every arrangement so far made between Captain Stirling and Mr Wheeler had been to the latter's advantage and if this one was not it would not be Mr Wheeler's fault.

Daisy entered the kitchen, too outworn by emotion and physical weariness to notice anything but the smell. All the stenches of which the people in the Avenue complained at times were concentrated here, and reinforced by the odour of dirty, sweaty clothing and stale cooking. Even to say "Good evening" and muster the ghost of a smile required an effort almost too great. The children stared and resumed feeding, less interested than pigs in a pen when a newcomer was pushed in. Mr Wheeler said, "Evening," without stirring. Mrs Wheeler, slightly more civilised, got wearily to her feet, said, "Set there," indicating the space on a bench, went to the stove and dished out a portion of the stew; a fair portion, one small cube of meat, a good deal of cabbage, onion and potato, a sodden dumpling, all swimming in a pale, grease-flecked liquid. Not in itself repulsive, not itself a meal which Daisy Holt, before she went into regular service, would have scorned, but in this foul-smelling place and in her state of exhaustion, quite repulsive.

"I'm sorry," she said, forcing a smile again. "I am too tired to eat. If I could go to my room; and perhaps a cup of tea?" Unconsciously she was being affected by the atmosphere, at best indifferent, at worst unfriendly, and she tilted the last words into a request, rather than

369

an order. Mrs Wheeler looked at her husband and he gave a just perceptible nod. Tea was still expensive and in the Wheeler household a rare luxury. Daisy was about to learn that the plentiful, willing service to which she had become accustomed was also a luxury, and here an unprocurable one. Nobody moved to show her to a bedroom. Mrs Wheeler made a pot of tea and took down three mugs. "Elsie, fetch some milk." She served her husband first, Daisy next and herself last. The tea, though weak, was harsh, the milk skimmed; but at least it was hot and to an extent restorative. Daisy revived sufficiently to take a look at the people into whose care Hugo had committed her.

It had sounded all right then . . .

"Wheeler," Hugo had said, "acts as caretaker to the house in exchange for the use of some land I didn't want to sell. It is a good arrangement and it's suits us both. I don't have to pay a caretaker and he doesn't have to pay rent. He's married — his wife was a cook . . . They'll look after you well. The house is a bit dilapidated — neither my father nor my brother ever had enough to spend on it . . . But the time will come . . ." Even he, vagrant-minded as he was, knew that a time came when every man must settle down and for him that time was drawing near. He'd squandered his substance on venturesome living, but, when he talked to Hebe, he was almost sure that this latest and most romantic adventure would be financially reward-ing — something he had hitherto given no thought to, though always at the back of his mind there'd been vague visions of Amblebury restored. But it was a long time since he had seen the place and he had no idea of the extent of Mr Wheeler's encroachments. Or of Mr Wheeler's ambitions, so far-flung as to be romantic. Mr Wheeler thought that given enough time, enough slave labour on the part of himself and his family, enough penny-pinching in every department of life, he could become a landowner. And the land he wanted was naturally that into which, for so many years, he had poured his sweat. He had already decided that the lady's stay at Amblebury was going to cost Captain Stirling dearly, while imposing the least possible extra work on anyone in the family.

Daisy thought Mr Wheeler a most unpleasant-looking fellow; he wore a permanent scowl between shaggy black eyebrows and his mouth was compressed into liplessness. Mrs Wheeler looked downtrodden and careworn; and the children were not like children at all. She did not intend to stay here a moment longer than necessary. One thing she was certain about was that Hugo had no idea of what the place was like — he had spoken of a garden . . . But really, she was too tired to think of anything just now. Nights of passionate love-making before Hugo sailed; nights of weeping since; a long journey and the feeling — ridiculous when examined closely — that everything was wrong, or was about to go wrong, had undermined her natural resilience. Almost her last words to Hugo had been, "You take my heart with you!" And she felt as though that had been not a mere figure of speech, but a physical fact.

"Now I must go to bed," she said.

Mrs Wheeler, who had sat down to drink her tea, rose again, with the same weary, forcing-herself-into-action look, and lighting one candle from another said, "This way." She opened a door and revealed a flight of bare wooden stairs — servants' stairs. At the top there was a passage. Mrs Wheeler turned left and through a doorway on to a wider passage, through another doorway and into a room. A big room and sweet-smelling.

Something, perhaps the tea, or being out of her husband's brooding presence, had loosened Mrs Wheeler's tongue.

"I put you in here, Mrs Johnson. It's a bit less lonely. I hope you'll be comfortable."

Daisy had almost forgotten that when her coming to Amblebury was under discussion Hugo had said that it wouldn't do to call herself Lady Overton. Charles would certainly try to trace her. And she'd thought of Margaret, and of the false name, already assumed, of the possibility of making closer contact with the child and said, all right, she'd be Mrs Johnson.

So now here she was; Mrs Johnson in a very peculiar place indeed. But she need not stay here because in her valise . . . God! Where was it?

She stood in the big room where one ordinary tallow candle lighted so small an area and she said, "I'm sorry, Mrs Wheeler. I left my valise downstairs."

Mrs Wheeler lighted the candle on the bedside table from the one she carried, and for a second the light of two candles illuminated the room. Then she went away and called from the top of the stairway, "Elsie! Elsie! Mrs Johnson left her valise down there. Bring it up."

The bed was all right, and the sheets, the pillow cover of smooth, lavender-scented linen, but it felt cold, and presently rather damp. (Upon such areas as the linen room at Amblebury Mr Wheeler had not encroached and if he had noticed that one of the many leaks which the old house suffered had been in a corner of the linen room, he would have dismissed it as not important.)

Daisy shivered for a little time and then fell asleep, slept for eight hours and woke, partially resuscitated. The curtains had not been closed overnight so the sunlight streamed in by the big window and fell across the bed and after a moment of confusion — Where am I? — she saw that she was in a pleasant room, comfortably furnished and at first glance, clean. Blue was the prevailing colour; curtains around the four-poster and at the window, carpet and upholstery were all faded, the woodwork had not been polished recently, but the whole room was in heartening contrast to the squalor of the kitchen. There were sounds of people astir, but nobody came near her. At eight o'clock she rang the bell. It was not answered. After half an hour she put on her thin silk wrapper and went down.

Mrs Wheeler was alone in the kitchen, kneading a great mass of greyish-looking dough on a floured area at one end of the kitchen table. Her sleeves were rolled up and Daisy noticed how thin her arms were between the knobbly elbows and the huge hands. Mrs Wheeler was, in fact, all out of proportion; a head too large on a stringy neck, a hollow chest, and then under the coarse sacking apron, a bulge.

She said, quite amiably, "Good morning. I hope you slept well." A merely formal courtesy, for without waiting for a reply, she went on, "The porridge is on the stove and everything else is there." She jerked her head at the dresser. "I expect you'd like some tea."

Leaving Daisy to wait upon herself, Mrs Wheeler took a knife and acting as though the dough were her sworn enemy, slashed it into lumps, hastily rounded them, stabbed each one, went to the brick oven in the wall near the stove, raked out the ashes of a faggot that had been burning in it for an hour, and put the loaves inside.

The boy who had stabled Dodger came in, a frothing milk pail in either hand. He went through to the dairy.

At Wichfield, in winter, porridge, with sugar and cream, was one of the acceptable breakfast dishes, but here, when Daisy said, "I can't find the sugar," Mrs Wheeler said, "We don't use it. There's salt somewhere."

Daisy had made the tea first, understanding why the beverage overnight had been so bad. What remained in the tin that was used as tea-caddy was mainly dust.

It seemed a little odd to offer Mrs Wheeler a cup of her own tea in her own kitchen, but Daisy did so and Mrs Wheeler, her harassed look increasing, said, "I'd like one, but I can't stop. So much to do. There's the cheeses to turn and . . ." Whatever the last word was it was lost as Mrs Wheeler went, quickly but heavily,

374

towards the dairy. Daisy tried the porridge unflavoured and then with salt which was an improvement. Quite unconsciously something inside herself was making tiny adjustments as it had done so many times before — to life in her own home without her mother; to the servants' quarters at the Hall; to Mrs Westcott's; to Kitty Hammond's; to Wichfield.

She changed her mind about leaving Amblebury immediately. She must stay at least until she had Hugo's letter. He had solemnly promised to write — from Funchal in Madeira, from the Canary Islands. Both places were on the rim of the unknown into which he was vanishing, but he said that any ship homeward bound would carry a letter and naturally he would address it to this place. Poor dear man, he couldn't possibly know what this place was like now, or he would never have sent her here. However, here she must wait at least until the letter or the letters came; and she must make herself as comfortable as possible during the waiting time. For that she needed money and although she had now nothing in coin of the realm, she had her trinkets. At that thought, the vision of Jack Skelton, long ago blurred and since her meeting with Hugo almost obliterated, cropped up. Faceless and meaningless, now, he had added to her overall knowledge of life by mentioning a pawnshop. What she must now do was to pawn — not sell — something. And to do that she must get into the centre of Birmingham again. There, once armed with money, something she had never thought about as being of paramount importance, she could shop for so many things. She needed clothes, having run away with so few; she needed proper Soo-Chung tea, and coffee and biscuits and wine. And all would be available, once she had some money. And another thought occurred to her — she could have Margaret now!

CHAPTER
TWO

Mrs Paske, with no experience in sleuth-work, but with her usual thoroughness, had combed Plymouth, beginning with the inns, ending with the boarding houses. Nobody had heard of Lady Overton or of Mrs Johnson. Nor, in any of the places at which she inquired — places where beds could be hired — had anybody heard of Captain Stirling. She could only come to the obvious conclusion — while in Plymouth he had slept aboard *The Mermaid,* Hebe had joined him there, and they'd all gone off — literally — into the blue, leaving no trace at all. And step by step, disappointment upon disappointment, rebuff after rebuff, some change took place inside her heart and her mind. From the moment of their first meeting she'd loved Hebe, and served her faithfully and well; and how had Hebe treated her? Shamefully! Confiding in her; think of the baby, smuggled out to Mrs Shillitoe; think of Margate . . . and now this. What Hebe had done for Mrs Paske could be utterly discounted and when at the end of the long, fruitless search, Mrs Paske found Harry and said, "We can go home now," it was almost as though Hebe had never existed so far as feeling was concerned. Other things were involved; self-preservation most of all.

Harry, thank God, was not inquisitive. He'd immensely enjoyed his stay in Plymouth. He'd seen the sea for the first time, talked to sailors and ostlers and grooms, eaten lobster straight from the sea. Like a horse wearing blinkers, Harry had a narrow and concentrated view, with which he was quite well pleased.

"You did not find her," Sir Charles said. Not a question, a statement.

"No." There was no other answer. "I did my best, Charles. Captain Stirling had sailed before I reached Plymouth and I fear Hebe went with him."

He was still suspicious of her, though he could not see what possible good she hoped to do herself by deceiving him. On the contrary, with Hebe gone, it would surely be to the woman's advantage to be on good terms with him. Not, he thought spitefully, that she would gain any lasting benefit.

He switched his mind to the problem which had been bothering him night and day ever since Mrs Paske had — all too late — told him the truth.

"What the devil are we to say to people?" Old as he was, infirm as he was, he still had his pride, and what he thought of as his good name, to protect.

"I have been asking myself that," Mrs Paske said. "She has left us in such a hopeless position . . . So far only you and I know the truth. She has run away, we don't know exactly where and we don't know for how long. But to say that she is dead — though to be frank she *is* dead to me, now, such behaviour has killed the affection I felt for her — could lead to difficulties later on. The man is already married. When this escapade ends . . . she . . . will . . . come . . . back."

They stared at each other in silence. Presently Sir Charles said, "Would you agree that leaving a good home where she had every consideration and running off with a married man with no roof to his head was the action of a mad woman?"

"Absolutely. She was . . . always . . . so kind, so considerate. To have done . . . this . . . Yes, she was demented."

"And such dementia can result from certain low fevers."

"That is well known."

"Very well. That is our story. She went to the bedside of a sick relative, fell ill herself, was restored to physical but not mental health and is now under restraint . . . Martha," and that was the first time he had used her Christian name since she had made her confession, "this whole affair has been a strain on me, a strain that no man in my state of health should be called upon to suffer. Help me to bed."

Bed was a refuge and he seldom left it again except to sit out for an hour in a chair by the window while the beautiful summer moved through its flowery stages. The news of what had happened to poor Lady Overton, poor Hebe, poor dear, seeped out slowly. It wasn't something to be advertised in the papers and even those faithful friends who, hearing, called to offer sympathy and commiseration were met by Mrs Paske who always said, "Please, no mention of Lady Overton; it simply upsets the poor man and does no good; ask after *his* health; be cheerful."

She could hardly say such things to Mr Copeland, Sir Charles's attorney, who came on the last day of June and had no doubt that Sir Charles was of sane mind and fully competent to make a new will, so clear and concise that it hardly took up half a page. Everything that was not entailed, Sir Charles left to George Skelton, a farmer in Lincolnshire . . .

"And now," Sir Charles said, "there is the matter of Mrs Paske. She has tended me very well, but she has been adequately rewarded . . . Perhaps a legacy, a token of regard, say a hundred pounds . . ."

Sir Charles was suffering from a common delusion, shared by many makers of wills; that the pattern thus being laid out would concern only the far future and when — if — it did eventually become actuality, he would in some way share it; see George Skelton's vast surprise and pleasure; see Mrs Paske's dismay and her realisation that she was being punished. That when this will was read he would be elsewhere, or nowhere, was almost unconceivable, one's own complete extinction being something — like infinite space and infinite time — outside the range of the ordinary human mind.

CHAPTER
THREE

Daisy did not know that away in Surrey she was being dubbed a lunatic and in effect disinherited. She was concerned with more immediate things. Fortified by porridge and bad tea she had carried what water remained in the black kettle upstairs and had a good wash. Then she had dressed, noting how even the best clothes, worn day after day, lost substance. She dived into her valise and took out a necklace of amethysts, a pretty thing, three gold links in a chain, a purple stone, three more links and another, and then a pendant, triangular, or heart-shaped, formed of slightly darker stones and some small pearls. She pushed it into her reticule and went down to the stable-yard. Dodger had, presumably, been fed and watered, but not groomed. Yesterday's sweat and dust formed a film over his should-be glimmering hide. She said what she immediately thought — "Poor old boy! We'll do better . . ." and then looked about for somebody to help with the harnessing and the hitching of the horse to the gig. A small wagon stood in the yard and as she watched Mr Wheeler came out of an adjoining stable, leading a thin horse which shared Mrs Wheeler's air of weary dispiritedness.

"Good morning, Mr Wheeler. I wonder could you help me, please. I've never harnessed a horse."

"You going into the city? Then you can give me and my stuff a lift. I ain't got a real load this morning." He pulled the gig out from the open-fronted shed and began transferring his produce; fowls ready dressed for table, eggs, baskets of prime asparagus, small young carrots, lettuces, spring onions, a basket covered with cheese-cloth. There was more than could be comfortably stowed in the gig's boot. The basket went down by the dashboard and one box on the seat. Mr Wheeler then harnessed Dodger and climbed into the driving seat. His face still wore its ill-tempered expression, but he was actually pleased; he was saving time by taking possession of the swifter vehicle and saving wear and tear on his own.

"Where'd you wanta go?" he asked as the suburbs merged into streets.

"Somewhere where I can shop."

"That'll suit me. Half of this is for the Central and half for the Regency. I'll drop you at the Central and pick you up there. How long'll you be?" For him that was actually quite a long speech and showed some rudimentary consideration for her convenience.

"I don't know. I have several purchases to make." Then it occurred to her that Mr Wheeler, who knew the city, might be helpful. "As a matter of fact, before I can buy anything, I must pawn something." She did not mind saying that for she did not value Mr Wheeler's opinion. She was surprised when he said, "Pawn?" in a slightly shocked tone.

382

"Yes, pawn. Captain Stirling . . ." And how odd it was that speaking his name, even to this surly, malodorous fellow, should be a pleasure. "Captain Stirling had so many expenses — making ready for a long voyage — and I was short of money. But I have money's worth."

"Pawnable stuff?" Mr Wheeler would never have dreamed of pawning anything for the simple reason that it was a process which plainly enriched somebody else; pawnbrokers weren't in business for the benefit of their customers. "What is it?" Daisy showed him, cupping the trinket in her hand. Neither of them had the slightest idea of its value, though Daisy knew that amethysts were only semi-precious, less valuable than diamonds or emeralds. Charles had bought her this pretty thing to go with a lilac-coloured dress. Away back, in another life.

"It'd be better to sell it," Mr Wheeler said. "Pawning is just another way of paying interest." He knew because he was the product of a Birmingham slum where women — the more respectable ones — pawned all the family's best clothes on Monday and redeemed them on Saturday — pay day — at about a hundred per cent. There'd been a woman, a good Methodist who believed in keeping the Sabbath holy; so she'd regularly pawned her iron and her sleeve board late on Saturday afternoon for sixpence, spent fourpence on food and put twopence into the collection plate on Sunday, and reclaimed the tools of her trade, paying tenpence, on Monday when the first customer of her busy week paid her for her labours in the preceding week. Mr Wheeler had never heard of the law of diminishing returns, but in practice he had seen it. He'd been lucky, he'd got away, gone to work for an uncle who hired a bit of land out at Amblebury, taken over the tenancy on his uncle's death and never looked back.

Daisy said, "I hadn't thought of selling anything. Just getting enough money to tide me over — for about a year." Unlike most people — but not all, for Hugo Stirling had convinced some — she believed that he would be back within a year and very rich.

Perhaps Sir Charles and Mrs Paske were not altogether wrong in thinking that she was demented.

Mr Wheeler said, "A year! Pawnbrokers can't wait that long! I don't know the ins and outs of the trade but if a thing ain't reclaimed, then they sell it."

"I didn't know that." She looked at the pretty thing and realised that it had no particular value to her. It belonged to the past, was directly connected with the lilac-coloured dress, not much worn, hanging in the clothes closet at Wichfield. "All right, I'll sell it. Where?"

"You'd better let me handle this," Mr Wheeler said. "I know where to go."

He would have been deeply offended had anyone called him a thief, but he knew where to go, because in any old house, inherited by members of the same family for generations and uncared for by its present owners, there were always cupboards and attics and cellars crammed with the debris of years, and amongst the rubbish hidden treasure. Soon after he was made caretaker of Amblebury and had taken up residence in

384

the house, Mr Wheeleer had come across a number of things which he was certain Captain Stirling had never seen and would never miss. A broken fan, a bent silver ladle, an odd earring in the back of a dressing-table drawer, an old belt with a silver buckle. And his taciturnity made him an expert haggler. Offered what he considered a silly price, he simply turned away, and nine times out of ten the man to whom he was trying to sell some small item would say, "Wait a minute". And up his offer.

On this morning he drove into the yard at the rear of the Central Hotel, delivered the produce, returned to the gig and found Daisy sitting where he had left her.

"You git out here. Do your shopping."

"But I can't shop until I have some money."

"All right." He dived into the pocket of his soiled, greasy breeches and pulled out a shining sovereign. "On account," he said.

They came from the same root stock, the rural poor, but they had followed different roads. To Mr Wheeler that one coin stood for a great deal and there had been a time when it would have meant almost the same to Daisy, but for her that time had passed. She had been debilitated by plenty, and looking at the sovereign she thought, not how much, but how little, it would buy. Nothing like the amount she wanted.

But it would buy some of the easement for which she craved. Wine — or better still, brandy — had helped her over several bumpy places; over losing her first love, over being deprived of her child. And she had lived, for more than a third of her life, in circumstances where alcoholic beverages were as common as water. That little glass — or two, if you liked — of sherry or madeira before lunch; white wine with fish or fowl, red wine with roast meat or game. The same at dinner. A little port wine to end off the repast. A nightcap on a specially chilly evening, or when a head cold threatened; brandy to ward off faintness; champagne on occasions.

There'd been wine at Plymouth, drunk with joy; then, after Hugo had left, brandy, enough to bring temporary oblivion from grief; but on the journey up to Birmingham she'd stayed cold sober for the simple reason that she could not afford liquor. As Sir Charles had remarked, she never had any money at the end of the month and she had refused what Hugo had offered. "You need every penny," she said; "and I have enough to get me to Birmingham." Enough, but only just, and on the last midday halt, Dodger had eaten, but she had not, which was only fair, since it was he who had to do the running.

The Central Hotel catered for many kinds of people, including ladies of the town who were properly dressed and knew the rudiments of good behaviour. It was still early in the morning and Daisy attracted no attention as she made her way to a velvet sofa under a potted palm and ordered brandy. Despite having eaten so little lately, she felt no hunger, and two brandies on a virtually empty stomach took almost instant effect. The old buoyancy did not return, but things seemed less depressing. She must stay at Amblebury until Hugo's letter arrived, but she would avoid that horrible kitchen; there were only three hundred and sixty-five days in a year — and Hugo had said that with luck he might be back earlier. She was even able to think what pleasure Mrs Wheeler would derive from a whole pound of tea!

In this lightened mood she went out into the busy street and found a grocer's shop. Tea, coffee, biscuits, rich fruit cake sold by the pound. She stopped spending only when the remains of her sovereign had run out, and naturally no such free-spending lady was expected to carry things. The grocer asked where could he send the goods, and Daisy almost made a slip. "To the Central Hotel. Lady Ov . . . Mrs Johnson's gig."

After that she walked for a little, looking in shop windows and planning what she would buy when Mr Wheeler gave her the money.

When she returned to the Central yard, he was waiting, his thunderous look darker than ever.

"Come on. Get in. I been waiting."

"I still have some purchases to make."

"That'll do another time. I gotta get back."

"Mr Wheeler, it is *my* gig."

"And my time."

Seeing no alternative, she gave in. "Let me collect what I have bought."

That consumed a little more of Mr Wheeler's precious time. There was a small room to the rear of the hotel where goods that had been delivered awaited collection. Daisy, a newcomer, did not know its whereabouts and went into the hotel to ask. Mr Wheeler, in many ways an irrational man, gave no consideration to the fact that even allowing for Mrs Johnson's delays, he would be back at work sooner than he would have been had he driven in his own wagon, and feeling aggrieved, as soon as they were out of the mainstream of traffic, took the whip from its socket and gave Dodger a stinging blow. "Giddup," he said.

In the world of which Daisy had so long been a part whips were almost decorative appurtenances; well-fed horses needed no urging, they needed controlling. Some whips were even decorated with ribbon bows and good drivers boasted that they could flick a bothersome fly from a horse's ear without the horse even knowing.

"Don't do that," Daisy said. "Dodger is nervous enough in any case."

"Too much corn." Saying that Mr Wheeler voiced not a mere prejudice, or a bit of his general parsimony, but a theory proved in practice. Thin cows gave more milk and calved more easily; thin pigs yielded more lean bacon — and nowadays all but the very poor, who in any case reared their own pigs, preferred lean to fat. It worked with people, too. Eighteen years ago, when he married Bella, she'd been plump and inclined to be argumentative. Look at her now!

Just to show this Mrs Johnson that he did not intend to be dictated to by her, he made to strike the horse again. But as Kitty Hammond had once said of Daisy Holt, "She has a *fluid* body." And a fondness for walking and for riding, and beyond all the acting and the dancing had preserved it. In a flash she leaned over, snatched the whip from his hand and sent it soaring over the hedge.

388

Mr Wheeler was annoyed, but not unduly perturbed. The whip was a very superior article, one of the best of its kind, silver-banded, and he marked where it fell. Nobody else could know, and tomorrow he would retrieve it and sell it, possibly for two pounds, to one of the men he knew who would buy anything and no questions asked. And that brought his mind back to the necklace. However, he knew the value of silence and silence was maintained between them until they turned into that disputed territory, Elm Avenue, and then she broke it.

"How much did you get for my necklace?"

"Ten pounds." That had been the dealer's starting price, and the fact that in the end he had paid fourteen was entirely due to Mr Wheeler's haggling ability; so the four pounds could be rightly regarded as well earned. Out of the corner of his eye he watched for any sign of displeasure, or approval or surprise — a guide to any similar occasion in future. Daisy's face did not change, but she said, "It cost a great deal more, I'm sure."

"New."

Mrs Wheeler, who had worked in the dairy during Daisy's absence, was back in the kitchen preparing the evening's stew. She viewed the groceries with concern rather than pleasure.

"Did Mr Wheeler buy all *that*?"

"No. I did."

"That ain't quite right. We're supposed to board you. Last night was a bit short commons, I know, but then we wasn't sure when you'd be here. I was going to get a few extras when the cart come this afternoon. A whole pound of tea!"

Even when talking and staring, Mrs Wheeler kept her hands busy, slicing onions and carrots — old ones.

"Would you like a cup *now*? Or coffee? And a piece of cake."

"I would." The poor woman's voice was positive, her glance dubious. "But I ain't finished in the dairy yet." She turned from the stew to a bowl in which nine large potatoes, scrubbed but not peeled, lay. She went to the brick oven and tugged open its heavy iron door. For a moment the good smell of baking bread overcame all the disagreeable odours in the kitchen. Mrs Wheeler put the potatoes among the loaves. "And then there's the milk," she said, with apparent inconsequence. Daisy, lifting down the teapot, said, "What about milk?"

"Tea, I always said, needs the whole milk. We never have any but the skim. And even with that I have to be careful — the pigs need it."

This was the kind of pinched poverty that Daisy had never experienced even under the rule of her stepmother; indeed, that bad manager had an extravagant streak where some things were concerned.

"Excuse me asking such a thing, but are you so very poor?"

"No. Just saving. Mr Wheeler . . ." She checked herself on the brink of a dangerous confidence. "He's a great saver," she said. "I'll get the milk."

"Would it be better if we took the tea to the dairy?"

"Oh, yes!"

A greater contrast between two places, part of the same house and in the hands of the same woman, could hardly be imagined. The kitchen was all cluttered and stinking, the dairy was specklessly clean. It had to be, for dairy products were so easily tainted. Just inside the dairy door hung a bibbed white apron which Mrs Wheeler put on over her poor old clothes, her sacking apron, before she began even to scrub and scald the implements and utensils which she had used earlier in the morning. The fresh, whole milk stood in wide shallow pans on a shelf made of slate. Cream, ripening towards the state where it would be ready for churning, stood in taller jars. The butter from this morning's churning lay, pearly golden and shapeless, awaiting attention. Mrs Wheeler had not finished in the dairy yet. Mrs Wheeler would, she felt, never be finished until she dropped dead. And sometimes when she gave way, she thought that could not be too soon; let it be in August when the next child was due. Because if it lived, and she lived, how on earth could she manage?

Mr Wheeler — it was quite inconceivable that she had once thought of him as Edward, and in intimate moments even called him Ted — had welcomed, in his way — quiet, she'd considered it — Bert, Betsy, Ted and Alfred. Lily and Elsie had not been welcome at all. And when, back in November, December, or perhaps even January — she had put it off as long as she could — she'd said, "I reckon I'm going to have another baby," he had been distinctly annoyed. He'd said, "Another mouth to feed! And you useless for a fortnight." Since then he had not mentioned her condition; nor had he spared her in any way.

She now drank her tea quickly and wolfed a slice of the pound cake.

"I'm eating for two these days," she said, shyly apologetic. "I expect you noticed."

"I did wonder." Daisy thought of her own pregnant time, the secrecy, the care, the cosseting. Poor woman! She made up her mind that for so long as she remained here, she would provide little treats, try to lighten the load in some way. She still regarded her stay here as a purely temporary arrangement; she must wait until Hugo's letter arrived. While she was here, she would do what she could. Beginning by washing these tea cups and anything else that had been used in the kitchen.

Washing up was a job generally avoided by all who had a chance to evade it; in the kitchen of the Hall at Talbot St Agnes Daisy had spent hours at the sink. At Mrs Westcott's she had sometimes helped Emily in the evening, when the children were asleep. In both places washing dishes had been a recognised part of household routine and there'd been cloths and mops and tea-towels, and soda to dispel grease; here, although almost all the things on the dresser and table seemed to need washing, little provision had been made for the job. Just several sour-smelling rags of varying size, all of which had started life in some other capacity — a monogramed but ragged table napkin, what looked like the sleeve of a shirt. And no soda.

392

Mrs Wheeler, hurriedly but skilfully weighing up and shaping the butter, remembered the bread and came, wearing her hunted-hare look, into the kitchen.

"Oh, you shouldn't have bothered, Mrs Johnson," she said, without halting on her way to the oven.

"I couldn't find any soda."

"We don't use it. It's bad for the pigs. Washing-up water," she explained, "goes in the swill pail, just outside the door."

She lifted out the bread loaves and tested the state of the baking potatoes by rolling one between her palms which were, apparently, inured to heat. As she did so she glanced at the tin clock on the dresser and seemed satisfied.

A potato, baked in its jacket, split, freely buttered, was an acceptable side dish, an accompaniment to a roast. But Daisy could remember baked potatoes, eaten without ceremony — and without butter, and, in cases where they had been part of a bonfire ritual, insufficiently cooked. But there'd always been some kind of merriment connected with them. Here there was neither butter nor merriment. The dourness emanating from the head of the household affected everything and everybody. Two of the boys and the biggest girl did not even sit down. They ate standing up. Again she thought of animals. Over the undercurrent of her own misery — now in the ascendant as the effects of the brandy wore off, and a year was a long time and who could say what might happen? — little surface waves broke. Poor things! It seemed to be the moment to produce the box of biscuits. Mrs Wheeler first, Mr

Wheeler. He took one, but he said, "Don't go spoiling them!" when she handed the biscuits on. Her ever-ready temper flared, the speck in her eye danced. She was ready to say, as she had said of the gig, that the biscuits were hers and surely she could do what she liked with them. But she happened to catch a glance at Mrs Wheeler's face; it wore an expression which could only be called imploring. It said, "Please don't anger him or we shall all suffer."

In the afternoon she amused herself by exploring the house. It was older than the one in which she had been a servant, and larger than the one of which she had been mistress, and she understood Mrs Wheeler's remark about the room assigned to her being less lonely. There were so many rooms, all dust-sheeted, damp-scented and bleak with the nobody-comes-here atmosphere. And how busy the spiders had been! They had woven webs almost as tough as fine muslin between dusty brocade curtains and unwashed window panes and between the banister rails of a fine staircase. There was evidence of roof leakages, dark stains on ceilings and walls; there were places where panelled walls bulged; other places on the walls from which pictures had been removed, leaving only the ghosts of their shapes. She felt rather like a ghost herself but she fought the feeling off, remembering that Hugo had said that, with luck, he would come back richer than Croesus. She had no idea who Croesus was, but Hugo had plainly meant that he would come back very rich indeed and all this poor house needed was a little

394

money and a good deal of labour and love expended upon it. Forcing herself to fend off the gloom, she came suddenly upon something which heartened her, a portrait of Hugo in naval uniform. Young! Just as she had been young when Jack Skelton had painted her as Hebe and there'd been all that fuss. But it was instantly recognisable; age and experience did things to people's faces, but only in a superficial way; nothing but a maiming accident, or that disease at which Mrs Bell had once hinted — "And you end with no nose!" — could alter the real structure of one's face.

You die with the bones you were born with. What a thought, now when she felt so low and had just found something that pleased her! I must not get disheartened or I shall not last out the year!

In this room individual pieces of furniture had not been covered; everything had been pushed to the centre of the room and shrouded by a sheet. Daisy fumbled about under the cover and pulled out a small gilt chair. Perched on it she could reach and lift down the portrait which she carried to her own room and hung opposite her bed, so that she could see it last thing at night and first thing in the morning. Then, prompted by the memory of church altars, she thought of flowers and went out in search.

Mr Wheeler's conversion of the pleasure garden into a utilitarian field had been thorough and systematic and his method of cultivation, which consisted of the relentless use of the hoe, had discouraged the growth of poppies, wild scabious, cornflowers and marguerite daisies; to him they were weeds and parasites. Daisy found what she wanted in the kitchen garden, reached by a gate in a wall. Except to root out a few things for which he could see no use and no demand in the market which he served, and to make the ground about twice as productive as it had been when two gardeners tended it, Mr Wheeler had kept the vegetable garden much as it had been. There were fruit trees espaliered on the walls and there were the greenhouses and the cold frames. One of the greenhouses had once been heated, but Mr Wheeler, carefully balancing expense against profit, had considered that a parasite, too — a rich man's whim to have melons and pineapples, just enough for the house, and some flowers, incapable of surviving without heat. What people wanted, and Mr Wheeler knew his market, was ordinary stuff, but a bit early. And this the greenhouses supplied, given nothing but shelter from the wind, the sunshine, plenty of water, plenty of muck. Just before Daisy's arrival he had picked the first sheltered strawberries and next week he could start lifting the indoor-grown potatoes — a good three weeks before even the earliest of the outdoor stuff was on the market. In an awkward little corner, just where the useful wall joined the useful greenhouse, there was something which had escaped Mr Wheeler's destructive attention, a climbing rose which, unpruned, uncared for, was reverting to the wild. It was not yet quite a hedge-rose, it was less open, less flat and the petals were not pink, they were striped, dappled, red and white. It was, in fact, the original Tudor rose and it was as old as the oldest part of the house. It was a survivor because unlike most roses it

396

grew not suckers but productive shoots from underground. It was very pretty and had a heavenly scent and a ferocious armament of spikes. Daisy realised that she needed scissors or a knife and turned back to the house.

At the kitchen door was what Mrs Wheeler had earlier in the day referred to as the cart. It was a travelling shop. The man who owned it and drove it was as fully attuned to his market as Mr Wheeler was to his; he sold everything that a housebound woman of limited means could possibly need; the cheaper cuts of meat, dried fish, flour, salt, candles, crockery, calico and flannel by the yard, needles, pins, thread, knitting wool, ribbon, tape. And what he could not supply from his meticulously arranged cart this week, you had only to bespeak and he would bring it on his next round. Boots, shoes, slippers hung in grapelike bunches from the awning of his cart, and along its sides lay spades and hoes, scythes and sickles.

There'd been a time when the new people in the new avenues and closes and terraces and such had been a bit shy and snobbish about buying stuff from a cart, but they'd come round because he gave value for money and had established himself not only as a good provider but as a character. He was always cheerful and — this was important when dealing with females of a certain kind — he was a lover of animals. His dapple-grey horse, a cross between a carthorse and a trotter, was something to see when so many workhorses looked half starved and utterly dejected; and his mongrel dog was as good as anything in a circus. Naturally, he never entrusted it with anything edible — that wouldn't be hygienic — but if a woman asked for a packet of candles or some such thing, the man would say, "Take it to the lady!" and the dog would enter wholeheartedly into the game, taking the package delicately between his teeth and depositing it neatly at the lady's feet. "Nobody ever had a better errand boy," the man would say.

Mrs Wheeler, poor woman, was taking in her usual supplies — all cheap. Two pounds of beef shin, twopenny worth of bones, pearl barley, four bloaters ... The travelling shop man had more than once wondered how so large a family managed on so little, and why they should be so pinched. Eight of them and four bloaters! And then he became aware of Daisy's presence.

"I want so many things," she said.

Somewhere between Plymouth and Birmingham, or more specifically in Plymouth where she had drunk herself into a merciful stupor, she had lost something, the bloom of youth; and her hair needed washing. The shining combination of beauty, youth and vitality had dimmed; yet she was pretty enough, and in contrast with Mrs Wheeler very pretty indeed. And what a potentially good customer! Wax candles, not tallow for her; furniture polish, silver polish, a pound of cooked salt beef; writing paper, ink, a pen; after a whispered consultation with Mrs Wheeler, five more bloaters. Then, at the end of a long list she said, "And a bottle of brandy."

It was not legal to hawk spirits, but it was not forbidden to carry them. Anything a customer cared to order he was allowed to transport, and under the seat of his van he had a bottle of whisky, ordered by a farmer whose wife disapproved of drinking. Every week he deposited a bottle under a bush, where the money was always waiting. He could let the lady have that, and buy another in the village.

"I could do you a whisky," he said, "and bring you a brandy next week, if you order it now. Then I ain't hawking, I'm doing a favour. See?"

Aware of Mrs Wheeler — though why she should mind her, Daisy did not know — she said, "I've never drunk whisky. Brandy is medicinal."

"So's whisky — in moderation." He went to the front of the cart and the dog leapt about. "No, Rough, you can't carry this. You take this to the lady." He entrusted the dog with the furniture polish. "Nobody ever had a better errand boy, did they?"

He drove away and Daisy put her five bloaters with the family's four.

"Now we can all have one each."

"I don't know what Mr Wheeler will say." Mrs Wheeler sounded nervous. "He called the biscuits spoiling."

"A little spoiling never did anybody any harm."

"About that, I ain't sure. You get used to things and then it come hard. Take me . . ."

"Captain Stirling told me that you used to be a cook."

"So I did, with everything you could want, and more. From the servants' table alone we threw out more in a day than I have to do with here in a week. It wasn't the right preparation." She turned away and resumed the work which the hawker had interrupted, tenderly washing eggs. Daisy borrowed a knife and went out to cut roses.

By supper time she had set up her little shrine. Below Hugo's portrait stood a newly polished table, bearing the roses in a bowl upheld by cherubs. The bowl was flanked by candlesticks, also decorated by cherubs holding wreaths of mixed flowers. When Daisy asked Mrs Wheeler for something to hold roses, Mrs Wheeler had directed her to the china room and told her to help herself. Shelves and cabinets there were full of beautiful things. Mr Wheeler had disposed of a few oddments unlikely ever to be missed, but the bulk of the china and silver was there, and the sight of a painted tea service had put into Daisy's head the idea of making tea in her own room. All she needed was a spirit kettle and she could buy that tomorrow. She was indeed beginning to settle in and now that the thought of living away from the family had occurred to her, she saw no reason for not having Margaret with her.

Mr Wheeler did not object to Daisy's supplementing his family's diet — it all helped — but his devotion to saving recoiled from the thought of waste, of such wanton extravagance as was implied by Bella's suggestion that the watery vegetable stew should be regarded as a first course and the salt beef should follow. No, he said, save the stew for tomorrow. He was equally adamant about the bloaters — they would make two meals. It had taken him quite a time to rid Bella of her extravagant notions and there must be no backsliding. If Mrs Johnson wanted to waste her money, that was her affair; he did not intend her to change the pattern of life which had worked, and was working, so well.

CHAPTER
FOUR

Miss Florence Reade said to her sister Edith, who was indubitably head of the school, "How very curious. Another letter concerning Margaret Walpole."

Yesterday's had been disturbing; it informed the Misses Reade that in future Charles Overton could not regard himself as responsible for the child; would pay no more fees or incidental expenses.

Despite her anger and disillusionment with Hebe, Mrs Paske had written — at Sir Charles's dictation — with regret. She had put up arguments against it, saying that the child should not be penalised for her mother's bad behaviour, and asking, "What will happen to the poor little thing?"

All quite useless. Sir Charles had been hurt, deeply, irrevocably, and needed to inflict hurt. Since Hebe was out of reach any whipping boy would do.

The letter had greatly troubled the Misses Reade, for it put them into a position of which they had no experience. They had always found that the people who assumed responsibility for children of slightly mysterious parentage were scrupulous about the payment of fees and other expenses, such as new clothing and medical attention. They realised that discretion must be

402

paid for. And to an extent the upkeep of a bastard could be regarded as a debt of honour.

The three sisters had worried about Margaret Walpole all day and conferred together about her in the evening. They would have been worried about any girl so abruptly abandoned, but Margaret was rather special, so very beautiful, which appealed to Miss Florence; so intelligent, which endeared her to Miss Edith; and so well-behaved, a fact appreciated by Miss Constance, who found most little girls rather boisterous and difficult to control. Now, what in the world was to happen to this beautiful, intelligent, docile child?

Miss Edith suggested writing a stiff letter to Sir Charles Overton — a letter in the third person, as his had been, demanding to know what plans he had in mind since the Misses Reade certainly could not be expected to assume responsibility.

Miss Constance produced a suggestion, well meant but impractical: put up all fees by some small amount and use the surplus for Margaret's support. Miss Florence, who kept the accounts and paid the bills, was doubtful about that; the fees were already high and an increase might lose pupils of the ordinary kind, the daughters of people who could pick and choose; had either of her sisters noticed how many so-called academies for young ladies had opened lately? And, she now remembered, there was another person besides Sir Charles Overton who had taken some kind of interest in Margaret Walpole. A woman who had been discouraged from writing; a Mrs . . . Mrs . . . Johnson, who had lived at the same address from which Sir Charles Overton wrote and who was, Miss Florence suspected, the child's mother, but an inferior person, judging from the handwriting.

"After all, she has a certain responsibility, too. I think I should write to *her* at the same time. Housekeepers and such people earn good wages and have no living expenses . . ."

Both the other sisters, willing to postpone the moment of decision, agreed that on the next morning Florence should write to Sir Charles Overton and to Mrs Johnson.

And now, lo and behold, the very next morning, was a letter from Mrs Johnson herself. Carefully written, but in the way which people who could only just write did write and with spelling faults. No matter. The fact that Mrs Johnson wished her god-child to spend a few weeks in the country with her and would call for her in the morning of the day after next was a relief to them all. Somebody cared, somebody was assuming responsibility and Miss Florence said, "How very curious, another letter concerning Margaret Walpole." She looked at the letter again.

"I judge by the post mark," Miss Florence said, "that Mrs Johnson is no longer in Surrey but in Birmingham." Three virgin spinsters jumped to the same conclusion — a loose woman had changed her allegiance or been chucked out. Yet there was nothing obviously wrong with the well-dressed, fairly young, but not too young woman who came to collect Margaret on the day appointed. The mysterious Mrs Johnson drove a good horse — Daisy had spent hours giving Dodger his long overdue grooming and seeing that he had oats; the gig was also first-class. Loose-living women, Miss Florence reflected, had the best of it in this world. She always saw to such things as comings and goings, and she forbore to mention to Edith and Constance, both so relieved about the way in which the problem of Margaret Walpole had resolved itself, if only for a time, that Mrs Johnson had smelt strongly of brandy. It would only upset them. Miss Florence also omitted another thing, which was to ask Mrs Johnson for her present address. The letter had been written on unheaded paper and Mrs Johnson had not written either the address or the date.

Mother and daughter eyed each other rather covertly at first. Margaret could remember the pretty, sweet-scented woman who had sometimes visited Mrs Shillitoe's, always bringing presents, sometimes taking her out for treats, but who had never come to Manchester and who ceased to write. This was the same woman but somehow different, in a way beyond the child's power to analyse. Certainly she smelt differently — not flowery any more. Daisy saw what had been a pretty, cuddlesome child grown very tall for her age, pretty still, very solemn, and not cuddlesome any more, stiff, reserved. The Misses Reade did not express their feelings in any physical way, or use endearments. They liked their pupils to behave like miniature women and what Miss Constance deplored as boisterous was the tendency on the part of the younger ones to relapse into childish behaviour.

"Where are we going, Mrs Johnson?"

Daisy wished she could say, "Home," but Amblebury was not that to her, yet.

"To a place where I am staying, darling. I hope you'll like it there and be happy."

"I shall do my best." How different it would have been if Charles had only given way and allowed her to have Margaret at Wichfield: that would have been a real homecoming.

"It's rather a peculiar place, but I have a nice room, with a smaller one opening out of it for you. There are other people there, but we need not see much of them." She could not say, as she could have done had they been on their way to Wichfield, that there was a lovely garden in which to play, that Margaret should have a pony, a piano. Still, Amblebury was only a stopping place. Daisy still intended to leave as soon as Hugo's letter came, as it must, it must soon. It was now almost a month since he sailed.

Mr Wheeler had raised no objection when Daisy proposed that her god-child, a little girl, eight years old, should come and stay with her. He had Captain Stirling's written assurance that any money outlaid on Mrs Johnson would be repaid. He had begun by intending to jot down on one page of his account book every penny Mrs Johnson cost him, but that did not make very impressive showing, so he had decided to charge a flat rate of two pounds a week; he would charge the same for the child.

Daisy stopped at a wayside inn for lunch, ordered brandy for herself and lemonade for Margaret. It was a comparatively humble place, but it could offer a choice in main dishes, roast chicken, steak and kidney pudding or hot boiled bacon. "Which would you like, darling?" The child seemed bewildered.

"Is roast chicken nice?" She had always been well fed by many standards, but she had always lived in cities where fowl was a luxury.

"Very nice. Try it. If you don't like it you can have something else."

"Oh, no," Margaret said, almost reprovingly. "One must always eat what is set before one." One was also supposed to leave a clean plate, but this plate contained so much; chicken and stuffing, a little roll of crisp bacon, a sausage, bread sauce, mashed potato.

"Well, do you like it?" Daisy asked.

"Very much, thank you. But . . . I'm afraid I shall not be able to finish it all."

"That doesn't matter in the least. You must leave some room for pudding."

This was the second time in her short life that Margaret had been called upon to make a sudden adjustment. School had been very different from Mrs Shillitoe's, and now everything seemed very different from school. Nicer — perhaps . . . But unconsciously she associated Daisy with brief, fleeting pleasure followed by brief misery. Even those romps on Margate beach, now forgotten at one level of the mind, had left a mark on a lower one and it was impossible for Margaret to derive from this kind, indulgent person the sense of security which school had provided. School, once one had settled in, had been easy; you must not do this, and, anxious to please, you did not do it; you must do that, and, anxious to please, you did it. Then all was well. Get a sum right and Miss Edith would say, "Correct." Do a bit of stitching or write neatly in one's copybook, and Miss Florence would say, "Very nice." Make one's bed tidily, keep one's drawer in order, walk sedately on the way to church or during the daily, dull, afternoon perambulation and Miss Constance would say, "Good girl." It was a small, narrow world in which Margaret had lived for three years, but it was orderly and secure. And happy; partly because of Phyllis, one of those who, like Margaret, never went home for holidays, had no parents or guardian, never got a sum right, made her bed in such a fashion that Miss Constance had once said she'd seen a haystack better made. Phyllis had, at least for Margaret, the great attraction of being amusing. Once on the daily walk they passed a shop window full of pans; there was a notice, "Guaranteed Copper Pans." Phyllis broke the rhythm of the brisk walk, stared for half a second and then said, "I'd never have taken them for anything else, would you?" It was this gift for twisting something quite ordinary into something else that had endeared Phyllis to Margaret, the more so because such remarks provoked a quiet inward laughter, not the kind apt to draw rebuke. Now she wondered if, or when, she would ever see Phyllis again.

Phyllis had also been a great teller of stories and a mine of information of the kind not to be gained from books. She was a year older than Margaret and until she was sent to the Misses Reade had spent her time entirely with servants. Phyllis knew the difference between a bastard and an orphan, and was willing to share her knowledge with those whom she imagined shared her state.

About this Margaret herself was not quite sure, when on the afternoon of the second day they arrived at Amblebury. They went through the kitchen, unoccupied at the moment, and up into Daisy's room where one of the first things she did was to arrange some fresh flowers — peonies bought in a small town where they had stopped for lunch and done some shopping — beneath the picture of a man. Two little memories, hitherto with no connection, slid into the child's mind; helping Miss Constance do the altar flowers just before Easter, and during that, or another holiday, going with Miss Constance to put flowers on a grave.

"Was that Mr Johnson?"

"No, dear. That is Captain Stirling. Hugo Stirling."

"Is he dead?"

"I hope to God . . . No, dear. As you can see, he is a sailor and he is away at sea just now."

Something in Mrs Johnson's manner bore out a school rule — it was rude to ask personal questions. Not that Mrs Johnson looked angry as one might expect, had one been rude, just very upset, and saying *God* like that.

"I apologise," Margaret said, "for asking a personal question."

"That's all right, darling." Daisy lit the little flame under the spirit kettle. "I'll just go down and get some milk. Then we'll have tea and unpack." In preparation for Margaret's coming, Daisy had made an arrangement with Mr Wheeler; she was to have two pints of whole milk each day, set ready in a brown jug in the dairy.

"Threepence a pint and paid for by the week," Mr Wheeler said, seizing a chance to make a little extra. Daisy thought it was a high charge, for in the heart of London, in Well House Close, milk had been twopence a pint, delivered to the door, but she was not the person to quibble over a penny . . .

Mrs Wheeler was in the kitchen when Daisy went down, working like a machine wiping the cut ends of a great pile of asparagus with a damp cloth and laying the stalks even, in dozens, ready to be tied. She'd spent much of the afternoon bent over, cutting the asparagus, culling carrots; her back ached, her legs ached, her head ached, but at the sight of Daisy she mustered a smile and said, "So you're back. Is the little girl all right?"

"Very well, thank you." One could hardly say to this so-busy, so-overworked woman, "Come and see her", since that meant climbing stairs. So Daisy called, "Margaret! Come here a minute." Margaret, well accustomed to instant obedience, came and stood beside Daisy at the foot of the stairs.

Daisy said, "This is my god-daughter, Margaret Walpole. Margaret, this is Mrs Wheeler."

410

Daisy had learned how to make an introduction; Margaret was schooled too. She made her little curtsey and said, "Good day, Mrs Wheeler."

Into the eyes of this drudge-horse of a woman there flashed the instant recognition which Sir Charles had dreaded. Nobody, nobody, not even Mrs Wheeler, seeing them together, could fail to notice the likeness, though both had changed since those days at Margate. However, in the case of Mrs Wheeler, though she recognised and realised what was obvious, it had no gossip value. She brushed the thing aside and speaking with absolute sincerity, said, "I'm glad you're back, Mrs Johnson. I did miss you."

Except for doing a bit of washing up, sharing a cup of tea and being friendly in a casual way, Daisy had done nothing to make Mrs Wheeler notice her absence, but the truth was that things seemed slightly better when Mrs Johnson was about. The old personal charm was still there.

Upstairs, in the little dressing-room which had been made ready for Margaret, they unpacked and, finding her winter clothes included, Margaret asked a natural question. She had never had a holiday, but other girls had gone home for the summer, or for Christmas, or Easter, taking with them clothes proper to the season, leaving others behind.

"Am I not going back to school, Mrs Johnson?"

"It all depends, dear." Miss Florence had explained the situation clearly, even showing Daisy Sir Charles's letter. If, she said, Margaret was to return to Stonebridge House in September *somebody* must assume the responsibility which Sir Charles had cast off; forty pounds was the fee for a term, and it *must* be paid in advance. Daisy's happy-go-lucky attitude towards money had enabled her to regard this as a minor consideration — what mattered was the child's happiness. So she had given an evasive answer and Miss Florence said that she must know by the end of June because then she would be considering applications.

So far Margaret had given no sign of increased happiness at her release from school. Even the food, which would have delighted many children, and would have meant so much to Daisy when she was eight, Margaret accepted gravely and made no comment until asked "Do you like it?" or "Are you enjoying it?" Then her answer was always the same, "Yes, thank you." No enthusiasm. Daisy suspected shyness, something from which she had never suffered, and thought that some less formal address would ease things.

"You need not call me Mrs Johnson, my dear. Call me Hebe." She remembered the look in Mrs Wheeler's eyes, "Better still, Cousin Hebe."

With the unpacking finished, Daisy suggested that they should walk through the house. She exerted herself to be entertaining, realising that Margaret had no experience of fine houses or how life was lived in them. She described, she mimicked. The child listened and watched but did not enter into the spirit of the thing. Once she shivered. It was a warm evening but even so these deserted rooms seemed chilly enough to warrant a shiver.

"Are you cold, darling?"

412

"No, Mrs — Cousin Hebe."

Sometimes shivers preceded an illness.

"Do you feel quite well?"

"Yes, thank you."

"Wouldn't this make a wonderful place for hide-and-seek?" It had occurred to Daisy that there were children in the Avenue. The poor little Wheelers she discounted as possible company for Margaret, they were always too busy and were not, strictly speaking, children.

"I do not wish to contradict," Margaret said, beginning in proper mannerly style and then giving way to some emotion, stronger than training. "No, it would be *horrible*! It's like a place where everybody is dead!"

"Oh, no. It's only waiting," Daisy said. Waiting for what? For Hugo's return, with plenty of money. She could discount money in day-to-day transactions, but she knew that to run a place like Amblebury in proper style, a great deal of money, something quite unrelated to mere pounds, shillings and pence, would be needed. But Hugo would have it and there would be servants and lights and huge fires. She also knew perfectly well that while Sir Charles and that woman in Jamaica lived, she and Hugo could not be legally married, but what did that matter? Irregular relationships, such as the one in which she and Jack Skelton had lived, could be very happy. It had ended unhappily, but that was Jack's fault. He had never truly loved her. And now, years after, saying, "Come along then, we'll go back to our rooms," the thought struck her that this seemingly meek little girl was Jack's child as well as hers. She could have inherited his unloving nature. No more her fault than the colour of her hair! Patience and understanding were needed. And it was possible of course that the child was tired.

"What time did you go to bed — at school, darling?"

"The really little ones went at half-past six. Then, Phyllis and I and some others, between seven and twelve, went at eight. The seniors at nine."

There was still some time to go.

"And what would you be doing now — at school?"

"Playing, with Phyllis, or some of the others."

"Playing what?"

"Phyllis and I played noughts and crosses, or draughts. Only two can play. It takes more for ludo, or twenty questions or dumb crambo. And sometimes Miss Constance read to us. Robinson Crusoe had just found that footprint . . ."

Margaret was too well-schooled to say the words that flew into her mind: *And now I shall never know.*

Incredible as it might seem to all those who had hated — sometimes with good reason — their schools, Margaret was not homesick, but school-sick. After the few first bewildered days there she had fallen in readily with the routine; every minute occupied, a standard of behaviour, strict but just, firmly laid down, a definite hierarchy established. And of course the company of her contemporaries — especially Phyllis.

And Daisy, willing as she was, could not give the whole of her mind to the problem immediately confronting her. She was waiting for the letter which must surely come, but didn't. Day after day. Sometimes she remembered with a horrible jerk of the heart the time when she had awaited a letter from Plenrerith. With John Skelton planning treachery all the time . . . Surely the same thing couldn't happen again? Lightning never struck in the same place twice.

She was preoccupied with thoughts of Hugo, and presently, for the first time in her life, with mercenary considerations. She'd spent the money from the sale of the amethyst necklace on what she considered necessities, a few bits and pieces, like the tea and the cake and the wax candles, and, of course, the brandy, and one new frock — an absolute necessity. And now incidental expenses were ticking up. Mr Wheeler said, with full justification, that he had undertaken to provide bed and board for a lady, but no mention had been made of a horse. If Mrs Johnson wanted — as she said she did — oats for her horse, then she should be prepared to pay what livery stables charged — fifteen pence a day.

It was quite useless to say, "But, Mr Wheeler, I am now providing my own food and that of my godchild. Could not the one be set off against the other?"

"That wasn't in the arrangement. Captain Stirling said that . . ."

Sell, through Mr Wheeler, the next trinket; another pretty thing, a bracelet of cameos set in a gold band. Buy a draught board set, a ludo set, books, crayons, paints and, because Margaret was growing so fast, some new clothes for her; pay Mr Wheeler for Dodger's oats, and for the extra milk. It was during the replenishment of Margaret's wardrobe that a warning note struck.

"It does suit her, doesn't it?" The saleswoman said. "And it only needs a little taking in, here and there." She extracted a pin from the little cushion which she wore on her left wrist like a bracelet. Colouring a little, Margaret said, "Am I going back to school, Cousin Hebe?"

"That all depends . . . Why do you ask?"

"Miss Constance would not approve of this dress. She dislikes frills."

Daisy almost said, "To hell with Miss Constance!" Her nerves were strained. No letter from Hugo; less than she had hoped for for the cameo bracelet, and whenever Margaret volunteered a statement it seemed to contain some reference to one of the Misses Reade, or to Phyllis. Daisy had not the experience to realise that Margaret was going through a natural and necessary process, in her case the more marked because for three years school had constituted her whole life.

"Never mind. It will do for parties."

A less disciplined child would have asked, "What parties?" Margaret said nothing, simply looked at her image in the long glass and wished that Phyllis — but not Miss Constance — could see the pretty dress with frills, and narrow ribbons slotted through at the yoke, the sleeves and skirt edge.

Daisy now made it her object to find Margaret some young company.

The women in the Avenue were aware that a female of ladylike appearance was living with the Wheelers up at the big house. She couldn't be a relative, they decided. Perhaps a boarder — but then who in her

416

right mind would wish to live *there*? The woman seemed to own a horse and a gig — enviable possessions which put her a little apart; one or two husbands who had caught a glimpse of her said she was good-looking. So beware! Now for some days whenever she went out she'd had a little girl with her, almost certainly her daughter. And there again, who in her right mind would take a child to live in that stinking hole? A mystery, best left alone.

Daisy set about making advances with her characteristic lack of shyness. She knew the rules — it was for people established in the neighbourhood to call upon newcomers, if they wished to strike up an acquaintanceship. Nobody had done so, so she must make the first move. Sauntering walks along the Avenue, a careful marking down of houses where there were little girls of about Margaret's age; and then a seemingly lucky encounter with the woman who had directed her on the evening of her arrival. The lupins were over now and the woman was cutting roses.

"Good evening. I think you were kind enough to direct me when I was lost."

"Yes. I remember."

"I always so greatly admire your garden. Oh, I'm Mrs Johnson and this is my young cousin, Margaret Walpole." Margaret made her little curtsey and smiled her stiff little smile.

"I'm Mrs Yates. Of course you have no garden up at the big house, now. Such a pity. Still, I shouldn't grumble. Mr Wheeler sold everything saleable . . ." She indicated a few things which she had bought. Talk drifted easily towards Margaret's need for company and Mrs Yates was again helpful. She herself had only boys, at present away at school, but Mrs Choat had two daughters, Mrs Tunbridge one and Mrs Wakefield three. "I know," she said, "if you'd come to tea tomorrow, I could introduce you."

It was a promising beginning and it led to what Daisy had hoped for, young friends for Margaret. But it brought her up against something of which she had no experience and with which she found it difficult to deal — suburban curiosity in other people's business. It had existed in Park Drive, but she had been only a servant there. It had existed, in a slightly different form, in Well House Close but she had been insulated from it. Here it was rampant and she was not prepared for what Miss Edith, Miss Florence and Miss Constance would have condemned as personal questions and therefore rude. She should have had some sort of story ready; if she were Mrs Johnson, then what of Mr Johnson? Alive or dead? What doing? Where? She'd slipped in and out of so many identities; Daisy Holt; Hebe Waywood; Lady Overton; Mrs Johnson. They'd all had backgrounds — even Mrs Johnson had been accepted without question by Mrs Shillitoe. Never before had Daisy been subjected to the scrutiny of inquisitive and basically snobbish women as hot on the trail of a putative mystery as a professional inquisitor tracking down heresy. And even more painful, in her present state of mind, was any reference to the Stirling family. Not all the Avenue dwellers were newcomers to Amblebury; two of them, Mrs Wakefield and Mrs Tunbridge, had been born and bred in the now engulfed village, had by fortunate marriages attained homes in the Avenue and knew more about Hugo than Daisy did herself. At the same time they were anxious to know exactly where Daisy fitted in.

"When we heard about your staying there," Mrs Wakefield said, "we wondered whether you could be a relative. A Grey or a Spanton. There were always so many young people staying there in the old days." It said, as clearly as it could, "Come on, tell us, *what* is your connection? *Why* are you staying in such an unlikely place?"

Daisy decided upon her role.

"Captain Stirling was an acquaintance of my late husband."

There was the slight hush, a tribute to bereavement. Recent? No sign of mourning! Most widows proclaimed their status in some way for years, wore grey or mauve if they ever discarded black, and always large lockets containing photographs.

"After my husband died I made my home with an aunt, but she died earlier this year. Then, at the house of a mutual friend, I met Captain Stirling again and was bewailing my homelessness and he said he had a huge house, running to seed and so . . ." A gesture completed the sentence.

Mrs Yates said, "He has not seen it lately!"

"Or smelt it!" somebody said.

"The part which I occupy is quite pleasant. One expects smells in a farmyard."

"Admittedly. What one does not expect is to have the farmyard moved to the end of one's avenue. My husband was saying only the other day that he wondered if Captain Stirling knew how much that man Wheeler had encroached."

"*Mister* Wheeler," the gayest of the women said. And laughed.

"Mrs Johnson will be able to inform him," Mrs Yates said. "I especially deplore what he has done to the garden."

"Not for some time, I'm afraid. When I last saw Captain Stirling he was about to go on a voyage that would take at least a year."

The lively one — Mrs Choat — said, "By that time there'll be pigs in the parlour!"

Much as Daisy disliked Mr Wheeler, she felt bound, partly in self-defence, to say, "I think that unlikely. Mr Wheeler takes his duties as caretaker quite seriously."

Just how seriously he took them, Daisy learned some days later, when, having taken tea with Mrs Choat, Mrs Tunbridge and Mrs Wakefield, she planned a return of hospitality, something simple and harmless; a combined party for mothers, who would play whist, and the six little girls, who could play hide-and-seek, or have a treasure hunt through the vast unoccupied spaces. For that she needed the use of the drawing-room.

A cunning encroacher himself, Mr Wheeler recognised another when he met one. He resented, in his dull, sullen way, Daisy's presence, which was unavoidable, and most of her behaviour, which included giving

biscuits and cakes to his children, and telling his wife —
in his hearing — that she should take things a bit easier,
considering her condition. As for the Avenue people, he
hated them, behaving so lordly and despising him
because he had muck on his boots. He had no intention
of having them or their brats in the house which he
even then regarded as his own. He was, as a rule, a
silent man, his wife and his children so trained that a
word, sometimes even a look, sufficed, but he could
when necessary, speak pungently.

"You don't know what you're talking about. Putting
on them dust-covers, laying that drugget over the
carpet, bagging up them chandeliers took two men two
days. You take them off, who puts them back? Me? In
the middle of haymaking? And s'pose something was
broke? When we moved in I told my lot, out of bounds,
and they respected it. None of mine ever set foot past
the baize door downstairs or the one in the passage
above. Captain Stirling in his letter said give you
accommodation, and food. He didn't mention no
horses, no children, no parties. So I say No, and I mean
it." The fleck in Daisy's eye danced and she was ready
to do battle; but all the heavy armaments were on Mr
Wheeler's side. "Come to the worst," he said, "I hold
the keys. I'll lock the whole place up."

He was sure of his ground now. This Mrs Johnson
kept on asking was there a letter? Had the postman
been? There had never been a letter for her, and Mr
Wheeler, capable of putting two and two together, had
arrived at a rough kind of truth. An unsettled man like
Captain Stirling was bound to have women, taken up,

lightly discarded; for this one he had made some sort of provision, the certainty of a roof over her head and food for her mouth, a few trinkets to sell — more than most men did for their kept women.

Daisy had a fleeting thought. At Wichfield if she had proposed entertaining cripples, village idiots, gypsies, the men who hawked Spanish onions . . . there would have been no opposition. The only person in the world who would not be welcome at Wichfield was Margaret. Now here she was not welcome exactly, but accepted.

And, let the truth be faced, damned awkward! Margaret hadn't really taken to any of the little girls from the Avenue. There was nothing wrong with them, except that they were not Phyllis.

Faced with the impossibility, in the face of Mr Wheeler's opposition, of returning hospitality, Daisy said, "Margaret, would you like to go back to school?" And then the spark which nothing, no endearments or indulgences had kindled, broke into a blaze and Margaret said, "Oh, yes, Cousin Hebe! I *would*! Phyllis is there and she will miss me as much as I miss her. And in the holidays Miss Constance . . ." She broke off, remembering amongst other things that comparisons were odious, that one should say the pleasant, but not the untrue, the true but not the unpleasant; remembering also the picnics, the puppet shows, the visits to the zoo, all the things which Miss Constance, or Miss Florence or Miss Edith had organised in order to make a holiday for those children who had no home, no parents.

422

"Very well," Daisy said, "you shall go back tomorrow. If you are *sure*." For God's sake let somebody, out of this whole sorry mess, be happy.

Margaret was sure. And Daisy needed forty pounds for this term; and for the next; and the next. For the first time in her life she thought of the future in terms of money and was deterred by the prospect until she remembered that Hugo would be back by the end of a year. Then everything would be all right.

"Fifty pounds!" Mr Wheeler said. "Thass a lot of money. I'd need to see its worth."

"I have it here. They are diamonds and worth far more than that." It was her engagement ring, a half-hoop of graduated stones, the centre one the size of a pea. It was the most valuable of the things she had brought away with her.

"Maybe and maybe not. We'll see. If not, then you'll owe me. I can just about manage it." Like most ignorant misers he distrusted banks and preferred to keep his hoard within reach, secret and safe. Long ago Amblebury had been moated; most of the moat had been filled in and become part of the garden; a section had remained as an ornamental pool full of water lilies, and shaded by weeping willows. More recently it had become a duck pond, muddy and dirty around most of its circumference, but with a bit of old stonework at one end. No thief, however eager, would regard a bit of wall, half-submerged, as a hiding place for treasure and no fire could threaten it. Oak didn't rot easily, and gold did not rust.

423

In addition to coming to the conclusion that Mrs Johnson was a discarded mistress, Mr Wheeler knew that she was addicted to drink. She might not remember very clearly. He felt quite safe in adding to the page of expenses incurred on her behalf: "Loan, £50". On the day of settlement, if she was still here, he'd argue her down.

With the perversity of childhood, Margaret grew more cheerful and expansive on the way *back* to school. She'd packed all the games and books and the crayons and paints — even the dubious frilly frock. "I'd like Phyllis just to *see* it, Cousin Hebe."

Daisy asked, "Why do you like Phyllis so much better than all the little girls in the Avenue?"

Margaret gave this question consideration and then said a hurtful thing.

"They all had mothers and fathers. Phyllis is different. She is like me. Phyllis says we're both bastards. Phyllis knows a lot about things, and she is very funny. She makes me laugh."

CHAPTER
FIVE

Forty pounds down, paid in advance until Christmas.
The child returned to school looking well, with rather
more baggage than she had left with, and positively
happy to be back. Miss Florence was glad to see her,
glad that a godmother was doing her duty. A term's fees
in advance, five pounds for incidental expenses.

Duty done, Daisy drove back to Amblebury, feeling
forlorn. Failed lover with John Skelton, failed mother
with Margaret, failed wife with Charles, even, when you
came to think about it, failed friend with Martha, and
none of it intentional. It had just happened. So far as
she knew she had never done anybody a bad turn or
acted maliciously. And this present situation could have
been avoided if only Charles had let her have Margaret
at Wichfield and if only she had been allowed to have
that one night in London with Hugo. One night, surely
not too much to ask. Denied it, she'd been forced to go
to Plymouth and explain and this was the result. In the
end she had been forced to betray them all — but not
until she had been betrayed. She was now even having
doubts about Hugo. The promised letter had never
come. And unless one chose to lie down and die of
despair, one must have recourse to brandy.

She was just inebriated enough to be calm through the violent thunderstorm which occurred towards the end of her journey back to Amblebury. Dodger disliked so many things, but most of all thunderstorms. At each flash and growl, he reared and then took sideways steps. Daisy left her seat in the gig and crouched by the dashboard, shortening the reins, reaching out, patting his rump: "It's all right, Dodger. All right! Good boy. Good Dodger." With him she failed too, and in fact a man, riding a placid cob and coming in the opposite direction, felt concerned enough to shout at her, "Lean back, missus! Use your whip!"

The thunderstorm ended with a heavy shower; the effect of the lunchtime brandy wore off and Daisy was damp and dispirited when she entered the kitchen at Amblebury, at no time a cheerful or inviting place, but this evening in the grip of some kind of tension. Mrs Wheeler and the biggest girl were not at the supper table, the youngest girl was crying and ignoring her food. Mr Wheeler and the rest of his family were eating but a shade less stolidly than usual.

"Where is Mrs Wheeler?"

"Having the baby. It's early."

"Who is with her?"

"Betsy. The woman we bespoke for August had another case."

"I see." Daisy went up the stairs and at the top hesitated. She felt no actual obligation to Mrs Wheeler, but the poor woman, out of her husband's presence, had been civil and grateful for the most casual bit of kindness. Daisy had borne Margaret, but that had not given her any very clear idea of the mechanics of the business; only the memory of pain and the need for secrecy remained. However, Martha Paske's reminiscent talk had, at least in the early days, often centred upon obstetric details and Daisy felt that perhaps she knew rather more about the business than a girl, how old? Fourteen? With the greatest reluctance, impelled by a sense of duty and by an instinct as old as time, at the head of the stairs Daisy turned right, not left.

Mrs Wheeler said, "Oh, thank God!" Then pain silenced her.

"Do you know what to do, Betsy?" Oh, let the answer be, "Yes." But Betsy, a work animal, a feeding animal, was now a frightened animal and said, "No. Me Mam was counting on Old Mother Saunders and she wan't there when Bert went to fetch her." None of the Wheeler children had seemed human to Daisy, but now this one suddenly did and Daisy felt obliged to comfort her, too. "It's all right, Betsy. Just do what I say."

So here I am now, almost at the end of my tether, striking another attitude. One with no entertainment value — calm, competent midwife.

Between the pangs which instead of increasing, seemed to ease off — a bad sign — Mrs Wheeler told what had happened. She'd been turning the cheeses on the top shelf in the dairy when the first pain struck and she'd thought she'd strained herself. By mid-afternoon she'd known differently and Bert had gone to fetch Mrs Saunders. "And she wasn't there . . . Aah! That was a good one. It shouldn't be long now . . . I've borne six and the last was as easy as wringing out a dishcloth . . .

Aah! And I thought it was over and done with. With my youngest eleven. But they do say . . . They say one last flash in the pan . . . Aah! Oh God!"

Bearing a dead child was a longer and more troublesome business than bearing a living one — there was no help from the child; but Daisy did not know enough to recognise the exact problem. She remembered one of Martha's rules; as little interference as possible until it was absolutely necessary. And another: the mother must be cheered and comforted. Daisy sent Betsy to make tea, and to fetch the brandy from her own room. She tipped generous measures of the spirit into two cups of tea and persuaded Mrs Wheeler to sip. "Do try, Mrs Wheeler, it'll strengthen you a bit. Betsy, drink your tea and then go to bed. I'll call you when I want you."

Mr Wheeler had looked in, more aggrieved than concerned. "It'd've been over now if we could've got Mrs Saunders." Even in her misery, Mrs Wheeler sensed a lack of gratitude in that remark and as soon as he plodded away to find a bed elsewhere, said, "*I'm* grateful to you. I'll never forget this."

When next she spoke it sounded ominous. "I don't mind dying. I been tired for so long."

Daisy's reply to that was strictly conventional. "You mustn't think like that. Think of your children." Visualising herself having a nice long rest in her grave, Mrs Wheeler had thought of her children, but from a practical rather than a sentimental view.

"Betsy can cook," she said. "I had time to teach her a bit before all this field work and the saving started. It's

428

hard to believe now, but we was almost like other people once." A pang came and went. "How I'm going to manage with a new baby, I just can't think. I'm more wore out than I was when I had the others."

"You mustn't worry about the future just now," Daisy said. She wished she could think of something positively cheerful to say, but she'd seen enough of Mrs Wheeler's life, so harassed and overworked, to share the poor woman's dismay at the thought of an added burden.

"I'll do what I can to help — while I am here. But that won't be long."

"I don't blame you. Thass worse in winter. I'd've done a bit more to make you comfortable, but there was never the time."

"I know. Don't worry about *that*, Mrs Wheeler. I've been all right. And I'm glad I'm here just now."

"So am I. I can't tell you . . ." Mrs Wheeler reached out her thin, work-hardened hand and took Daisy by the wrist. "When it comes, don't call Betsy . . . You and me can manage . . . She is a bit young . . ."

Actually no midwife's satellite was needed. Nobody needed to see to the baby while somebody else saw to the mother. The baby was dead, purplish, yellowish, like a dying bruise.

"I'm afraid, Mrs Wheeler . . . The baby is dead."

Mrs Wheeler said, "Be glad. I am," and sank into the post-childbirth sleep.

By this time the early-rising household was astir and Mr Wheeler, who had slept well in Bert's bed while Bert slept on the floor, looked in, morose, treating the whole thing — the long night of agony — as though it had almost nothing to do with him.

"Well?"

"It was still-born."

"Just as well. She all right?"

"I hope so."

"Then I'll bury it."

It! Poor little scrap of unwanted humanity, not even granted the distinction of sex, "he" or "she" which preceded the christening and the given names. A flash of the old Daisy Holt, that almost forgotten creature who had been insolent to Mrs Westcott and outfaced Kitty Hammond, knew a brief resurrection.

"And you're to blame. If she hadn't been so overworked, and standing on a stool, turning cheeses, he . . . it was a boy . . . would have been all right. And so would . . ."

She was unable to complete her denunciation; suddenly a wave of nausea hit her and she was obliged to run to the window and open it and be sick.

It was humiliating, but it meant nothing. Any woman who had dealt, single-handed and ignorant, with a still-birth might well be sickened. And this humiliation was nothing compared with that she had suffered years ago, in Well House Close when she'd been so ill. And anybody who in twenty-four hours had eaten so little and drunk so much brandy, must expect to be sick.

But there was something else to be considered. Time. And there again it was possible, it was *necessary* to think, to think of all she had been through in the last few weeks. Finding Hugo, losing him; losing Wichfield;

430

finding Margaret, losing her; trying to adapt to Amblebury, even planning a party. My God, no wonder I'm late!

Hugo's letter, so long and so eagerly awaited, came just when suspicion had hardened into certainty. It was, in many ways, a good and satisfactory letter, written in instalments, sure proof that he had thought of her often. It began. "At Sea. Two days out of Plymouth. Darling, I can't tell you how I hated leaving you or how much I wish you were here. I've said goodbye to a lot of people in my time, but I've never minded like this, but then I've never known anybody like you and doubt if I ever shall." Daisy, who had never received a love letter, read and reread these words with a glow of pleasure and skimmed the next piece which was impersonal; all about the bad, unseasonable weather and the buffeting which the poor old *Mermaid* had taken. Then the personal note again. "My love, I hope that you have settled at Amblebury and that the Wheelers are looking after you well. I like to think of you there. The funny thing is I've so often thought of getting rid of the place and never could bring myself to do it. Now I know why. I'm sorry I sold the best pictures. Never mind, if my treasure hunt succeeds we can buy others."

This assumption that they would have a shared future was heartening. Then there was another reference to the bad weather. "So, darling, although I wish you were here, I'm glad you are not.

"I've been thinking about the future. I suppose I could divorce Eugénie. She left me; in law that constitutes desertion. On the other hand I agreed, settled money on her and never even asked her to come back. That may complicate things after all these years. I'll try to get it sorted out when I reach Jamaica. I know that even if Eugénie . . ." He'd crossed through the last six words, and begun again. "That leaves Sir Charles, would he divorce you? Or he may die. Does that sound too brutal? After all, he is getting on and he has had your company and the joy of looking at you, if nothing else. Enviable, really! Goodnight, my dearest."

Then came a page, headed Las Palmas and the writing showing signs of haste. "Darling, I'm ashore and have just time to write to you and get the letter off by *The Pelican,* sailing tomorrow morning. The Romans called the Canaries the Fortunate Isles and so they have proved for me. Damage to poor old *Mermaid* was superficial and we should be away the day after next. And can you believe it? One of the first people I ran into was a fellow to whom on my way home to enter into my inheritance, all those years ago, I lent ten pounds. He's Spanish, though he speaks English, and Spaniards set great store by their dignity. He said he had always regarded the loan as an investment — he grows indigo now and is wealthy. He insisted upon giving me two hundred pounds, compound interest he called it. I need a hundred, for the repairs and to replace the stores ruined. The other hundred, tell Wheeler, will be sent to Selby's Bank, placed to his credit. For the house and for you. I wrote him such a hurried letter that day from Plymouth so that he should be ready for you. Now, at least he will have money for coal, and, darling, anything you need, just ask. It isn't much, I know, but Wheeler is a careful spender . . ."

Daisy read all what she called the loving parts of the letter again, trying to feel cheered, elated. There was nothing wrong with it, plenty of endearments, plans for the future. It was a wonderful letter, but it did not dispel the gloom which clouded her spirits; in fact Hugo's happy assumption that she was comfortable and well looked after inspired in her a bitterness to which she was almost a stranger. Little did he know! Anything you need, darling, just ask! . . . a careful spender!

She thought of the struggles of the last month — the second, she now knew, of her own pregnancy.

Mr Wheeler had seen no reason why his wife should not be up and doing after a couple of days; she always had been before and this time there was no baby to feed.

"She must stay in bed for a week at least," Daisy said. "I'll do her work."

Then, for the first and only time in all her acquaintance with him, Mr Wheeler laughed. Not a pleasant laugh.

"You ever pluck and dress a fowl?"

"No. But surely that could wait one week."

Sombre-faced again, he said, "Don't talk ignorant! A weekly customer is a weekly customer." It was consideration for the customer that prevented him making Daisy pluck and dress fowls. Everything else which Mrs Wheeler did, Daisy was supposed to manage and it was simply too much, though Daisy was so much younger than Mrs Wheeler, and, as she had once boasted, strong. Instructed by Mrs Wheeler, lying abed and feeling guilty, she managed the dairy work, even the butter-making. She picked peas and raspberries, gathered and washed the eggs. She cooked; perhaps the most difficult task, since what she had to use was meagre in quantity and of the worst possible quality.

"This piece of bacon is quite green, Mr Wheeler."

"I'll bury it," he said in exactly the way he had spoken of the dead baby. With so many pigs and fowls about, that sounded rather extravagant and Daisy, never sarcastic until now, said, "Couldn't the pigs eat it?"

"We shall," he said. "Two days in the ground and it'll be sweet as a nut."

Then there was the question of invalid diet. Daisy remembered all the delicacies she had enjoyed after Margaret's birth. Impossible here, but at least Mrs Wheeler should have beef extract, red wine and chicken broth. Good milk was available since Daisy had never cancelled her private order for milk while Margaret was there. A tough cockerel was provided, with the utmost reluctance, by Mr Wheeler; the beef extract, the red wine and brandy which she herself needed, Daisy bought with the last of her ring money. She needed the brandy, as never before, working as she was, and still waiting for Hugo's letter, and slowly realising that now that she was pregnant, she was tied to Amblebury. That was a deadly thought.

She had always intended to stay here only until Hugo's letter came and then find a lodging elsewhere.

434

At first she had believed that her jewels would keep her, but obviously she had greatly over-rated not their value, but what they would fetch. Very well, then, she could work. As always when she tried to plan for the future, her notions were vague and she did not know exactly where or at what she would work, but she would find something. Then next year, in May, when Hugo was due back, she would return to Amblebury. Being pregnant altered all that; she must stay where accommodation and food of a kind were provided, hoard her remaining resources and be patient. And she must stop drinking. Now that she had Hugo's letter there was no excuse for swigging brandy. Spirits were supposed to be bad for pregnant women. And she could not afford to buy liquor any longer.

By the time the letter arrived, harvest was in full swing, Mrs Wheeler was up and about again and Daisy was still saying, "Sit down, I'll do that." Unless Mr Wheeler were in the offing, Mrs Wheeler generally accepted offers of help, but unwillingly, sometimes even tearfully.

"I don't know why, but I ain't picking up like I should. I'm still as weak as water."

"Well, it's only a month. And you got up too soon."

"Mr Wheeler don't think so. He say I laid abed too long. Laying abed might make you weak, perhaps, but it wouldn't make your back ache all the time — different from the tired ache, I mean. Nor it wouldn't . . ." She mentioned an alarming symptom.

"Mrs Wheeler, you should see a doctor."

"Oh no!" Had Daisy suggested an interview with a rabid dog Mrs Wheeler could hardly have looked more scared. "Think what it would cost."

"I'll pay," Daisy said recklessly.

"I don't think Mr Wheeler would like it."

After all these years she knew her husband imperfectly. So long as he did not have to pay, he had no objection to calling a doctor who just possibly might put a bit of life into Bella. And ladies being the poor feeble things they were, the entry "Doctor £2", would attract no particular notice in the final account which he meant to present. But before Daisy could contemplate paying a doctor seven and sixpence for a house call, she must get some money. Some for herself.

"Mr Wheeler, I need five pounds. Out of Captain Stirling's money."

"What money?"

"I showed you that part of his letter. He said he was sending a hundred pounds so that I could have anything I needed."

"Money don't fly," Mr Wheeler said, thinking but not bothering to say so, Except one way, outwards with feckless women like this one. "It may take months. I said so at the time. If you need five pounds, I'll lend it and that'll be fifty-five."

"I don't understand you. You lent me fifty pounds, but I gave you my diamond ring in exchange. It was worth far more."

"No denying that. But you gotta find a market. Thing like that . . . *after* harvest is the time to sell."

436

"If you couldn't sell it, where is it? Give it back to me. I'll try myself."

"Can't do that," Mr Wheeler said. "Man I hoped would buy it took it to London where he might do better. I ain't heard from him yet. So you owe me fifty pounds. See?"

"All right! Lend me five now." And to hell with you, Mr Wheeler! You just wait until Captain Stirling comes back!

Against Captain Stirling's return, Mr Wheeler had been preparing for a long time; ever since he had been made caretaker. His original holding, leasehold, twenty pounds a year, lay well to the rear of the big house, separated from it by two meadows once used as pasture for the Stirling horses and now used by Mr Wheeler's cows. The holding was provided with a small house, the one in which all Mrs Wheeler's children had been born, and with the ordinary farm buildings, a barn, byre, pig-sty, stable and cartshed. Of these Mr Wheeler had retained the use, so that he was virtually running two establishments at some distance from each other; the small house he had let on a weekly tenancy, so that whatever happened the Wheelers would not be homeless. Mr Wheeler hoped, however, that he would not be obliged to return there. When Captain Stirling came back, Mr Wheeler had his story ready; the twenty pounds a year which he had gained through not paying rent had been totally insufficient to keep the big house in good order, therefore it had been necessary to make the garden earn its living; and even then only the most urgent repairs could be made, though naturally Mr

Wheeler had done his best, had even denied himself and his family. Faced with a dilapidated house and no garden, in a situation now completely unsuited to a gentleman's residence, Mr Wheeler reckoned that Captain Stirling would be open to the offer which he was prepared to make . . . And then a crazy dream, conceived at an age when boys were susceptible to such things, would come true. Mr Wheeler would own Amblebury.

Twenty years earlier in any place, and now, in a more rural area or in the hands of a more conservative doctor, Mrs Wheeler would have been condemned to the life of semi-invalidism which so often followed a bad childbirth, or too many, too close. A female complaint, as they called it. But the century was in its sixth decade, the place was Birmingham, and the doctor whom Daisy had chosen blindly was young, ready to experiment, and quite free from the old and lingering prejudice against anything concerned with obstetrics.

He examined Mrs Wheeler in Daisy's room, in Daisy's bed, wearing Daisy's nightdress, for as Mrs Wheeler had truly said of her own, "They're a bit shameful. I mean, for an outsider to see . . ." She no longer regarded Daisy as an outsider.

Actually it would none of it have mattered, for Doctor Acey took no notice of irrelevancies. He saw only a woman, of very weak physique, mother of six — he had asked — who had borne what he called a menopause child, dead — he had asked about that, too

— and was now suffering from the results. In any activity the same thing could happen; a child could suffer a sprain and be running about within a week; the sprain could disable an older person for weeks and leave a permanent weakness.

About this particular ailment, however, something could be done and the young doctor was prepared to do it, but it would mean Mrs Wheeler going to hospital, probably for a fortnight. "And think, dear, what a complete rest that will be," Daisy said.

"Yes. But what about you?"

"I shall be all right. And I shall look after the family *well*."

The emphasis was intentional. During the time when Mrs Wheeler was in bed and Daisy had been in charge she had hesitated to do or say anything which might annoy the man. He would, she sensed, take it out on his wife. Mrs Wheeler's utter submission, her cowed appearance, her fear of being caught sitting down, drinking an untimely cup of tea, or merely chatting, indicated a long period of intimidation. So did the children's behaviour. Daisy had never seen Mr Wheeler act violently, he seldom raised his voice, but everybody in the house was afraid of him. Except me, Daisy thought.

Mrs Wheeler had not been in hospital for more than twenty-four hours before Daisy was afraid of him, too.

She had done the bread baking, as usual, but not until the afternoon because she had driven Mrs Wheeler to the hospital. And now, instead of the baked potatoes which were always thriftily cooked along with the bread, she produced eight mutton pasties. Despite feeling unaccountably low-spirited, she had regained her appetite and of all things, for no known reason, she had hungered for a mutton pasty, something her own mother had made superbly and something which people with every comestible at their command did not despise — though in proper households the pastry was better because white flour was more suitable.

"Whass this?" Mr Wheeler asked when he, head of the household, received his first.

"A mutton pasty, Mr Wheeler. We have one each."

"Mutton!" That meant bought meat. Mr Wheeler reared some sheep, they were never home-killed, they went to the butcher in what had once been the village shop; and Mr Wheeler took, as a minute part of the payment, the very inferior part known as scrag. But he hadn't sent a sheep there lately; therefore this must have been bought. Thoughtfully he halved his pasty, the good odour of best mutton with just a touch of onion, and some gravy oozed out. "Half each," Mr Wheeler said. "The rest'll make dockey tomorrow." Dockey, Daisy now knew, was a bite of food taken and eaten in the harvest field, or at any other work which prevented coming home for the midday meal.

Obediently the children halved their pasties and rebelliously Daisy accepted half of Mr Wheeler's. But that was not the end of it. Mr Wheeler said to his family, "Off to bed with you," and they scuttled. To Daisy he said, "I want a word with you."

The word was not precisely about the buying of mutton.

440

"Now, look, we'd better get things straight, Mrs Johnson. I don't take no interference. And you have been an interferer ever since you come here. You interfered when my wife was having the baby — and a fine mess you made of it. No argument! The baby dead and now she's in hospital. See? Now you're interfering with the feeding. Running up a butcher's bill and putting fancy ideas into their heads. I tell you straight, I won't have it. Captain Stirling, he wrote to me and asked me to give a lady bed and board. And that I did. But it don't suit you. All right. This don't suit you, go elsewhere. But first pay what you owe."

"I don't owe you anything, Mr Wheeler."

"Oh. Then let's see." He was not yet sure that she was fully subdued so he did not say, "Hand me my book, it's in the dresser drawer." Instead he rose and lumbered across, opened the drawer, took out a book and, licking his thumb, turned some pages and began to read out a number of things, carefully edited, some true — yes, she had ordered milk and proper feeding for Dodger — but in the main false.

"Mr Wheeler, you know as well as I do . . . for every penny . . . there was the necklace and the bracelet and the ring."

"There it'd be your word against mine, wouldn't it?"

Daisy realised, in a flash, the extent of Mr Wheeler's ruthlessness and her own helplessness and was appalled. Not a friend in the world. Just Hugo, far away and out of reach and not due back until next May, and the baby due in — count on your fingers — February.

CHAPTER
SIX

Mrs Paske had not a lot of friends, but a great many putative employers once Sir Charles was dead and everybody knew how shabbily he had treated her. After all that devoted service, a mere hundred pounds! But everybody, everybody had some old relative who needed the kind nursing and the management of a biggish house which Mrs Paske provided at Wichfield. Such a wide choice was bewildering, but her decision was almost predestined; she had retained her professional respect for doctors and went to look after Doctor McGibbon's sister, only mildly disabled by rheumatism.

The George Skeltons moved in, and under Lucy's firm command everything went according to plan. Having inherited so much, they could hardly grudge whatever must be paid for the keep of poor Lady Overton at a place called Petwick. "Of course," Lucy said, "we don't yet know what the charges will be. If they are exorbitant we could find somewhere cheaper."

"No. We must stick to the terms of the will," George said. They expected to receive a bill at the end of the quarter. None came. Nor at the end of six months. This slightly worried George who even in his struggling days

442

had never owed a penny to anybody and one day, calling upon Mr Copeland about another matter, he raised the subject.

"I know nothing of it," the lawyer said. "Apart from making provision for Lady Overton, Sir Charles never mentioned what must, after all, have been a great grief to him and it was not for me to talk about it."

"Where is this place, Petwick?"

"I am not absolutely sure. Somewhere in Kent, I think. Would you care for me to make a few inquiries?"

"My wife'll see to it. She's good at that kind of thing."

Lucy, after a bit of prodding, wrote a cool letter of inquiry and in due time received a reply; no Lady Overton was at present residing in the establishment at Petwick, nor did the records reveal that a Lady Overton had ever been there. With this Lucy was quite satisfied, but George worried a little. Once he said, "After all, my dear, I can't get it out of my mind that her misfortune was our fortune." And he could not guess how near the truth he was. He would have been extremely perturbed, if during one of the little talks about Hebe — I wonder what happened; did Charles put her in there under another name? did she die? did she recover and go away? — he could have seen, by some magical means, exactly what had happened to Lady Overton.

CHAPTER
SEVEN

Nobody, with all the goodwill in the world, with energy, with strength, with determination could do much about the kitchen at Amblebury; it smelt much the same as it had done when Daisy first entered it. Scrub the floor and in they all came with muck and mud on their boots; scrub the table, the dresser, and in no time at all they'd be soiled again, chickens to be plucked and dressed for the good weekly customers, a dead rabbit, some pigeons for family consumption. The everlasting onions and the smell of boiling potato peelings which, mixed with meal, fed the fowls which were so well-fleshed and in such demand.

Nobody, with all the goodwill in the world and at first willing to fight Mr Wheeler's parsimony, could do anything about the food. Mr Wheeler was a careful spender still and intended to remain so until the day came when he could make what he thought of as an irresistible offer. That that day was delayed suited him well, it gave him more time for saving and made his victory more certain. In fact the stars in their courses had fought — and were still fighting — for Mr Wheeler.

Mrs Wheeler had died on the operating table. The use of chloroform was still a hit and miss affair and the eager young doctor, the only one who knew anything about it, could have misjudged; or perhaps Mrs Wheeler seeing, at last, the chance of eternal rest, had seized it and slipped away.

"Now," Mr Wheeler said, "you see what come of interference!" His pride compelled him to give his wife a decent funeral, but he grudged every penny, though he entered most of the cost on Mrs Johnson's page as "Various Expenses".

His hold over Daisy encroached as steadily as had his hold upon Amblebury. By September her condition was beginning to show and it was typical of him that the moment he realised it he decided that anybody with the use of their eyes and their hands could pluck a fowl, and anyone who could pluck one could pluck a dozen. The fact that his guest was pregnant confirmed his suspicion that she was a discarded mistress, of no real importance to anyone; and this was made cruelly evident by the failure of the promised money to arrive. Week by week Mr Wheeler lumbered into Selby's Bank, that untrustworthy place, and asked about the hundred pounds which Captain Stirling had promised to place to his credit. At first he was met by polite explanations; money paid into a foreign bank took a little time to appear in Birmingham in English currency. Then as the weeks passed civility frayed and it was simply, "No, Mr Wheeler."

Of course, Mr Wheeler thought sourly, there was no hundred pounds; there never had been! And there again he was not far wrong in his reckoning. The Spaniards, as Hugo Stirling had rightly observed, set great store by their dignity, and that of an unnamed Spaniard in Las Palmas, suddenly confronted, as by a ghost, by a man who had once, long ago, lent him ten pounds, had been preserved by a promise. A promise; two hundred pounds; compound interest; indigo; they all sounded well during that chance encounter, but they were only words as Hugo had found out, after he had sent his letter by *The Pelican*.

"There you are," Mr Wheeler said. "Don't it pay to be cautious? S'pose I'd just gone ordering coal . . ."

By that time Daisy had passed through the first, inevitable, doubtful and dismaying days of early pregnancy, into the euphoric phase. This child was Hugo's, born of the ecstasy amongst the bluebells, on the thyme-scented grass, in a bed in Plymouth. He — she always thought of the baby as a boy, a miniature Hugo — must be properly treated, before, at, and after birth.

She had never been very handy with a needle, but after all, anybody who could pluck and dress a fowl to Mr Wheeler's satisfaction, could do almost anything — given the materials . . .

"Mr Wheeler, I really must have some money. Has that ring been sold yet?"

"Thass my affair. You had the value of it."

It was true, in a way. But now she was suspicious of Mr Wheeler and decided to try to dispose of what was left herself; a pair of earrings in what, three or four years ago, had been the latest fashion; tassels, five little gold chains each weighted with a pearl; a brooch, a special birthday present in the time when Charles was

446

still infatuated with her. A very curly "H" for Hebe; as he had said at the time, "Designed especially for you." And since, because inside the golden curlicues the initial, in small sapphires, was still an initial, the value of it was decreased. "As you see, madam, it would only be an acceptable gift to a lady whose name began with the same letter . . ."

On the whole Daisy's transactions were not much more profitable than Mr Wheeler's. But she had enough to buy flannel and linen and muslin, all that a baby would need during the first months of life.

A more serious demand drew near as the year declined. The next forty pounds for Margaret's school fees.

"It's a good gig," Mr Wheeler said. "Could fetch fifteen pounds. *Rightly* handled." Only the slightest emphasis was needed to inform her that he knew about her attempts to sell things herself and the way she'd been diddled. "And," he said, in what sounded like a burst of generosity, "I'll give you fifteen pounds for the horse."

"And keep him here?" Even in that moment of desperation this seemed of importance to her; she didn't want Dodger sold into slavery. Here at least she could occasionally filch him a handful of hay or an apple, pat him, call him by name. He had no oats, though "Fodder for Horse" appeared regularly in Mr Wheeler's account book; still, so far his work had been light.

"Why not? My old nag is about done for." It was not a propitious omen for Dodger's future, but Daisy had no choice.

"Very well." Then of course Mr Wheeler said he would deduct the fifteen pounds from what she owed him. At that some remnant of spirit flared and she said, "No. That would be useless to me. I must have at least forty pounds by Christmas. And I think if I sold Dodger and the gig together I might get it."

She certainly would — and Mr Wheeler would lose the chance of a good young horse, cheap.

"All right, then; in cash. Then you'll have thirty. The other ten I'll lend."

That would ensure Margaret's safety until Easter. Beyond that Daisy refused to consider anything except that in May Hugo would be back and everything would be all right. What she must think about more immediately, was the need for engaging Mrs Saunders, who must, of course, be paid.

Not yet sufficiently subdued, Daisy tackled Mr Wheeler on the subject of wages. His surly, brooding expression seldom changed, but it did then, registering amazement.

"You earn your keep."

"I earn far more and you know it. You wouldn't find another woman in the world who would do what I do just for a bed and some very bad food! Besides, Captain Stirling promised to pay you."

"The same as he promised that hundred pounds. There's another thing, how do we know when he will be back, or whether he'll come back at all."

That reduced her not only to silence but to tears. After a good howl, as he called it, women came to heel — he'd learned that with Bella. So he let Daisy cry for a bit and then said roughly, "When're you expecting?"

"February. Towards the end."

"Then I'll bespeak Mrs Saunders. We don't want no more accidents."

For that she almost thanked him.

CHAPTER
EIGHT

Had Captain Hugo Stirling been capable of thought as he lay dying of blackwater fever just outside Maracaibo, he would have thought, How ironic! Here I am, hot on a trail almost three hundred years old and practically certain, and within arm's reach, and too weak to stand.

He had, however, no such thought; nor, judging by what he managed to mutter to the one member of his crew who remained faithful, did his last thoughts drift towards his home, or his love. What he had on his mind was frigates. We need more frigates. Where are the frigates? Soon he ceased even to fret about them; and died.

His was too common a fate to attract any attention in a primitive and unorganised area and he had since leaving the Navy led such a peripatetic existence, accountable to no one, that he dropped out of life causing little more stir, and leaving almost as little gap as would a leaf, falling from a tree. Even what he left in England — a mouldering house and rather less than a hundred acres of land — was of interest to no one except Mr Wheeler. His natural heir was young Lord Fenstanton, who had all the land and all the money he needed, and would have had difficulty in finding Birmingham on a map.

Only Daisy, counting weeks and months, and — eventually — years, cherished a memory which outlasted hope, though hope died hard.

Her baby, a boy, was born in February and Mr Wheeler, unusually indulgent, engaged Mrs Saunders for a fortnight, entering in his book: "Baby etc £10". Daisy would have thought that the kitchen could not possibly grow worse, but during Mrs Saunders's reign it did, so Daisy returned to a squalid world and must face what Bella Wheeler had regarded as a nightmare — all this work, with the added burden of a baby. But there was a difference; she did not regard the baby as a burden; it was a joy, an unfailing source of pleasure during a particularly hard time beginning just before Easter when she tentatively approached Mr Wheeler for another loan — forty pounds for Margaret's school fees. Mr Wheeler said, "No," very firmly. By his book she was already deeply in debt.

"But this is April, Mr Wheeler. And next month Captain Stirling will be back. He said a year, or less if he could make it sooner."

"Then we can wait, can't we?" he said, with something of a sneer.

"But you don't understand. I promised to pay in advance. If I don't they won't keep her. She'll have to come back here."

"Where's the harm in that? She can make herself useful."

Another child-slave! A thing to be avoided at all costs. Daisy wrote to Miss Florence apologising for the delay; some money due to her had not yet come in, but the fees should be paid at the end of May, at latest. The sisters held a consultation and agreed to wait.

May came; the month whose very name had shone like a light at the end of a long dark tunnel. Despite her harassed life, Daisy began to pay more attention to her looks. A weekly egg-shampoo — the eggs purloined — and conscientious brushing at night when her whole body craved for bed, restored the lustrous sheen of her hair; but her face and figure had, she thought, deteriorated. She was thinner and now and then, looking anxiously at herself in the glass, she fancied that she saw a disturbing resemblance to Mrs Wheeler. That, she thought, is because I look worried. Mustn't look worried. She smoothed her brow with her fingertips, forced her mouth into a smile. Mustn't stoop, either. From time to time during the seemingly endless days she would straighten up, correcting that look of leaning forward to the next job before this one was half-finished.

She took great joy in the baby and often comforted herself with the thought that even if Hugo found her less pretty than he remembered, she had his son to show, a lovely, plump, amenable child. Daydreams were a comfort, too; Hugo would come back; Sir Charles was dead, or would die, and Eugénie would allow herself to be divorced. Then Hugo and she could marry and be happy ever after.

452

May, all thirty-one days of it, drained away into the past and it was June. Daisy was disappointed, but not despairing. With such long distances, and such uncertain things as ships involved, a delay was not necessarily sinister. She longed to have someone with whom she could talk, who would share her speculations, her hopes, and as time went on, her fears. But Mr Wheeler confined his remarks to, "We shall hear soon enough," or "Mebbe something's happened."

About making her another loan he was adamant and more talkative.

"You seem to reckon I'm made of money. Well, I ain't. I can't go on loaning and lending. Most of what I already done weren't in the agreement. And no certainty of ever being paid back. Weeks overdue now and we ain't heard nothing, hev we? I'm stretching things to say I'll take the girl in."

Last year she'd had Dodger and the gig. Now she had nothing. Humbly she said, "There'd be the train fare."

"That I can just about manage, but thass the end."

It was also the beginning of such a nightmare time that even the most wretched days of the past year seemed happy in retrospect. The light at the end of the tunnel faded; the hope of rescue receded. Daisy was now as cut off from the world as though she were marooned on a desert island. Even the cart had ceased to call. Prices had gone up, little by little, but steadily. Mr Wheeler chose to ignore this and laid the blame on Daisy's bad management. It was useless to say, "But look, Mr Wheeler, I've bought exactly what I did last

453

week, but the same things cost fourpence more." Then sixpence; then tenpence.

"He's cheating us," Mr Wheeler said, "knowing we ain't handy for the shops. In future I'll do the buying when I take stuff in. Waste of time, but a saving in the long run."

And there was the problem of Margaret. She'd hated Amblebury when she had enjoyed guest status. Now everything had changed, greatly for the worse. The girl had outgrown her strength, become tall and rather frail, but Mr Wheeler, horrible man, said sitting over a desk never helped anybody; work in the open would do her good. "She ain't handy, but she'll learn," he said. In his school unhandy people soon learned; otherwise they didn't eat. He made that clear one evening when Daisy was dishing out portions of rabbit pie — a rare treat.

"No," he said, reaching out a long arm and taking Margaret's plate away. "She ain't earned her salt today, leave alone meat."

"She can have my portion."

"You need your strength. Siddown. We don't want no arguments." The new, sadly changed Cousin Hebe sat down.

"Give her a slice of bread," Mr Wheeler said.

Margaret accepted it, with apathy, with dignity. Daisy, watching her, remembered Jack Skelton, now almost forgotten though tending to appear now and again in dreams, better banished on waking, since they were all concerned with happy days which could never come again. Jack had never cared what or when or if he ate; perhaps his daughter suffered less from this petty deprivation than her mother did.

The truth was that Margaret now had worse things to bear than the loss of a supper. There was the behaviour of the Wheeler children, now that she was reduced to their level. To Daisy and to Margaret they had never seemed like children, they were prematurely old, undersized adults, working like ants at their pre-arranged tasks. But they were children at heart, unhappy, deprived children, eager to make the newcomer unhappy, too. On her former brief visit Margaret had had very little to do with them, now she was working alongside them, and though they had little time or energy to spare for physical bullying, they jeered at her, made the most of her mistakes, imitated her manner of speech and of eating. Never, of course, in their father's presence.

Margaret bore a great deal without complaining to Cousin Hebe, in whom she now had little confidence; but presently, into the occasional rough handling, a more sinister element crept. Bert Wheeler was rising seventeen; he knew that he mustn't fool about with his sisters, but Margaret was not his sister, and she was very pretty . . . One day Margaret ran into the kitchen, crying, a thing rare enough to take Daisy's whole attention, busy as she was.

"Darling, what is the matter?"

"Bert Wheeler. I'm frightened of him." In an agony of embarrassment she explained why. It was a situation common enough in backward rural communities, and in urban slums, but one which Daisy herself had never

455

been called upon to face; she had been taught not to act so that men or boys took liberties, but she was Carpenter's daughter and Benjamin Holt was both respected and feared and from his protection she had passed into that of Sir Alfred Langton, which meant that she was practically sacrosanct . . . She listened, with understanding and a kind of horror, to the child's gasped-out tale. At first all the Wheelers had been horrid; when her job had been helping to load one of the handcarts which Betsy and Elsie trundled around the neighbourhood, they'd push it so that she was pinned against the wall; or they ran it over her toes; and when they were picking potatoes they'd take hers and put them into their sacks. A lot of petty persecutions inflicted upon one who was not of their tribe. And then Bert had turned friendly . . . had seemed friendly, until he'd taken her into the stable . . . "He said he had something to show me. But it wasn't that. Cousin Hebe, he said . . . he said . . ."

"Did he *do* anything?"

No. There had been no time. In fact Bert's clumsy first attempt at sexual play had not gone beyond, "Let's see your drawers", when Mr Wheeler, back from profitable selling and parsimonious buying, had driven into the yard.

"Then it's all right, Margaret. It won't happen again. I promise I shall speak to Mr Wheeler."

Margaret gulped and said, "If you could . . . without mentioning drawers . . . We were supposed never to use the word."

456

Daisy spoke to Mr Wheeler, who spoke to Bert, mentioning the strap.

"You get randy, with her or anybody else, my boy, and I'll take the strap to you."

This instrument of correction was seldom used, seldom mentioned, but it was always there; the ultimate sanction. Whatever rather piteous attempts at sexual experiment had inspired Bert Wheeler were adequately quelled by the use of one word. Yet the incident played its small part.

Sex had never played much part in Mr Wheeler's life. He'd married Bella because a man needed a wife and, looking forward, a son to carry on the work when, as all men must, he himself grew old. Also Bella had a good reputation as a cook, and was not bad-looking and didn't argue. After a few months of marriage intercourse with her had meant little more than an evacuation of the bowels.

The idea that he might one day marry Mrs Johnson had occurred to him from time to time, but first he must see how she shaped — which was well; and, of course, if things went the way he hoped and he obtained possession of Amblebury, he might do better for himself. So apart from a lecherous thought or two he'd let the matter slide. Now, with Bert's attempt to frolic with Daisy's daughter — there had never for a moment been any doubt about the relationship — Mr Wheeler's mind turned to the mother.

"Well," he said, one evening, "getting on for Christmas again and we ain't heard nothing."

"No," Daisy said dully. She was engaged in some of her clumsy needlework and therefore bound to sit in the kitchen, which was at least warm. Mr Wheeler seldom stayed up long after supper and unless he had some rebuke to administer, rarely talked. Tonight he did.

"I was never told much. Just that he wanted you here. I don't even know if you're widowed or not."

"Does it matter?"

"It might." He tried again. "I noticed you named the boy for *him*."

That seemed to require no answer and she made none, stitching away and in her mind seeing the tunnel stretch on and on for ever, with no light at its end.

"As I see it," Mr Wheeler said coarsely, "he got you into trouble. And maybe you didn't know he was married."

Lady Overton said, "Naturally I knew. Mrs Stirling found the English climate intolerable and chose to return to Jamaica."

Mr Wheeler was surprised that she knew, and affronted — but at the same time obscurely pleased — by her manner.

"What I'm getting at . . . He couldn't marry you even if he wanted to. Not without fuss. And it could be he went to Jamaica, and stayed there. Did that ever strike you?"

It was, of all the things which a torturing seven months' belatedness had suggested to her mind, the very last thing. She'd imagined shipwrecks, illnesses, even lately, in the dead days of winter with hope

458

running out, death. But the idea that Hugo, going to Jamaica to discuss divorce, might instead have mended his marriage, had never occurred to her. For a moment she was deprived of sight, of breath, of movement. Then something new, wily and self-seeking, was born in her.

"It is a possibility. Would he not have let you know?"

"Why? None of my business."

Whose business? Who would know? Who can tell us anything?

"I should have thought that it was, Mr Wheeler. What about the money you have laid out on *me*? Perhaps Captain Stirling's lawyer . . ."

"He never had none lately. He did, when he was selling some land; but they had words. No, I shall be out of pocket, having you, *and* the baby, and now the girl, but . . ." Mr Wheeler knew the value of the dramatic pause. ". . . That don't concern nobody except you and me. And maybe we could come to terms. Eh?" The meaning was clear enough.

CHAPTER
NINE

Without knowing it, she had been fortunate for once. The thought that Hugo had deserted her might have broken her entirely had she had time to sit down and think about it; as it was she was not only over-busy physically, but desperately preoccupied in mind. She, Margaret and Hugo must get away, and in order to do that she must have money.

She began seriously to consider Mr Wheeler's finances. His was the only money to which she had any hope of access and if she could find it she would not have the slightest scruple about taking it.

A great deal of money came into the house, little went out and he did not use a bank. So where was it? She began every time when she could be certain of his absence, to make a thorough search. Mrs Wheeler's ghost went with her, for there had been times when Bella had thought that out of a hoard, if only she could find it, a half-sovereign would not be missed or at least not immediately. The big largely unoccupied house offered innumerable hiding places and it was not until the end of February that Daisy was satisfied that the money was not *in* the place. Then where? She began to take note, for the first time, of Mr Wheeler's evening routine.

There was the business — common on all farms — of racking up, seeing that everything was safe for the night. As a general rule this last duty was left to Bert and Ted, but every now and then Mr Wheeler said, "I'll rack up," took the lantern and went out. When he did so he was always out longer than the boys. He could assume this duty any night of the week, but *always* on market day.

Early March, the moon fairly bright but often obscured by scudding clouds. The lantern was easy to follow. Mr Wheeler did not give even the most perfunctory attention to the buildings or to the animals they housed. He went straight to the upper end of the horse-pond; Daisy took cover behind the nearest building, the stable, and watched. He set down the lantern and knelt and seemed to be groping about in the water. She could not see very clearly, for the moon had clouded over, the radius of light from the lantern was small and for a moment the man was out of it. Then he was in again, faintly illumined as he opened what looked like a large box, placed something inside it, closed the lid, and then became invisible again. He stood up, lifted the lantern and started to come back. Daisy sped, lightfoot, to the house.

Now she knew!

She had, during the first days of her internment here, been interested in the house, because it was Hugo's, and under the prod of what she could now look back upon and call sickly sentiment, she had gone in search of flowers and found the kitchen garden. Apart from that she had done no exploring and for her the pond was merely a place where ducks lived and bred. And if anything could be more disgusting than dressing a fowl for table, it was dressing a duck!

Now she was obliged to wait before she could study the pond, because Mr Wheeler was preparing to plant one of his catch-crops, early potatoes. The traditional time for such planting was Good Friday, but he was no slave to tradition and had proved that a pound of potatoes, three weeks or even a fortnight earlier than most was worth twice as much . . .

She was obliged to wait until next market day before she could inspect the hiding place. The bit of stone wall dropped sheer down into the water, and it looked very solid; but she knelt, as approximately as she could guess, where Mr Wheeler had knelt, and reached down, felt about, feeling for a loose slab of stone. When she found it it came away easily, but was so heavy that she almost pitched forward into the water. Laying it carefully aside, she reached into the cavity and hauled out the box, solid, brass-bound; the kind of box used for keeping cutlery in neat compartments. The fitments had been removed and the box now held a number of small canvas bags, all but one tied at the neck with string. The one which was still open was waiting for the next contribution. Mr Wheeler was methodical in his saving; each full bag contained exactly a hundred sovereigns.

She replaced the box fairly easily, the stone with more difficulty, but she managed it and stood up, breathing as though she had been running. The problem had now switched from Where? to When? And how to make sure that she had the maximum start. She felt reasonably certain that if she could get to London she could mingle, unnoticed, with the crowds. Some place, she thought, rather like the neighbourhood where Jack Skelton had had his studio; everybody in such places was so intent upon scratching a living they took little interest in other people. She must not make the mistake of spending too freely at first, thieves were often caught that way, and of course Mr Wheeler would have every policeman in the country on the look-out for her.

The suburb was served by a horse-bus nicely timed to meet the needs of the inhabitants. The earliest one left the opening of Elm Avenue at a quarter past eight and took men to their offices and businesses; the next was at half-past ten and took ladies into the city to shop. And to catch that, without Mr Wheeler knowing, she must wait until next market day when he was sure to be absent from the house . . . No, that wouldn't do, because it was always after market day that he went to add to his hoard, therefore he would discover his loss immediately and connect it with her absence and so cut short her start. Also she did not want to wait another week; it was now some time since Mr Wheeler had mentioned coming to some arrangement and since then, though he had never actually said anything or done anything, he had *looked*. So much so that she had deliberately made herself look as unattractive, as drab and slatternly as possible, just as, while a tiny hope remained, she had done her best, with so little material resource, to preserve her looks.

She had never been good at planning forward, but now she must and it was like some other person thinking, not in a day-dreaming way, something beautiful just around the corner, but hard and clear.

She had never been inventive, but now she must be. And for a novice it was not a bad plan.

Mr Wheeler came home, worked so long as the light lasted in the potato field, ate the inevitable stew, making only one comment, intended as a compliment. "You make a good dumpling." After that he did not speak again until he said, "I'll rack up." The children scattered and here they were, alone except for the good amenable baby asleep in what had once been a cradle and was now no more than a brokendown basket.

Daisy said, "I had a letter this morning, from Margaret's school . . . They want her back. No fees, nothing to pay."

"How is that?"

"Oh, some kind of fund for promising girls. I am so glad, for her sake."

"Well," Mr Wheeler said, "maybe it's as well. She ain't shaping up here. When?"

"Tomorrow. The sooner the better, I thought. There isn't much to pack. I'll just go down and see her on to the horse-bus. Could you, would you, lend me sixpence? The Miss Reade who wrote to me said that the train fare could be paid for at the other end."

"They didn't say that last time. I had to pay to get her back."

464

"I know. But this is different."

"All right. There's your sixpence." He put it on the table and Daisy said, "Thank you." She then seemed to give her attention to the black bowl in which the morning porridge would go through a process more gentle than simmering, overnight, on the cooling stove. Mr Wheeler lit his lantern and went out.

Now, she thought triumphantly, I have an excuse for leaving the house, with Margaret and with the baby; but I must lay some kind of false clue. She went upstairs to her room, carrying the makeshift cradle.

No wax candles now, no flowers, no shrine. Once she had looked Hugo's portrait full in the face and said, "You might have told me!" and broken down into a passion of tears. But that was all over now. Now all she had to do was to hold Mr Wheeler off for a little.

"Deer Mr Weeler, I'm gone to manchester with Margaret. Theres jobs there and I mite as well work for pay as for nothing." Under stress all that she had learned at Wichfield, fled away, leaving her with no more than the half-literate cook at Talbot St Agnes had tried to pass on. But it was enough. He'd understand and be angered, but he might not — please God he would not — immediately suspect that his money had gone with her. She proposed to leave the note on the kitchen table.

She packed, just absolute necessities for Hugo, Margaret and herself in the light wicker hold-all which Margaret had brought from Manchester; her own valise, a sturdier article, would carry the gold. She heard Mr Wheeler mount the stairs and then, after only the slightest hesitation, plod along to his own room. She had no means of telling the time, her pretty little watch had followed the rest of her valuables. So she counted. Sixty seconds to the minute. Give him ten minutes to shrug off his horrible clothes and drop into work-animal sleep.

The clouds of last night had shed their rain in the afternoon of this momentous day, and tonight the moon rode high and clear. She could manage without the lantern. The house was now so still that the sound of one creaking stair sounded as loud as a pistol shot. Across the kitchen. The bolt on the door shrieked — she should have greased it. Out into the yard, the eerie black and white of moonlight. Around the horse-pond the ground was slippery with mud, but she walked carefully, reached the bit of wall and knelt down, groping. The stone came away more easily than it had done when first she tried it, and the box, because she now knew its size and shape and weight, was more quickly withdrawn. Her hands, though vibrating to the thud of her heart, were swift and sure, transferring, robbing, making away with . . . And then, in this eerie black and white world, something was suddenly blacker.

"So thass it!" Mr Wheeler said. "You gotta a lot to learn. Think to fool *me*!" He had not believed one word of the story about Margaret going back to school at no cost except sixpence for the fare on the horse-bus. He had retained, because he was primitive, something of primitive man's extra sense.

466

He'd been prepared for something, vaguely connected with the girl's return to Manchester; some bit of trickery. Nothing like this, of course, not even when the stair creaked and the bolt on the kitchen door squealed. He'd gone to his window which overlooked the yard and seen Daisy disappear around the end of the stable block. The pond! The possibility of suicide leaped to his mind. He'd run out without bothering to put on his trousers or lace his boots.

Now his state of mind was divided between shock — his so cleverly contrived hiding place found and being raided by a stupid woman — and something as near humour as his grim nature permitted.

"Well! Well! Looks like it's *you* I'll have to take the strap to!"

He made a clumsy, near playful move towards her, and Daisy, caught, completely shattered, incapable of thought, made an instinctive move away so that where she had been there was empty space. Mr Wheeler lost balance and the greasy state of the pond's edge did the rest. He fell into the water.

Even here, at its upper and untrodden end, the pond was no more than four feet deep, but the mud below it, silt and dead leaves, an accumulation centuries old, was as deep again, a gluey quagmire. It sucked at him, he wallowed, fought for his life; once even managed to get his hands into the cavity which the removal of the stone had left, but it offered only a slippery handhold, the pull of the mud was stronger.

Daisy could have saved him then; but she chose not to do so. She, once so tender-hearted that she could not bear to hear of unwanted kittens being drowned, watched with callous detachment. And Bella Wheeler's ghost was equally inactive. When the last guggle-guggle sound died down and Mr Wheeler ceased to fight, gave in and drowned, Daisy finished what she had come out to do, the transference of the hoard into the valise. The box she replaced, and also the stone. Nobody would ever know that behind that stone had once lain, translated into currency of the realm, a man's ambition, the life of a woman, the childhood of six children.

Daisy gave her last public performance in the coroner's court where all sudden, accidental deaths must be fully investigated.

Soberly clad, clean and neat, well-spoken, pretty, and with charm of manner, she appeared to be exactly what she claimed; no relative to the dead man; just a lodger who after Mrs Wheeler's death had stayed on to do what she could for the family.

Mr Wheeler, she said, had been very much depressed since the death of his wife and while not actually suspecting him of suicidal intentions, she had kept an eye on him and on the night in question, hearing him go out later than usual and not hearing him return, she had gone to investigate. Upon finding Mr Wheeler in the horse-pond, she had called Bert and together they had dragged him from the water.

So far as Bert Wheeler was concerned, this was exactly what had happened; he said, "Yes, sir," and "No, sir," in answer to questions, and once volunteered a statement, rancid with old grudges. "He been daft for a long time, sir."

Accident seemed to be ruled out by the fact that Mr Wheeler had been wearing only shirt and boots.

CHAPTER
TEN

The affair caused a little local stir. There was interest and curiosity, but not of the kind to cause Daisy any embarrassment. Mr Wheeler had owed no man a penny, nor was a penny owed to him. People who had been in contact with him in the way of business — and found him surly and unpleasant — thought it strange that he should have acted so emotionally, but in the main the interest centred about the question, What will happen next?

It was Bert Wheeler who actually voiced the question. He did so over the supper table at which a luxury — unheard of in Mr Wheeler's day — fried sausages — two per person — had just been served.

"Whass gonna happen now, Mrs Johnson?"

"That rather depends upon you, Bert."

"Whaddya mean?" Bert knew his place, eldest son, seventeen years old and in his own estimation a man; but nothing in his downtrodden life had prepared him for the shouldering of responsibility or for making plans.

"I mean that I see no reason for any great change — provided we all work as before." Not that she intended ever to dress a fowl again! There would be changes,

470

great changes, but they would come gradually, and have no ostensible connection with the money now safely locked away in her own room.

"I'm useta work," Bert said. He chewed mediatively on a piece of sausage. "But I been thinking. Me Dad musta left some money. He was a saving man."

"I know nothing about that."

"Maybe the bank?" Bert said, venturing into unknown territory.

"Maybe. You could ask. You'll have to take in the weekly orders now, you know."

"Couldn't you?" Bert asked, retreating, handing over authority.

"Deliver the orders? How could I, with all I have to do here?"

"I meant go to the bank." In all his life he had been into the city only twice; he reckoned he could just about make the deliveries, manage to face the market, but the idea of a bank intimidated him.

"I suppose I could," Daisy said obligingly.

CHAPTER
ELEVEN

And so she slipped into the position of head of the family, governing with the full consent of the governed, who, now that the glooming presence of Mr Wheeler was removed, moved timidly and tentatively towards becoming, not quite normal children, it was too late for that, but individuals with personalities. Nobody questioned the new way of life, the extra food, the comforts which Daisy gradually introduced; it seemed natural enough that now Dad was not there to take, for instance, every penny which Lily and Elsie brought in from their rounds, there was money for good meat, and sugar to put on porridge and things like new boots when they were needed.

Daisy never lost sight of the fact that much of Mr Wheeler's savings — slightly under fifteen hundred pounds — was the result of these children's labour and privation; she meant to deal fairly with them, all in good time. The one thing which was most urgent was Margaret's return to school.

"Darling, would you like to go back to Stonebridge House?"

"Not much. No, I don't think so."

"Why not?"

"Phyllis has left. It was dull without her."

"Well, perhaps we could find another school, not so far away. You might find another Phyllis."

Margaret's expression implied that she thought that unlikely. On the other hand anything would be better than staying here. Things had improved since that horrible man died but she still hated and feared the Wheeler children. And Daisy was always conscious of the threat constituted by Bert. She could hardly take a strap to him and all her long-term plans depended to some extent upon his willing co-operation which an open row might ruin.

"We'll go into the city tomorrow," Daisy told Margaret, "and buy some clothes, and make inquiries about schools. Betsy can look after Hugo for a day." That chance remark virtually settled Betsy's future; she said, "Thass what I always wanted to do, really. Work indoors, not like a man in the fields. Now Lily . . ." She broke off, one confidence was enough for one day.

"What about Lily?"

"One place where she go in the village — with eggs and stuff — there's a dressmaker. Miss Bramble. Lily always said she'd like to work there. But that mean you don't earn nothing for three years."

"I think that could be managed. Don't say anything to Lily until I have made some inquiries."

In arranging for Lily's future, Daisy met with an obstacle.

"Oh yes, of course I know Lily Wheeler. I have always felt sorry for those girls — out in all weathers and so poorly clad. But frankly, Mrs Johnson, she is hardly the *type* of girl . . ."

"Certainly there is room for improvement. But I'm sure that, granted the wish of her heart, she would improve — rapidly."

"Perhaps. And I realise that she is an orphan . . ." Miss Bramble cogitated and then said, "No. I'm sorry, but I have customers to consider."

"Need there be contact until she was more presentable?" Some memory of the Barsham dressmaker whom Charles had liked her to patronise flowed back. "And of course there would be no trouble about the premium."

"I have never accepted a premium," Miss Bramble said with an air of conscious virtue. "Nor a resident apprentice."

"Oh, of course Lily would continue living at home. I was thinking rather in terms of spoiled materials — and of course the necessity of correcting Lily's speech as well as her stitches. I thought twenty pounds for a trial period."

There was a little silence. Miss Bramble seemed to be reckoning how much stitching and fitting must be done to earn twenty pounds. Then she said, making a great concession, "I should wish to be the last person to deny the poor girl a chance."

There was a great deal of Mr Wheeler in Bert and as soon as he became more sure of himself, had discovered his inborn ability to haggle, sold an old cow, a young steer and several pigs in the cattle market,

474

where, oddly, he felt quite at his ease, he was less disposed to submit tamely to the mild, though somewhat revolutionary rule which had taken the place of his father's iron hand. One evening after supper he said, sounding very much like his father, "I gotta talk to you, Mrs Johnson. Haymaking is coming up and I'm three short. First there was Margaret away to school; there's Betsy always indoors and now Lily gone to the dressmaking. Not to mention me Dad dead. How'm I supposed to manage?"

"As other people do — hire some labour."

"That'd mean paying out."

"Of course. You can't hope to run the farm on forced labour for ever. As a matter of fact, as soon as the harvest is in, Ted is being apprenticed to a carpenter."

"Thass all your doing. Trying to ruin me."

"Betsy and Lily and Ted are doing what they wished. Elsie and Alfie seem content at the moment, but they may choose something else later."

"And you encourage them," he said bitterly.

"Of course. I believe in people being as happy as they can."

He glared at her sullenly.

"And there's another thing! They're saying Mrs Bramble was paid to take Lily."

"That is correct. Twenty pounds."

"Where'd it come from?"

"I paid it. Out of my own purse." This was sensitive ground but she stood on it firmly. "I imagine you doubt that I have money of my own. Just because I chose to live here — and out of the kindness of my heart help your mother, and then after her death do my best to keep the family together. You are quite wrong. I am well provided for and I sometimes wonder why I stay here and take the trouble to teach Betsy how to keep house and manage the dairy. If you wish to be unpleasant, I can leave tomorrow."

"No. No," he said hastily. "I wouldn't want that. I was only saying, about being shorthanded. Now *you* say pay out. Which I suppose I must. What beat me," he said, coming back to the subject that had bothered him ever since his father's death, "what did he *do* with his money? Me Dad. He was a saving man. *You* asked about at banks ..." And he had checked, once his timidity in formal places had been mastered. "*I've* looked about, everywhere I could think of. And not a penny piece. Ain't that a mystery? I mean, every week, regular customers for the fresh stuff; every day Lily and Elsie with the barrows, and selling livestock and corn. Where did it all *go*?"

"It is useless to ask me, my dear boy. Misers are supposed to bury their treasures." And this seemed to her the right moment to mention Dodger. "While we are talking about money, or money's worth, Bert, I want my horse back."

"What horse?"

"Bert Wheeler, if you deliberately act like a stupid yokel, everybody will take advantage of you. You know perfectly well what horse. The horse I brought with me and which I *lent* to your father, when his poor thing failed. I want it back. You must buy yourself another

476

horse, more thickset. And at the same time you can buy me a gig — for that I will give you the money."

He supposed it was all right. He remembered her arrival — and she had appeared to have money then, buying cakes and biscuits and tea. But that was some time ago, lately she'd seemed to have nothing and to be as much under his father's thumb as the rest of them. All very puzzling. He said, discontentedly, "So now I gotta buy a horse and hire labour. How'm I ever going to save anything?"

"Do you *want* to? I should have thought you'd have seen enough of saving. Look at your father! No pleasure in life, no comfort. Working himself and everybody to death, and for what? In the end he was so miserable that he drowned himself. At the inquest you said he was daft. Do you want to go daft in the same way — and then leave your money hidden in a hole in the ground, or under a stack?"

"No, not exactly. But you gotta think about the future, Mrs Johnson."

"Up to a point, but not to the extent of making yourself and everybody else miserable. And this I must tell you, if you start on that tack, I shall just go away and then you'll have to hire either a cook or a dairymaid. Betsy couldn't manage alone — *yet*."

"No. I suppose not. I wouldn't want . . . to do anything to offend you, Mrs Johnson."

"No? Then I'll tell you one thing which does offend me. People coming in with mud and filth on their boots. It makes it impossible to keep the kitchen clean." An artful thought struck her. "If I buy everybody a pair of slippers, *out of my own money*, will you see that they change?"

The chance to exercise his authority was irresistible. "Out in the shed, you mean?"

From such a modest start the civilisation of Amblebury began. Washing hands before meals, fairly frequent changing of clothing; new clothes. Daisy said often — but not too often — "If I use my own money . . ." or "If I pay for it . . ." Such an introduction to any expenditure made Bert's co-operation certain and after all, as Daisy thought wryly, it was their own money, and doing them far more good than it would have done, hidden away and being saved for some unknown purpose — unknown because Mr Wheeler had never shared his dream with anyone. The money was buying not only material things, but happiness. In this house no young Wheeler's birthday had ever been celebrated; Christmas except for extra work on chickens had been completely ignored. All was different now.

One day Daisy proposed an innovation which drew a protest from Bert.

"I don't see why we should use all this old cracked, chipped crockery when there is a whole roomful of china just there."

"But we mustn't touch that, Mrs Johnson." He was the only one who remembered Captain Stirling, or had been old enough at the time to understand, though rather vaguely, the arrangement about caretaking in lieu of rent. "Thass all Captain Stirling's stuff and in a way me Dad was paid to look after it. Maybe you didn't

478

know. I mean, if Captain Stirling come back and found us using his stuff, there'd be a row."

"I'd take the blame, Bert. In fact there would be no row."

For who was Hugo Stirling? Look back and think. To begin with a sharer of ineffable joy, the promoter of madness, enough to disrupt her whole life; the subject of yearning memories, and hope. One letter and then silence. Worse than death, really — one could at least tend a grave. The two ladies in the Avenue who had said, carefully prefacing bygones with the words, "Of course, I was only a child at the time," had said that Mrs Stirling was very pretty. And then Mr Wheeler had reckoned that he had gone back to his wife in a place called Jamaica. So for the second — no, the third time — in her life loving had failed her. Jack Skelton, Margaret, Hugo Stirling. All lost. Margaret had recently written saying that she wanted to accept an invitation to spend holidays with her new, best friend, Stephanie Oakes.

None of my loves prosper.

But there are other things. I have my baby and although, fourteen hundred and seventy pounds will not last for ever, the house is crammed with treasures.

How strange; Hugo went to hunt for treasure and consigned me here to poverty and misery. I found treasure, right under my nose.

While Daisy thought, Bert Wheeler had been thinking too. He was not a stupid boy, he had simply been suppressed, worked into exhaustion and afraid of his father. Now his mind ran about, drawing some

479

correct and some erroneous conclusions. She'd called the baby Hugo . . . And she was making free with the contents of the china room.

"Did he die and leave everything to you, Mrs Johnson? Captain Stirling, I mean."

"That is one way of looking at it. Yes."

Bert looked thoughtful, creasing his forehead into a scowl very reminiscent of his father's. Then he said slowly, "Do that mean *you're* my landlord now? And living here, doing your own caretaking? You want me . . ." he almost choked on the words, "to pay *rent*?"

She waited just long enough to frighten him slightly; to allow him to think about paying hired help, buying another horse and paying rent! During that pause his expression changed and became more like that of his poor mother; the hunted-hare look.

"Of course not, Bert. I shouldn't dream of it. We'll go on as we have done — with a few improvements. I should like the pigs moved away from the house. And part of the garden restored. I like flowers. All I ask of you is to keep the place going and help me to make everybody happy."

She heard the last words as though somebody else had spoken them; and they sounded like things people said about the dead — or put on gravestones. At the thought, the tough, lively spirit which had carried her through so many ups and downs sprang up, all the stronger for having been so long subjugated to her wish to please, her desire to be loved, her need to survive. She thought, I'm not dead. I'm not even *old* yet. I've still got some living to do! She saw Amblebury

480

transformed, a place where Hugo could grow up happily, a place to which Margaret would one day return, and to which she would be pleased to invite her friends.

Alongside the practical thought something else struggled and, like an escaped butterfly, took wing; the assurance of something wonderful awaiting her. Just round the next corner . . .

The Town House

Norah Lofts

The Suffolk Trilogy, Book 1

"It was in the first week of October in the year 1391 that I first came face to face with the man who owned me . . . the man whose lightest word was to us, his villeins, weightier than the King's law or the edicts of our Holy Father . . . "

So began the story of Martin Reed — a serf whose resentment of the automatic rule of his feudal lord finally flared into open defiance. Encouraged by the woman he loved, Martin Reed began a new life — a life which was to culminate in the building of the House, and the founding of the dynasty who were to live there.

ISBN 978-0-7531-8828-6 (hb)
ISBN 978-0-7531-8829-3 (pb)

The House at Old Vine

Norah Lofts

The Suffolk Trilogy, Book 2

The House at Old Vine is the second in a trilogy of novels about the inhabitants of a Suffolk house. Covering the turbulent years of 1496 to 1680, it follows six generations of the descendants of Martin Reed, who founded the "House" dynasty. As the house becomes briefly an Inn and then a school for boys we meet those who lived within its walls. First there is Josiana Greenwood, who marries into the house and witnesses her lover burnt at the stake for heresy. Then there is Barbara Kentwoode who saw the house transformed into an Inn during the time of the Civil War. And finally Antony Flowerdew, who would run the house as a school. Over the years The House at Old Vine would be home to many intriguing characters who lived and died for what they believed in.

ISBN 978-0-7531-8830-9 (hb)
ISBN 978-0-7531-8831-6 (pb)